CHASING THE WRONG BRIDE

A BLINGWOOD BILLIONAIRES NOVEL
BOOK TWO

EMILY JAMES

STALK EMILY JAMES:

Facebook
  Goodreads
  Amazon
  Newsletter
  Bookbub

ALSO BY EMILY JAMES:

The Blingwood Billionaires series

Book 1—Sorry. Not Sorry

Book 2 – Chasing the Wrong Bride

Book 3 – Catch a Falling Star

The Love in Short series

Book 1—Operation My Fake Girlfriend

Book 2—Sexy With Attitude Too

Book 3—You Only Love Once

Book 4—Leaving Out Love

The Power of Ten series

Book 1—Ten Dates

Book 2—Ten Dares

Book 3—Ten Lies

PROLOGUE

LAYLA

"*Y*ou would have looked better if you lost those five pounds we talked about," Mom says, fussing with the train of my dress that's so long she had to bunch it up in her arms to close the door of the vestry.

A mirror takes up most of the wall, forcing me to stare at my reflection. Trussed up in white, it's like the dress is wearing me. "I'm no bigger than the day I started working with Jonathon. If you can't be nice, be quiet," I say, even though she's incapable of both.

"I'm sorry, darling, you look lovely. Hips and breasts are back in fashion, so at least you're current. Unlike Jonathon's sister on her wedding day. Honestly, I've seen scarecrows with better style."

"Mom, I'm nervous and your constant chatter isn't helping. And can you please refrain from commenting on Jonathon's sister's weight. She's been trying really hard to cut down."

Her lips purse. "Darling, are you suggesting I'm insensitive?" She sounds offended. The irony would have me belly laughing if my nerves weren't already doing the cha-cha.

"Please try not to upset anyone today, I'm nervous enough already."

On the wall next to me, a bright red emergency exit sign flickers. I turn my attention back to the mirror and take a deep breath in. After three hours with the stylist, I look like a nicer, more expensive version of myself. My dark hair is long and loose, curled into perfect waves that fall halfway down my back, and pretty pink lips pout back at me.

"If you don't pull yourself together, you're going to smudge your eye makeup," Mom warns.

"Good thing you ordered the stylist to use waterproof mascara then," I reply more curtly than I mean to.

"People cry at weddings. It was the safe choice."

"I didn't think it was supposed to be the bride who cried."

Mom takes my hand in hers and smiles placatingly. "Sweetie, as soon as you see your fiancé standing at the end of the aisle, all your doubts will wash away."

"Did your doubt wash away when you saw your groom?"

She nods.

"What about during your second, third, and fourth marriages? Did you have a handle on your emotions by your fifth marriage?" It's a low blow that goes over my mother's head.

Mom drops my hand and checks her perfectly manicured fingers. "Yes. The more times you do it, the less nervous you feel."

"I only plan to do it once, Mom."

"So did your father and I," she replies. "But we don't always know what or *who* is around the corner."

Dad's been gone six months but the grief still grips me every time I think of him.

Mom takes a step closer and steel-gray eyes pin me to the spot. "There's a reporter from *The Herald* out there. Do you want the pictures they print to show you with messy black tears streaming down your face?"

"Why is a reporter here?"

"The wedding is big news for the town. Jonathon's the son of a retired professional football player, and he's marrying a local nobody. It's like a fairy tale."

"Mom, he's marrying *me*. Your daughter. Since when am I a nobody?"

"Oh honey, you're not a nobody. You know what I mean. Jonathon's father got a great deal on the photographer so long as they could cover the story. You're getting all the photographs for free!"

If that's the case, I wonder why Jonathon took seven hundred dollars from our joint checking account to pay the photographer.

Mom pushes me out of the way so she can look at herself in the mirror while she talks to me. "The stress you're feeling, it's really just excitement. Before you came home to take care of your father, you were in a new town or city every few months. Always moving around, you forgot how to settle in one place, but I know Jonathon is going to take care of you, just like Brian takes care of me."

I narrow my eyes, watching as Mom reapplies fuchsia lipstick.

"Brian was your last husband. You're married to Roy now."

Mom laughs. "It's a good thing Brian—I mean Roy, didn't hear that." She watches me through the mirror as I bite my lip. "Are you still worried about the condom?"

I shake my pounding head. "The lead up to the wedding has been tense. Jonathon was distant but we haven't had a single fight since he swore he knows nothing about it."

Seeing the condom strewn against the trash can in our

office was a shock. Jonathon and I don't use condoms. We got checked out and now I'm on the pill. He blamed the cleaning couple, and I'm inclined to believe him since they literally can't keep their hands off each other—even when I'm still in the office Jonathon and I share at his father's recruitment company.

Jonathon wouldn't cheat on me.

He wouldn't.

I pull my cell from my silk purse and check my inbox to distract myself while I wait for Jonathon's sisters to come tell me it's time. Yesterday I meticulously replied and deleted my inbox in preparation for my absence from the office, so I'm annoyed to see I have a new email.

"No work today, Layla. It's your wedding day," Mom says, but my finger hovers over the message.

Jonathon and I will be flying to Bora Bora straight after the party and, now might be my only chance to deal with it. "It might be important," I say, opening the email.

Mom has never had a job, whereas my work history is vast. Before settling in my hometown for the past two years while I cared for Dad, I worked temp positions right across the country, and I loved it so much it's taken a great deal of effort to ignore my recent itchy feet.

I remind Mom what I do now, in case she forgot. "We specialize in hotel recruitment and it's peak season, so we've been super busy. The email won't take a minute to deal with, and since I'm trapped in this airless room anyway...."

As soon as I see who the sender is, I regret loading the email.

To: Layla Bowers

From: Skyla Blingwood

4

Subject: SOS Logan Blingwood requires an URGENT PA

Please send me whoever you have—he's desperate!

GOOD LUCK WITH THAT! I inwardly cringe.

Skyla is the HR manager of the Blingwood Beach Resort in Santa Barbara. They just opened a new resort in Miami and I've been helping them recruit for the open positions. However, lately, my focus has been finding a suitable PA for Mr. Blingwood, who's located in their Santa Barbara location. Unfortunately, his fierce reputation puts most people off from applying. I've sent three PA's to Mr. Blingwood and not one has lasted longer than a month—all of them leaving and complaining of a grouchy boss who is impossible to work for.

Skyla is supposed to be on her honeymoon, not working, and as of tonight, I'll be with Jonathon on ours.

Not my problem.

I switch on my out-of-office reply and take a deep breath.

No more work.

I need to focus on my impending wedding. Before I can put my phone into my purse, it starts to ring.

"Oh honey. Turn it off," Mom says. "The last thing you want is the phone you insisted on carrying with you ringing during your vows. That happened to the pastor during my third wedding and it was very embarrassing!"

Mom peers down at the screen. "Why is Jonathon calling you? He can't speak to you before the wedding, it's bad luck. Hang up."

The phone weighs heavy in my hand. *Should I accept super-*

stitious wedding advice from a person who's been divorced four times?

"What if it's an emergency? Maybe the pastor had a heart attack and we have to call off the wedding."

I swipe to connect the call and press the loud speaker, trying not to enjoy the look of disdain on my mother's face. Jonathon's voice comes through the speaker before I have the chance to say hello. *"I have to go through with it. Everyone is already here."*

Mom's smile drops by a centimeter before she catches it, but her lips remain frozen in a forced, reassuring position as she listens.

"Of course, it's you I want. But my grandparents came all the way from Michigan."

Jonathon is talking to someone else. His voice is quiet, like his phone is too far from his mouth.

Did he butt-dial me?

There's a muffled response, higher pitched than his. I can't understand what the woman he is talking to is saying.

"Baby, forget about the bride—concentrate on what I'm saying. It's just a wedding. It doesn't affect how I feel about you."

It's definitely Jonathon's voice, but it doesn't sound like him. He's never once, in two years, called me baby. I bite my tongue to stop a string of expletives forcing their way past my lips and stare at my mother incredulously. My shaking fist clutches the phone like it's his neck.

Outside of this room, my entire family is sitting on pews. My school friends! Even perfect Penny Tucker from my old cheerleading team! Every. Single. Person. I. Know. They're all here to watch me get married.

Jonathon proposed right after my dad died. Maybe he thought it'd cheer me up or maybe he couldn't cope with all my crying, but it was *his* idea. I don't even remember saying yes, but I remember feeling like I should. He had, after all, supported me as I cared for my dad.

"Let me say I do, and then in a few months I'll say I don't."

The room is spinning like a tornado and everything blurs. My mother's face contorts and the color of her pallor mixes with the red from the emergency exit sign. The sunlight streaming through the window gleams from my mother's car keys—haphazardly thrown down on the table—which are only there because Jonathon thought we shouldn't waste money on a limousine.

Like divine intervention, it sets off a chain of events.

"Mom, I need to borrow your car."

"Why would you want to do that, honey? The service is starting in just a moment."

"I can't do it," I stutter, my head shaking from side to side as though I can shake away this nightmare.

"Honey, Jonathon is right. Everyone has come all this way and you're here now. It'd only be for a few months, and Jonathon's father is rich! The best way to get revenge on him is in the settlement. You get nothing if you walk away now—"

I shake my head more violently.

"No, Mom. I can't do it. Tell Nanna I'm sorry she canceled bridge club to come today. I'll make it up to her."

"Nanna won't care about that. She wants to see a wedding—"

I don't stop to listen. Instead, I claw at the snaps that connect the train to my dress and yank until it's unfastened, and then I fire myself toward the emergency exit, snatching the keys as I go.

CHAPTER 1

LAYLA

*T*he *Blingwood Beach Resort: Escape, unwind, and experience paradise.*

I ROLL my eyes at the hotel website's tall claims and then tuck my phone back into the silk pouch of my wedding purse.

After fleeing the wedding, I drove around aimlessly wondering where to go. I even slept in my car last night while I figured it out. I can't face returning to Jonathon's condo, and I can't go to my mother's. Her husband Roy has a model railway taking up most of their guest room and my mother's cats sleep in the other spare room. Besides, after her insisting I marry Jonathon, even after we had proof he cheated, I'm too angry to even answer her calls.

In a moment of utter desperation, I call Skyla, and even though she is on her honeymoon, she answers. I confirm Mr. Blingwood still needs a PA and that the job still includes the on-site apartment. The excitement in her voice should be deterring me, but I am too grateful to allow my concern to overwhelm me.

Here I am, Sunday morning, the day after fleeing my wedding, and I'm rolling toward the resort still in my wedding dress. The ocean view outside my open window is so breathtaking it brings heavy, fat tears to my eyes.

I've been a fool.

My foot presses down on the gas and suddenly I no longer know if I am speeding away from my past or speeding toward something new, but I stop when I see my destination.

Atop of huge, white marbled pillars stands the sign marking the Blingwood Beach Resort. And if I wasn't intimidated by that, what lies beyond it surely rattles my insides. Manicured gardens, untarnished by even a single dandelion, weaves a meandering path to the beach, which is set up with an altar and seating for a lavish wedding.

It seems like a sick joke, speeding away from my own wedding, only to arrive at someone else's.

I don't dither or dissect how my life became such a shit show. Instead, I follow the road that snakes around the ornamental water feature to the building marked Reception. I stop behind a line of cars—Mercedes, Lamborghinis, and Aston Martins—each car and their owners are being attended to by sharply dressed valets. My cell vibrates across the passenger seat from inside my purse, so I turn it off and get out of the car, tossing the keys to the valet and taking the ticket he gives me.

"Welcome to the Blingwood Resort, ma'am," the concierge says. "Are you the bride for today's wedding?"

"No, that's not my wedding," I reply gesturing to the wedding paraphernalia outside.

He stares at me, confused.

"Are you meeting your husband here?" he asks, once again gawking down at my wedding dress and shoes.

"Nope. No husband."

Unfortunately his questions continue. "Have you stayed with us here in Santa Barbara before?"

"No, but the internet speaks very highly of you," I reply and then glance down at his badge and politely tack on his name *Doug*. He's a big guy with an even bigger smile and I wonder what he's so happy about.

"Come right this way. Sally will get you checked in." He looks down at the ground, confusion simmers on his face. "Ma'am, did the valet take your luggage from the car?"

"I don't have any luggage." I stare down at the white, floor-length dress and cringe.

What was I thinking, coming here?

He chuckles awkwardly. Behind him, a lady in a maid's uniform with a hotel badge fastened to it stops walking and she eyes me curiously—which is no wonder, really, since I am standing here in a wedding dress with no groom, and looking disheveled, I'm clearly not the bride for the impending wedding.

"I'm here about the job," I tell Doug. "I spoke to Skyla on the phone earlier and she said I should come right away."

Doug stares at me blankly, then says. "Skyla's on her honeymoon."

The woman in the maid uniform makes no effort to hide her eavesdropping.

"Mr. Blingwood *is* still in need of an assistant?" I ask Doug.

Either nerves or the fact I haven't eaten since yesterday has me lightheaded. I'm homeless—unless I want to go back and face the man I jilted at the wedding. I'm jobless—unless I want to go back to work in my almost father-in-law's business. And I'm frazzled—and in desperate need of space from everyone I know.

I turn to the blonde woman who has now joined Doug and me. Her badge reads: *Jessie Yates. Head of Housekeeping.* I pray she can offer more assistance than Doug, who appears to have become mute.

Thankfully, she smiles with recognition and I feel momentarily reassured, until her eyes dip down to my attire, her brows shoot up, and she starts to laugh. "Holy eggplants! You're her?! When Skyla called me to say there was an applicant on her way, I didn't realize she meant you! Do you know you are a walking beacon of Mr. Blingwood's own personal brand of hell?"

My mouth pops open.

Personal brand of hell?

She guffaws like she just can't help herself and gestures to my dress, then looks around like we might be being spied on. "I don't know what you're doing here in a bridal gown, but if Logan sees you dressed like that, he'll hate you on sight and there ain't no way he'll give you a job."

My cheeks warm. "I… It was a last-minute decision to take the position. I heard Mr. Blingwood was in urgent need and… I'm in urgent need of a job with housing."

"You a bridal model or something?" Doug asks, perplexed.

"Or something," I reply, then I turn to Jessie who seems more in tune with my predicament. "I emailed Skyla my resume…."

Jessie holds out her hand. "Skyla's not back from her honeymoon for another week, but I can help you." She has a caring yet concerned look and I can't blame her. Here I am, no doubt looking like a tired and crumpled Halloween bride on the brink of a mental health breakdown. "Come with me."

She starts walking, but I'm too stunned and remain still.

"Don't forget the bride!" Doug calls after her and she turns her head in annoyance.

"You have to keep up. He can't see you like this!"

I follow her down a staff corridor and say, "I don't normally turn up to job interviews dressed like this." I pull up my dress so I can walk a little faster and keep up with Jessie. "Yeah, so it's been kind of a crazy since yesterday. I should be on a beach in Bora Bora with a fruity drink in my hand, not here asking for a job."

"Secret's safe with me." She holds open the door to the ladies' bathroom and I enter.

"If I don't secure this position, I'll have no choice but to return to my mother—the woman who thought I should go ahead with the wedding—and that is not going to be good for anyone. Is there a hotel store I can buy a change of clothes, and please can you confirm there is a vacant apartment as part of the job?"

Jessie gives me a measured stare. She must invariably feel sorry for me, because without judgment she says, "Logan hates weddings and he hates brides even more. The apartment right beneath mine is vacant, so if you get the job, it's yours. But we've got to fix you up first." Her head bobs up and down as she takes me in. "Size four?" she asks and I nod. "I'll go find you what you need, but for sausage's sake, stay hidden!"

"I won't move," I promise. "Why does the boss hate weddings so much? I mean, it looks like there's one taking place right outside."

There's a flash of sympathy on her face before she checks her watch. "I don't have time to give you the deets. Bottom line: Logan's a brilliant businessman, but he's gonna work himself and the rest of us into an early grave if he doesn't get some help. Stay here until I come back."

CHAPTER 2

LOGAN

*I*t's only when my stomach growls furiously that I realize it's well past noon. It prompts a shorter than usual response from me to Mike in accounting.

"Handle it," I bark and take strides in the direction of the staff cafeteria.

This late in the afternoon, I'll be lucky to find so much as a scrap to eat for lunch. Of course, as the CEO of Blingwood Beach Resort, I could have one of the kitchen staff fix me something, but there's a big event today that they'll be busy attending to. Some socialite and her fiancé are using the resort for their nuptials, and a centerfold spread is being photographed for *Celebrity Magazine,* not that I care at all about it, but it'll be good publicity for the resort.

A wedding.

I roll my eyes.

Fools!

If we didn't make such generous profits from hosting

weddings, I would ban them altogether. The irony of hating them isn't lost on me, though. After all, I was almost married at this very resort just a few months ago—fortunately I had a lucky escape.

These days, one might say, I'm married to the resort.

At least she doesn't lie, cheat, and try to con me out of everything I have worked for.

In the cafeteria, I see Sandy, my HR Manager's assistant, filling her plate.

"Just the person," I say by way of a greeting and she almost drops her plate.

"Mr. Blingwood." Sandy gawks at me from atop the black rimmed spectacles that have slid down her nose. I don't miss the nervous flick of her eyes as she notices my firm stance.

Sandy knows she has an important piece of work outstanding—not to mention the fact that I've told her to call me Logan enough times but she insists on calling me Mr. Blingwood.

I don't have the patience to prompt a more casual dialogue between us so I cut to the chase. "P.A." There's a draconian sternness to my voice that is drawn directly from my famished state.

Sandy's plate clatters against the metal counter as she drops it down and turns to me. Then she drops eye contact while she straightens an imaginary crease in her skirt, buying time while she considers how to break bad news, no doubt.

"Well, you see…. Skyla was dealing with your PA replacement, but then she went on her honeymoon…. She put out an emergency ad for a temporary PA to support you over the peak season, but we haven't secured anyone yet. The temp person I thought I had lined up to be your assistant didn't show up and now—"

"No shows? We're the best resort in Santa Barbara! How can you possibly be having problems with recruitment?"

She bites her lip nervously and so I relax my stance and cease glaring at her. "Is it the pay? Do we need to offer a more generous salary?"

She shakes her head sympathetically. "The pay is well above market rates."

A chef walks past us with a tray of piping hot goodness and my stomach clenches with need.

"Then what is it? I've been without an assistant for weeks. I've got work backing up because I'm inundated with stuff I should be delegating."

Her throat bobs as she swallows and then she suddenly stands taller, as though mustering all her strength. "Why did Joanna leave?"

"Beats me." I shrug. "She wasn't suited for the position. She couldn't operate the photocopier and left food crumbs on the files she passed to me."

Sandy is still waiting for a more appropriate answer, and I want my lunch so I placate her. "I don't know why Joanna left... politics?"

I stare into Sandy's eyes as they dart about the place while she wrestles with whatever she is about to say. "It wasn't politics."

"What was it, then?"

"It was... I think she thought... perhaps you were a bit... Well, since... you know, you've been a little—"

"A little what?" I interrupt and Sandy shrinks back.

I know what she's getting at. Since the almost wedding—where I was set up to be left standing at the altar, high and dry... humiliated—I have been a little difficult to be around but I have remained professional. I can't afford any further negative press, not when I have already been subjected to public rumors and gossip. I have a business to run and customers can be fickle when it comes to negative press. So, I remain professional at all times—even when people annoy the shit out of me.

"Are competent staff too much to ask for, Sandy?"

All around me, various staff are on their breaks, eavesdropping while filling their plates with the freshly delivered lasagna that has my name written all over it.

I pin Sandy with a stare that demands she cut to the chase.

"Your last assistant reviewed her position here as, 'would not recommend,' stating 'management' as the source of the conflict."

My jaw clenches. She can't be implying I am the source of the negative review. I was perfectly nice to my assistant, even if she was borderline useless.

"Who within management isn't performing appropriately? We're entering peak season. I haven't got time for staffing shortages on top of everything else. I don't care how you do it, but find me someone. And find them today!" I step around her to the counter and see the freshly baked right-out-of-the-oven tray of lasagna has been devoured.

"B-b-but Mr. Blingwood, it's Sunday. I won't be able to find anyone on a Sunday," Sandy says from beside me, but my reply is stalled as we get interrupted by Jessie, the newly appointed head of housekeeping.

"Sandy, you're needed in reception. Mr. Blingwood, Simon from security asked that he borrow you for a moment."

Jessie looks at me with the kind of sympathy that makes me not want to be around her. She was the one who alerted me about my ex's trap, so I haven't the heart to tell her to inform Simon to go deal with whatever it is himself. Turning on my heel and keeping my mouth shut, I head to the security desk, knowing there is no chance of me getting lunch now.

* * *

AFTER SORTING OUT MULTIPLE ISSUES—A near paralytic wedding guest pouring soap in the fountain and a lost child —I get back to the staff cafeteria to find it is shut down until dinner. Anger rolls down my back, and hangrier than ever, I stalk to my office in the hope that there is a protein bar in my drawer that can keep starvation at bay.

Entering my office, I smell her before I see her—Chanel N°. 5 mixed with a subtle hint of kennel. Her back straightens as the door slams behind me and she rushes to me as though she hasn't seen me in years rather than weeks.

"Mom. What are you doing here? Why aren't you at the animal shelter?" I ask, since she's almost always there; I set her up with the non-profit of her dreams to keep her busy after Dad died. "Is something wrong?" I drop my 6'2" frame down onto the Eames chair I splurged on.

"Logi, what kind of welcome is that?" She grins and leans in to kiss my temple, her almost white, curly hair tickling my face. "Nothing is wrong. I missed my middle son, that's all."

"I've got a lot to get through," I reply, leaning away. "I haven't got time to—"

"To what? See your own mother. To attend brunch with the family. To answer my calls or reply to my texts?"

Mom takes a seat opposite my desk and crosses her arms over her baggy T-shirt. Her stance as well as the disappointed expression on her face takes me right back to memories of childhood admonishments.

I hit the On button and boot up the computer while I wait for her to voice her annoyance with me—and it's coming, not that I haven't earned it.

My emails have doubled since I checked them this morning. My eyes bug out as I read the first line of an email—the Blingwood Resort has been nominated by the Gee Foundation for the best resort award. I pick up my pen, then throw it down. *It must be some kind of sick joke.* The Gee Foundation was set up by my ex almost-father-in law and a board of hoteliers.

Donald Gee is a prominent hotelier in New York, and there's no way he allowed my resort to be listed as a finalist unless he plans for me to lose publicly to humiliate me following my breakup from his daughter.

Mom clears her throat. I'd almost forgotten she was there.

Stress radiates through my entire body.

When I look up, she raises a silver brow at me and I'm hit with how much older she looks—still stunning, and a smart and confident woman, but the creases between her brows are more prominent, the lines around her mouth deeper. When Dad died, it was like her hair went completely white overnight—I suppose grief will do that to a person.

I take my hand off the computer mouse and give her my attention. I haven't been there for her as much as I meant to be. I can't remember the last time I called her. And I know there are a few dozen text messages from her that I haven't had a chance to reply to.

Damn.

I'm letting her down. I promised I'd take care of her. I invested in the charity she set up—but that's just money. I haven't been truly present in a while—not since shit went down with Dana, and Mom knows it.

"Mom—"

"You're busy, I know. So are your brothers. Tate's off on a film set somewhere, and Drew's on his honeymoon but even when he's not, he's busy with Skyla—though *he* stays in touch. Today is Sunday. It's time you took some time away from the office on the weekends, Logan. You used to come to Sunday brunch at the house. You have to stop punishing yourself with work. Life shouldn't be all work and no play."

I grimace and her stern stare softens. No matter how much I disappoint her, her heart stays full and pure with love for her family. "I'll come by next Sunday," I agree.

Mom's lips tip into a fond smile. "Lecture over. I popped by with this sandwich." She holds the brown paper bag in the air and suddenly my stomach growls.

"Thank you, Mom. I'm starving. What's in it?"

"Chicken and avocado on rye."

I hold out my hand to take it but she pulls it out of my reach.

"It's got a squirt of lemon mayonnaise too," she adds, and my mouth is already watering. "But obviously, you're too busy for a late lunch. I'll just—" Her voice trails off and she stands.

"Mom, sit. It's been too long since I saw you. I'm sorry. Things have been crazy here but that's not your fault. Staffing has been a problem. I know it's no excuse. I'll make more time for you, I promise."

"No. Being busy is not a good excuse—everyone is busy. I've missed you." She clutches the bag tightly and brings it down to rest on her lap as she reseats herself.

"I'll do better. I don't have an assistant right now which means I'm having to do everything myself. I'll have more time when the new one arrives."

"Oh, and when will that be?"

I shrug and expel a frustrated breath. "With Skyla on her honeymoon, Sandy is doing her best to find me one, but so far the search has been fruitless."

Mom nods. "What happened to Joanna?"

My head tips in surprise. "You knew my assistant's name?"

"Logi, I spend more time talking to your assistant than I do you."

Mom's got a point. I'm spread pretty thin.

"I don't know, she left. Like I said, staffing has been an issue of late."

"You were nice to her, weren't you?"

"What? Of course I was nice to my assistant."

"Don't give me those innocent eyes, you know how you get when you're stressed. You're even worse with an empty stomach. I saw a review that said one of the managers here was a 'gorilla.'"

"Yes, I saw that too. But it doesn't mean they were referring to me. There's a whole management team. I can't run this place single-handed, even if I feel like I am most days. You think *I'm* the gorilla?"

"No." Mom breaks eye contact to glance down at her manicured hands and I know damn well she thinks I'm the problem. "It's just…" Her chin tilts up and she looks at me through lashes that are thick despite not wearing makeup and her stare becomes watery. "Since Dana left, you haven't been yourself."

She went there.

Even though she knows we don't talk about *her*, she went there.

"How is the rescue center?" I ask, deftly changing the subject. Getting Mom to talk about the animal shelter is always a good distraction and anything beats talking about *her*. As suspected, Mom's face lights up and her arms open animatedly as she prepares to gush about her charity. Then I notice something disturbing. "Mom, your T-shirt… it reads: *Gone dogging.* Are you aware what dogging is?"

Mom coyly grins while she picks a stray dog hair from her sweatpants. "The shelter is doing amazing, and of course I know what the T-shirt means, it's fun! You know I love getting out and getting those pooches exercised! We just got a new boy I think you'll love. His owner left him tied to a post outside the clinic. Abandoned him! I don't know how people can do that. I've been calling him Logi… I mean, Yogi, like the bear." She chuckles, and I check my watch, wondering how long until I can escape. "He's all grumpy and didn't enjoy the vet visit, but I think he'll be a great big softie once he receives some love. He reminds me of someone."

"Mom, did you name this dog after me?"

"No. It was just a slip of the tongue. He's called Yogi, like the bear, son, not at all like you." Her smile falters. At least she has the decency to look remorseful.

"You've named the dog after me?"

She bites her lip sheepishly. "He's a teddy bear. Why wouldn't I think he was like my sweet second-born son! Besides, a little love and stability is all you both need. Come to the park on Saturday. We're having a recruitment drive to find some new volunteer dog walkers. I swear, once you meet him, you won't want to send him back to the pound."

"Why can't you be like a normal mom and try set me up with women instead of dogs?" Mom laughs and I smile back at her. "It's weird."

"Ha! I have no concerns you'll meet exactly the right woman at exactly the right time. You're a good man, Logan Blingwood."

"Mom. I'm done. Please don't meddle. If I learned one thing from my experience with Dana, it's that I'm not cut out for relationships. They're too much work and I have enough work to do here." After what she put me through, I doubt I'll ever be able to trust another partner again. Not after Dana lied to me, faked a pregnancy, and tried to trap me into a wedding so that she'd be financially set after her father disinherited her—if he even did. With the hotel nomination, I'm now questioning if it was all a setup. Maybe her father was in on her plan to dupe me into marriage. It's a known fact that Donald Gee has been stressing over who to leave his lifetime's work and legacy to. Dana lacks the competence to manage her father's resorts and hotels. Even with a team of expert support, she'd run them straight into the ground and Donald knows it. Regardless, it's of no consequence to me, my dalliances with marriage are over. Been there, chose the rings, grateful I escaped with only my reputation in tatters after Dana published her lies on social media.

My cell starts to ring and Mom stands to leave. "Don't write off love. It'll happen for you just like it did for your brother." She pulls down her glasses and pierces me with a worried stare. "Don't work so hard that you forget to make a life."

I nod but my attention is squarely fixed on the bag that contains my sandwich as she holds it teasingly close. With one of my hands ready to answer the call and the other outstretched to take the sandwich, Mom says, "Saturday, 9 a.m. You'll be at the park?" She pulls the sandwich back, just out of my reach until I answer.

"Deal," I reply.

Mom whispers good-bye as I answer the call and she lays the bag with the sandwich on her chair.

I answer the call fast, hoping it'll be a short conversation so I can finally eat.

It's Simon from security. "You need to come quick. The socialite bride got drunk and is in the fountain throwing up. She's refusing to move, and the journalist and photographer are due here at any moment."

"What?! She's supposed to be getting married in half an hour. This won't look good for the resort."

"I know, boss. I thought you'd want to know."

"This is more evidence why weddings are a total waste of time. Simon?"

23

"Yeah, boss?"

"If I'm ever involved with another wedding, shoot me. Okay?"

Simon chuckles then replies, "You got it, boss."

I hang up my phone, say a silent good-bye to my sandwich, and go sort out another damn crisis.

CHAPTER 3

LAYLA

*W*hen she returns, Jessie hands me a black pencil skirt and a shirt that smells like it came from the lost and found.

"I've ordered security to keep Logan busy. It should give you time to change and prepare yourself for the interview. Sandy's making space in his calendar and then she will bring him to collect you from the breakroom. If he has any sense, he'll hire you on the spot."

"Skyla said she was emailing her assistant the resume I sent her."

"Yes, Sandy's already printed it and she's putting it on Logan's desk, and with Logan's sister-in-law vouching for you, the interview should be straightforward."

"Sister-in-law?" I ask, and tug against the fabric of the dress, sweating trying to free myself of it.

"Skyla married Drew Blingwood, Logan's brother."

"I notice her name on her email changed from Manning

to Blingwood but I didn't realize she married her boss's brother."

"Yeah, those two had it bad for one another, and now they're married. Turns out, happily ever afters do happen."

I try not to scoff while I turn around and ask, "Can you help me? Damn dress doesn't want to come off."

Jessie steps forward and wrestles with the zip. "Stubborn little turnip doesn't want to—" She tugs again and the audible sound of splitting fabric cuts through the air. "Oops. Sorry," she says and when I turn to look at her over my shoulder, her mouth is fixed with a grimace.

"It's fine. The dress is going in the trash the first chance I get." I pull the tiny, single diamond engagement ring off my finger and hold it up to the light where it shimmers, then tuck it into my purse.

"So, you left the groom at the altar? You could always pawn the ring."

I nod. "I have no idea if Jonathon made it as far as the altar before he realized I wasn't going to turn up. My mom is going to kill me when I finally face her."

Jessie helps me tug the dress down over my hips and says, "Moms have a tendency to get over things pretty quickly. Take my mom, when I got enough courage to tell her I was knocked up by a guy who wasn't interested, she was chill about the whole thing in like… eight months."

I chuckle along with her for a moment until the laughter is gone and I am left feeling sad. It must suck to have the baby daddy not stick around to help. In my own situation, at least there's no chance of me being pregnant, thanks to the pill that I never forget to take.

"Macy's two, and I wouldn't change any of it. I'm sure you and your mom will get over what happened. The Blingwood Resort is a great place for starting over."

When I'm out of the dress, I toss it on the floor and

change into the clothes Jessie brought me. Then I step in front of the mirror above the sink. The gauzy white shirt is at least a size too small to fit over my generous chest, and it's just transparent enough that my sexy wedding bra is visible beneath.

"Maybe if I keep my arms down the seams won't split," I say, gesturing with my hands to the stretched material. "The skirt's also a little tight, but if I don't bend, then nobody will see the stockings and garter belt."

Jessie smiles reassuringly. "Lady, you look hot! Logan won't know what hit him."

She agrees to put the pile of white satin and tulle in a dumpster and then she points to the pearl hair accessory the stylist plugged into my curled dark hair. I nod for Jessie to have at it.

"Thank you. I know this isn't normal practice."

"No problem. You're going to be fine." She turns the wedding accessory over in her hands.

I nod, hoping she's right.

"Is he really as bad as everyone says?" I ask, remembering my earlier problems recruiting for the position. Logan Blingwood's reputation is as lousy as my mood.

Jessie's mouth forms a perfect straight line. "He used to be nice."

"*Used to be*. Great." My tone is sarcastic.

"The shoes will have to do. I don't think mine will fit you." I glance at Jessie's pint-sized height and tiny feet. "He's unlikely to notice they're bridal shoes. I'll go find Mr. Blingwood to give him the good news that you're here. When you're ready, grab yourself a coffee in the breakroom at the end of the hall. Sandy will bring Mr. Blingwood to come find you."

* * *

27

WHEN I'VE STRAIGHTENED out my hair and wiped off as much of the excess makeup as I can, I pull out my cell and google the company—ignoring the now half dozen missed calls from my mom.

I'm irked that Jonathon hasn't called and at least tried to apologize. I wonder if he even realizes I know what he's been up to, and then I decide I don't care.

I never want to see him again.

Scrap that, I hope he never gets a boner again! Then I think of what him cheating could mean for me. I know I'm definitely not pregnant, but I need to get myself checked out so I google a clinic. Then, out of sheer interest and a healthy dose of intuition, I check our joint checking account.

Apart from about fifty bucks, all the money from our joint account is gone!

When I look through the list of transactions on the online banking app, I see payments to restaurants, bars, holiday companies and Victoria Secret.

Fury rages a fire through my veins and I text him:

> Where is the money?

I haven't checked the account in a while, but I deposited the check from my father's estate into our joint account just last month. There was three thousand dollars left after we paid for the wedding.

I'm going to kill him. Which might be frowned upon but it'll solve my two biggest problems: I won't need to worry about a job or accommodation because I'll be rotting in jail.

Scratch that, I look awful in orange and I don't think I could eat prison food.

I take a deep breath and try to keep my shit locked down.

I need to deal with the problem at hand: the interview.

I start by searching job recruitment websites for the

Blingwood Resort. I'm hoping to find honest reviews from previous employees.

Don't even bother! This place is hell on earth. NOT PARADISE. The manager is a gorilla!

You could donate a kidney to this asshole and he'd still fire you.

If I had one piece of advice it would be: don't work here.

My gut twists while I click on the link to read more. As the screen whirls, nausea spins my empty stomach.

What am I doing here?

I dash to the cubicle and when I'm certain I won't be sick, I take some tissues and tuck them beneath my arms. Sweaty pits certainly won't improve my interview.

"Oops. Sorry, I didn't realise anyone was in here," a lady dressed in sweatpants, sneakers, and a baggy T-shirt that reads: *Gone Dogging*, says as she walks in. She has wonderful silvery white hair that's stylish despite its wild curls. She steps around me to wash her hands at the sink and then grabs a towel, dries her hands and then uses it to brush away tiny white hairs from her clothes. "Dog hair. I swear, you think you got it all and then..." Her gaze shifts to mine and then she pauses. "Are you okay? You look shaken."

She has one of those sweet smiles that draw you in, and so I explain, "I'm fine. I mean, I just got here after the worst experience of my life and now I have to interview for a position as assistant to the CEO who, might I add, is famed to be a 'gorilla'." I take two more paper towels and squeeze them beneath my arms. The lady looks at me curiously. "Are you warm? I'm boiling."

She smiles and holds out her hand. "I'm Cassandra."

"Layla," I provide.

Cassandra pulls out an unopened bottle of Evian from the bag slung across her shoulder and hands it to me. "You're probably dehydrated and your nerves are getting the better of you, but you're going to ace this interview. I have it on good authority the CEO just ate a good lunch and he's feeling bright and friendly. Close your eyes."

I do as she asks since she's got such a calming, kind vibe.

"Repeat after me," she says and I nod. "I am a valuable member of the team." I repeat the sentence but my voice sounds doubtful. "Visualize yourself being Mr. Blingwood's right-hand woman. When he is stressed and in need of a calm voice in a stormy environment, you are that person. You are the one who will anticipate his needs and help him find the very solution to his problems, and in return he will respect and value your support."

I imagine myself dashing through reception holding the important document he couldn't find and imagine how warm my insides will feel when he thanks me for saving the day.

It beats returning to the small town in Oregon to face my mother and my cheating ex.

"And, this is the most important part, repeat after me, 'I've got this, and I ain't taking no crap. Logan Blingwood needs me!'" My eyes blink open to find Cassandra winking at me. "It's true. He's desperate and stressed and you're going to be just the person to help him. You're going into that interview and you will tell him your worth and demand a fair shot!"

Her faithful pep talk helps provide me with a sense of control.

He needs me.

This *gorilla*, whether he likes me or not, needs an assistant.

And I need this job and the apartment that comes with it.

"Better?" she asks.

My hands are no longer shaking and I feel cooler, less like I'm about to spontaneously combust.

"Yes, thank you!"

"Here, take this in case you feel yourself getting clammy."

She hands me a white cotton hankie with a picture of a dog embroidered into the corner. "It was a gift from my son. He's useless at buying gifts, but his heart is in the right place."

"Thank you. You've been very gracious. Hopefully I'll see you around, if I get the job."

"Oh, you'll see me around. Now, what are you doing Saturday?"

I shrug my shoulders. "I only just got here. I have no plans for Saturday or any day for that matter."

"Wonderful," she says. "Here's my card. Come see me Saturday at nine." She presses a white card into my hand that's embossed with the logo: Free Spirit Pound Rescue. "We're looking for dog walkers."

I stare down at the card. "I've never walked a dog before."

"Beginners are welcome." Her smile is warm and inviting, and I instantly decide that she's the kind of person I'd like to spend time with.

"Thank you. I'd love to help." And I might as well since I am in a new place with no plans, no friends, and no family to call upon. "So long as I get the job. What if he's an awful gorilla like the review says?"

"Oh honey, a beautiful young woman like you, he'll be putty in your hands. And besides, even if he is the grumpiest of gorillas, give him a chance, okay? Even King Kong was just a cuddly bear underneath it all once he was in the hands of the right woman."

* * *

I ENTER the breakroom through a large opening off the corridor. A television on the wall is playing the news and there are two black leather sofas, but otherwise the room is similarly styled to the rest of the resort with modern white walls and polished marble floors.

When I spot a coffee machine over by the window, so I fill a cup while I wait for Mr. Blingwood. After a few minutes of watching a weather reporter announce record July temperatures, a guy walks into the room, empty coffee cup in hand, startling me.

As he pours coffee, his eyes lazily flick to mine and his lips tip up at the edges. "You must be new around here since I never forget a face, especially not one as pretty as yours."

He crosses the room, his left hand outstretched for me to shake. As I put my hand in his, he looks at my hand. My finger feels bare without the ring I've been wearing the past six months. The guy—who I am guessing is an employee—is around my age, maybe a year or two older and dressed in a flawless white shirt and black chinos without socks. His hair is glossy and black and he's freshly shaven.

"My name's Layla. I'm interviewing for the CEO's assistant position."

He pulls a face that is not comforting at all and I pull my hand from his firm grip. "Oh, you're going to be *his* assistant?"

"Well, yes, if I get the job. Should I be worried?" I put my coffee cup down on the table and rub my palms against my skirt.

He casually sits beside me. "I'm Mike. You'll probably be fine." His smile becomes strained. "It's just—"

"What?"

"Logan is known around here for being an asshole. But who hasn't had an asshole boss before, right?" He chuckles smoothly but I don't laugh. "Don't sweat it. I'll watch your back."

Unease and exhaustion grip me. My emotions have been thrown back and forth so much that I've got whiplash.

"Once you get used to it here, you'll find most of us are friendly. Will you be living at the resort?"

I nod. "Housing comes with the job, right?"

"Right. At the moment, I'm living with my mom but I plan to move out soon. Perhaps when I do, we'll be neighbors." He pulls out his cell, then smoothly slides his elbow to rest on the back of the sofa we are sitting on, bringing him even closer to me. "Give me your number and I'll show you around. I could take you for a drink to celebrate your new job."

Mike's eyes are twinkly. He's good-looking but I've only been single for a day so I decide it's best to let him down gently.

"Miss Bowers? Mr. Blingwood will see you now."

I'm startled by the sudden voice inside the room and glance behind me to see the woman, whom I assume is Skyla's assistant, Sandy, gesturing to the man beside her. He's tall enough to cast her in a shadow and so thickly built that his shirt pulls taut over his shoulders and biceps.

He's *very* good-looking.

Scratch that, he's gorgeous.

So appealing, it's jarring. Unsettling even. Suddenly my hands don't know what to do with themselves and I feel self-conscious, especially when I look down at my ridiculous bridal shoes. Still, I can't help turn back and gaze in wonder at him like one would a spectacular sunset or a shooting star. Men like him are normally in magazines or on television, not in the standard American workplace.

His deep brown eyes, strained by an arrogant stare complete a full appraisal of me. It's impossible to tell if he approves of me, but his glower is so powerful it commands me to stand at attention.

He's so... intimidating.

Every inch of the boss of the Blingwood Resort looks tense—bordering furious, except his glossy hair that's the color of spun caramel and silky enough to model in shampoo commercials. He's in his mid-thirties and wearing a black shirt rolled to his elbows revealing tan skin covering thick chords of muscle that ooze brute strength and power. But what dries my throat and makes it difficult to swallow is how his lips look when he speaks. Soft and full, yet 100 percent masculine.

Inviting.

I should probably introduce myself or go and shake his hand—that's the professional thing to do in this situation. But I feel like I just laid eyes on Channing Tatum's better looking brother, and if I blink or even move an inch, I'll miss the part where he rips off his clothes and grinds his body against mine.

"Miss Bowers?" His tone is so deep and measured that the hairs on the back of my neck stand on end and the skin against my panties quivers.

I clear my throat and almost choke on my saliva at the sexy tone he uses to say my name.

His stare becomes impatient. "Can you tear yourself away from Mike, or should I book an appointment for when you're ready?"

CHAPTER 4

LOGAN

*H*er eyes widen and her mouth pops open like she's in a state of shock.

Mike was asking for her number when I walked in, I could tell from the way he had his phone in his hand, ready to enter the digits. No wonder he's lavishing attention on her —she's striking.

Innocently beautiful. Like she hasn't realized it yet.

She's got this flock of black hair that makes her turquoise doe eyes stand out and sparkle. Her lips are full and pink, conjuring up powerful images of how they might look around my...

Her skirt is short—much shorter than normal for the office—and I swear I can see a hint of a garter belt at the top of her lithe thighs. The shirt that's tightly pulled across the impressive swell of her breasts threatens to eject the buttons and expose her assets.

My cock twitches.

Mike stands and hands her a white silken pouch too small to hold much other than a cell phone. He's staring at her breasts too and it makes me want to break his face. She thanks him and begins the ten steps toward me, slowly, like she's trying to regain her composure.

Mike walks beside her, too close. But what's making me even more uncomfortable is Miss Bowers doesn't seem in the least bit wary of the predator beside her. Hell, maybe he's not a predator. All I know is he was a dick to my sister-in-law before she married my brother. Last time I checked, Skyla said Mike avoids her where possible and when they do have to work together, he is professional and Mike'd better keep it that way or else I'll be introducing him to my boot as I kick his ass out of the door. I don't trust him. Leopards don't change their spots and I intend to get rid of him as soon as I can fire him without a lawsuit.

"Mike, have you completed the mid-month report?" My voice is icy but I don't give a damn. He pisses me off.

"I—"

I interrupt his stuttering. "On my desk by the end of the day." Mike widens his eyes at the woman as though trying to communicate something, so I cut them off by barking, "Back to work, Mike!"

I enjoy it more than I should when he jumps at the sound of my voice. Then Mike slowly walks away, trying to keep his cool in front of the woman. I glare at his back until he is out of the room.

Beside me, Sandy shifts her weight onto the other foot. Her voice is an octave higher, a few shades friendlier than usual as she takes short steps toward the new PA. "It's so nice to meet you. Thank you for waiting patiently. If you'd like to come with us."

I remain at the edge of the room as they walk toward each other. I'm against the wall, sizing up Miss Bowers's slender five-foot-six frame. Her over-the-top, white strappy heels might increase her inches, but they aren't increasing her confidence.

"*Layla*," Sandy emphasizes the woman's name for my benefit, "you don't need to be nervous. We'll go easy on you, won't we, Mr. Blingwood?"

"Logan," I correct. Last thing I want is this new office woman calling me *Mister* every five damn minutes.

Layla stares up at me through impossibly thick, dark lashes. She's got a sexy vibe but she looks exhausted. Spent. And not in a good way. Perhaps she had a long journey here.

"Skyla emailed me and Mr. Blingwood to say she's confident you'll be a great addition to the team. Let's complete a short interview and get you settled into your apartment. I'm sure you're tired and in need of a rest before you get started tomorrow."

"I'll be the judge of whether she's joining the team, thank you, Sandy." I gesture in the direction of my office. "Come with me."

"I thought we'd interview Layla together—"

I turn to Sandy and she stops talking mid-sentence.

"Sandy, please go inform my three o'clock I'll be late."

"But I was going to—"

"That won't be necessary. I'm not an evil dictator, and I'm sure Layla doesn't need you to hold her hand." Sandy looks uneasy, Layla even more so.

I inhale deeply. A mouth-watering vanilla scent flavors the air as Layla shifts closer to me. It reminds me I still haven't had lunch and I'm starving. Sandy throws Layla a helpless look which I find annoying. I'm not a grouchy boss even if the reviews say otherwise.

"Follow me," I tell Layla and lead the way to my office, her shoes tap across the marble so lightly it's like she's made of air and her sweet scent irritates my nostrils the entire way.

When we get to my corner office, I open the door and gesture for her to go inside then I sit down and notice that Sandy has helpfully placed Layla's resume on my desk. I pick it up to look at it while Layla cautiously lowers herself into the chair in front of my desk, but as she sits, the sound of paper crunching fills the quiet office.

I immediately stand and lean over the mahogany desk that forms a partition between us. "Did you just sit on my sandwich?" My tone is incredulous. The words leave my mouth through gritted teeth and instead of an innocent question it sounds like, "DID. YOU. JUST. SIT. ON. MY. SANDWICH?"

Layla's jaw drops and she immediately stands and swivels her body to lift the now flattened paper bag. She picks it up between her delicate fingers and holds it out between us.

The lemon-spiced mayonnaise has seeped through the wrapper. It drips on the polished wood of my desk and my stomach clenches. My body tenses and for just a second, and I swear my vision clouds red.

Layla's expression is apologetic, but it does little to quell my hunger as she pulls a white handkerchief from the ridiculous silk pouch she carries and uses it to smear the mayonnaise across my desk.

"I'll just clean that up. I'm sorry. I didn't notice the sandwich. I'm sure it's still edible." She opens the bag and looks inside. Her face tells me everything I need to know. "The filling has all squished out but it'll taste better than it looks. I can get you a spoon?"

"A spoon?" I choke out a laugh and then take the bag from her outstretched hand and fling it in the trash can.

If I had an assistant already, I'd ask them to bring me two Tylenol and a jug of water—scratch that, a beer.

"I really am sorry. I—"

"Forget it," I say more sharply than I mean to. It was an accident, I remind myself.

An accident that cost me my lunch!

I lift her resume and distract myself with the task in hand.

Layla stands opposite me, bobbing nervously from one foot to the other—her breasts jiggling like they might break free from the fabric. It's making me dizzy. "Please, sit."

She does as I ask and I can feel her gaze as I skim the multiple pages of her resume.

"I know it looks bad on paper but I've gained a lot of experience."

I put her resume down and watch her cheeks flame. She's certainly pleasing to the eye and has this little-lost-girl vibe that she probably uses in all manner of ways to get what she wants. But thanks to Dana, I am accustomed to deception and it won't work on me.

Not anymore. I'm immune.

"What exactly looks bad? Gracelessly destroying a man's lunch or having such a vast work history."

While she squirms in her seat, I read aloud. "Aside from your last position that lasted two years, you've moved jobs every six months—sometimes more often. A car insurance center, a school office, Sleep Tight funeral home. Before that a train conductor."

Her smile weakens and I can tell she was worried I'd pick up on her flightiness.

"I can't picture you as a train conductor," I mutter dryly. But as I force the image of Layla in a hat and uniform into my mind, I think I discover a new kink.

"It was fun riding that train but some days, it was so hot I was desperate to get off." She continues innocently, having no clue that my thoughts are heating at the mention of hot rides and getting off. "I had to collect the money, check everyone had a ticket, and that they were adhering to safety guidance. People don't realize, there's a lot more to conducting folks than you might think. At the end of each trip, I did the accounts and banked the money. I've developed a number of abilities, including dealing with difficult customers and my skills are all transferable to this position. I'm sure they'd give me a good reference if you called them."

I glance down at her resume again. "So you were a conductor?" She shrugs her shoulders and throws me a nervous smile that does little to distract me from the unsuitability of her work history. If it weren't for the fact I'm desperate, and her most recent job is more aligned—albeit vaguely—with the skills needed for this position, I'd have already kicked her out. "It says you left for *health reasons.*" The corner of my right brow tips up. Her skin has a light sheen like she's suddenly too warm.

"The chiropractor suggested I give my two-weeks' notice. The track was bumpy and well… I have large breasts and the movement was giving me a backache, not to mention motion sickness on a bumpy ride for eight hours a day."

Suddenly my eyes fix on her breasts and I have to drag them away. They are indeed large, squashed beneath her shirt and threatening to make the buttons redundant. The image of her bouncing around on a bumpy ride has my balls suddenly aching.

I shift in my seat and read aloud the position she held before that. "Receptionist in an adult assisted living facility. You managed seven months there, well done," I say more sarcastically than intended. "Reason for leaving: *Stress.*" I tilt my chin up and stare into her impossibly turquoise eyes then look away. If she can't handle the stress of working in a retirement village, then she'll have ulcers before the day is out working with me.

"I loved that job. The residents were wonderful and I got to know all of them so well, but… um, some don't live very

CHASING THE WRONG BRIDE

long and I found saying good-bye really hard. It was just too difficult and it was making me sad. I'm not good at good-byes."

"Yet you say good-bye so often," I deadpan. "Why did you leave your last position?"

Layla bites down on her lower lip, making it plump either side of her front teeth. There's a vulnerability that unsettles my soul and I suddenly wish I hadn't asked—whatever it was, judging from her expression, it was bad.

"Difference of opinion with management."

I think aloud as I finger the pages. "There are no pauses between positions, so I deduce it's not your work ethic that's at fault—you just can't seem to settle anywhere—apart from the last place. How is it you managed to stay there two *whole* years?" Again, I can't keep the sarcasm from my voice, which I'm going to blame on the fact I have no sandwich to eat and my stomach is starting to eat itself.

She looks away, then up at the ceiling. Her hesitation has me impatiently waiting to hear her speak again. Furthermore, it annoys me that I'm so interested in this woman's transient ways, especially given its triggering effect on me. The last thing I need is another flighty, potentially untrustworthy woman in my life, even if she's just my PA.

Finally, Layla tilts her jaw and squares me straight in the eyes with a *fuck-you* glare. "My father was sick and undergoing cancer treatment, so I moved to my hometown to help take care of him. As you can see from my resume, I worked in recruitment for *'two whole years'* while I cared for him."

Way to put your foot in your mouth, asshole.

I soften my tone. "Sorry to hear that. I hope he won the battle."

"He didn't," she replies curtly and I fucking deserve it.

"Losing a father is tough," I reply softly and then pause as

I shuffle the pages of her resume before putting them down in front of me.

She's not what I'm looking for and yet I can't help but keep the conversation going. "Tell me why you want the job and what can you bring to the role."

When I draw my gaze back to her, she's looking up through her lashes—her jaw set in a way that confirms she's still pissed with me, but carefully considering her reply. "I want a new challenge." She smiles through her formulaic answer, though I can tell it's fake. "I'm creative and diligent and I think you'll benefit from my help. You are, after all, in need of assistance."

"I'll benefit from your help. Really? I must have missed that particular quality when you sat on my lunch." I curl my lips sinfully, fully aware it was a low blow but my low blood sugars and her sweet scent are playing havoc with my ability to be rational.

She ignores my joke and continues. "You'll see from my excellent references that when I commit to a role—"

"For those few short months that you commit—" I interrupt and she scowls angrily at me.

"—for however long I may be in a position, I commit and I work hard. Any of my previous employers will tell you as much. I'm flexible…" *God, I bet she is.* "I can work hard and as often you need." *I fucking hope so.*

I pinch my eyes closed and when I look up, she huffs out a frustrated breath.

"It's the sandwich, isn't it? You're going to hold it against me." At her mentioning me holding *it* against her, I imagine myself doing exactly that. Holding myself against her and covering her tiny body with mine. I shake away the thought.

I need an assistant I don't have the desire to fuck.

"Miss Bowers. You have neither the staying power nor the experience for the role."

She raises her jaw with irritation, then closes her eyes. Her lips twitch momentarily as though speaking to herself. It reminds me of when my mom spouts her affirmations crap.

Layla sits taller in her seat and pierces me with those punch-you-in-the-gut, bright turquoise eyes. "Mr. Blingwood, I'm having a bad day, so perhaps I am not giving off my normal good vibes." She shakes her head. "Actually it seems to me, we are both having a bad day, but you can't hold my being a 'temp' against me for the *temp position* you are trying to fill. I have it on good authority that I have way more experience for this role than your last three assistants." I wonder how she knows that but I don't get the chance to press because she rolls right into the rest of her verbal assault. "Perhaps it is *I* who should be interviewing *you*. Your company's reputation has some questionable reviews regarding working for you. Maybe *I* should be wary of *your* history." She sits taller, finding her confidence in our sparring.

I shut her down. "Those reviews are most likely fake. The Blingwood Resort is a wonderful place to work. And actually, I need a permanent assistant. We are having temporary recruitment issues, so I am having to make do with a temp until a good candidate presents themselves."

Her expression turns smug. "Really? You're having recruitment issues. But you're so welcoming. I wonder what could possibly be deterring people from working with you?" Her smirk is sarcastic and sexy as hell. My back stiffens as I brace for her next challenge. "Tell me, why did your last assistant leave?"

"Beats me," I say.

"I'll consider the role on a trial basis, but I have other options. It's peak season, after all. There are resorts up and down the coast crying out for staff."

"Crying out for *good* staff, you mean."

"You need me. If you don't give me a chance, then you'll be without an assistant for even longer than you have been already. Can you afford that?"

She sucks in a breath as though she just mustered the last of her energy to berate me. But she does have a point. I just opened a new resort and am busier than ever. Even if she just answered the phones and dealt with my calendar and the constant bullshit, it'd be a help.

"Your trial period is six weeks." I decide on the spot to give in. I'm starving, exhausted, and frustrated—in a pants tightening kind of way. "I'll consider offering you a permanent position at that point if it works out. Unless six weeks is too long for you?"

"That length sounds perfect," she replies with a saccharine smile. Then she crosses one slender leg over the other. Her white shoes look like they belong on a child's dress-up doll. "So, the job is mine?"

"I'm probably going to regret this," I reply and she bites her lip to keep from smiling. Then I hear Mike in the corridor, loudly talking into his cell, and my shoulders stiffen. "You should know that we have a strict non-fraternization policy here at Blingwood. No dating between the staff." It's an outright lie, but if it somehow protects her from getting used by the likes of Mike then it's a worthy twist of the truth.

She lets out a whooping laugh. "Fine by me!"

"You start tomorrow." I stand and hold out my hand to shake and Layla puts her tiny hand in mine. The spike of adrenaline that pulses through my palm almost knocks me off my feet. I put the entire feeling down to my famished state.

"Thank you." Layla stares directly into my eyes and looks so relieved her mouth tips up into a dazzling grin that catches me off guard. I let go of her hand and take a step back, sending my leather office chair scuttling back along the marble floor. "I mean it," she says. "I'll be the best six-week assistant you ever had."

"Or the most troublesome," I whisper, then watch her hips sway as she walks away, her skirt temptingly sliding up her thighs to reveal a glimpse of a garter belt.

Sweet baby Jesus!

And even long after Layla has gone, I can't get the image of her turquoise eyes and tempting curves out of my head.

What the hell I have gotten myself into?

CHAPTER 5

LAYLA

*M*y legs are still shaking as I approach Sandy in the resort lobby.

Noticing my uneasy grin, she assures me, "He's not so bad when you get to know him. A pussy cat really."

I resist the urge to laugh. Sandy didn't look like she was petting a kitten when she was dealing with Mr. Blingwood, more like coaxing a lion.

"I sat on his sandwich," I admit.

Her face looks stricken. "You what? But Mr. Blingwood gets cranky when he's hungry." She laughs but tries to cover the sound with a cough. "Well, I guess it broke the ice?"

"It definitely broke something." *Like his willingness to give me a chance.* "For a second, I thought he was going to eat me." My cheeks warm as I remember the way his eyes fixed on mine and the things it did to my body. Suddenly I was too hot with the image of him bending me over his desk for a spanking.

"He'll have forgotten all about it by tomorrow. I'll order room service to have a snack ready and waiting for him when he gets back to the penthouse."

"Mr. Blingwood lives at the hotel?"

"Oh, yes. The finest penthouse suite in the resort. Perks of being the owner, I suppose. But you'll be comfortable in the staff apartments. In fact, we ought to get you moved in now that you're authorized." She peers over my shoulder and then waves her hand to someone. "Jessie, are you clocking out?"

Behind me, Jessie replies, "Yeah. I'm headed home now."

"Could you be a doll and show our newest employee where her apartment is?"

"Sure."

Sandy gives me a set of keys and I follow Jessie to a golf cart that's so loaded down with toilet paper and cleaning supplies I can barely fit in the passenger seat.

"Hold on!" she calls out and then drives the cart like we are being chased by the police. "Don't worry. I've been driving this thing for almost two years and I'm getting really good at handling it. Our apartments are the farthest back, but we'll be there in no time."

I hold on tight as we snake through the winding roads, passing three story hotel buildings and quaint little bungalows.

"Housekeeping is that building over there. It's where you can do your laundry in the evenings. And over there, that's the staff cafeteria," she calls over the sound of the motor.

We pass the tennis and basketball courts as we head inland away from the ocean. It's quieter the farther back we drive, with less people milling about, and those that are around appear to be staff in their various uniforms.

At the end of a block of small apartments, Jessie pulls to a complete stop. "This is you," she says, walking me right up to the door.

I fumble with the key and jimmy the handle a little until it opens.

"The staff accommodations aren't as fancy as the guests' but they're clean."

We step inside and I ask, "Have you worked here long?"

"For the last two years. Macy and I love it. We've got the beach right out front and the shops aren't far. There's so much to do here you'll never be bored and well, you can't beat the sunshine, right?"

"Macy. That's your daughter?"

"Yes. She's at daycare, but you'll meet her soon enough. We're in the apartment right above you."

"It'll be nice to have a friendly face nearby."

"Once you're settled, we'll show you around."

"Thank you. That sounds great."

We step farther inside and Jessie opens the blinds and windows. A flood of warm, late afternoon sun lights the room and I notice that is all it is.

Noticing my expression, Jessie says, "It's compact but has everything you need. The bathroom is through here," she points and I follow her to see the square shower cubicle, the sink and toilet, "and over here is the closet and bed." The bed is already made up with what look to be very nice hotel sheets. There's a small sofa opposite the bed that faces a coffee table and a television, and that completes my studio apartment.

"It's comfortable enough, but where do I cook?" I check. "There's no kitchen."

"Didn't anybody tell you?" I shake my head. "Staff meals are included in the perks. We all have meals in the cafeteria."

"Oh. No cooking."

"Free food," Jessie cheerfully replies. "Right, I'll leave you to unpack. I've got to pick up Macy at Betty's."

I look at her questioningly, as I have no idea who Betty is.

"Oh, right you've never met. Betty recently retired from the resort but still lives close by. She loves having Macy and Macy loves her too. Okay, holler if you need anything."

"Actually, there is one thing." Jessie waits for me to continue. "Is there a Target or Goodwill nearby? Perhaps a pawn store?" I pull the diamond ring from my pouch and then gesture to my tightly fitting blouse. "I need clothes, shoes and underwear."

Jessie's mouth pouts with concern. "Of course, I forgot, you turned up in just a wedding dress." She blows a strand of blonde hair out of her eyes and shakes her head. "Come with me. We can get you everything you need to get started down at the Second Chance Emporium. It's on the way to get Macy, and just wait until you meet Betty!"

JESSIE WAS RIGHT. Betty, who is in her seventies, is an utter hoot. I've never met a woman like her. As embarrassed as I was that she was asking about my sex life, she was hilarious and I hope I see her again.

After seeing Betty, Jessie showed me the way into town. The nice thing about living in fancy-ass towns are the thrift stores! They have way better stuff than the usual offerings in the other towns where I have lived and worked. I managed to get $500 bucks for my engagement ring, and so I stock up on underwear and a swimsuit from the new section and find a small collection of items to get me started.

If I want my clothes and shoes back from Jonathon's place, then I'm going to need to face him and right now, I can't deal with him—not when I'm this angry. But I do text him again to tell him I want my money back but I get no reply and when I call him, it rings like he's overseas. The idea that he's taken the woman he was cheating with to Bora Bora pops into my head and I force myself to block out all thoughts of him or else I'll drive myself crazy.

I'm about to take a shower when there's a loud knock on my door.

"You got the job!" Mike bellows enthusiastically from just outside the doorway.

"For now, but it was pretty hairy for a while."

"I was about to go to the cafeteria and I wondered if you'd eaten yet? I can show you the way, if you'd like?" He looks past me into the room, his eyes gazing around lazily.

The thought of food has my stomach responding with a growl so I grab my keys and agree to join him. By the time I have my new-to-me sandals on, he's taken a step inside my little studio.

"Is that your cell?" He nods his head to the little metal table with a glass top next to the sofa.

"Oh yeah. I've been so busy…" My voice trails off as I pick it up and see I have seven new missed calls.

"Someone's popular," he says and smooths his hand through his dark and shiny hair.

I slip my cell into my bra, wishing I wasn't popular at all. My mother is probably wondering when she will get her car back. "Annoying telemarketers or robo calls, probably," I say and then usher him out the door into the balmy evening air.

He leads the way. "Let me guess, you're one of those chicks who leaves her phone on silent all the time?"

I chuckle at the accuracy of his assumption, even if his use of the word chick is slightly irritating. "The sound of the buttons annoys me," I reply.

"It's a risk though, right? What if you miss an important call, like from me. Which reminds me, I still don't have your number."

"Oh, that would be truly awful… to miss a call from you!"

I joke, though get the impression that if that happened Mike would just call the next woman on his list.

We pass the laundry and tennis courts, and the smell of spices and warm food increases until my mouth begins to salivate.

Mike opens the door. "After you," he says and I walk inside the cafeteria to be met by a flurry of activity with what appears to be the entire resort staff loading plates and chefs in white jackets and caps filling up platters of food in multiple buffet areas.

Mike introduces me to a few people as we get in line, like Simon from security who tells me the location of his office in case I need of anything. Overall the people are friendly, especially Mike who helps load my plate and grabs me an extra roll from the baked goods section after I mention how I haven't had the chance to eat today. But he doesn't take any food for himself, explaining that his mom already made him dinner—which makes me wonder why he came by if he didn't plan to eat.

I look around for a place to sit but every seat is taken.

"A chair will free up soon. The night staff will be starting their shifts around seven. It'll be a mass exodus and then there'll be plenty of spaces."

Mike's phone rings and he looks at the screen. His lips curve up like he sees something tantalizing and then he looks guiltily at me and says, "I got to take this call. It's my mother. I'll catch up with you later."

"Yeah, no problem. Thanks for showing me the way," I reply but he dashes off.

My guess is he got a better offer, and I'm only mildly jealous he will be getting some tonight and I most definitely will not.

Still standing with my plate full of spoils, I spot someone vacating a chair and rush to take it before somebody else does. I put my plate on the table and lower myself down into the plastic chair and glance at my neighbor who looks at me apologetically before rushing off to start the night shift.

And so, without anyone to talk to, I pull out my phone and check my missed calls while I wait for my pasta to cool.

It's just as I thought.

And it's bad.

I now have eleven missed calls from my mom, and one from my ex, as well as five voicemails. I put the phone on the table and fork piping hot meatballs into my mouth. After a few bites, the vacant seat beside me is suddenly loomed over by an enormous shadow.

I flick my gaze upward.

He's wearing black shorts and a workout shirt that confirms exactly how muscular his broad shoulders are from what I'd assumed when I saw him in the button-down earlier.

"Mr. Blingwood," I greet him with a mouthful of balls.

"Bowers." He says my last name in a tone that is gravelly and deep and it makes my pulse quicken. The post-workout sheen he has going on is making him look more ripped male model than grouchy asshole boss than I'd like to admit. It's obnoxious he can look so tasty when he's moody and mean. His close proximity increases my annoyance.

"Is it safe for me to eat my meal here or should I acquire some PPE first?"

I quell my desire to shoo him away like an annoying child and smile saccharinely. "You're quite safe. My vendetta against your lunch is thoroughly dealt with now."

Logan Blingwood sits beside me and though it is clear to see that he has had a hard workout, he smells divine. On his plate are the meatballs from the hot food section, only his portion is twice the size of mine. Perks of being the boss, I guess.

"Good. Tomorrow you'll bring me lunch at twelve sharp. I'll be taking a Zoom call in the morning and I will be hungry by the time I'm done." He forks a meatball into his mouth and lightly groans an almost undetectable sigh of appreciation. Still, I kind of hope he chokes. "Unless you've already decided it's time to move on?"

I wasn't expecting to see him until work tomorrow, and I had hoped by then I would have showered and be feeling stronger. As it is, I'm tired and hangry and just want to eat my dinner in peace and then get some sleep before day *uno* of hell commences.

"You'll be glad to hear, I'm sticking around for now. So, of course, *boss.*" I say the word boss like it's mean and dirty. "I'll bring you whatever you'd like for lunch, and no worries of me sitting on it first."

I fork another meatball down like it's done me harm, but it tastes so good I'm unable to keep my pleasure at bay and let out a satisfactory sigh.

He points his fork at me. "Don't mess with a man's food, Bowers."

"It was a one-time thing, Blingwood."

We eat in companionable silence for a while. Both of us are seemingly too hangry to waste another second bickering until our plates are almost empty and the cafeteria has all but emptied out. But every now and then, I feel him watching me.

"I see Mike showed you the way here."

"Yes. He came and got me in case I got lost. Good thing really, as there isn't a kitchen in the room, and I had no idea we get free meals."

"That should have been noted in the job listing. None of the apartments have much by the way of cooking, except for the apartment for the head of housekeeping, who has a kid. Hers has an extra bedroom and a small kitchen." He takes another bite and licks his lower lip free from sauce. I do the same and hope there is no tomato sauce around my mouth. "It was very good of Mike to call on you," he says in a way that suggests he does not think it was "good of him" at all. His voice deepens. "You do remember the non-frat policy?"

"Yes. And there is nothing to worry about. I have no intention of…" I stop talking as my cell starts to vibrate across the table.

Logan's head twitches as he looks at the caller display. "*Jonathon* is calling you," he points out.

"I'm still eating. I'll call him back once I'm done."

Finally, my cell stops vibrating.

Until it starts again.

"Looks like *Jonathon* really wants to speak to you."

"Jonathon knows eating is important. He's very understanding." I switch the phone off and tuck it in my bra under the watchful eye of my boss.

Logan leans back in his chair and rests his hands on the flat of his stomach. From the corner of my eye, I can feel him staring at me but I refuse to meet his glare so instead, I take my plate and say, "I'll see you tomorrow, *Mr. Blingwood.*"

"It's Logan, and don't be late!" he calls after me, but I don't dignify him with a response.

Layla Bowers is never late!

THE NEXT MORNING does not go as planned, which I blame entirely on my poor night's sleep, and I find myself running late at the coffee shop at the edge of the resort waiting in line.

I was too stressed to sleep, so I texted Jonathon and told him not to bother calling me. I don't want to speak to him, I just want my $3,000 back. I don't even care about the stuff I have at his apartment. I'm used to traveling light, having moved around so much, and there isn't anything at his place that I feel particularly attached to—especially him. Then I logged into social media and saw Jonathon had marked himself as single. On his feed were dozens of messages from the women in town offering to help him through his hour of need "in any way he needs."

It royally pissed me off, so in a moment I am labeling as "unsmart decisions," I re-established my online dating profile, blocking Jonathon, who was live on the site, and set my location to Santa Barbara. After all, *I* have done nothing wrong and two can play at that game.

Hence, I forgot to set my alarm and now I'm at the coffee shop, dancing precariously with tardiness after I was specifically told *not* to be late.

"A double-spiced latte for Layla please, and a strong straight coffee for my asshole boss," I say, noticing the line of freshly baked muffins behind the counter. "I'll take two blueberry muffins too, please. One for me and one for him. Apparently, he's less of a gorilla when he's fed."

The woman behind the counter lets out a raspy laugh and tells me, "You got an asshole boss, too? Urgh, those creeps are everywhere!"

"I wouldn't say Logan's a creep, he's… highly strung." Yes, he's a little grumpy and seems perpetually stressed, but after a whole night ruminating about my asshole ex, I feel much less annoyed by my new, moderately assholic boss.

Logan Blingwood is a creative, corporate personality type and perhaps his passion can come across as gorilla-*ish*. He's bound to soften toward me once he sees how hard I work. We just got off on the wrong foot is all.

Today is a new day.

"Is he hot? Just makes it worse if he's using his sexual

power against you. They're the worse kind of boss. Don't worry, I got your back, sister!"

Hot?

He's a freaking volcano—not that I am interested. I would never go there—I had my fingers well and truly burned by Jonathon. Besides, Logan Blingwood emphasized the non-frat policy enough times that it's clear he would never go there either.

"I can tell by your blushes that's a yes—he's a hot asshole." She turns her back to me and pours the coffees while I reaffirm Logan Blingwood is as off-limits as it gets. "My boss is an asshole too. That's why today is my last day. Honey, you don't like that arrogant mofo... you find a way outta there fast."

I take the coffees and muffins from her and say thank you. I appreciate her negative positivity this early on a Monday morning. And she's right, this job is only to tide me over. If I don't like it, I can leave. In fact, I make a mental note to register with a new recruitment agency later and ask them to notify me of new vacancies, just in case.

I dash across the resort in my new-to-me, thrift-bought heels, shirt, and skirt, passing security—who let me into the office since no one else is here yet—and I seat myself at the assistant's desk, overlooking *his* office through a large glass wall with six and a half minutes to spare.

Since I haven't been shown what to do yet, I congratulate myself for getting here early despite all odds, and as a reward I pull out my cell and wait for Logan or Sandy to arrive.

I have a text from my mother asking when I am returning her car—like she doesn't have three others—and I wonder how I can get it back to her without actually having to see her, preferably before she reports it stolen.

Then I waste time and log into Tinder to see if anyone has matched my updated profile.

I have a notification!

I press on the icon but it takes a moment to load.

"You're still here. Congratulations," Logan says in a disinterested tone as he enters the room wearing a well-fitted suit that probably costs more than my entire wardrobe.

I drop my cell phone and jump up from behind my desk, coffee in hand.

Last night I vowed not to let Logan's gorilla-like qualities deter me from my quest. I can do a good job. I know I can. And I am in paradise with free food and lodging, and that is not to be snubbed just because I have to spend ten hours a day with this miserable son of a gun. So, I'm going to be a good employee and make the most of my time here until I can get my money back from Jonathon, save some cash, and move on.

"I bought you a coffee and a muffin. You know how you get when you're hungry." I smile sweetly and thrust them in his hand so fast he has to take a step back or risk being burned.

He takes the coffee and muffin with an air of suspicion. "And how exactly do I get when I'm hungry?"

"Not a morning person either, I see?" I chuckle good-naturedly but he looks pissed so I change the subject. "Looks like another sunny day."

"Like every day in California."

My cell vibrates across my desk. Logan stares in the direction of the device and narrows his gaze to the screen of my phone. "Miss Bowers, is that a dick pic on your phone screen?"

I spin around with such gusto I almost lose my balance.

There in all its glory is a closely taken photograph of an enormous penis, right on the screen of my phone, with a bunch of purple emoji and the message: *Wanna hook up?*

"It's not... I didn't... you see—"

"Company policy is phones *off* during work hours," he booms and then he storms into his office, shoving the glass door closed with enough force I'm shocked it didn't shatter.

When I look at the clock above the door, it reads eight-oh-one, and I cuss then block the big-membered bastard that sent me his "eggplant" just a minute into my very first shift.

CHAPTER 6

LOGAN

I log into the computer and prepare for my Zoom meeting but my mind is far away.

Who sent Layla the dick pic? Is she being reckless with her safety? She's obviously logged into a dating app, so is she searching for a hook up? And who was that guy calling her yesterday?

Jonathon. Is he her boyfriend?

A boyfriend would be the safest person to be sending her intimate photographs, but it still irks me. She didn't want to answer his calls at dinner last night, and the picture today was clearly from an app, not a text from a boyfriend.

Did she not answer because I was there or is it because he's some asshole who doesn't treat her right?

Questions buzz about my mind like flies I want to swat. I also want to squash the asshole who sent her the dick pic even though it isn't my place.

Why am I so bothered?

She is just my temporary assistant.

I sip the now tepid coffee and my stomach grumbles. I'm getting hangry. I unwrap the muffin she bought me and take a bite. It's good and I immediately feel shitty for not thanking her, but then I spot the muffin has something etched in sharpie on the wrapper: **Gorilla.**

So, she wants to play games.

I glance above my computer screen and see her talking to Sandy, probably completing the mundane new-starter stuff —fire drills, emergency contacts and computer log-ins. Layla looks over her computer screen and beams a smile which I return with a glare before ducking beneath my own screen and taking another secret bite of the muffin.

I'd like to assert I am more principled than eating some-thing that has been scrawled with childish messages, but I didn't have time for breakfast—I'm famished, which leads my decision to eat the vandalized muffin anyway.

Why would she even bother to get me the muffin in the first place if her plan was to use it as nutritional warfare?

Okay, so I was a little snarky in her interview yesterday, but everyone gets a little cranky when they're hungry, stressed, and in need of an assistant who is competent.

However, this act of rebellion will not go unpunished.

* * *

AN HOUR LATER, as I am about to join my Zoom meeting, I get a text from my brother Tate:

> You around, man? I really need to talk to you.

It's unlike Tate to send an SOS, so I immediately video call him.

"What's up? Mom said she's barely spoken to you. Everything okay?"

I recognize the background behind Tate as the trailer he uses between takes on the movie set.

"I think I fucked up," he says. Behind him, the background moves. He's pacing and his expression is worrisome.

"Nothing's that bad. What happened?"

"It's all over the internet. Everyone is laughing at me. I look like a complete fool."

"What happened?"

"Logan, someone made a meme of it. They're calling me *Triptastic Tate*."

A chuckle forces its way passed my lips and I disguise it with a cough. Making fun of my younger brother is anything but helpful right now, so I try to rein in my laughter.

Tate takes a deep breath, his face turning red with embarrassment. "I was out for dinner with Stella—my co-star and a bunch of the guys from the set, right? We're having a good time and I decide to show off a little. I attempted this stunt." He rolls his eyes, presumably at himself and shakes his head. "I just did it to make the people in the restaurant laugh."

"What kind of stunt are we talking about here?"

Tate squirms uncomfortably.

"I thought I could juggle some lemons while balancing a spoon on my nose. I'd had a few cocktails and it was supposed to be a silly little trick, but I ended up knocking over a whole table of drinks. It was a complete disaster."

I burst into laughter myself. "Did someone capture it on video? Please tell me they did. I need to see this."

Tate wipes his face with his hand. "Someone was recording it and they posted it online. The trolls dialed in on it and now there are memes! They've racked up thirty million views."

"Price of fame, brother. At least you weren't caught taking a leak like last time."

"I can't do anything anymore. Every move I make is captured by someone and ridiculed. Loag, it's getting to me."

The smile slips from my face. My normally carefree brother looks tired, his eyes downcast. Mostly the press coverage of him is positive, but after my own recent negative press following my ex accusing me of being a workaholic and an insensitive asshole, unbothered by a miscarriage—all lies I might add—I have a new understanding of how intrusive and unwelcome media coverage can be.

"Hey, your fans love you. And the haters, well they'll move on to the next viral video soon enough. When are you coming home?"

"As soon as we wrap filming in a month or two. Mom has been on my back about visiting and well, you know Mom."

"Yes, she's been on my back too. I thought I was being pragmatic, setting her up with the rescue center, while also keeping her busy and off my back, but now she wants me to be a volunteer mutt walker." I laugh half-heartedly. "I love seeing Mom happy, but I might have thought twice about buying her the non-profit if I'd known her new vocation would land me with a hobby I neither want nor have the time for."

"She's worried about you and enlisting you to walk the rescue dogs is a way of spending time with you. Since the wedding—"

"Give me a call when you're ready to come home and I'll charter the jet for you."

Realizing I have deftly changed the subject, Tate moves onto other news. "Have you heard from Drew?"

Drew, our older brother, just got married. "He's due back from his honeymoon in a few days," I inform Tate.

"Cool. I like Skyla, she's good for him. Makes me wonder

if you and I should take a leaf out of his tree and find something serious."

"Not me, Tate. I'm done with women but you can't be short on offers being an A-List movie star."

Tate grins. "Not short on offers. Just can't find the one. There was this one woman I met back before my career took off, but I didn't get her number and now I have no idea how to find her."

I laugh loudly. "Hollywood God Tate Blingwood got ghosted. Bet she's kicking herself now."

"No, man. She wasn't like that." He shrugs and expels a sigh. "Guess I'll never know if she might have wanted me for me. All I know is her first name, and quite honestly, if she got in touch now, I suppose I'd have to question why she wasn't interested in giving me her phone number when I was a nobody."

"There'll be other women but keep your wits about you, okay? I'd hate to see you fall victim to some scam like I did."

"Have you heard from Dana?"

My body tenses. "Not personally, but I'm still getting requests from journalists to comment on the demise of our relationship. Meanwhile, she's stopped posting outright lies on social media but continues to allude to the fact there was a pregnancy despite our proof that she lied. And now, the latest, if you will, her father's organization nominated the Blingwood Resort for an award."

Tate's mouth pops open. "Doesn't the guy hate you?"

I nod. "It's suspect. The awards are held annually and we've only ever been nominated once. Reading through the regulations by the Gee Foundation, it notes that votes are cast by the public and not by the organizers, still, I can't decide if I should go. An award like that will certainly provide proof of our quality. The accolade would be splashed on every booking website worldwide and it'd be brilliant, free marketing but…" I consider I'll probably come face-to-face with Dana and her father. Donald said he was disinheriting Dana, which is why she moved to my resort and how we ended up dating. As soon as she fled the wedding, Dana went to him so I guess they got over it. "It could be a ploy to have me lose out to some roadside motel and humiliate me further, or for Dana to spin it as some kind of story on her socials. If you'd asked me a year ago if I wanted the award, I would have bitten your hand off for it. Now… I just don't trust them."

Tate gives me a measuring stare and tips his head. "Or you could just attend with a beauty on your arm as a big *Fuck You* to Dana and the rest of the Gees."

I chuckle at Tate's poetic response. "That would be most deserved and it might end the media speculation about a reunion for Dana and me."

I take a sip of my now cold coffee.

"What's that on your cup?" Tate asks.

I lift the cup. "It's just coffee. My new assistant brought it in for me this morning."

"I know it's coffee! But what does it say on the cup?"

I lift and twist it in my hands until I find more offensive scribbling. "That, brother, says **Asshole Boss**." Anger straightens my spine. "I think my new assistant is pulling another prank."

Tate's cheeks rise up like he's holding back his laughter, and I realize how much I've missed spending time with him. We're both always so busy that seeing each other seems to only occur at mandatory family events.

"She sounds like fun. I'd love to meet her if she's showing you a thing or two. Is she hot?" he asks, and if he were here in person, I'd already have him in a headlock.

"No. She's irritating and frankly unqualified for the job."

"So, she's hot, then?"

I glance at Layla, sitting at her desk, following Sandy's instructions. She stares back at me and smiles. "She's doing her best to annoy me to death, that's what she is."

I hang up with Tate just as Sandy knocks on the door and asks if she can steal Layla away to go fix some IT issues. Behind her Layla is still smiling. The smile doesn't appear sinister, but she vandalized my breakfast and coffee with her scribblings, so she must be hiding her smugness.

"Sure," I say, my tone deceptively mild. "But Layla, when you return, I want to see you in my office."

"Me?" Layla asks, her face paling despite her upturned lips. "But you have a Zoom business call."

"Yes, you," I reply, unable to stop my lips from turning up wolfishly. "Don't fret, I'll make time to deal with you."

I have the pleasure of watching the smile wipe right from Layla's pretty face before she and Sandy turn to leave.

CHAPTER 7

LAYLA

"*W*hat is his problem?" I ask Sandy "I bought him coffee and a breakfast muffin as a peace offering. He's barely even seen me all morning. What could I possibly have done—apart from breathe—to have earned his ire now?"

She lowers her voice to barely a whisper and leads me down a corridor. "Man, I could sure eat a muffin. I'm on this diet and..." She looks down at herself in a disappointed manner. Sandy's got curves and she's beautiful. I'm about to tell her as much when she continues, "He's under a lot of pressure. He just opened a new resort and rumor has it, our Santa Barbara resort here has been nominated for the Gee Award. After what happened to him, well it's no wonder he's stressed."

"What happened?"

"You must have heard? It was in all the newspapers." I shake my head. I don't follow the rich or famous. "Oh. The most awful thing happened." She pulls her clipboard from beneath her arm and completely changes the subject. "We'll start in reception, complete a tour of the necessary departments and then circle back to IT to get your log-in set up. As Mr. Blingwood's assistant, you'll need access to your own calendar and his." She pastes a smile on her lips that I don't have the energy to return.

What happened to him?

It seems more important than ever I find out if I am to figure a way not to strangle him while I am his employee.

"How about on the way through the resort, we pop into the cafeteria and grab an early lunch. A big plate of fries and we'll both feel heaps better," Sandy offers.

"Okay, you're on. And I'll do my best to keep smiling. I don't know why he makes me so darn nervous."

Sandy snorts and says beneath her hand, "Because he is gorgeous. He's like a delicious dream and a mean fantasy all rolled into one."

"I hear ya!" I reply, "At least the mean fantasy part, anyway."

"You'll find a way to work with him," Sandy replies and she's right. Not everyone hates him. In fact, during our tour of the grounds, I notice that people seem to actually like Logan. Except Mike, he's made it quite clear he hates our boss.

So, if most people seem to respect and get along with Logan Blingwood, *what's wrong with me?*

* * *

SANDY SHOWS me the swimming pool and the gym, which will hopefully help me deal with some of the frustration I am carrying. Then we take a walk along the white sand while she points out the relaxation spots and double-canopied beds that are available for guests to rent. The view is stunning and picturesque, and I should be feeling happier, but my nerves are frayed.

Why did he sound so mean when he said he wanted to see me in his office?

I eat a chicken salad for lunch, and for balance I follow it with rich chocolate cake. Remembering that Logan told me to bring him lunch in his office, I grab him a turkey and cheese baguette and an apple.

When I enter my workspace, Logan's rich cologne scents the air, but the bosshole himself is nowhere to be seen—I guess he finished his Zoom call and then got called away from his desk. So I seat myself at my desk that directly faces his, though it is separated by a wall of glass.

I'm tempted to check my phone, but it's probably just full of messages from my mother noting how *disappointed* she is with me. And since I got caught with a dick pic on my screen earlier, I don't dare pick up my phone. Besides, the device feels dirty to me now, like I might catch some kind of venereal disease through the screen. I'll delete the dating app and sage the office later—receiving a dick pic in front of my boss is all the bad juju I need.

I leave Logan's lunch on the edge of my desk and follow the instructions to sign into the computer system. My first email is from Mike:

> Welcome to the team.
>
> Hope Bossman isn't being a dick!
>
> Want to grab a drink later?

SHAKING my head at his stupidity using his work email to call the boss a dick, I fire off a quick reply:

> Thanks, but I'm going for a walk with Jessie and her daughter. Another time?

I DECIDE against inviting Mike to come along with Jessie and me on our walk. I really want her to dish the dirt on Logan, and she might not talk freely if Mike is there.

MIKE'S REPLY IS IMMEDIATE:

> Another time for sure!

THEN I OPEN the next email. It's from Logan:

> See attached to-do list.

> Have it done by 6.

NO PLEASE AND no thank you. I open the attachment and my first thought is how long the list is, but equally I am grateful to have some tasks to busy myself with. I'm also glad that I don't need to bother Logan by asking him what I should do. It makes me wonder if I can find a way to communicate with him solely by email.

Now there's a thought.

I email him back:

> Yes, BOSS

The next hour passes in a flurry of activity while I complete the first section of my to-do list:

1. Call Simon from maintenance and ask him to repair the east entrance signage.
2. Arrange dinner for two at 8 p.m. next Thursday at Le Bateau.
3. Print monthly reports and put them on his desk ready for his meeting with accounts.

As I look over the list, I'm grateful to see that Logan has helpfully linked the company telephone directory so I can easily check off the first task.

Item number two isn't quite so easy since the company phone directory doesn't list the restaurant number, but thanks to an internet search, I manage to book the reservation. However, booking dinner for him has me wondering if he will be eating with a woman and if so, who said woman might be. Logan Blingwood is a multi-millionaire. Billionaire possibly. What type of women do men like him date? Certainly not a lowly office worker. No, I'll bet she's a socialite, model, Barbie lookalike with her own clothing line, or maybe even a Hollywood superstar—his brother is a movie star, so he mixes in the right circles to date an actress. She's probably five foot eleven with a waist the size of my thigh. Imagining such a woman on his arm sends a flare of annoyance through me. He must act entirely differently with her than he does with me or else why would any woman date him?

Because he's gorgeous and he has this powerful, sexy vibe going on that makes me feel like a very naughty girl who needs taking in hand.

And item number three is pretty easy, assuming he means *Mike.* Seems the dislike goes both ways.

CHASING THE WRONG BRIDE

I congratulate myself for navigating the printer easily and then walk into Logan's office with his lunch, ready to place both it and the freshly printed paperwork on his desk. But first, while he is gone, I complete a closer, unfettered inspection of his office.

The walls are decorated in the usual bright white but placed atop the perfect smoothness is varying awards of excellence for hotel, leisure, and tourism-type dalliances. There's a picture of Logan—looking mouth-wateringly hot in a sharp suit—with some other guy and the words at the bottom of the frame state "Business Man of the Year."

I inch along the impressive display but then I start to feel jittery that he might walk in and catch me snooping, so I turn around to put his lunch and paperwork on his desk and plan to leave when something catches my eye.

Atop his enormous shiny desk, laid out like a voodoo sacrifice, is the crumpled peace offering that got me no kudos whatsoever. The empty coffee cup and the paper muffin bag, side by side, placed carefully on a neatly spread-out napkin to save drips or crumbs.

Weird.

I take a closer look, sitting in Logan's leather throne that's almost as tall as I am, and then I see it:

Gorilla is written on the muffin wrapper and **Bossy Asshole** is scribed on the side of the coffee cup in a large cursive handwriting.

But why would he write that?

Unless.

Oh Fuck!

No wonder he was throwing daggers at me earlier. He must think I wrote it or that it's what I told the server she should write. I remember the woman in the coffee shop. Scorned by her own boss, she must have thought she was helping me fight the cause of asshole bosses everywhere, but little does she realize she has landed me in massive doo-doo.

"Comfortable?" Logan says, leaning against the doorframe, with his chocolatey brown eyes laser focused on mine and his brutish jaw set in a way that sends a shiver down my spine. He grins wolfishly. "You seem surprised, Layla. Not expecting the *bossy asshole* to return so soon?"

CHAPTER 8

LOGAN

*L*ayla looks stricken and I'm tempted to go easy on her. The way my chair swamps her tiny frame, makes her appear vulnerable. *Innocent and sweet.* But she isn't innocent and is obviously not sweet, and I'm tired of people thinking they can fuck with me.

I take long strides and cross the room in three steps, startling Layla. I loom over her until my hand is on the back of the chair and I can smell the sweet vanilla on her skin.

Anger fills me up from my toes but there is something else intermingled.

Want.

I'm overtaken with the desire to pin her by her shoulders against the chair and show her exactly how I feel she should be punished. I wonder if she'd be a good girl and take it all and if her magnificent blue eyes would water as she did.

"Admiring your creation, I see." I swivel the chair so she has no choice but to gaze up my body to look at me. The top of her head is practically level with my junk, and the way she looks at me with her invitingly full lips popped open is sending my pulse into overdrive. I lean back until her scent is less invasive and cross my arms over my chest, resisting my desires and forcing myself to stay professional.

Touching my index finger to my mouth as though pondering, she waits for me to speak. "Would you describe this as expressionism or pop art, perhaps?"

"I….I…"

I tip my lips up sinfully. "Didn't you expect me to notice? Did you think it would give the others a laugh in the office? Or was your aim to make me look like a fool in the Zoom meeting?"

"No! I… this wasn't me. It's a big misunderstanding, you see, I didn't write those messages."

"You got me the coffee and muffin?"

"Yes. I ordered it, and I brought it to you but—"

"Who do you suggest wrote it, if it wasn't you?"

"The barista." Despite being nervous, her voice is velvet. Then she brushes the back of her neck self-consciously, flicking her long—so dark it's almost ebony hair—across the breast of her shirt and all logical thoughts fly right out my head. "I would never write that. The coffee and the muffin, they were peace offerings. I was trying to win you over."

I nod slowly and her shoulders lower just an inch as she relaxes.

Layla picks up the offending items and stands so we are just inches apart. She's wearing leg lengthening heels, but her head barely reaches the top of my chest and I have to stoop my own head to meet her guilt-ridden eyes.

"Interesting descriptions the barista chose. What might have made them choose such insults, I wonder." Her ears pinken. "No need to come up with an excuse. I know exactly how the barista knew what to write." Her mouth pops open as she waits for me to explain. "So that's what you call me?"

She's looking up at me through her thick, dark lashes. Striking blue eyes capable of disabling a man's mind. "It was a slip of the tongue."

As if prompted, her tongue dips out to moisten her full lower lip and I swear her gaze flicks to my own lips. The air between us is tense but not as tense as my cock in my pants.

"Knock. Knock," Mike says from the doorway but my eyes stay fixed on Layla.

I lower my voice to a growl. "That's strike one. Don't push me again."

I hear her gulp as she slowly nods her head. Then she ducks away fast to get out of my sight. And while I should have fired her—I had grounds to fire her—all I can think about is how badly I want to teach her lesson.

CHAPTER 9

LAYLA

J'm in the bathroom flustered and way too warm for comfort.

What was that?!

Rather than being reprimanded, it began to feel like a prelude to some kind of very hot and very forbidden encounter. I've never felt such a need before. The way he looked at me, like I was something to eat and he was starving, had my knees shaking and my pussy whimpering.

I toss the coffee and muffin wrappers in the trash and run cold water, splashing it up my arms and on my cheeks.

Just breathe, Layla. Logan was peeved with you, that's all.

It wasn't some kind of hot foreplay, and he wasn't going to bend me over his desk and spank me—no matter how much I might have wanted him to.

I feel bad. Mean messages are not cool, even if they are somewhat deserved.

It takes me another few minutes to muster the strength to

return to my desk and get on with my to-do list. And every single time I dare look above my computer screen, there he is with his soft, dirty blond, tousled hair and serious brown eyes, staring at me like he doesn't know whether to fire me or fuck me.

And honestly, it has me so tightly wound I can barely breathe.

I want him.

It's ridiculous! I just fled my own wedding not two days ago. I've only known Logan Blingwood less than twenty-four hours, and he hasn't shown me an ounce of kindness. Okay, so I haven't exactly been a model employee so far either, but still, I can't allow myself to ponder red-hot fantasies about my boss.

His steely gaze is so jarring I have no choice but to lift my computer screen to block him out just so I can think clearly. I pull up a blank email and fire a message to the recruitment agency:

SOS. Please find me another position. ASAP!

* * *

I'm almost done transcribing the penetration report for Logan when Mike leaves his office.

"You okay?" Mike asks, putting the palm of his hand on my desk and leaning toward me as though a fellow conspirator. "That asshole in there is in a particularly shitty mood today."

Before I reply, I chance a glance toward Logan's desk to check he's still in his office, since knowing my luck he'd be standing right beside us listening.

Thankfully he is still at his desk, though he catches me looking.

"I fucked up," I tell Mike. "I'm fine though."

"Really, because when I walked in his office earlier you looked like you were about to fall apart."

"It was honestly all my fault. I'm not getting off to a very good start here." *And that is putting it mildly!* "It's so frustrating. I've always been proud of my ability to slip into a new job and make friends with everyone, you know?"

Mike leans in further. "Hey, don't sweat it. Everyone else here thinks you're great. Don't let that asshole get to you. Come out for a drink with me tonight?"

"I can't tonight, I already have plans."

Above my screen, Logan's eyes bore into mine. Then an antiquated intercom that's wired to my desk and doesn't match its sleek surroundings crackles before Logan's gruff voice orders: "Layla, I take my coffee at three. It's five past."

Mike shakes his head. "Asshole."

"I better get the boss a coffee," I reply, brushing my skirt down as I stand.

"Let me know when you're free. I promise we'll have a great night."

"Layla! Coffee," Logan barks and I instinctively push the button on the intercom down hard and it sticks a little. I stare at him as I reply, "I'm doing it right now, boss!"

"Would it hurt him to say please?" Mike says. "We could get a coffee one night, if you don't want to go to a bar?"

"I'll let you know when I'm free."

Logan barely even makes eye contact when I deliver his coffee but he does mutter, "Thanks," beneath his breath while he works on his computer.

I spend the rest of the afternoon fielding calls and taking messages while doing my best to restrain myself from looking at Logan. By the time six o'clock comes, my body aches and my nerves are frayed from the tension caused by *him* sitting right opposite me, aware of my every move.

I pray the agency comes through for me soon because much more of this, and I won't need a new job, I'll need Valium and a straitjacket.

* * *

PINNED to my apartment door when I get back is a note from Jessie: *Gone to the doctor's office with Macy. She's fine. Will meet up soon!*

I'm a little disappointed since I was looking forward to debunking my day with a friendly face but more concerned that Jessie's child is sick. I take out a scrap of paper from my purse, scribble my number on it, and a note to say that I hope Macy is okay. I slip it beneath Jessie's door. Once I'm inside my apartment, I plug my cell in to charge and shower off the tension of my day.

Having changed into my comfies, I flick on the TV but am unable to concentrate so I pick up my cell and go through my latest voicemails. The first three are from my mom:

SWEETIE, I spoke with Jonathon. It was all a big misunderstanding. Call me!

DELETE.

I had dinner with Jonathon and his father. Such lovely people. I honestly think he'll take you back if you come home.

DELETE.

Honey, you can't ignore me forever. You have my car. When are you coming home?

DELETE.

. . .

WHILE I WAIT for the next voice message, I wonder if it is acceptable to block my own mother.

The final message is from Jonathon:

"Layla. Hi. I spoke with your mother. She thinks you overheard some stuff that made you think I cheated. I would never cheat on you, you obviously heard wrong. I'm not going to lie; I don't know if we can come back from this. You left me standing at the altar. My grandparents came all the way from Michigan to watch me get married. Reporters were there and covered the whole story in the Herald. You humiliated me. All I ever did was try to help you after your father died and this is how you repay me? Anyway, call me."

DELETE.

I close my eyes to the sound of his voice and imagine Jonathon's blue eyes over blinking like they do when he is trying to be persuasive. His voice sounds strained on the voicemail, and it has me immediately questioning what I thought I heard when he butt dialed me at the chapel. But as soon as he mentions his grandparents and Michigan, it sounds exactly the same as he'd said to "her", and I know I heard right. How could I hear and understand that so clearly and the rest be wrong?

It can't.

He cheated and he's still lying about it.

My eyes snap open as I drag deep breaths into my lungs.

Resigning myself to the fact I will never see the money Jonathon took from me, I open Facebook and find a local community group where I find someone to deliver my mother's car back to her tomorrow. It's going to cost me the last of the money from pawning my engagement ring, but it's a small price to pay if it means my mother gives me space to process the last few days. Then I throw the phone down on the bed and stare at it.

I'm angry as hell but also lonely and I feel the pull of home even though all I have in Oregon is a man who cheated on me and a mother who thinks that's okay—that a cheater is good enough for her only daughter.

My eyes land on the swimsuit I didn't get around to putting away yesterday.

A distraction, that's what I need.

* * *

ON MY WAY to the pool, I see the woman from yesterday who talked me off the ledge when I was preparing for the job interview. She's wearing a T-shirt that reads: *I wish men were as easy to train as dogs,* and she's holding a tiny, grumpy dog by a lead. I lean down to stroke him. He growls at first and then leans into my hand, so I kneel for a moment and give him a good scratching behind his ear.

"You got the job?!" Her singsong like voice is truly positive so I try to match it.

"Yes." I smile through my uncertainty. Cassandra is so charmingly enthusiastic it's difficult to be grumpy around her. "I'm not entirely sure why he gave me the job, though." *Since I'm almost certain he hates me.*

I stand to face her and the dog shows me his disappointment at my ceasing the ear scratch by sitting on my foot.

"He's abrupt and he lacks manners sometimes, but he's learning," Cassandra says nodding her head to the dog.

"Same could be said for my boss," I reply, only half joking.

"Is he being a pain?"

I'm about to ask if she knows him but since he's the boss around here, it seems obvious. "I hear unanesthetized open-heart surgery is less painful than working with him."

She puts her arm across my shoulder. "What's he done now?"

I walk with her along the path toward the beach with the setting sun in the distance and suddenly his actions don't feel so bad. "It's more how he makes me feel. I made a few mistakes today. He disapproves of my long job history and well, he thinks I'm flaky."

"Why would he think that?"

"Well, because I'm a little flaky," I say and we both laugh.

"There are worse things to be than free. I think he'll see you for who you are just fine in no time at all." Her point resonates with me as we walk for a while. I haven't really had someone see me or appreciate just me for me... maybe ever.

Putting that morose thought away on top of the hellish couple of days I've had, I tell her I'm on my way to the pool for a swim and she offers to walk me there. Meanwhile, she tells me about Yogi, the dog she is training. "Sometimes you've just got to show them who's boss. Assert control. Don't let them boss you around. They have big egos, you see. You need to nip that behavior right in the bud or they'll think they can get away with whatever they like."

"Sounds like advice for dealing with my boss."

She smirks. "Demonstrate patience while you train the bad behavior right out of him and you'll be glad you persevered."

We stop as we reach the building that houses the gym and the changing rooms for the outside pool. Beyond it, the sun has finally seen fit to set on this most awful of days.

"Give it time. I don't believe any man could resist your charms for very long. Now, have a lovely swim, and don't forget, 9 a.m. Saturday. I've got the perfect girl in mind for you."

I thank Cassandra and after I have gone through the doors to the changing room, I realize, I never asked what part of the hotel she works at. Still, I suppose I'm bound to see her again.

After changing into my swimsuit, I put my towel and cell on the bench to the side of the pool and set a thirty-minute timer. The evening is warm and the water looks like a refreshing balm to ease my overheated body and mind. I rinse off beneath the outdoor shower and step into the pool, gliding onto my back and wetting my hair. Then I flip over and swim breast stroke to try and clear my head and leave behind all thoughts of absent mothers, ex fiancés, and sexy bossholes intent on driving me crazy.

CHAPTER 10

LOGAN

*W*hen her workday was done, she left without saying good-bye.

I don't blame her. Now that hours have passed, I think I actually believe her when she said she didn't write asshole boss on my coffee cup.

Maybe I was too hard on her.

Two hours of going through reports with Mike, followed by tiresome meetings with her sitting opposite me taking notes while trying not to look at me, felt like it lasted twelve hours instead of two. It became a game. I'd feel her gaze and though I was determined not to look at her, I'd seek her out moments later.

Flawless.

Her face is flawless.

Perfectly full, red lips. Hair so dark it should make her look pale but it doesn't; her skin glows with not a single imperfection. And her legs... Her legs are long without her being conventionally tall. Add in her 5-inch heels, and she has legs for miles. I've never noticed a woman's legs in this way before, but hers are so lithe and strong, like they could clamp around me and hold me prisoner. When we were arguing at my desk and she stood—almost up against me—I wanted to pick her up. See if she is as light as she looks, feel her weight in my arms and press her against me.

And Mike, the utter prick, asked her out. I saw his lips move as he asked her and saw her shake her head. I wanted to march in there and stick his head through the monitor.

She said no.

He'll keep trying, though.

She thinks there's a non-fraternization policy. That's why she said no. When she finds out no such policy exists, she'll say yes to him.

And it is none of my business.

I throw down the pen I have been holding for the past hour and switch off my computer screen.

I am not interested.

She is my assistant not my plaything.

Mike can have her. None of my business. He'll probably turn up at her apartment the second he gets off work. They'll chat about what an asshole I am and then he'll tell her that there is no policy with employees dating. In fact, there are already quite a few ongoing relationships in the resort. Living and working together like we all do; some might say it's inevitable.

I ponder this for a moment and then switch my computer screen back on and pull up my direct messages, finding Mike in the company address book. The little green light next to his name reassures me he'll get my message immediately.

> Mike. I need the last three years profit and loss accounts data on my desk first thing tomorrow.

There's a moment's pause before the swirling icon appears to indicate he is typing a reply.

> What? But I stayed late last month. That'll take me all night.

> On. My. Desk. By. Morning.

HE STARTS TYPING a reply and then must delete the message.

I log off from the system, turn off the computer, and then grab my workout gear. I need to spend some energy. And I need to get Layla out of my head.

As I pass Layla's desk, the scent of her perfume still hangs in the air.

Fuck me.

* * *

MINUTES INTO MY WORKOUT, erasing Layla from my thoughts becomes even more difficult.

She's right there. At the side of pool!

And she's wearing a sexy little red two piece that shows off all her curves.

I keep pummeling the treadmill as I watch her from the window that overlooks the outdoor swimming pool as she puts her phone on the bench, showers off beneath the moonlight, and descends the steps into the water.

She's the only person in the pool, not that she seems aware of her surroundings.

She's intriguing to watch. Deep in thought, swishing the water over her shoulders and acclimating to the pool temperature.

Replaying her disastrous first day at work?

Layla rolls onto her back, closing her eyes as though luxuriating in the pleasure of the cool water against the balmy night and wetting her long hair so it fans out around her. She moves her limbs gently to keep herself afloat. Under the soft glow of the outside lighting, her body—all her delicate curves—are illuminated.

I check side to side to see if anyone else in the row of treadmills is watching, but it's a quiet night and the only other person here is grunting as they stare at the built-in television.

Layla flips back onto her front and darts forward while I increase my pace to a sprint. She completes several lengths of the pool and her technique is impressive. I toy with going outside for a swim. I don't normally use the pool, but part of me wants to see her mouth pop open when she notices me. When there is barely a breath left in my body, I hit Stop on the machine but I can't tear myself away. She's getting out of the pool and the water clings to her like a shimmering second skin. Her body glows like a siren sent to destroy me.

Layla grabs her towel from the bench, wraps it around her and then picks up her cell.

"Nice night for a swim, huh?" The guy beside me says having stepped off the treadmill to watch Layla and chug water.

A growl escapes my lips.

"Might go for a swim myself," he adds.

Then he nudges me with his elbow and winks so I nudge him back, harder, and tell him, "Pool's closed!"

Five minutes later, I'm showered and heading into the pool. I don't look in her direction but I do show off my best dive and then I front crawl all the way to the other side and back again. I do a few lengths before I wonder what the hell I am doing.

When I get out, she's gone. And I have no idea if she saw my dive or was impressed with my physique, or if she even noticed it was me at all.

"Get a fucking grip, Logan," I mutter beneath my breath as I leave the pool to go change.

CHAPTER 11

LAYLA

I get to the office early with coffee and without any dick pics on my phone. I should be feeling good but I'm jittery.

Did Logan see me last night in the pool?

I saw him.

Diving in like a member of the national swim team. The light illuminating every hard, ripped muscle like he was sculpted entirely for my viewing pleasure. I couldn't tear my eyes away—if he caught me, I'd probably be in BIG trouble.

Am I subconsciously intent on getting my ass fired?

Hiding behind a giant potted palm tree while perving on my boss will get me recognition but not the type that will get me a pay raise or a promotion—no, it's more likely to get me arrested!

Get it together, Layla. You need this job and the housing that comes with it.

I put Logan's coffee on his desk along with a white

chocolate and raspberry muffin. The server was someone different today, but I still double and triple checked it wasn't scribed with any *special* messages.

"Is everything set for my eight-thirty?" Logan asks, striding into the room. His suit is black. His shirt is black. His eyes look black from lack of sleep, his dirty-blond hair unrulier than its usual impeccably finished style.

He speaks to me as though commanding, "Everything had better be ready for my eight-thirty or your ass is out of here."

Great.

Instead of hangry and grumpy Mr. Blingwood, today I get tired, hangry, and grumpy Mr. Blingwood.

I push my freshly painted lips upward. "Everything is ready. I've printed the transcripts you asked for and have moved your ten o'clock to ten-thirty so you're not interrupted by the 10 a.m. fire drill."

He pauses in the doorway, as though deciding whether I did a good job or not. Meanwhile, I'm picturing him in his swim shorts. A man with a body like his should definitely wear swimwear at every possible opportunity. Not that that it would help me complete my duties. No, even in a conservative, well-cut suit, it's difficult to think straight in his presence.

"Good."

"There's a coffee and a muffin on your desk."

He clears his throat and I wish I hadn't mentioned it. "Thank you."

I almost choke.

"Are you okay? You look startled," Logan says.

"Yes, I'm fine. It's just you said, thank you."

His nose crinkles. "I say thank you all the time."

Not to me you don't.

His eyes fix on mine and my heart thuds against my ribcage. "Thank you for the coffee and muffin, Layla."

"You're very welcome, Mr. Blingwood."

His nostrils flare. "It's Logan, and I'll be in my office."

When he leaves the room, closing the door behind him, it's like the air is suddenly returned to the room and I suck in a breath. Logan seats himself behind his desk, glances down at a file Mike slipped on his desk earlier, and then gets up and throws it in the confidential trash bin. Then he brings his computer to life.

I try not to watch his every move, but it's impossible. I am hyperaware of him.

My intercom crackles. "Layla, you've booked an eight-thirty for me with a Mr. Valeska. Who is he?"

I booked the meeting in yesterday. "Beats me. He said he needed a meeting with The Boss."

At the time, it felt like the right thing to do, but judging by the glare he's throwing me through the glass wall, I messed up.

AN INSTANT MESSAGE pings on my screen from Sally in reception:

> Hi Layla. Mr. Valeska is here for Mr. Blingwood. Can you come down and get him?

I KEEP my gaze trained on the wall and go meet the visitor, praying I didn't just arrange a meeting with the head of the local cult recruitment service.

My heels clip-clop across the marble and I greet the visitor. He has a professional-looking briefcase and is wearing a well-worn suit with a logo on the breast pocket. I let out a sigh of relief he doesn't seem to be affiliated to any religious group and lead him to Logan's office.

"And you are?" Logan's voice is professionally courteous yet cautious.

"Marvin Valeska. Your assistant kindly booked me in. I'm here to discuss your photocopying needs."

The pit of my stomach plummets. Logan's eyes darken and his jaw twitches.

"Come right in, Mr. Valeska. You came at a most crucial moment. Our photocopying needs have been keeping me awake. Nothing is as important as this matter—not the thirty-million-dollar resort I have recently opened, or the intensity of peak season of my business. No. Let's talk printer ink."

Logan hammers a stare at me over Valeska's shoulder, which he follows with a smile that is anything but friendly.

"Should I bring you more coffee?" I ask. My voice is a squeak, my legs are jelly.

Logan's nostrils flare as he replies, "I think that is the least you can do."

* * *

AFTER A SHORT, seven-minute meeting that's over before I get the chance to serve the coffee, Logan shows Mr. Valeska out, and then he stands over my desk as his long fingers massage his temple.

"Layla, when you book appointments into my calendar, you must first check who they are and what they want. If you are unsure whether they are a good use of my time, check with me first."

"I'm sorry. I didn't—"

"No, you didn't. There are a number of companies who would like to sell us any number of useless items and waste my time. We have already sourced the very best deals in all our business paraphernalia. Hell, I have procurement staff that look after that side of the business. I don't have time to deal with such matters. Understood?"

"Perfectly."

He turns and takes a long step toward his office.

"Logan."

He looks back at me over his shoulder and my stomach somersaults.

"Should I bring you a cookie with your coffee?"

His lips quip up in a half-smile. "I think that would be best." He takes another step, then turns back to me. "Thank you."

"You're very welcome," I reply with a grin.

* * *

THE MORNING GOES without any further hitches and by lunch time, I feel calmer. At twelve on the dot, I pull out my phone and see I have a message from Jessie:

> Did you put the comic book beneath my door? Thank you! Macy loved it. Meet me in the cafeteria at lunch?

I TYPE a quick reply and tell her yes, I got the magazine from the gift shop on the way back from the pool last night. It had a free picture book attached to the front and, betting that Jessie is the type of mom who reads a bedtime story to her kid, I couldn't resist picking it up.

I used to have bedtime stories all the time—until Dad left

and Mom was usually out every night at the country club. It's no big deal; it was just the simple act of a story before sleep. I don't even know why it matters to me. By the time I was six, I had learned to read enough that I could manage the little board books Dad bought me, but I vow that if I'm ever lucky enough to have children, they'll get a bedtime story every single night.

"Wasting time on Tinder?"

Startled, I look up and blink before answering. Logan has one of his thick brows raised and he's removed his suit jacket. His shirt sleeves are rolled to his elbows, revealing his toned forearms. I tear my eyes away and glance at the clock. I don't dignify his dig about online dating. Instead, I reply, "It's my lunchbreak."

"And are you going to lunch?" He studies me like I am a puzzle. "You looked deep in thought." He shakes his head and dismissively says, "You should eat. We have a busy afternoon."

I take my lipstick out of my purse and apply it using the timed-out black monitor as a mirror. He makes no effort to move. I add a spritz of perfume and stand, the whole time I can feel him watching me.

"I'm meeting a friend for lunch," I say, having no idea why I said such a thing except perhaps to demonstrate that there is someone who likes me—even if he cannot stand me.

As I walk forward, he does too and our arms touch as we attempt to leave through the door. He stops and gestures for me to go first. "I wasn't suggesting we have lunch together," he provides.

I glance at him from the corner of my eye. He has a deep crease between his brows. We continue to walk toward the cafeteria, neither apart nor together.

"Let me guess, you're eating with the shmuck from accounting?"

I'm almost expecting him to throw the nonfraternization policy in my face but instead he stops walking and so I do too. We're staring at each other like it's some kind of tense stand-off.

"You really ought to learn the names of your staff, *Mr. Blingwood.*"

His jaw tenses with frustration. "There are over one hundred staff here, *Miss* Bowers. I can't possibly be expected to know each of their names."

"No. You're right. Perhaps you should give everyone a number and have them communicate with you by email only. It may save you more of your precious time." I grin playfully.

He returns my grin with a scornful smirk. "Great suggestion, Bowers. Write me a two-thousand-word proposal on the benefits of your suggestion with estimates of the time and money it will save. Have it on my desk by 6 p.m."

His eyes are deadly serious so I play along, holding my smile steady.

"Yes, Mr. Blingwood." I continue walking and he does too. "I'll clear my calendar this afternoon and visit each department to take an inventory of names and positions. Maybe Mike from accounting will be able to help me. He does deal with payroll after all. He's bound to know everyone's name."

Logan bares his perfectly white, straight teeth. "I was joking, Layla. Keep to the duties on your to-do list."

"Sure thing, *Blingwood.*" I'm unable to wipe the satisfied grin from my face as we turn into the cafeteria to find Jessie waving at me to get my attention.

CHAPTER 12

LOGAN

*L*ayla was having lunch with Jessie, my head of housekeeping. She could have just said as much, but no, she enjoys winding me up too much for that.

As we walk in, numerous staff welcome her and say hello. I, too, am greeted, but the atmosphere stiffens around me. Not that I care. I have no desire to be liked, only that people do their jobs to the best of their abilities. Still, I can't help notice how everyone gushes over the new girl, and I find myself oddly curious about her.

She's becoming a strange mystery I want to solve. She's my assistant, no good can come of wanting her and certainly no good will come of pursuing her. I don't have time for anything other than no-strings fun, and that'll only make things more complicated in the office.

No. I'm done with these games.

My fascination stops now.

Layla sits beside Jessie, and they share the lunch Jessie has already picked for her while I get in line and hope there's something left by the time I reach the counter. I end up with a plate of meat and potatoes and wind up taking one of the empty tables at the back of the room. Perks of being the boss is that no one, literally no one wants to sit with you at lunch.

Which is fine by me!

Whatever Jessie says has Layla laughing hard enough for it to be heard above the rabble of the cafeteria. She then takes out her cell and the two scroll through her phone with the fascination and dedication of a military operation.

I narrow my eyes, wishing I could see the screen.

After that Jonathon guy was calling her at dinner the other night, I was curious. Is he her ex? Her friend? Her brother? No, that can't be right, she said in the interview that she was an only child. No father; that sucks. I know from losing my own just how much that hurts. Maybe the guy is her cousin.

None of your business, Logan!

She leaves her lunch date at twelve fifty-five and I do the same. We walk side by side but not together back to the office where she kicks off her shoes once she is seated and rubs the toes on each foot with the other.

"Can I get you anything, Logan?" she asks. Her voice is sexy. Sultry.

"No. See to the rest of the to-do list for today. I'll prepare another one for tomorrow."

"As you wish."

I sit at my desk and begin pouring through emails.

When I look up, Layla's head is tucked down, studiously staring at her monitor screen. I find myself watching the clock. Yesterday, I told her I take my coffee at three. It's only one-forty-five and she hasn't looked up from her screen since we got back from lunch.

I punch the speaker button that goes through to her

office. It's an antiquated device that somehow survived the remodel of the resort but I'm glad of it.

"Layla, I'll take my 3 p.m. coffee now." I wait for her to lift her head to look at me through the glass like she normally does. One, two, three seconds pass. I'm about to punch the button again to make sure it's working but then sure enough, her pretty little head pops up and she looks at me sternly.

"Anything else?" she asks through the speaker.

"No. That will be all."

A barely detectable huff muffles through the intercom.

"Is there a problem?"

"Nope. No problem at all." She stares at me placatingly while her wrist moves across the desk to switch the intercom off. Then I hear her mumble, "No problem except your manners, asshole!"

My mouth hangs open, but in front of me she's sporting a sweet smile that doesn't match the comment she made. Her chair squeaks as she stands to get the coffee and I realize the button of the intercom is stuck.

A few minutes later, she brings me my coffee, bending a little curtsy as she places it in front of me.

"Your coffee, Mr. Blingwood," she says with the most saccharine of smiles.

I smirk. "Finally," I reply even though she took no time at all.

She narrows those turquoise eyes of hers. "Anything else?"

I have two options here. I can say thank you and apologize for not saying please earlier, or I can get her back for calling me an asshole and toy with her some more. I decide on the latter.

"Yes. I'd like some cookies."

She raises her brows while she awaits a please.

"Anything else?" she says through her teeth.

"Nope," I repeat the word in just the exact way she said it to me earlier, making sure to enunciate the *P*, and a spike of adrenaline rushes through me as I watch her react.

"Cookies. Coming up." She grits her teeth belligerently and marches from the room, swinging her hips. The intercom rustles as she walks past it. I shouldn't be enjoying her ire as much as I am, but damn if her ass isn't the ripest peach I've ever seen. If pissing her off causes her to stomp around the office, swaying her butt like that, it's going to be almost impossible not to deliberately annoy her.

When she returns with a plate full of cookies, high enough to fall off the tiny paper plate, her face is flushed and the tips of her ears are a warm shade of pink.

"Here are your cookies." She bends again as she puts the tower of chocolate on my desk. My hand rests on the arm of my chair and I'm sorely tempted to brush my fingers against her ass just to check if it is as firm as it looks.

What the fuck has gotten into me?!

By the time I have my mind out of the gutter, she's sitting back at her desk scowling at me. I pull up an instant message addressed to her and watch as she reads it:

Thank you.

SHE REPLIES INSTANTLY:

You're welcome.

99

THEN LAYLA LOOKS me straight in the eyes, above the computer monitor she purposely lifted to block me out, and she shoots me a real smile this time—it renders me dizzy.

* * *

IT REQUIRES all of my focus to stay on task when I can hear Layla's voice every time she answers a call or makes small talk with another employee as they pass by her desk. She's effortless in the way she communicates with the rest of the team, whereas whenever we talk, there's an underlying tension.

Seeing this other side of her is interesting and has me thinking positive thoughts... until Mike walks into her office.

"How's it going?" I hear him say to her through the intercom that remains stuck in its on position. He's got his arms crossed like he's trying to be casual, but from his side profile his smile is unnaturally wide.

"Yeah, it's going good. Grouchy said, 'Thank you,' earlier, so that's an improvement." She giggles.

I'm not grouchy.

"Yeah, he's a piece of work, isn't he?"

Layla's eyes flick to mine and her pretty mouth flattens. I'm leaning into the intercom; she still has no idea I can hear her.

"You know, he's not so bad. Oh and Jessie told me at lunch there's a bonus program. I never had a bonus before! How cool is that?"

Mike grumbles. "Yeah, if you meet your targets. Doubt I'll be getting one this year. Blingwood has it in for me."

I narrow my eyes at him, but he's too busy looking down Layla's cleavage to notice. *Bet your ass you won't be getting a bonus. Your reports are half-assed and late every damn month.*

He's on his last warning and will be gone just as soon as he messes up again.

"I'm sure he doesn't have it in for you," Layla says, tucking a stray tendril of dark hair behind her ear and leaning back—blocking his eyes from seeing down her shirt.

Good girl.

"I better get on with some work. I don't know where today went, but it feels like I only sat down in the office five minutes ago and already the day is almost done."

Mike doesn't take the hint. Instead, he perches on the corner of Layla's desk. I'm seconds from jumping up and reminding him that I pay him good money to work, not hit on my assistant, when he says, "So, I noticed from your work file you have a lot of previous addresses."

She snaps her head up, righteously pissed at the intrusion.

He quickly adds, "I had to look up your file to arrange payroll."

Layla seems uncomfortable, her shoulders tense and she's not her usual carefree self like she is with the rest of the team. I'm holding onto the chair ready to pounce but equally curious to know more about her and how she will react. She looks down at her notepad, not responding.

"So why do you move so often?"

"I..." The sound trails off and I can tell she's uncomfortable but instead of Mike telling her it doesn't matter, that he's just being a nosey fucker, he waits. "Well... um, I guess I'm just used to new places. Old habits die hard..."

"Oh?" Mike prompts.

She glances at me and I pretend to be invested in something on my computer screen.

"Well, my dad worked as a photographer and when I used to visit him, he was always on location someplace exciting. I guess I caught the bug." Her voice sounds pained.

Mike doesn't notice, instead, he pushes. "And you traveled alone?"

She pushes her silken hair up and fans her neck like she's too warm—the air conditioning is working just fine.

"Mostly." Her voice is singsong. Fake. She tips her lips into a smile that doesn't reach her eyes.

"I love to travel too. But I haven't lived many places." He laughs, trying to make himself sound interesting, but I know the sad fuck still lives at home with his mommy and has a picture of Chewbacca on his desk. "So, did you want to grab that drink with me. I'm free tonight—"

I'm up and out of my chair and standing in front of Layla's desk in a half-second.

"Mike." I bare my teeth. "The reports that were on my desk this morning, you forgot the quarterlies."

"I... I—"

"It's not comprehensive enough. It's lacking. You'll need to work on it tonight. I need them by morning, latest."

"Logan—"

"Mr. Blingwood," I assert. "By first thing." I fold my arms across my chest and wait for him to try to squirm out of doing the work.

"Yes, Mr. Blingwood." He shuffles out the room like a weasel and I let out a satisfied breath.

"Coffee?" I ask Layla and her face lights up.

"Yes." The dimples in her cheeks deepen. "Yes, please."

* * *

THE REST of the day passes quietly and I wipe away all thoughts of Layla and her foibles. She is my assistant. That. Is. All.

Later, my office phone rings. "Mr. Blingwood, I have a call for you on line two," Layla says. If I take the call, she'll hear my voice coming through both the phone and the anti-quated speaker and realize the button is stuck in the on position. So, I speak quietly into the receiver and hope the sound isn't picked up by the intercom. "I'll call them back. Do that with all my calls today, please."

GREAT. *Now my fascination is affecting my normal work duties.*

Once she's gone home for the day, I'll fix the stuck speaker button.

I'm almost certain I will.

CHAPTER 13

LAYLA

I'm retelling yesterday's office antics as I chat with Jessie in line at the coffee shop.

"It was like he was jealous but he can't be. He barely tolerates me. I can't do anything right. Okay, so he watches me sometimes, intimately, and I get the impression he likes what he sees. Maybe he is attracted to me, but I doubt it. It'd be like pairing a pedigree Pointer with a non-discriminate cross breed."

"Shut the fluff up, lady! You are beautiful. A goddess. And he is a mere Blingwood. He'd be a fool not to love you."

"Love me? HA! I'd be happy if he just said please and thank you."

"Why do you think a man like Logan won't love you? I mean, I know there's the shitshow of your almost wedding, but that hasn't soured all romantic relationships for you, has it?"

It's an honest question, asked with a frown of concern. I'm speaking before I've even given thought to the answer. "It hasn't soured them but I am going to be more cautious in the future. Not that I plan to date my asshole boss—even if he did start being kinder to me—he is off-limits. I'm… Jonathon cheated. My own mother thinks I am capable of nothing more than being arm candy to a businessman. I'll see out my position here and then see what happens in the next place. It's too soon for me to even consider a love interest, let alone one who is dangerously mean."

"Sorry, but your mom sounds like a dick," Jessie says, handing over some cash for the coffees, oblivious of my mouth wide open until she side-eyes my expression. "You think I shouldn't say that about your mom?"

I ponder briefly then reply, "I think dick sums her latest behavior up. It's just… it's not often you find someone this honest," I laugh.

"It's better to be honest. And Logan isn't dangerously mean. He's been through shit just like you have. He'll come around in time."

"Shit?" I leave the question dangling and wait for her to fill me in.

"You don't know?"

"No. Sandy mentioned something but she never expanded. What happened?"

"This place thrives on gossip, yet their lips are locked tight when it matters. I'm proud the staff here didn't spill right away." Jessie nods her satisfaction. "But you need to know. It'll explain why he's such a grumpy ass."

"I'm all ears."

"Dana Gee. You heard of her?"

I shake my head.

"She's a fake celebrity. More like a daddy-rich girl who is

trying to land her next paycheck. Logan was engaged to her. She wanted them to be the next celebrity couple. Like Blake and Ryan but they ended up more like Justin and Selena except, he never cheated. He was good to her, you know."

I find myself nodding, even though she loses me with the celebrity references. Logan can be a grumpy bastard, but he strikes me as a loyal grumpy bastard.

"They're not together now, though. What happened?"

"She said she was pregnant."

"And he didn't want a baby?"

"No. He wanted the baby. He was single-minded, in fact. Getting books on parenting delivered to his office, looking after her… he was… everything you'd want from the father." Jessie's face is thoughtful. I suppose seeing a man behave like that when your own baby daddy deserted you has got to sting.

"Then what went wrong?"

"This is top secret. Only a few people know the real truth."

"I won't tell anyone."

Her eyes study every part of my face, checking for signs of dishonesty. "I believe you. There was no baby."

My mouth drops open. "What?"

"She lied about it all. Her father had disinherited her. She'd moved to the resort to 'find herself.' Next thing you know, she's hanging out with Logan at every opportunity and then, BAM! She announces she's pregnant and suddenly he's doing what he thinks is the right thing and proposing."

The image of Logan being treated in such a vile way has my heart breaking for him.

"So, she was using him?"

"And some. It gets worse."

"What can be worse than that?" I shudder.

"The whole time she was trying to get pregnant, she was giving interviews anywhere that'd print her lies, gushing about her, Logan and their baby—a baby that only existed in her warped imagination. The day of the wedding I found a half a dozen pregnancy tests in her room. *Negative pregnancy tests*. She knew she'd been caught, and she probably had good reason to suspect I'd tell so she fled. Took Logan's private plane and went back to her daddy."

"She left him at the altar?"

"Almost. I got to him in time to save him from that particular humiliation. We covered it up and pretended like there was no wedding, but even though it wasn't printed, people knew they were supposed to marry and that she left him. Poor man is still getting awkward questions and press intrusion into his life."

"I had no idea. I mean, I'm glad she's gone but to not tell him she was leaving, that she'd lied about it all—it's beyond cruel. Thank God he didn't marry her. It's a horrible thing she did to him, but he's better off, right? Without someone like her in his life."

Jessie pushes her sunglasses up her nose as we approach our respective work buildings. "She put a post on her Insta account detailing what a cold, work-obsessed man he was and said the stress brought on a miscarriage."

I pull Jessie to a stop. "What?!"

"She frickin' did! She's lucky she got on that plane when she did because if I got my hands on her, she wouldn't be using a straw for the lines of coke she sniffs, she'd be using one to breathe."

"How have I never read about all of this?"

"Dana was threatened with a lawsuit and the post got deleted. But it was up long enough to do some pretty hefty damage. Nowadays, her posts are a little kinder—to herself.

She keeps Logan's name off her profile but still, she says crap, 'taking time to find myself after my tragic breakup.' If I bump into her, she'll need time all right—time to find her teeth after I knock them out!"

I'm reeling from how awful this must have been for Logan. No wonder he's seemed so grumpy and preoccupied. My heart breaks as I imagine him in his wedding suit, prepared to marry a woman who was not who she pretended to be, and a cold shiver runs up my spine.

"When I got here... the dress. You said he must never know I was a runaway bride."

Jessie's face pales. "Man practically left at the altar meets woman who left a man at the altar. You wouldn't have gotten as far as the interview. He can't ever find out what you did." She examines my face then rubs my arm. "You did the right thing for you. None of this is your fault—it's Dana's. She and Jonathon are the enemy. But the last thing you need is for Logan to think you're anything like her."

My head bobs up and down then shakes from side to side. "He can't ever know."

"Nope," Jessie agrees. "But, back to you, you've still got to be open to love. That thing that happened with your ex, you deserve better and I'm proud of you for loving yourself enough not to tolerate anything less than you deserve. You'll find the one."

"What about you? Are you open to love?"

"I already got love. Macy and I don't need some fake-ass man making promises his bank won't cash. We got each other, and now we have you too." Jessie grins but it doesn't light up her eyes. Then, with it almost time to start work, we agree to catch up later and we head in the direction of our offices.

* * *

By the following week, I'm more settled and even have a new routine for the weekend. On Saturdays, I volunteer walking Cassandra's rescue dogs, and on Sundays I do my laundry and swim. I even start to think I'm going to like it here, even if there are only five weeks left of my contract.

It's Wednesday and the morning passes quickly, and I'm still smiling after Logan said please and thank you to me not once but twice, *and* he said I was doing a good job. Okay, so he didn't actually *say* I was doing a good job, but I had the transcripts on his desk from his meeting before he'd even asked for them and when he noticed, he said, "Good."

"You're still here!" A lady who I have never met in person, though I have spoken to numerous times on the telephone, says as she walks into my office. "I'm Skyla," she sings and from the corner of my eye I see Logan's head rise up like a meerkat and then tips his hand to wave hello before he dips his head back down to study his computer screen.

He's so attuned he literally seems to sense every movement that happens in my office.

"I'm still here," I reply, my voice a few octaves higher than normal. "I'm actually really enjoying the role now that I'm getting the hang of it."

"I knew you'd love it here!" She deposits a bunch of files in my In tray. "I came by to drop these off for Logan and to check how you were doing. It's my first day back from our honeymoon and I'm trying to get back into work mode and catch up on all the goss from while I was away."

I ask Skyla if she enjoyed her honeymoon and her face lights up as she describes the white sands of Mexico before returning to chatting about business.

"Some of the guys in the office had a bet running whether you'd last to the end of the first week, but I knew you'd still be here. If you stay the full six weeks, then I am on course to win thirty big ones."

I muster a shallow chuckle. "I'll try extra hard to go the distance for you if there's thirty big ones at stake."

"Tell me, has Logan mentioned the annual office party?" She flicks her hair over her shoulder as she glances through the glass at Logan whose eyes are trained on his computer. Skyla covers her mouth as she speaks as though conspiring. "He normally has his assistant arrange a staff party to commemorate the resort's birthday. It's three years this year and I already bought the perfect dress since finding good ones is stressful on a deadline."

"I haven't heard him mention it. How lovely, though!" He may be a grumpy asshole sometimes, but a staff party is a nice touch not to mention the bonuses, free food, apartment... the list goes on. "I'm surprised this place gets such a bad rap from employment reviews. I've worked at a lot of places and not many treat their staff this well." *Bad manners aside.*

"I love it here. Logan's a good boss and I heard the resort has been nominated for an award. Layla, this is big. If Logan wins, it'll show everyone that we're the best and all that nonsense they printed in the papers was just that —nonsense."

At her mentioning Logan, I look up at him and find him staring back. He's running the tip of his pen along his delectable lips as though deep in thought. I remember my conversation with Jessie and my heart aches for him. When I look at Skyla, she too looks saddened as she glances Logan's way.

"Everyone here works so hard—they deserve an award. I'll mention the party to Logan. He seems to be in a nice mood today. I wonder if it was the banana I brought him to eat with his breakfast. Maybe he's a man who needs a good dose of potassium in the morning."

"Or he had a good dose of something else this morning?" Skyla winks one of her big brown eyes at me and my blood runs cold.

"Is he… is he dating someone? I'm mean, not that I care." I try to keep my voice casual but Skyla's mouth tips up at the edges like she can tell right away how I'm much too interested in her answer.

"Drew hasn't mentioned that Logan is dating again. But Logan's a man. A very good-looking and rich man in his prime, it'd be criminal if he wasn't getting some somewhere."

It reminds me how he asked me to book the table at Le Bateau. It's tonight at eight. I already checked his calendar to see if he added his dinner guest's name but he hasn't.

"Are you… still single?" Skyla asks, though I know she is aware I was supposed to be married from our calls back when I was working for Jonathon and we were trying to help her staff the new resort. She also knows I left the guy at the altar after I found out he was a cheating rat. It's sweet of her to put it so kindly, so I just nod in response, setting her at ease.

"We should go out for drinks. We'll have to plan a night when Jessie can get a babysitter."

"I'd love that." It would be so good to have a couple of girlfriends to hang out with. Since taking care of my dad and then being with Jonathon, I haven't had the chance to forge any female relationships—something sorely missing in my life. "And yeah, I suppose I ought to get back out there and into dating hell again," I say on a forced laugh.

Skyla's mouth tips down. "Were you with Jonathon long?"

Across from me, Logan's back to staring at me over-the-top of his computer screen. It's like he knows exactly the subject I'm talking about and is vested in my answer. Thank God our offices are separated by a three inch wall of glass.

"Two years."

"Oh, honey, you'll meet someone else. Hopefully, we can find Jessie a man too!"

"It'll have to be quite a guy to handle Jessie, she's wild," I reply. "She took twenty big ones off Simon from security yesterday. Man, can she win an arm-wrestling competition."

Skyla lets out high-pitched laughter. "Don't ever place a bet with Jessie. You will lose every time!"

We both laugh and I hold my hand over my mouth so Logan doesn't hear me having fun during office hours.

"Well, I better skedaddle," Skyla says. "Hopefully Logan will let you plan the office party. We'll have a blast!"

I say goodbye and am in the midst of planning how to broach this subject with Logan when I receive an instant message from him:

Layla,

Please plan the annual resort birthday party.

You can find details of previous events in the team building section of my files. My calendar is free on Saturday the 29th.

THE TIMING of Logan's message is so eerily spooky I read it twice just to check I am not imagining it. I guess it just goes to show that Logan Blingwood is a man with his finger on the pulse of what needs to be done.

I consider all that's involved in planning a staff party and get a pang of excitement that pushes a wide grin on my face. I never arranged a party before. Hell, I never *had* a party before.

Sure. What's the budget or should I speak to Mike?

HIS REPLY IS INSTANT.

I'll handle the funding. Just let me know what you need.

MY REPLY IS SWIFT.

What is the theme?

Theme?

Yes. Would you prefer a particular theme, a style of music or food perhaps?

I WATCH as he taps his finger to his chin before the reply blinks onto my screen.

Theme: Fun. Food/music/entertainment: Whatever you decide.

THEN I MESSAGE Skyla and Jessie:

> Staff party is go!! 29th okay for you?

SKYLA'S the first to respond:

> WOOHOO! I love it when I hire the right person for the job :)

CHAPTER 14

LOGAN

*L*ayla's gloriously happy. She hasn't stopped smiling since I asked her to arrange the party.

I'm not sure how I missed the date, but I find myself looking forward to it as long as I don't allow myself to think about who I brought last year.

Cue a steady stream of messages:

> Should I arrange a band?

> > Yes, Layla. Music is deemed quite appropriate for a party.

> Food?

> > I'll be hangry if there is nothing to eat.

> Definitely food then. Lots of food.

> Absolutely.

Can we have party bags for the guests?

> If you wish.

Yay! What about a photobooth?

I imagine her grinning for the camera.

> That is permissible.

Balloons? What else?

> If you like. Standard party stuff. Have you never been to a party before?

The typing icon shows and then it stops and does this on repeat, so I look up from my computer to see her nibbling the corner of her thumb while she ponders her reply.

I'm so excited. Can we have a champagne fountain?

It's not a party without champagne.

> I'll make it the best party you ever had!

I'm sure you will.

> Can we bring plus-ones?

Layla, I have work to do. Staff only.

As I FINISH up for the day and plan to head to the gym, I decide I might incorporate a swim too.

Layla is at the pool most nights—in her same red swimsuit that makes my balls ache, and while I mostly refrain from joining her, tonight I refuse to be excluded from my own pool just because my assistant happens to be in there.

Before I can shut down my computer, Layla sends me a message reminding me not to forget my *date* at Le Bateau tonight—which she specifically italicized in the message.

Interesting.

It unfortunately scraps my immediate plans of the gym and a late-night swim.

Date.

I chuckle to myself. I'm not sure a meal with my long neglected mother counts as a date, but I'm too proud to correct her.

CHAPTER 15

LAYLA

"*Y*ou look exhausted," Jessie says at the coffee shop the next morning. "Trouble sleeping?"

"I barely slept a wink. Today would have been my dad's birthday."

Jessie's hand reaches out and she cups my shoulder. "I'm sorry. What was he like?"

A watery smile lifts my lips. "Pretty great. My mom was always a little prickly. She cared, but she didn't know how to show it. Whereas my dad was the opposite. He lived his life pursuing exactly what made him happy, which took him away from me, but he was happiest in the middle of the jungle photographing wildlife." I smile, remembering our summer in Africa. "I was with him at the end and he said he had no regrets."

"Sounds kinda selfish. I mean, I like margaritas and desert islands, but I wouldn't ditch my daughter to go get them."

Jessie orders her coffee and I have to stop myself from

118

immediately defending him. Is she right? Was following his dream selfish? Leaving me to be raised by my mother when he knew how she could be.

"Maybe it would have been selfish of me to ask him to stay at the expense of his career?" I wonder aloud.

"Kids are entitled to be selfish when it comes to their care." She shrugs and I wonder why she has such a stick up her ass about it.

"Well, when I did see him, he was a good father."

"MMhuh." We walk to work and are quieter than usual.

Jessie checks her phone and tuts at whatever she has found while I ponder the complex emotions of losing a parent who wasn't perfect but still loved me.

As we turn the corner and the hotel comes in to view, Jessie slings her phone in her purse and says, "I shouldn't have said that about your dad. People have complicated lives and just because he was absent doesn't mean he was bad. I'm putting my own shit spin of fathers on you."

"What happened with your dad?"

"Macy and I got more in common than DNA. My dad skipped out too. Guess I never really had much luck with father figures. Doesn't mean yours was a douchebag, though. I am sorry for what I said."

"That's okay. There were a lot of questions I wanted to ask Dad that I never really got the chance to. Like, why did he leave me with my mother when he knew I was unhappy? I suppose I could have asked him while he was sick and I was seeing him every day, but instead I decided to let it rest with him."

"I could use some practice at letting things rest." She laughs and I chuckle too. "You going to be okay today? I can tell Logan you got your period and need to go home and rest. Ain't no man going to argue with a lady on her cycle."

At the mention of Logan my heart thuds.

Last night, when the sadness got too much and I tried to think of other things, my mind kept drifting to Logan, who was out on a date.

It should not bother me.

"I'm fine. Hopefully our boss will be in a good mood today. It's Friday, after all."

If he is in a good mood, does that mean his date went well?

"Okay, well if you need me, dial five and I will be there."

I REACH the office at one minute past eight and as though an alarm went off, Logan's gaze flicks in my direction, his face stony. I put my purse on the coat hook and before I even log into the computer, I wordlessly take him his coffee, muffin, and banana.

I can't muster the energy for small talk, so instead of greeting him like I normally do, I pull my lips into a forced, polite smile. Mostly I try not to get down about the absence of family in my life, but some days it tugs at me harder.

I feel Logan watching me and wonder if he can tell I'm feeling low. I'm almost at the exit when he says my name.

I turn back.

"Thank you," he says and his eyes are sparkly and warm, which I chalk up to my replenishing his calorie deficit.

"You're welcome," I reply, ignoring the stirring in my chest.

"Are you okay?"

"I'm fine." I take a calming breath and nod to affirm that I am indeed okay, but I can tell from the way he studies me he doesn't believe my lie.

Once I'm seated at my desk, the first email I read is from Logan, sent at 9:04 p.m. last night:

> For future reference, when I ask you to book Le Bateau, I mean the restaurant on Abbots not the burlesque bar on Gambit.

HEAT WARMS my cheeks and I fire back an immediate apology.

The number for Le Bateau was at the top of the search bar, and because I was so utterly thrilled that my many first tasks were going smoothly, I didn't double-check the venue.

One step forward, two back.

As always.

His reply is instantaneous.

> It's fine. My mother quite enjoyed it. I, on the other hand...

MY JAW DROPS and I stare up at Logan and belly laugh at the image of him in a burlesque bar with his mother! Then he winks and I stop laughing; my cheeks flame and I bite my lip to stop my mouth popping open.

Damn.

Why does my grouchy bosshole have to be so damn sexy?!

CHAPTER 16

LOGAN

She's not herself today. Her body is crouched inward, protectively so. Her breezy smile is smaller, contained. And her big blue eyes that normally pop appear worrisome, as though the threat of tears is not far away.

Last night after the staff explained there are two Le Bateaus in town and we realized Layla's mistake, Mom insisted our driver take us and I couldn't argue since I forgot to show up for dog walking last Saturday. I didn't realize it was burlesque until we got there, and by then wild horses wouldn't have driven my mother away. She was glowing and firmly in her element. It was good to see. Witnessing her dancing along with the acts, however, may haunt me for eternity.

Now my mother plans to book another table when my sister comes to town in a few months—another image I could live without. But I can't muster the effort to be annoyed with Layla, not when she seems so down and vulnerable today.

Why is she so sad?

I want to ask her but doubt she'd tell me, of all people, her asshole boss, her problems.

The issue is distracting me from work. Instead of looking through the profit data of a venture I am considering, I send a group email to Layla, Jessie, and Skyla, and include the head chef of our best restaurant:

> Ladies, please attend The Bay restaurant at 7 p.m. this evening.

> Layla needs to approve the catering and wine list for the staff party, and I'm not sure I can trust her with this decision alone.

> Fernando, have the menu prepared. I'm authorizing unrestricted access to the wine list.

> Thank you

MESSAGES BEGIN FLYING BACK and forth with Jessie calling the evening: Girls Night! So, I graciously leave the conversation.

Layla smiles at me widely enough that it crinkles the skin around her eyes and a strange warmth spreads in my chest. I chalk it up to the coffee, but then, I accidentally wink at her again.

Which is weird because I've never been a man who winks. I had thought winking was reserved for fathers giving clandestine approval to matters that mothers would never permit, and pervy old guys—neither of which are categories I identify with. Yet I have done it twice in the past hour and basked both times in Layla's exuberant responses.

* * *

LATER THAT MORNING Layla once again tries to put a call through but I tell her I am not to be disturbed. Once she goes on her break, I'll go fix the button on the intercom so that normalcy can resume and I can stop feeling guilty.

When Mike pops his head into Layla's office and asks her if she wants to catch *that* drink tonight, she politely tells him no. Of course, he doesn't let it rest there and asks if she wants him to show her how to surf, but she explains she already knows (impressive!) and that she already has plans Saturday—hopefully nursing a light hangover after a fun night with her friends.

When she gets a call from reception, I can only hear one side of the conversation. "For me? Are you sure? I'm not expecting any personal calls."

"Okay, put him through."

"Hello," Layla puts on an accent. I'm not sure what accent it is supposed to be since it is utterly terrible but still she continues the pretense.

"No. She no work here. This is Laura Bower. No Layla. Okee. Byee."

Then I watch as she cradles her head with her palms. I'm out of my seat and standing at the doorway between our offices before I've actively thought about doing so. "You okay?" I ask her.

She lowers her hands and looks up at me through her lashes, abashed. "Yeah, I just—" She shakes her head as though she can't believe she just used such a lame attempt to quell the interest of whoever it was.

"Boyfriend?"

"Ex," she supplies.

"You need me to block his number? I can tell security to make sure he can't get to you here." A strange protective instinct washes over me and my hands have balled into fists.

"It's nothing like that. Jonathon wouldn't hurt me...."

"Yet you don't want to see him or for him to know where you work?"

I'd like to get my hands on this guy. There'd be nothing left of him once I'm done with him.

"He lived in my last town. We broke up, you know?"

I have no idea, but I want her to keep talking so I nod.

"I don't know how he found me here."

"Forwarding address at your last place?" I ponder aloud.

"I never gave a forwarding address. Clean break, that's best."

"You move around a lot?" I ask it as a question but I already know it as fact.

"I haven't found anywhere to settle. I'll know when I find the right place."

I remember Layla stating as much during her interview. At the time I thought she was flighty and irresponsible, now I'm quite sure it's something different.

"Hey, thanks for arranging the meal with Jessie and Skyla. You wouldn't believe how stressed I was getting over the catering options for the party. I mean, it's like a week away and there's so much to arrange."

"No problem." I'm tempted to return the conversation to why she moves around so much but since she changed the subject, I'm reluctant to scare her off from talking by pushing her for answers so I, too, create a subject change.

"I forgot to add a task to your to-do list today. I need you to book us rooms at Gee Towers in New York. It's the annual tourism awards and I'm going to need you to come with me. I wasn't going to go but the resort has been nominated...."
My voice trails off. I'd decided not to go, and then I decided I would go and deal with it for the sake of the staff who

deserve this award. The compromise I made with myself was I'd go alone without mentioning it to the staff in case it got their hopes up, and quite frankly I'd save myself from any more embarrassment.

So then, why did I just tell her she's coming?

"I'll need my assistant with me. We have to fly out on the thirtieth. The day after the staff party. I trust that will be okay?"

She doesn't have to say yes.

I want her to say yes.

She blinks slowly, then lifts her flock of ebony hair that fans her slender neck.

"An awards ceremony."

My jaw twitches. She's not going to want to spend seventy-two hours with me.

"I've never been to an awards ceremony before. What'll I wear?"

You'll look stunning in anything.

"Whatever you like. Most women wear a cocktail dress but choose whatever will make you feel comfortable."

Her face lifts into a huge, shit-eating grin. "New York. Really?"

My lips tip up but I cover it with a stoic nod.

"Separate rooms?"

"Of course. I normally book the penthouse suite that has three bedrooms, but it may be too short notice so just get the best rooms you can."

"New York, here we come!" She does a cute little jig and I feel oddly happy to go to the event now that Layla is coming, even though *she* will most likely be there too.

CHAPTER 17

LAYLA

"Holy crap! I'm going to the Big Apple!" I blurt, and Jessie and Skyla raise their glasses.

We're on our fifth glass of bubbly and have completely forgotten which ones we'd prefer for the party.

"You have the best boss in the entire world!" Jessie says.

"Hey, he's your boss too," I counter.

"Ain't taking me to New York though, is he!" We all laugh and I feel elated.

"I need to find a cocktail dress and figure out what the heck I'm going to do with my hair." I'm excited but nervous too. I've never been to an awards event and I don't want to let Logan down.

"Fernando! We need to sample cocktails!" Skyla calls out. She's getting rowdier with every sip, and it's good to see the quiet one of our newly assembled crew letting her hair down.

"Yes, ma'am! I'll get the mixologist to rustle you some up. He has a brand-new menu I think you'll love."

"This is the best day ever!" I say and then feel a tinge of sadness wash over me. Celebrating feels wrong, but also right. Dad wouldn't have wanted me to spend the day crying; he was a firm believer in making the most of opportunities and doing what makes you happy. It's funny how a day—a life, even—can turn around when the universe intervenes, especially when I don't even remember asking the universe to take me across the country to New York.

"He's hot though, isn't he?" Jessie says.

I stare at Fernando. He's an older gentleman with the body of a salsa dancer. "I suppose he is quite handsome, but I wouldn't describe him as 'hot.'"

"Not Fernando, silly. Mr. Blingwood!"

"Oh. Well, I mean, he's okay," I reply warily.

"Girl, you blind?"

I cover my blushes with a sip of the crisp white we're sampling.

"He's more than just hot. He's sweet and the best boss. I mean, we're getting a free meal with unlimited wine. You're getting a work trip to New York," Skyla says. "Not to mention you get to look at him all day through the window." She and Jessie high five and I begin to feel self-conscious.

Staring at the impressive Logan Blingwood all day is just one aspect of my incredibly varied and professional position. Impeccable view aside, dealing with him can be perilous.

"He might be fine to look at, but I swear he oscillates back and forth from grumpy to sweet so often I get whiplash. Might I remind you, the trip to New York is just work. It's not like he's my boyfriend or even a contender." *Or rather, I am not a contender for his heart.* "We are oil and water. He is a fine wine and I am a McDonalds' milkshake." I shake my head. "He is absolutely not my type."

"I'd choose a milkshake over wine any day. Hey, do you think he has a Big Mac?" Skyla snorts, the alcohol now at its full effect. "His brother does." Her complexion pinkens by three shades.

"I bet she'd love a taste of his Big Mac, wouldn't ya, Layla?"

Jessie gets the giggles and I await the next fast food innuendo while the mixologist stacks our table with cocktails.

Once the server has left, I order Skyla and Jessie to, "Stop teasing me or else I'll never be able to look Logan in the eye ever again. It's my job not a relationship. And you are both clearly jealous of my New York City trip and drunk, very drunk!" Then, as if to hammer the sentiment home, I hiccup and we all burst into giggles.

"Okay, so he's off-limits, we get it. But what does your ideal man actually look like, Layla?" Jessie asks.

I consider it for a moment and then reply generically. "Tall, dark, handsome."

Jessie narrows her eyes on me suspiciously. "I'm going to need more than that. What's your type?"

"I don't think I have one."

She huffs out a frustrated breath. "What was your ex like?"

"He was tall-ish but not as tall as Logan. Blonde. Complete cock—I mean, jock." I pause and think of the few relationships I've had and deduce they've all been very different. "My boyfriend before that was a banker. He was short but he was so funny. And then, the one before was medium height and he mostly just liked to bet on the horses, but he had this gorgeous cat and made the most amazing waffles for breakfast."

Both women look confused.

"He had a nice cat?" Jessie laughs. "What about his cock?"

"Don't forget he made waffles," Skyla adds laughing

equally hard.

"But what did you like about them? What did they have in common?"

I shake my head not seeing where this is going. Their mouths pop open as though hit by realization.

"You've never been in love before?" Skyla says with a look of understanding.

Jessie straightens her expression and tries to cover the sadness in her eyes by sliding another cocktail in front of me.

"Of course, I've…" It hits me. Have I really gotten to twenty-six years old without falling in love? Yeah, I've had boyfriends who liked me and I liked them too, but not like you see in movies when you're so utterly taken by another person that they hold your heart entirely captive. "With Jonathon, he kind of scooped me up while I was taking care of Dad. He told my mom and dad he'd take care of me and they seemed to approve. It seemed like a solid plan. Have you both been in love?"

They both nod and then Skyla says, "I hadn't been in love until I met Drew, but now I can't imagine a life without him."

"That sounds nice," I reply, trying not to allow my lack of love to bring down my mood. "I guess I have to be patient."

They both seem to be deep in thought for a moment and then Skyla breaks the silence and says, "I propose we drink these lovely cocktails and then go dance away the calories down at the beach bar."

"Ooh. Great plan! I hardly ever get a child-free night so we must."

"Who's looking after Macy?" I ask feeling relieved by the change of subject.

"Macy's with Betty. I swear, without Betty I'd be a basket-case with literally no rest!"

"To Betty," I say, raising a toast.

"And to Big Mac's!" Skyla cackles.

CHAPTER 18

LOGAN

I'm drinking a beer on the wraparound balcony of the penthouse, wondering how Layla's night is going while the sun sets on the horizon. The prospect of a meal and some drinks with friends seemed to return the smile to her face, and for that I was glad. Still, I return to the question of why she seemed so sad.

I tell myself anyone would feel bad to see their employee down, but it was more than that. Her pain was palpable. My throat ached and my gut twisted. In that moment, I would have done whatever it took to see her smile.

Perhaps it's because she's younger than me by a few years. Maybe it's because she's all alone at the resort, her father's dead, and her family probably miles away. But really, I know that I am becoming fond of her strength, and the way she stands up to me, and also her tenacity for getting out of tight spots. And it doesn't hurt that she has the kind of face you can't look away from.

I knew right away she was pretty. What I didn't realize was that she would soon become even more beautiful each time I looked at her. By now I'm pretty much captivated, staring at her each day, trying not to look and congratulating myself when I manage ten minutes... by darting my gaze to hers and hoping she doesn't catch me.

Fucks sake, Logan. Stop thinking about her!

A couple of hundred yards away, the beach bar begins to fill with revelers out for the evening. Guests and locals mix, all looking to have some fun, and I consider walking over to my local haunt to see if any of my buddies are over there.

The music is loud and I hear the DJ announce that karaoke will begin soon, which would normally put me off, but tonight I feel like I need a distraction. I'm about to get ready to wander over when my phone rings.

"Tate. You're alive!" I say, resting my elbows on the balcony, watching a group of people stumble down the wooden slats that form a path in the sand and lead to the tiki hut that houses the bar.

"Brother! How are you? How's Mom?"

There's a lick of unease in Tate's voice so I quickly reassure him. "We're all fine, I'm seeing Mom again tomorrow. I was supposed to walk a dog for the rescue center last week but I forgot, so she texted me every day this week to remind me I have to do it tomorrow. She made me promise. What's going on with you?"

"Me? Nothing, dude. I'm fine. Why do you ask?" I listen carefully for any sign that my younger brother has been drinking his troubles away but he sounds sober.

"Stella Brimworth mentioned you in an interview. I wondered if it was true?" I reply.

"If what's true? I've been on a diving expedition near where we shot the movie. Today is the first time I've had a signal for a few days. What did Stella say?"

"She said you two were an item on an E interview. I wouldn't know anything about it, but our niece sent me a link. I didn't think you were into your co-star?"

"What? We are not dating. We share the same agent, but apart from that we have nothing in common. Wait, she said we were dating?"

"You fell in love on set, apparently."

"Hmph. I must have been out of it if we did because I don't remember shit about that," Tate replies.

I resist the urge to laugh. "You don't sound too upset that she lied."

"I'm not upset, I am annoyed though. We start promo for the movie in a couple of months. Jason, our agent thought if the media thought we were in a relationship, it'd sell more movie tickets, but I told him no. Jason gets overly concerned about our popularity. Tells me all the time, 'You're only one bad movie away from getting canceled.'"

"You better speak to Mom. She thinks you met a woman and didn't introduce her."

Tate sighs. "Mom'll think I've been keeping some great romance from her and whoop my ass next time I see her. I'll call her after we hang up and tell Stella to can it..." His voice continues but my attention is taken by a development near the beach bar.

I hear loud, voracious laughter coming from the beach. A trio of woman are headed up to the bar but one of them has fallen in the sand. The other two are trying to help her up, but she's spaghetti in their hands and they're all cackling like the amusement is splitting their sides.

"Hey, bro, you listening?" Tate says through the phone.

"What? Yeah, I'm listening. There's this woman—"

"Dude, you got a woman with you?"

"No. She's on her way to the beach bar. Clearly drunk. She fell over, though she's back on her feet now. She's taken off her heels and she's stumbling toward the bar with her friends, and hell, can you hear her singing?"

I listen carefully while staring intently, wishing the sun wasn't so close to setting so I could see better.

Her singing is completely out of tune and she keeps getting the words wrong, but it's fucking cute at the same time. Worse still, I know that voice and wish I wasn't smiling as hard as I am.

Layla.

"I'll talk to you later, Tate."

CHAPTER 19

LAYLA

I can't remember why I'm limping but we're all still laughing about it.

Skyla lines up shots, which is hilarious because I thought she was uptight when I first talked to her, and yet here she is slamming shots and telling us we need to get up and dance on the table.

"Karaoke!" Skyla orders. "We've all got to take a turn!"

The flashing disco lights and the setting sun in the distance give everyone's faces an orange hue. I hold onto the barstool to keep from stumbling. Then I notice my feet are bare, which is strange because I almost never leave the house without shoes.

We down the shots and then Skyla puts the song menu in front of me. Just that small gesture, and I suddenly feel like I'm part of this amazing sisterhood and these girls have my back. It's wonderful!

"I'm going to sing and I'm going to dedicate it to my

unbelievably gorgeous husband," Skyla shouts for the world to hear.

"I'm going to sing, too, but I'm going to dedicate my song to my beautiful baby girl," Jessie yells above the music and pushes her blonde hair away from her dewy skin.

"I'm going to sing too," I call out and then hesitate as I realize I have no one to dedicate my song to.

"You can dedicate yours to your grouchy boss!" Jessie replies.

As though a perfect sign, I immediately see *the* song—the one that sums everything up. It's an epiphany. Almost biblical in its brilliance. I stomp to the stage with determination and purpose, yelling the song I'd like to sing to the DJ. He hands me the microphone and I move to stand center stage and curtsey to the girls before I announce, "I dedicate this belter to my A'hole boss. He's grumpy and he grates on my last nerve, but my God is he *GORGEOUS!*"

And then, blinded by the spotlight and with the added trickiness of a room that won't stop spinning, I sing my heart out for the cheering crowd of equally inebriated party people.

I yell it. I scream it. And the crowd goes wild... or maybe they're just fans of Soft Cell and they like to sing along, but I belt out "Tainted Love" as though my life depends on it.

And when the spotlight dims, the floor stills, and the final phosphenes politely stop dancing in front of my eyes, there he is.

As if I manifested him right from the core of the universe.

Logan Blingwood stands right in front of me.

And I think I'm going to throw up.

CHAPTER 20

LOGAN

I manage to help Layla outside before she violently pukes in the bushes.

"Oh dear," I hear Skyla stumble over her words from behind us. "Mr. Blingwood, I mean Logan, uh, brother-in-law. What are you doing here?"

"Oh nooo. Mr. Blingwood," Jessie slurs. "You weren't supposed to hear Layla's song. This is baaaaad."

"No, I don't suppose I was meant to hear that. I can't say it's how I imagined being serenaded," I reply, playing the part of the big bad wolf, while holding Layla's hair back as she purges another stomach-crunching pint of alcohol from her gut.

"I'm sorr—" Layla's interrupted by more retching.

"She okay?" I hear my buddy Matt say. He must have seen me walk in, though I didn't even get the chance to say hi or order a drink before Miss Sassy Pants began her song. "Shall I get her some water?"

"No. Can you call my brother to pick up Skyla then take Jessie home. I'll deal with this one once she's stopped throwing up," I reply to Matt.

Matt props a lady up beneath each of his arms while I wait for Layla to start breathing normally, then I help her up onto her bare feet. "Where are your shoes?"

She looks down at her pretty pink little toes and a puzzled expression takes over her face. "I must have left them at home." She cackles loudly. "Home. Haha!"

"Come on, I'm taking you back to your apartment."

She stumbles and falls straight into me.

At this rate, it'll take all night to make sure she gets home safe.

"This is never going to work." I scoop her up until she's a dead weight in my arms. The material of her cotton dress rides up to reveal smooth thighs and her toned arms drape around my neck. She nestles the top of her head against my chest and I pull her in tight to make sure she's secure.

"No. It can't work. You're a pedigree and I'm just a mongrel."

"What?" I ask but she changes the subject.

"I can walk. Just as soon as the world stops spinning you can put me right back on my feet...." Her eyes close then open then close again and, for a second, I think she might fall asleep but then she says, "Where are my shoes?"

"We'll get you new shoes, sassy pants."

Her eyes flutter closed again and when she opens them, she looks right into my eyes with her baby blues. "Thank you, Blingwood."

"I got you, Bowers."

WE GET MOST of the way to Layla's apartment with her lightly snoring into my shoulder.

Part of me wants to rip her a new one that she got so

138

drunk she put herself at risk. I'm also pissed she announced to an entire bar full of people that I am "grouchy and grating" but, since she also said I was gorgeous—which had every hair on my body standing on end like it was trying to catch some of her electricity—I wonder if I should let that slide.

It's not the first time I've heard someone say I'm gorgeous *or* grouchy, but it's the first time it's had me smiling like a fool. The song choice was odd though, and I couldn't help noticing the way she emphasized, *run away* by shouting the words in the song.

Is that what she does?

Layla rubs her cheek against my shoulder and inhales. "Mmm… I like this pillow; it smells like something I want to eat. Can I have a banana for breakfast? My boss eats bananas. The potassassassium stops him being grumpy. I like him when he's not grumpy," she mumbles and it's adorably cute.

As we near her apartment, I decide I'm going in with her. She's been sick and I'm not risking her being unwell in the night with no one to care for her. In her purse, I find her keys and let us both in. Then I switch on the bedside lamp and pull back the covers, gently lowering Layla onto the bed. Her fingers latch onto my collar, clinging to me and pulling me toward her until I am laying down beside her.

God, even post puke, she smells divine.

"You can sleep now. You're home," I tell her and wait for her fingers to loosen themselves from my shirt.

"Home," she repeats without opening her eyes, like she's somewhere between awake and asleep. "Layla doesn't have a home."

Her bottom lip quivers and my throat aches in response.

"Layla has a home and people who love her, right?" I check, suddenly wondering if I heard right.

"Unwanted. Unloveable. That's Layla Bowers."

Her eyes are half-closed, our bodies side on side, she

snuggles closer to me, wrapping her arms around my neck until she is nestled perfectly into my body.

"You are most loveable," I whisper, and she lets out a light muffled sigh and her eyes seal shut. "You are wanted. Sleep now, sassy pants." Then I lightly press my lips to the top of her head.

CHAPTER 21

LAYLA

a siren or something equally annoying is playing bongos on my eardrums, so I pull the pillow over my head and groan into the mattress.

Someone, please, make that noise go away.

It doesn't stop.

It gets louder.

Then it stops.

Then it starts again!

I bolt up in bed and swing my head around, searching for the thing I need to kill.

The alarm on my phone.

But it's not an alarm, it's the reminder I set.

Today must be Saturday, and I promised I'd walk one of Cassandra's rescue dogs. I enjoyed it last week. Cassandra handed me a loveable pooch and then I walked the route set out by the other walkers.

I force my feet out of bed and down onto the cold tile. My

head thumps like I hit it off every wall when I got home last night. My tongue is coated in a mixture of cocktail flavors, bile and some kind of fur, but on my nightstand is life sustaining water—that's cold enough that it still has condensation dripping down the side of the bottle. Next to it is a box of Tylenol, a banana, and a muffin.

Worse than that, there's a note:

Layla,
Thanks for an… enlightening evening.
See you Monday.
Logan

My stomach lurches, and if I wasn't certain it was entirely empty of contents, then I know I'd throw up.

I do an inventory of my body.

I'm fully clothed but my skirt has risen up in the night and I am displaying a hefty amount of ass cheek, and judging by the way my skin feels and my mouth tastes, I neither took my makeup off nor brushed my teeth.

Urgh. But I don't feel like I had sex.

I'd remember if I banged my boss, right?

Of course, I'd remember.

I suspect sex with Logan Blingwood would feel like the universe collided with the stars, giving birth to fireworks, rockets, and unicorns. The world would surely stop turning and glitter would cling to all that is.

No.

I definitely did not sleep with my boss.

Phew.

There's a gentle knock at the door and I tentatively get up, wipe away eye dust, pull my clothes into place to cover the essentials, and go answer it.

"Tainted Love" is playing somewhere in the distance. I pull open the door and Jessie is standing before me. Appearing fresh from the shower, her long blonde hair drips water, and her arm is outstretched with the phone that is playing the offending song.

And then I gasp.

"I dedicated that song to Logan *and* he heard every word of it!"

"Yeah, you did." Jessie's grinning like the fool I feel. "I thought you might be feeling bad about that."

"Bad. I feel terrible."

"It's not so bad. Bossman knocked on my door as he was leaving. He stayed with you all night! I think he'll get over it." She clamps her perfect teeth down on her lips that are itching to pucker into a smile.

"He stayed all night?"

Jessie nods, her eyes alive with mischief.

"But we didn't…" I shake my head and widen my eyes until she gets my drift.

"You didn't bang the boss? I'm not surprised, you were way too drunk to bang anything apart from your head on the bush you threw up on."

I cringe. He saw me throw up. "Logan's never going to let me live this down."

"No, I doubt he will. He told me to come check you didn't die. Then he said we should all be grateful we've still got jobs —that we're lucky someone didn't end up dead. Total overreaction, but he seemed more worried than pissed. Like, he was really worried about you."

"Worried about me? I doubt that very much." I bring my hand to my mouth and can smell the faint scent of his cologne on my fingers. "Nah. He's pissed we lowered the standard at the beach bar and probably annoyed that I survived my alcohol-induced coma. Dammit he was probably tempted to kill me himself. I'm so embarrassed!"

"Layla, you lost your dad and just got out of a toxic relationship. So, you went wild—you're a grown-ass woman who makes her own decisions. Lots of girls let their hair down and get their titties out to let off steam—"

All my blood leaves my head and I feel like I am in danger of imploding. "Tell me I did not flash my boobs at Logan?!"

Jessie creases up with laughter. "No. There was no flashing. It was more like an accidental slippage."

Shit!

"You can report back to Logan that I did, in fact, die. I can feel it happening right now," I whimper.

* * *

IF MORTIFICATION HAD PHYSICAL SYMPTOMS, I'd likely be in a medically induced coma right now while I heal from the trauma. But since my body is still working, I keep to my word and meet Cassandra, hoping that the fresh air will clear my head enough to decide whether to skip town today or wait until tomorrow.

"You came!" Cassandra calls as she sees me heading over toward the huge array of dogs and their walkers.

"I'm sorry I'm late. I—" My voice is whipped away by the wind and I freeze, mouth agape.

Standing beside Cassandra, wearing sportswear that shows off his muscular shoulders and tan skin, is Logan Blingwood.

Suddenly I'm nauseous again.

"Meet my son, Logan," Cassandra says with a grin so warm it could heat custard.

"Mr. Blingwood, I-I wasn't expecting to see you."

Logan's lips pucker up smugly. "Miss Bowers, how's the head?"

My hands reach up to check it's still there because I swear I am, in fact, losing my head.

Cassandra scans both of our faces, the warmness of her smile unwavering. "There'll be no Mr. or Miss today, you two. You're not at work, you're here to destress and do a good deed. Try to enjoy it." Her smile turns to a devilish grin while Logan's eyes flick between his mother and me like he hasn't got a clue how we know each other.

I smile at them both politely but inside I am freaking out. I've complained to Cassandra on numerous occasions about how awful my boss is, only to find out he is her son. And last night I threw up in front of him and he quite possibly saw my breast—I don't even know if he saw the good one.

Cassandra's hand slides onto my forearm and she grips me in a way that is reassuring while she whispers, "All your secrets are safe with me." Then she winks and my skin warms. "Now, you two. I'll just head to the truck and bring you your companions. Layla, I've got a perfect girl for you today."

"Thank you, I can't wait to meet her," I reply angelically.

Cassandra nods approvingly and then turns to Logan and says, "Logi" with such affection, I grin at the cuteness of his nickname. Cassandra continues, "I know you're experienced so I'm going to give you our newest boy. Don't you dare be grumpy with him, understood?" She gives "Logi" a steely gaze that cuts right through his stoic expression and then she skips off to get our dogs.

"What are you smirking at, Bowers?"

I let out a light chuckle. "I'm not smirking, *Logi*."

The moment is so light that I almost forget about the karaoke.

Almost.

"Look, about last night…," I start.

"You think I'm a grumpy asshole, I get it," he says though he doesn't seem angry, which is even more unnerving.

"No. I don't think…"

When I dare meet his eyes, he's cocking a thick brow at me.

"Okay, so yes, you can be a little grouchy sometimes." I hold my hand up to demonstrate just an inch. "But the dedication to you, that was just for fun. All the girls had people to dedicate their songs to and—"

"And you have no one else you could have dedicated your song to?" He doesn't look angry; rather invested in my answer.

"I… I'm not seeing anyone right now." Logan's mouth twitches and a flash of annoyance spikes up my spine. "Is it funny that I'm single? I suppose you think I deserve to be alone. Are you still upset about the sandwich?"

His two front teeth grip the plumpness of his bottom lip as though to erase his smile and then his expression returns to neutral.

"No, I don't think it's funny you're single. But should you decide to change your situation, perhaps hold off from deploying the screeching you call singing while on the first date—it'd put off even the most ardent of suitors."

I take a calming breath to stop myself jabbing him in his ribs and defend my voice. "Hey, I got a standing ovation."

"I think the crowd was just pleased it was over."

"I was choir leader in high school. I can sing!"

"You couldn't find the right note if you had a GPS," he replies with a tone so light I can tell he is enjoying our back and forth teasing.

I cock my brow at him and feign annoyance. "You're clearly and certifiably tone deaf."

"It's quite possible since listening to your unique singing

voice. I fear the damage may be irreversible." Logan mockingly rubs his right ear causing me to snort.

"Seems you hate it so much, Blingwood, maybe I'll break into song right now. Music is, after all, great therapy and God knows you could use some."

He rolls his eyes as though he's annoyed but a small, boyish grin lifts his cheeks. "Please don't. The dogs will struggle to cover their ears and walk at the same time."

"Next time I sing for a man he's going to feel lucky to get my song!" I say, ignoring his jibe.

Logan's stare suddenly hardens and I wonder if he's more pissed off about the dedication than he's letting on, so I try to let it go and calmly smooth things over. "The dedication, it wasn't personal. In the moment it seemed fun, but I apologize. I promise to never dedicate a song to you ever again."

His eyes are fixed on me, making my legs turn to jelly but I refuse to look away. My mouth goes dry and his utterly breathtaking good looks make it difficult to swallow. Still, I try to talk my way out of the mess I'm in and hope we can move on—like to separate sides of the country.

"I've explained and I've apologized, so I think it's best if we never, ever, ever, talk of the dedication, the song or the singing, or the puking ever, ever again. Clear?" I smile and put my hand out confidently and hope he takes my hand in silent agreement.

"Oh, sassy pants," he says, but takes my hand in his, spiking my blood pressure, "where would be the fun in that?"

"Blingwood, you tease me about this and I'll sit on your face. I MEANT LUNCH! I'll sit on your lunch."

His eyes crinkle with mirth. "You sit on my lunch, and I'll set up the big screen and play your entire performance to the whole cafeteria."

"You didn't record it?" I pull my hand out from his.

He wouldn't have recorded it, would he?

The look he's giving me is so smug, I'd like to... well, I'd like to kiss it off his face. "I guess the decision you need to make is if you're ready to find out."

"You wouldn't do that," I say more confidently than I feel. "I know that even though you are grouchy—"

"And gorgeous."

My face flames.

Damn. I said that. Forget it. No more thoughts of kissing.

"Even though you are many, many things, you wouldn't stoop that low."

"You're right. I would never *taint* myself like that, *love.*"

We're staring at each other, hard. The tension is palpable. Torn between the desire to strangle each other and other more carnal things... Thankfully, Cassandra is being pulled our way by two excitable dogs and it makes us both straighten our scornful expressions and behave.

I concentrate on Cassandra intently, glad of her return. The first dog she holds is some kind of Mastiff that's absolutely enormous and the second is a grumpy-looking Chihuahua. I hold my hand out for the small dog that is busy growling at Logan's ankles but Cassandra pulls the lead out of my reach.

"Oh, no, Layla, darling. You're not ready for Yogi. He needs a more experienced handler." She hands me the beast of a Mastiff that weighs more than I do. "Now, don't worry. Cindy might be tall and strong but she's a perfect softie, aren't you, girl?" She pets Cindy's head and Cindy leans up into her hand. Then she hands the Chihuahua to Logan, but he pulls his hand away and takes a step back.

"Hell, no. I'm not walking that thing! If you're making me do this, I want a real dog."

Cassandra's affronted and her tone turns stern. Pleasure zings through my body to see Logan put in his place. "Son, Yogi *is* a real dog. Now stop hurting his feelings and take him." Logan doesn't show any sign of relenting and so his mother steps forward. "Logi bear, would you refuse this poor little man who was left tied to a post near the rising tide? Would you? Is that the boy I raised?"

Logan sighs heavily. "Mom, you've got twenty dogs in that van, please go get me a real one."

"I can—" I gesture with my other hand an offer to take Yogi but Cassandra and Logan both put their hands up to pause me.

"Logan Anthony Blingwood. Do we discriminate based on gender or size? Would you honestly neglect or deny someone based on their appearance? Are you not comfortable enough with your own rugged manliness to be seen walking a chihuahua?"

I'm stifling a laugh.

Logan snatches the lead from his mother. "Fine, but if it bites me on the ankle, you're paying for the tetanus shot."

CHAPTER 22

LOGAN

"That's my boy!"

My mother is practically bursting with pride as she hugs the side of my body.

"Now, you two. Keep these little babies on their leads, we're still working on their recall." She holds out her hand to me. "Here are some bags in case nature calls, and Logi, no talking business. I want both my charges to have a lovely, stress-free time—which means no bickering, okay?" Mom looks at me like *I'm* the problem.

To my side, Layla is sporting an angelic smile, but beneath it I know she is lapping up the motherly embarrassment.

"Mother, do you know Layla is in fact the one with anger issues? She sat on the sandwich you bought me."

Mom grabs my chin. "Logi, are you tattle-tailing? Please behave nicely. I want lovely Layla to come back next time and she won't if you're unpleasant to her."

"I'm always pleasant!"

I huff but Mom takes it as agreement and replies, "Good boy."

Without even looking at her, I feel Layla's inward laughter.

"This way," I say in a cold, mirthless tone, eager to get away from my mother, and Layla follows me along the trail.

It's a sunny day with only a mild breeze and Layla's hair, still slightly damp from her morning shower, looks longer than usual. When the wind catches it, I'm hit with the sweet scent of peaches that catches in my throat.

She's opted for tight workout shorts and a cami. The tightness of her body takes me straight back to last night when she was glued to me like a cat clings to a tree.

I spent most of the night watching her to make sure she didn't choke if she was sick, but I couldn't help notice how utterly adorable she looked as she lightly snuffled beside me. I stayed all night and ordered room service to her apartment since I knew she would need sustenance when she woke. She was so peaceful and vulnerable, a total opposite to the sparring partner I have grown fond of, yet still as appealing.

When she side-eyes me, I nod my head at the sign pointing to the coastal path and explain the trail loops back through the woods to where we started but she doesn't answer. I wonder if she's embarrassed and if she even remembers me carrying her home.

"Come on," she pleads with her dog, "can't you up the pace?" She encourages Cindy to speed up so they can walk ahead, but the dog just plods along beside me in no hurry at all.

"Mastiff's have a tendency to set the speed," I explain and Layla pouts, seemingly frustrated, like the last place she wants to be today is here with me.

"You can hand me the leash if you'd rather go home and

sleep off your hangover," I offer, giving her the opportunity to leave.

"I promised your mother I would walk one of her dogs and I am a woman of my word. Besides," she smirks, "who wouldn't want to hang out with their boss on a Saturday?" She gives me a smile that has my heart rate hitching and I can't resist teasing her.

"Yes, hanging out with your *gorgeous* boss. It is a gift, no?"

"*Yogi Bear*, you obviously misheard; what I said was *grumpy*."

"If you say so, sassy pants." The smirk I'm sporting makes my cheeks ache but the pain is worth it when she snorts.

"I think we should walk in silence. It'll be less stressful for the dogs."

I glance down. Yogi is chasing his tail yet still moving in line with us—like a cyclone on a forward trajectory—and Cindy looks more chilled than a hippy in a dope factory.

"I think the dogs can handle it, besides we have so much to discuss that it will keep the walk interesting. Tell me, are you concerned I'll mention the screeching or the snoring most?"

Her eyes bore into mine but my grin refuses to shift.

"Embarrassed, Bowers?"

"Will we be traveling near any cliffs?" she asks innocently and I shake my head. "Oh, that's a shame. I was going to push you off one and pretend you fell." She holds her palm up to demonstrate the push, like she just can't help herself. "It'd be easily explained. A self-righteous, big head, walking near a vast height—being so top-heavy and all, people would understand how easy it'd be for you to lose your balance." She smiles sweetly but I keep my expression neutral.

"No cliffs, I'm afraid. You'll be pleased to hear the ground is quite flat. Probably for the best since your breathing is so easily exerted. You were snoring so loud last night I wondered if your nostrils had collapsed."

"What?! *Logan Anthony Blingwood*, I *do not* snore."

"You *do* snore."

"I didn't ask you to take me back to my apartment. I was perfectly capable of getting there myself."

"Oh, you were?" She's glowering at me now; even hungover and angry she manages to look beautiful.

"Yes, I was fine. I can handle myself. Believe it or not, I've been taking care of myself my whole life."

"The collapse of your nostrils must be causing a lack of oxygen to your brain because last night you could barely walk, never mind getting yourself home safe." I dread to think what could have happened if anyone less scrupulous had found her in that state. "The lack of oxygen might also explain why you decided, against any good measure of judgment, to get obliterated drunk. You're a slight woman who probably can't take much alcohol before it affects her. How much did you drink?"

She looks annoyed, but our sparring is turning me on.

"I wasn't obliterated. Sounds to me like you're more worried about the bar bill than my welfare. I didn't ask you to pay for the drinks. In fact, I'll pay. Just tell me how much and I'll—"

"Fourteen hundred and eleven dollars," I say knowing she's unlikely to have much recourse. Her salary is generous. I don't pay beneath a good living wage, but I'd bet she'd struggle to find that kind of money for just one night's drinking.

She stops walking and stares at me incredulously. "Are you out of your mind?" Her voice is a shriek. "How the heck—"

"It's a Michelin star restaurant, sassy pants—they're expensive. But I don't care about the cost. I was taking you

153

home because you were in a hopeless state. I could have been anyone!"

"Sassy pants," she repeats.

"You're being sassy."

"You're being annoying."

"And perhaps even a little right."

She's suddenly quiet, petting her dog until she realizes it's about to answer nature's call. She sidesteps to the left.

"I'm sorry if I lowered the tone in your fancy resort."

"You didn't 'lower the tone' but you put yourself at risk. Layla, we don't vet the guests and any member of the public can use the beach bar." Now I'm wondering if we should vet the guests and increase security. "What if there had been a rapist or murderer, you wouldn't have been able to defend yourself."

"Hey, don't hypothetically victim blame me. No matter what state I was in, I should be safe."

My hand goes into my hair in frustration. "I'm not victim blaming, I'm—"

"You're putting this on me. I didn't need saving." She's looking at me fiercely. But then her gaze flicks down to beside her where Cindy is taking a dump. "Can you get that?" She points her thumb to the fresh mound left by Cindy. "I don't think my stomach can cope."

When I glance down. I feel in danger of losing my own breakfast. "You're doing the next one."

"Fine," she hisses.

When we continue walking, I consider what she said. She's right. Layla could have thrown up and stumbled back to her place with her friends—but it was I who wasn't prepared to take the chance. I don't know what came over me. Seeing her vulnerable, it had me taken over by need to know that she was safe.

"I suppose you'll go back to work after we've finished the

walk?" she asks, changing the subject. I wonder if she thinks I'm so dull I have nothing else to do on a Saturday, and so I find myself correcting her assumption.

"There's a lot more to me than just working all the time, Layla."

She has a coy expression as she arches her delicate brow. "Oh, so what are your plans?"

"Well," *I was going to head straight to the office and work on a new investment I have been considering,* "I am going to go shopping, actually. I need a new tux for the awards."

She guffaws. "Logan Anthony Blingwood does not do his own shopping."

"You're right," I say quite seriously. "I have an assistant for that. I'll email you the list."

"What? It's Saturday!" She looks affronted so I continue to play along.

"Layla, it's company policy, if I request additional hours—"

"You're not serious?" Layla's uneasy expression has me putting her out of her misery.

"I'm not serious. Though I do need to go and get a tux. Have you bought your dress for the awards ceremony?"

"No. I feel—" Her nose scrunches up.

"You feel?"

"Well, I'm waiting for Jessie or Skyla to be free so they can come with me. I don't want to go into the fancy stores alone…" Her voice trails off and she seems uncomfortable.

"Layla, what is the problem?"

She doesn't answer. Instead, she sports a frown that I'm not used to seeing. We're approaching the finishing point and my mother is already waving her hands about looking excited to see us.

"Are you busy now? I need a tux anyway. We can shop together and both get what we need."

The crease of her frown vanishes and her full pink lips tip up at the edges. "If you don't mind, I'd like that. Should I change first?" She looks down at the Lycra fabric with an unsure expression.

"You look fine just as you are. Where is your car?"

She shakes her head. "I don't have one."

"How did you get here?"

"I rode the bus."

"The bus?"

"Yes, Logan. Public transportation. I'm sure you've heard of it."

I find myself chuckling. "Yes, sassy pants, I've heard of it. I just didn't expect you to wake up early enough to get yourself all the way over here on the bus."

"When I commit to something, I commit to it," she says proudly.

"We can take my car."

We reach my mother and she coos over the dogs and fusses with them like they were dancing with death by her allowing us to take them.

"Will you both be back next week?"

We are both railroaded into another Saturday of volunteering and then we set off toward the parking lot and I suddenly wish I hadn't brought the Bugatti. It looks utterly ostentatious nestled in between my mom's rescue wagon and all the soccer moms' cars.

"This is your car?" Layla asks when we reach it, her expression delighted.

"Yep."

"Can I drive?" she asks sweetly.

"Not a chance, sassy pants," I reply.

CHAPTER 23

LAYLA

"*Y*our car is so fancy." One part of me wants to stroke my hand over the soft, supple leather of the seat. My other instinct is to reach out and touch the rugged perfection of the man driving it.

"It's getting quite old now, I have a new one on order," he replies even though the car looks brand new.

Logan guides the car down the hill that takes us away from the park. With each push on the gas pedal, the engine purrs and my core heats. Sitting so close to him in the confined space means that with every breath, I'm inhaling more of him.

"Are you showing off?" I ask him when we get on the freeway and leave all the other cars behind.

"No." He smirks but there's a fire in his eyes that tells me otherwise. "I don't leave the resort all that often these days, and it's nice to open her up."

I don't complain. The speed is exhilarating and my heart races as I watch the scenery blur past.

"You don't own a car?" he asks casually.

"No," I admit. When my last car broke down, Jonathon drove me to work since he was going there anyway. "I'll save up and get another one eventually."

His chin juts a fraction to acknowledge my answer while he concentrates on the road up ahead, but I can tell he's listening because he continues to ask me about the cars I have owned. And while our car histories are not at all similar, he doesn't make me feel cheap; moreover, he seems to approve of the early hybrid options I have owned.

"You know, we've reduced the carbon footprint of the resort to 20 percent below industry standard. In the remodel we switched to mostly solar and the business pages printed a few pieces stating we were industry leaders in revolutionizing green initiatives." Then, as though realizing he sounds like a nerd, he turns to me and bashfully smiles. It's cute, which is not a word I would have used to describe my boss just two weeks ago.

"It makes my eco-warrior mother and sister happy, at least."

"Yes, you have two brothers and a sister. Must be nice having a big family," I reply, recalling the article in which he was deemed "Business Man of the Year" where the writer referred to his family as a "Financial Powerhouse."

"It is good—when we're not fighting. In that respect, we're just like any other family. It's better now that we don't live together, but growing up my mother used to put us all in separate rooms when the arguing got bad and she demanded we don't talk to each other until we could be nice. Sometimes we'd go days without speaking." He chuckles fondly and tells me about a time he managed to lock his brother inside his bedroom, and it was hours before his mother realized Tate wasn't just sulking, he was stuck! I wish I could ask him to continue to describe his family life in rich, delicious detail. Somehow, even detailing the arguments has me yearning for a more typical childhood.

"What about you, only child? How was that?"

"It was… lonely at times. I read a lot and joined all the extra-curricular clubs."

"Really? So you were in the cheer team?"

I laugh. "No. I was on the choir, soccer, chess, and debate teams."

"Ah. Now, I can see you on the debate team. You're quite skilled in truculence."

I take it as a compliment. "I'm well practiced at holding my own and talking myself out of situations when the need arises."

Logan pulls into a space right outside the clothing store and throws the valet the keys like he didn't just hand over about a half a million dollars.

"Mr. Blingwood," the assistant sings as we walk inside, and I imagine she just saw her commission go up by 200 percent. "Can I get you a coffee? A champagne perhaps?"

"I'll take a water please and Layla will have…"

The assistant looks me up and down in my thrift store workout gear, and I suddenly feel too hot and much smaller than I was just a second ago.

I order a champagne because—why the hell not—and sip it carefully, remembering how quickly the bubbles went to my head last night. As I enjoy my champagne, Logan explains to the assistant he needs to be fitted for a tux, while I am here to choose a dress.

His no-nonsense tone and stature has all the assistants suddenly running around after me, advising me that yes,

Jennifer wears this designer, or how about this one, Kim has it in blue.

I run my fingers along the row of dresses delighting in the satins and silks. And while Logan goes to be fitted for his tux, the assistants help me into a dress I paused to look at for a minute too long.

It's beautiful and somehow manages to make me appear taller, leaner and more elegant than I ever have before—including how I looked in the wedding dress my mom helped me choose.

It's surreal.

I send a photograph to Jessie and Skyla as I stand on a platform like a runway model, and they both reply immediately and gush at the azure-blue dress with gold lining, telling me that it compliments my eyes and skin tone perfectly.

"So you'll take it?" the store assistant with the razor-sharp bob asks.

"That's definitely the dress for you," her colleague adds, smiling more widely than can be considered natural.

"I love it," I gush, running my fingers over it and worrying that I'll somehow contaminate the flawless fabric.

"You'll look like a million dollars," bob-lady adds. "Shall I box it up for you?"

Both women are nodding which has the opposite effect on me and I shake my head.

"I didn't see a price tag. How much is it?" I check.

"It's Dior," smiley-face says, "a timeless classic."

"How much would one pay for a timeless classic?" I inquire.

"It'll probably fetch three times the price tag if you decide to donate it to a charity event later down the line."

"I can't imagine I'll ever be able to part with it," I reply. "But still, what does it cost?"

The women happen to glance at each other at the same time and I catch a momentary sneer passed between them.

"It's absolutely worth it—"

"The cost is very economical when you look at the crafts-manship," the other interjects.

"How much?" My voice bites through them gushing about French designers and haute couture while they point at the lace overlay on the hem of the dress.

Bob-lady lets go of the dress and stares up at me. "The dress you're wearing is $22,000. Would you like the shoes also? They're in the promotion for $3,400."

I almost choke on my own saliva.

"That's more than half my salary!" Suddenly the dress is suffocating and I reach for the zipper but I've lost all feeling in my fingers.

"You're with Mr. Blingwood." She blinks three times like she's trying to get her head around the fact I can't afford a dress like this. "We assumed you were..." Smiley-face is apparently so confused she forgets what she was saying and stares at her partner.

"I'll get the zipper for you," bob-lady says, sliding it down in one swoop.

"Let me help you out of those shoes," smiley-face adds, almost causing me to lose my balance as she pulls on my ankle to liberate the crystal encrusted sandal from my poor-ass-foot.

I slide back into my clothes as quickly as I can and chastise myself for not checking the price before I put on the dress. I head back out into the showroom and quickly glance around for the clearance rack—to no avail. Heading back to the row of dresses, I slide my fingers along them determined to find something cheaper when bob-lady appears over my shoulder and says, "We'd prefer it if you didn't finger the gowns."

I instantly pull my hand back.

I don't remember fingering being a problem when they thought I'd be splashing the cash here.

"How much is this one?" I point to a deep red gown with fabric as soft as silk, even though the label says it's a cotton-blend.

"That one is eleven."

"Hundred?" I ask hopefully, but my credence is dashed as she curtly replies, "Thousand."

The atmosphere changes like a storm cloud passing over a pristine white beach.

"I don't suppose you have anything cheaper?" I ask with renewed conviction because surely not everything in this store costs a fortune.

"Maybe you'd be better heading over to Target?" Bob-lady replies, passing her colleague a look that is so disparaging it creates a wave of irritation to crash over me.

"No," I reply curtly. "I'm choosing a dress from here just as soon as I can find something in an acceptable price range."

She shrugs as though to say "whatever" and turns her back to me.

I've been dismissed.

Metal hangers screech as I rummage the rails. But it's hopeless. I have no idea how much anything is or whether they have it in my size, so I approach the assistant with the bob and force myself to ask, "Do you have a sale rack?"

"It's over there," she brusquely says, nodding her head to the back of the store.

"Would you mind helping me, please? I don't know the prices."

"We're really very busy. The cheapest ones will be marked as damaged on the label." Then she walks over to smiley-face and the two women whisper between themselves. No doubt laughing at me—even though I doubt they could afford dresses here either.

I follow the direction bob-lady nodded, feeling dejected. Not long ago I was standing on the podium texting photos of me all dressed up to my friends, and now, here I am rummaging the sale rack and wondering if the dress with the split to the navel can be safety pinned together.

"How is Miss Bowers doing?" I hear Logan's voice a little while later and when I look, I am almost knocked off my feet.

"Is it too much? It is, isn't it." Logan pulls at the collar of his shirt. "I look like a damn penguin—"

"No! It's... you look... I think..."

I'm truly lost for words. Logan in a tux is the most exquisite thing I have ever laid eyes on. But his usual confidence is suspended, replaced by an unsure, wonky smile that is as endearing as it is bashful.

"Don't look so doubtful, Blingwood. You wear it well," I say, finally able to make coherent sentences, and he rewards me by widening his smile and making my knees tremble.

"You managed to find anything?"

I look over at the assistants who are feigning busy by moving hangers an inch at a time on the rail.

"It's very expensive here," I say, my voice barely a whisper.

Logan steps closer until he's right before me and he shrugs. "You're worth it."

I smile back at him, because honestly, I can't restrain myself. "I can't afford any of these dresses."

He shrugs again. "Layla, this is a work expense. I'm paying."

"I didn't know. I thought...." I relax a little and then move to my next concern. "Logan, some of these dresses are more than twenty grand." I widen my eyes as I hiss the number and his eyes crinkle with amusement.

"Well, shit. I thought they'd be expensive."

"Logan, twenty-fucking-grand on a dress, are you crazy?"

This time he laughs outright. "Dana used to spend twice that. What's your point?"

"I'm just your employee, though. You don't want to waste all that on me."

He loops his fingers around my wrist and the warm current of his touch pulls me in toward him. "Layla, I appreciate you attending the event with me. I want you to feel at your most confident. There will be predators at the awards who hate me, and I have been led to believe that for a woman, a good dress is like a suit of armor—which you may well need. Forget about the cost, it is of no consequence to me. Money is just numbers on screens that we shift around here and there."

I nod seriously. "It helps not to think about the price tag as real money."

Logan clasps my wrist more tightly in his hand and my heart rate gallops. "Don't ever suggest that anything is wasted on you. You're a valuable asset, worth considerably more than some rags in a store."

My mouth goes dry and the only response I can muster is a slow nod.

He drops my wrist and gestures at the row of dresses. "Have you tried anything on?"

I meet Logan's chocolatey brown eyes, grinning like a fool but I don't care.

"I found one that was nice. I mean, Skyla and Jessie thought it was the one, but... the lighting is quite flattering in here and the angle from the podium probably made me look taller than I will on the night."

Logan studies my expression for a second and his gaze narrows. "Layla, did you like the dress? Did it make you feel good?"

I grin because until I began thinking about the cost, I felt like a million bucks.

"That's settled then." He glances over to where the store assistants are standing and says, "Can I get some assistance over here, please?" And then he turns to me, "Have they been this unhelpful the whole time?"

I shrug then nod and shake my head. I'm a fully grown woman, I don't need to rat them out.

He makes a, *Hmph!* sound from his nostrils and I immediately jump to their defense. "They were being very helpful. I think we got off on the wrong foot. It's fine."

Logan asks me to tell the assistants which dress I have chosen and bob-lady helpfully asks if I want the shoes, too, to which Logan tells her we do.

"I feel like a princess," I sing to him and realize, I didn't just sing the words, I bobbed like a dancer too.

He chuckles deeply. "You'll look like one, too."

While Logan goes to change out of his tux, I take the dress from bob-lady and drape it over my shoulder so it doesn't touch the floor and then tuck the shoe box under my arm. Then I loiter in the store, busying myself by checking out the framed prints on the walls until Logan returns.

I haven't noticed a cashier counter so I ask him, "Where do we pay?"

Noticing Logan, bob-lady immediately joins us. Her stare is measuring, like she can't decide if I'm a love interest or a pity fuck. Seemingly she decides I'm no competition and she sidles closer to Logan adoringly and snickers. "Normally, Dana would leave all her apparel hanging in the fitting room, then we'd package and courier them to the penthouse. Of course, Miss Gee would never stop at one dress, she'd choose a dozen." She puts her hand on my forearm. Her tone is one that might be used on a child. "You've never shopped at Superfluity before, have you? You leave the important stuff to us." She winks at Logan, making me feel superfluous to the conversation.

Logan's glare cuts right through the air between us. He takes the dress and shoes from me and pushes them into bob-lady's unsuspecting hands. "The tone of this store has declined and I'll be sure to inform my good friend and your boss Tom that improvements are needed. I don't bring my guests here to have them weighed down with garments and treated like bell-boys. Have this wrapped and delivered to the penthouse by five. Oh, and be sure to add a matching purse to the collection—no expense spared." My mouth is agape but I don't have time to process the way in which he chastised bob-lady for her treatment of me because he takes my hand and says, "Come on, darling, let's go!"

I don't let go of his hand until he has led me to the car and I notice the valet holding the door open, waiting for me to get inside.

"I could have taken care of her," I tell him, stalling at the driver's side of the car.

He grins confidently. "You'd have eaten her alive, sassy pants, but you shouldn't have to. Besides, if you waste your energy arguing with her, it might deplete your reserves when it comes to arguing with me."

His stare is warm brown and devious, and it gives me a thrill.

"You like it when I fight with you?" I check.

"I approve of you standing up for yourself, Bowers. Now, get in. I'm starving and you're taking me for lunch." He nods his head to the driver's seat. The keys are dangling in the ignition.

"You're letting me drive this baby?" I don't dare hope. He'd be crazy to let me drive it.

"You scratch her paintwork and I'll spank you," he replies,

but the threat of his statement is at complete odds with the hunger in his eyes.

I shiver.

"You better put on your seatbelt, Blingwood!"

I hop in and press my foot against the gas, feeling the engine purr right through my core, and before he has even shut his door we're speeding away.

CHAPTER 24

LOGAN

*W*hy did I just pretend I was Layla's boyfriend?

I've never called a woman *darling* in my entire life. In fact, people who do such things make me queasy. But I couldn't help myself. When I saw that woman— if one can call her that—treating Layla like some kind of second-class citizen, it had me wanting to buy the store just so I could fire her!

I watch as her manicured fingers navigate the wheel of my favorite car. The smile doesn't leave her face. She's sexy and carefree, gushing about how awesome it is to get to drive my car.

"You know I might not give it back," she says, raising her brow and grinning.

"Oh, you'll give it back all right. You're too pretty to go to jail."

She bites her lip. "You think I'm pretty, Blingwood?"

"So pretty that the inmates would have a field day with

you. Better to stay on the right side of the law, for your own safety."

"Logan Blingwood, thinks I'm pretty and he's worried over my safety. It's touching." She holds the palm of her hand against her chest and I try not to stare at how her breasts bulge.

"You sure you like the dress you picked? We could go someplace else for you to choose one." I change the subject. Talking about her being pretty is just making me realize how utterly beautiful she is.

"Oh my god, do I like it?!" Her smile lights up the entire car. "It's the most beautiful dress I've ever seen. Ever!" She does an adorable jig in her seat to show her excitement. "I won't ever be able to take it off. People'll see me, swanning about the place like the Queen, marching around the resort, doing laundry or going to the pool, and there I'll be, wearing an exclusive dress from the brand new summer collection."

Her happiness is catching and I feel oddly content. Ahead of us is the sign to turn left for the resort, to the right the road leads along the coastline. But I don't want to go back yet. "You hungry?"

"Starving," she replies. "Where do you want to go?"

"Your choice."

She careens right before she answers. "You need to eat before you become hangry. I think I saw a sign for the perfect place on the way out to the store. I think you'll approve."

My usual demanding hunger takes a backseat to something else that feels strange and uncomfortable. Something I thought was a myth or exaggeration.

And I think that thing might be what women sometimes refer to as butterflies.

CHAPTER 25

LAYLA

"*W*ell, this is a first."

"What is?" Logan asks.

"I'm eating a McDonald's from a drive-through in a Bugatti."

"I find it makes my Big Mac taste even more mouth-watering."

Big Mac.

At his mention of it, my eyes move to his crotch and I quickly squeeze my eyes shut.

Don't think of my boss's junk.

Don't think of my boss's junk.

Don't think of my boss's junk.

I'm thinking of my boss's junk and I could quite literally kill Jessie and Skyla for linking popular fast-food to Logan's manhood.

My Coke does little to cool me down.

"Good?" he asks, watching me intently as my eyes flutter

closed.

"So good." My gaze drifts downward again and I have to force myself to stare into his chocolatey brown eyes.

Inside the car, this close to him, I'm practically inhaling him. And he tastes divine.

"Have you made plans for the rest of the weekend?" he asks casually, focusing on dipping his fries into his sundae, then eating them three at a time.

"I'll probably do laundry tomorrow, maybe I'll go for a swim. You?"

His lips curl sinfully. "Same."

"You do not do your own laundry." I shake my head. I know he doesn't since I've heard housekeeping flapping about starching Mr. Blingwood's shirts *just right.*

"Hey, I can do my own laundry if I want to." He looks a little affronted.

"I know you can, but... why when you don't have to?"

"It isn't like that. I don't outsource it because I don't like doing it or I think I'm too good for the task, I just rarely have free time."

"I get it, don't worry; I know you don't think of yourself as above such things. I've seen you pick up litter as you pass it in the hotel lobby when you could just easily dial for the cleaning service. You muck in like everyone else, but you are just one person—you can't possibly do it all."

"You noticed that?"

"Logan, I spend more time with you than I do any other human on earth. I probably know your habits better than you do."

He puts his burger wrapper back in the paper bag and runs his tongue self-consciously over his teeth even though there are no food remnants. He looks perfect.

"And how are my habits? Do people still think I'm a bossy

asshole?" Suddenly he seems fragile, despite his powerhouse status.

"Do you care?"

"No." He shakes his head then nods glibly. "I mean, no one wants to be hated, do they?"

"They don't hate you." He raises a thick brow disbelievingly so I continue. "You're in charge of all the people, it's only natural there's friction at times. You're the most hands-on boss I have ever worked for—and as you know, I have had a lot of bosses, plenty to compare you to. But everyone likes you."

Logan grins at my admission and my heart flutters beneath my chest. I focus my gaze to the line of cars heading out of the parking lot.

"They don't hate me. I'm surprised. I've been unbearable," he admits.

When I meet his eyes, I'm taken aback by how different he looks. He's the same man, who two weeks ago, threatened to fire me first chance he got, yet now I've gotten to know him, I see through his bossman act to a man who is human beneath it all. A man who cares if he is liked and seems to want to do better.

"You've been through a personal trauma. The people who work for you understand that and honestly, they support you. I've seen firsthand how much is demanded of your time, and that's despite you having a line of managers beneath you to lighten the load. Cut yourself some slack, Blingwood, you're doing okay."

"Okay." He crinkles his nose with distaste. "Sassy pants, I can do better than okay."

With the sun lowering itself in the sky and our meal finished, Logan tosses our empty food bags into the trash as I drive past the garbage bin and then I head in the direction of the resort, and I feel a pang of disappointment our day together is almost over.

"Home sweet home," he says as I pull up in front of my block and switch off the engine. "Is the room... comfortable enough for you?"

"Oh yes. The mattress is firm—but I guess you know that. The space has all I need."

"It was difficult to get comfortable on Friday night, what with all the snoring." He winks and my heart flutters. "If you need anything let me know, okay?"

I nod. "See you Monday." We both get out of the car, but before I head inside, I stop and tell him, "Thank you. The dress, the purse, and the shoes—I never had anything designer before—I can't wait to wear them."

His cheeks lift with his grin making him look deliciously handsome. "My pleasure." Then he drives away and it takes a full hour before the exuberant grin on my face returns to normal.

* * *

THE NEXT DAY I order a dress for the office party and some new underwear—wearing cheap cotton briefs from the new section at the thrift store feels criminal beneath designer fancy dresses.

I then do laundry and complete more internet searches of last-minute entertainment for the company party. The options comprise of singing quartets that jump out of cakes, petting zoos, and an assortment of games.

Once I've made the bookings, I get so excited for the party that I've already added it up and I send Logan an email before I've even thought to stop myself before disturbing him on a Sunday.

His reply:

All sounds great.

Go wild.

Are you having a nice Sunday?

I reply instantly, wondering what he's up to and if I might accidentally run into him today:

Not many ways I can dress up laundry. Haha!

Logan's reply seems smug:

And working. Party planning on a Sunday is still working, Layla.

Don't work too hard.

I am enjoying it so much that planning more aspects to the party hasn't even seemed like work.

I hope you're having a nice Sunday, too.

He responds:

Lunch with my mother and her menagerie. I might go for a swim later...

THE GREEN LIGHT that indicates he is online goes off and I wonder if it's an invitation, then I slap myself upside the head.

Layla Bowers, get this into your thick skull, your hot boss is not into you!

Any of his nice treatment has only been in an official capacity. He needs me to go to New York with him as his assistant. There are probably all kinds of assistant-like things he needs me to do. The amazing, twenty-grand dress is to make him look good, not me. And carrying me home drunk from the beach bar was probably to avoid some kind of lawsuit—not that I would ever sue him, but he doesn't know that—because he doesn't know me, not really.

I distract myself by reading when there's a knock at the door.

It's Jessie ready to make good on her promise to take me out of the resort to show me around. We walk along the shore to the public beach with her little girl—two-year-old Macy in her stroller. She's got her Mommy's phone and is watching a video of some guy juggling lemons. With her dark curls and big blue eyes, she is the most adorable little girl I have ever set eyes on.

"She just loves that video," Jessie explains, pointing at her cell. "I had to edit the part after the juggling and put it on a loop, but she could watch it for hours."

"It's the one of Tate Blingwood, isn't it?"

Jessie nods.

"It's pretty funny, especially the part after the juggling when he takes out a table full of drinks," I reply. "I hear he's getting a hard time online because of it."

Jessie bites down on her lip and then, as our feet hit the sand, she takes the device from Macy and passes her a little plastic shovel to play with in the sand. "Tate Blingwood is a spoiled star, I'm sure he can handle it. If he thinks that's hard, he should try pulling double shifts around a two-year-old with a temper!"

I chuckle then ask, "Has Macy ever seen her father? I know you said you were a single mom, but does her father have any involvement in her care?"

"Not in person. I reached out when I found out I was pregnant and got precisely nothing in return."

I watch as Macy digs in the sand, her soft hair flapping in the gentle breeze. "How could anyone do such a thing?" Even as I ask the question, I already know that people do such things all the time.

"We were both young. I guess this isn't what he signed up for." Jessie smiles fondly at Macy, but I can see beneath it her heart is breaking as she watches her daughter play.

I admire Jessie's strength, doing the hardest job on earth alone.

Then Jessie turns back to me and adds, "I guess I had a lucky escape, too, since I never signed up for a lazy, shirking, lowlife..." She stops, seeming to catch her increasing annoyance of the topic and lowers her voice. "He's a jerk and he doesn't deserve her. But she'll never lack love, I'll make damned sure of that."

The pit of my stomach aches for them even though they are both doing just fine.

"Don't look so glum. We're okay. It's me and Macy against the world and I wouldn't have it any other way. You can't depend on people."

I nod. "You're right."

"Oh no. Not you. You can depend on people. You've got to get out there and meet someone, but me, I'm keeping myself just for Macy. She ain't never gonna get anything less than 100 percent from me and that doesn't leave room for anyone else. But you've got no excuse to get out there and date. And with bossman as hot as he is, I think your first target has revealed himself."

I shake my head and then tell Jessie all about yesterday—leaving out the parts where my heart thumped harder with every glance, smile and touch and how he pretended to be my boyfriend to stop the store assistant acting like a jerk.

"No way! He spent all that money on a dress for you? That is insane!"

"Logan told me to buy what I liked, but honestly I didn't choose the most expensive—they were all crazy prices. And the shoes… you should have seen the selection; it was like I died and went to heaven."

Jessie hands Macy some kind of kid friendly potato chip and watches her while she eats. "Do you think you'll see him again?" Jessie asks.

"Well, yeah. He's my boss. He'll be sitting right opposite me all day tomorrow."

"No, silly. Like outside of work. What you guys got up to yesterday, it sounds dangerously like date territory. Not that I blame you, he is utterly gorgeous, and rich, and quite funny sometimes, and—"

"And my boss!" I nudge her. "Logan Blingwood is utterly and completely off-limits."

"So, you don't know if he has a Big Mac yet?" Jessie waggles her brows. "You can't say never to a man as tempting as him." She has this cheeky look on her face that has me blushing.

"I'm saying never," I insist.

"That's a shame. It'd be nice to see Mr. Blingwood happy. After what that bitch did to him, it's no wonder he's been grumpy and difficult to be around. Maybe he's finally snapping out of it."

"Dana Gee certainly sounds like a piece of work."

"She is, but you wouldn't think it if you read her posts all over the internet. She makes out she's a saint but it's all fake." Jessie pulls out her cell, takes a quick snap of Macy looking adorable before typing in the woman's name and showing me the screen.

Dana's face is blended by the overuse of a dozen filters, making her look flawless. Artificial. Fake.

"Dana's the heir to the Gee millions or bajillions. A hotelier mogul's only child. She spends her time in Aspen during the holidays, Dubai in the winter, Marbella in the spring… you get the idea. Her daddy has hotels all over the world."

"Nice work if you can get it," I joke. "But if she's that awful, why did Logan even date her?" It's the question that's been bothering me most.

"Dana pursued him. Moved into the resort and was suddenly everywhere Logan was."

I lean in, more interested in the details than I'm comfortable admitting.

"Her daddy did a Forbes interview stating he categorically would not hand over his company if Dana didn't learn the business or marry someone who could run it for her when he passes. I think she didn't want to do the work and learn the business, so she set her sights on Logan and was this close to getting him to marry her and run the whole empire to keep her daddy sweet. It's no secret Logan wants to build his brand so maybe he would've liked the Gee hotels in his arsenal too. On paper, he and Dana made complete sense, aside from the fact she's a manipulative bitch."

I think about that for a moment and silently thank the universe from saving Logan from what I now realize would have been a sham of a marriage. "Seems like after you found the negative pregnancy tests, her house of cards imploded."

Jessie grins euphorically. "I should probably ask Logan for a raise."

We both chuckle but there's a sadness beneath it. "Must be hard for him to trust people. To be used in such a way must really hurt."

"He'll trust the right person when he wants the rewards of it badly enough."

"I hope so," I say with a sigh.

We both join Macy digging in the sand, and as I watch her, and note how absolutely enamored Jessie is with her daughter, I can't help feel angered on Logan's behalf. "He thought he was getting this. A child. He must have been heartbroken to find out it was all a lie."

Jessie nods and her voice cracks as she speaks, "He was."

It's not hard to visualize Logan, looking dashing in his tux, ready and waiting for his bride, but his expression when he realized she wasn't coming, that is unimaginable and it tears me up inside.

"How'd he react? I mean, it's public humiliation, right? He must have been devastated."

"You'd think, but he just went right back to work that afternoon and if anyone dared ask, he told them to mind their own damn business. Of course Dana moved on. Last I saw in Celebrity Gossip Magazine, she was dating some oil tycoon with a net worth to match Musk's. Typical, her next victim is someone even richer. You think it hurt his ego?"

"That she's dating someone richer?"

Jessie nods.

I think back to him dipping his fries into his chocolate sundae, and I think no. "I doubt he cares how much cash the dude has, but then, every day I see how driven he is to open another resort and succeed in business, and so perhaps net worth is something that matters to him." I shrug. "The whole sorry affair reminds me of my mother. She's had five husbands and each of them has been richer than the last." I stop talking. I feel bad slamming my mother. I'm sure she didn't pick my step dads based on their bank accounts. At least I hope not.

"Maybe your mom can talk to mine." Jessie chuckles before she continues, "I love my mother dearly but I'm the oldest of six girls. We all got different daddies and each of the chosen baby daddies has been poorer than his predecessor. Being poor is in my DNA."

"I'd rather be poor than give up my morals."

"Get with your hot boss and you could be rich and grounded?"

I picture Logan's flawless face with his too straight nose and chiseled jaw. I imagine my hands gripping his biceps as he…. I need new panties. He's gorgeous and I'd be lying to myself if I pretended I didn't want him, but I immediately brush my desire away with trivial reality.

"Not going to happen. I have four more weeks left of my contract and then I am off to pastures new. Besides, from all you've said it confirms that Logan Blingwood stays in his lane. He dates rich chicks that can match him round for round, drink for drink. I couldn't even afford the bar bill from our night out let alone the dress. I can't be further from his type."

I breathe out a relieved laugh.

It's ridiculous to even entertain such a notion.

CHAPTER 26

LOGAN

I tell myself, being at the office two hours earlier than normal is due to my unusually social weekend eating into my work schedule and not my strange yearning to see Layla. After all, no time off goes unpunished. I have a lot to get through, and without Layla sitting opposite me, crossing and uncrossing her legs in that way she does, I should be able to power through work undistracted.

But it doesn't quite go like that, and by the time she walks into the office—soaked from the tropical rainstorm and looking sexy as hell, carrying her usual order of a coffee, a banana, and a muffin, all for me—I have literally achieved nothing except a to-do list for her that includes everything she needs to get through before we go away on Saturday. And while I was thinking of what I need her to do, my mind wandered to things that I *would like to do to her*. And entertaining such thoughts is making working with her much *harder*.

"Didn't you get anything for yourself?" I ask as Layla wanders into my office, doing her usual slight bend of her knees as she places my breakfast on my desk, rounding her plump ass to delicious proportions, before standing and throwing me a perfect smile.

"I had mine at the coffee shop. I started chatting, and since I was early I ate there."

My jaw tenses but I cover it with a forced smile. "Chatting with someone? Sounds nice."

"It was nice." She smiles and it's truly breathtaking. "I wasn't late this morning, was I?" She glances at the clock above the door, satisfying herself that she was punctual.

"Perfectly on time, despite your breakfast date." My expression turns stoic. "I'm emailing you a list. I need you to have it done by the end of the day." Her expression turns sour and she swivels on her heels. "Please," I mutter, feeling like a jealous asshole.

It's not my business who she has coffee with or who she dates!

* * *

I'M STILL FEELING guilty about my comments to Layla hours later and so, on my way back to my desk, through the hotel lobby, I toy with a plan to rectify my behavior.

I notice the suggestion box is overflowing and remark for Sally to deal with it, *please*. Then, I head to the break room in search of something to make good with Layla. I settle on a latte and a plate piled high with cookies and am rewarded when Layla smiles as I place them on her desk. It sends a thrill right through me before returning to my office to try and focus on work—though focusing on anything that doesn't involve my assistant is becoming increasingly difficult as each day passes.

Later, I'm about to follow Layla to the cafeteria when I'm

met with a delivery guy who is standing right in front of Layla's desk.

Her sweet scent still flavors the air.

"Layla here?" the delivery guy asks. He's soaked from the rain and it's dripping onto the marble. I've noticed him before, bringing in parcels and making Layla sign for them—smiling his face off at her. It's pathetic. "Or am I too late today and she's already gone to lunch?" The asshole looks disappointed.

"Miss Bowers isn't here. You seem very familiar with my assistant." I notice his badge and the logo of the company he works for on the pocket of his jacket. "Is it your company policy to take such an interest in the women you deliver packages to?"

He looks abashed. "I was just being—"

"Overbearing? Give me the package, I'll sign for it myself."

I snatch the box from him and scribble my name on his handheld machine.

"This one's for Lay—Miss Bowers, sir." He seems to hover, checking behind him, looking for her.

"I'll see that she gets it," I say with an air of finality. "Was there anything else you wanted, aside from flirting with my assistant?"

His throat bobs with his swallow. "No, sir."

"Good." He turns to leave. "Oh, and Gary," he swings back around to face me, "I'll be watching you. If you do not conduct yourself with complete professionalism in my assistant's presence, I will see your delivery round does not include my premises."

He nods once then leaves, and even though I know I am being a dick, I can't help myself. She's too good for an asshole like him. Even more she's too good for an asshole like me.

Once Gary's gone, I place the package on Layla's desk and the wet paper packaging rips. Silky material the exact same color as Layla's eyes slides out. I hold it between my finger and thumb, rubbing back and forth, and my mind conjures an image of her in the underwear. Beneath that set is another in red and my mouth waters.

A growl escapes my lips and then I take the package, storm from the room, and head to the bathroom for some privacy.

CHAPTER 27

LAYLA

"*L*ogan was in a funny mood all day. If he didn't go out on that errand and give me some respite this afternoon, I think I would have had a seizure from the stress," I tell Jessie as we walk back to our apartments after work.

"What was he moody about this time?"

"That's just it, I don't think he was moody, more like frustrated, but I don't know why."

Jessie chokes out a laugh. "Yeah, he's frustrated. Logan's gone from bosshole groucho to knight in shining armor all in a matter of weeks. Frustration is the next phase. He must have it bad."

I wish she'd stop hinting that he likes me because it just has me wanting him!

"He's like the weather. I thought this morning's rainstorm would never end but look at the sky now, it's like the storm never existed." I stare up at the beautiful sky, not a rain cloud in sight. "Tomorrow there'll probably be a tornado or a hurricane."

"Maybe there'll be an earthquake." Jessie winks and elbows me. "Don't tell me you haven't been thinking about what it'd be like for him to make the earth move."

I shake my head and dismiss her comment, not daring to give it headspace.

"I've wondered if the ground would open up and swallow me when I'm around him, if that's what you mean?" She laughs and then I continue, "He's so unpredictable. This morning he was in a good mood. I mentioned I'd been at the coffee shop and then his mood turned sour. He even brought me cookies—which was odd. He's usually happier after lunch, but today he was restless." I huff, still annoyed that I couldn't figure out why he was grumpy.

"Maybe tomorrow he'll be back to scorching hot sunshine."

I roll my eyes. "Sunshine? At best he'll be dry and over-bearing, and that's only if he's not stormy."

"Stormy could be fun. Just imagine him getting you wet." Jessie's cackle rips through the air and I bite my lip to keep from grinning.

Now there's a thought.

"That's odd," I say as we approach my door, then I bend to pick up the package on the doorstep and rip open the water-proof wrapper. Inside is the new underwear I ordered. "I thought I marked my order for delivery to the office."

"Reception probably directed the delivery guy here. Anyway, I'm off to grab Macy from daycare. Sweet dreams," she says in a whistling tone.

And strangely my dreams are sweet and steamy. Too steamy. And that's when I know, I'm in BIG trouble.

* * *

THE NEXT DAY Logan is still holed up in his office and insisting I don't put calls through. I've never had a boss who refuses to take work calls. Instead, it's always the same, I email him the name and number of the caller and at some point he calls them back. He's also started taking his meetings in the boardroom, even when it's just him and one other person.

I, on the other hand, have a steady flow of people entering my office ever since I sent out the email invites to Saturday's party. They want all the details, and wherever I go there's a buzz of excitement. I try not to allow the pressure of pleasing everyone with a perfect party get to me, but since it's the first party I've ever planned, I can't help myself.

What if I let everyone down?

"So, you bringing anyone?" Mike asks after stopping by at my desk like he often does.

"Oh, it's just staff, no plus ones."

From the corner of my eye, I see Logan shift in his chair and I can feel his intense eyes burning on me. Meanwhile, Mike's gaze floats down toward my chest and I instinctively cover my cleavage with my hand. I give him a pointed stare and say, "I'll be going with Skyla and Jessie."

He chuckles. "I'll see you there."

Suddenly, the door to Logan's office flies open. "Did you need something, Mike?"

"Nope. Just checking on the party."

Logan's jaw twitches. "It's not lunchtime for another forty-five minutes. This is exactly what I was talking to you about in your quarterly appraisal."

"I'll get back to work," Mike says and leaves with his tail between his legs.

Logan turns to me and my breath catches in my throat.

"Great work on those transcriptions by the way." He smiles widely and I'm so flustered I can't speak. "Are you okay?" he asks. "You need me to ban Mike from the office? Say the word and I'll do it."

I chuckle lightly and shake my head. "I can handle Mike. It's… you said my work was *great."*

He fixes me with a serious stare. "I compliment your work all the time. You're doing great."

"Maybe I didn't notice." I shrug.

I mean, he brought me cookies and he says thank you more often. The pay is good and the perks are decent. What more am I expecting exactly?

Cunnilingus?

I clamp my eyes shut like he just heard my embarrassing thought. As though erasing my view of Logan will erase the idea.

When I open my eyes, Logan's biting his lip contemplatively. "Sweet Jesus, I'm sorry. I get so caught up in my workload that I don't give you the credit you deserve." He hesitates, like what he is about to say is going to be difficult but then he decides to say it anyway, "Layla, I apologize if I don't say it enough, but thank you. I appreciate you and I noticed you are working hard and fulfilling all your tasks to the highest standard."

He continues to stand there, his hand idly in the pocket of his pants, his gorgeous face set to a sweet smile and I feel myself melting.

"Really?" I try not to sound too shocked, but getting a heartfelt compliment from my boss has me jigging with pride and letting the compliment go straight to my head. "I mean, I am amazing. I'm just surprised it took you so long to see it. I'm probably the best you'll ever have. I'm not saying you *have* to get me a trophy or a plaque, but I'd totally understand if you couldn't help yourself."

His lips quip up into a broader smile like he's enjoying my reaction while I'm already excited for his comeback.

"I'd love to give you a token of my appreciation, Bowers, but we both know you'd sit on it."

Our mouths fall open at the same time.

I know he's referring to me sitting on his sandwich.

He knows he's referring to me sitting on his sandwich.

Yet we're both imagining me sitting on something entirely different.

"I better get back to work," he says, smoothing his hair back and leaving it in a tangle, much like my panties.

* * *

THAT NIGHT I go for a swim to try and relieve the tension in my body.

Logan Blingwood is an enigma; a complicated conundrum I can't work out. Some days, I feel like he likes me, like he *really* likes me. He looks at me like I'm special and he's enjoying my company and then other days, for no apparent reason, I'm certain he can't even stand to be in the same room as me.

Earlier today I got an email from the agency alerting me to a position I could start right away in Alaska, and I was sorely tempted to take it. But then Logan said my work was "great" and suddenly I am putty in his hands and I decide to stay for the term of my contract.

But my decision to stay isn't just about Logan. I'm really enjoying getting to know Skyla and Jessie and the rest of the staff. The resort has a family feel to it that I've never experienced before, and it'd be easy to get used to something like this. I'm not staying because of the enormous crush I've developed on my grouchy boss!

I complete twenty lengths and am about to get out of the pool when I see him in red swim shorts and a filthy grin.

"Layla, beautiful night for a swim, huh?"

"Sure is," I reply and watch as he dives perfectly into the pool with barely a splash. I try not to ogle his thick arms and rugged shoulders as they power him up and down the pool. His length is impressive. Then he swims over, holding onto the ledge beside me. His wet hair looks almost black beneath the moonlight but his eyes are luminously warm.

I hold onto the ledge of the pool, too, since the way Logan's looking at me is making me lightheaded and I'm in danger of forgetting how to tread water.

"Great work today, Layla. You're really proving your abilities."

"Thank you," I reply, smugly pleased with my two compliments from Logan in one day. "I'm enjoying the challenge."

"You're approaching the end of your third week, and if you continue this way we'll definitely be looking to extend your contract."

I try not to look too floored by this news. A compliment and a potential offer of an extension all in one conversation —part of me wonders if it is just wishful thinking.

"Thank you," I stutter and he rewards me with an ardent smile.

Somehow, we've floated closer to one another and are now only inches apart. The temptation to reach out and dig my fingers into the tanned skin of his broad, muscular shoulders and pull myself closer to him is overwhelming, and from the way he's looking at me, like he can't drag his gaze away, he feels it too.

The sound of furniture being dragged across concrete has both our heads twisting in the direction of the noise and then one of the pool guys says, "Sorry, boss. Didn't realize anyone was still in the pool."

We pull away and then I tell Logan I'll see him tomorrow. I swim to the steps and get out, dripping water everywhere until I can pull my towel around me. When I look back, he's watching me and even when he knows he's been seen, he continues watching, instead of turning and finishing his swim—like he can't help himself and I know exactly how he feels.

And it's terrifying.

CHAPTER 28

LOGAN

J wasn't sure whether it was the chlorine or how beautiful she looked, but it hurt my eyes to watch her walk away.

Working opposite her, listening to her cute laugh and the way she sweetly placates the often annoying questions from some staff, she captivates me and my resolve to remain professional is unfastening quicker than the fly of my pants —especially after seeing the silky panties she had delivered to the office.

I've been observing her mannerisms and routines. Like right now, how she's parting her full lips while she applies a fresh application of red lipstick. In a moment she'll spritz some tantalizing scent as she prepares to go for lunch. She'll then come into my office, smile a heart-stopping smile, and sweetly ask if I'd like her to get me anything, and it takes every part of my restraint not to tell her exactly what I want to eat—what I now dream about eating. Any more of this and

I'll need to replace the breakroom with a personal room since I can't get her off my mind.

"What are you doing here?" I hear her ask through the intercom that I have yet to fix.

The sound of her elevated pitch has me immediately checking to see who is bothering her. It's a guy. He's around Layla's age, but I don't know him from the resort. I immediately stand, ready to act and watch her eyes flick to mine as she shakes her head subtly as though letting me know she is okay.

Still, I don't like it, not one bit.

"Your mother said you had her car delivered back to her and this was the location the driver gave as your work address. I tried calling but some of the staff here don't speak good English."

He's the asshole she faked the accent for?

I move closer to the door, not to eavesdrop—I can hear every word through the intercom. No, I want to be close enough to rip the door open and tear his head off if he so much as raises his voice to her.

"Jonathon, you shouldn't have come all this way. We broke up and I don't want to see you." Her voice is quieter than usual, less sure. Her shoulders are hunched and she looks... hurt.

"I'm not communicating with you by text and you won't answer your phone. Besides, I wanted to see you for myself. The way you left me. You humiliated me. I never knew you could be such a bitch...." Jonathon's tone is sharp.

How dare he speak to her like that.

He sounds really fucking pissed and the feeling is rubbing off on me.

"The way I left you?" She sounds angry, *good girl.* Though exactly what this asshole has done to earn her ire has my thoughts racing.

"Layla, come on. You fucking left me standing there like an idiot! Were you so stupid to think I wouldn't come after you to have it out? You made me look a fool. After everything I've done for you—"

"Everything you've done for me? Get out!"

"I'm not going anywhere until you—"

I'm through the door and have a hold of him by the lapel of his cheap suit.

"Go, NOW!" I growl.

Jonathon's eyes bore into mine like he's tempted to fight me and adrenaline shoots through me.

Bring it on, motherfucker!

I jolt him back a step so there's no chance of Layla getting caught in the tussle and then tell him, "You ever come near Layla again and I will end you, understand?" I shove his back against the wall and the air heaves from his chest. "Understood?"

Layla steps forward and puts her delicate hand on my bicep. "Logan, really. It's fine. Jonathon is going."

My body is so tightly wound I couldn't let go of him even if I tried.

"I'm going," Jonathon finally replies, side glaring a sneering look at Layla. "You can have her."

It fuels my anger and I pull him forward then smash his back into the wall again. "I'm going," he whines.

I smile, feeling better. "Yes, you are."

Fucking weasel.

Simon from the security detail enters the room along with one of the employees from his staff and I shove Jonathon in his direction. "Get rid of him and then I want a full report on my desk within the next hour detailing how this fuck found his way unfettered into Layla's office."

"Yes, boss," Simon replies, grabbing Jonathon by the arm

and roughly directing him into the doorframe on his way out.

When I turn to Layla, she is sheet white and clearly shaken. I step forward toward her, my head dipped trying to make myself smaller.

"Are you okay?" I ask.

"I'm sorry he showed up here. I wasn't expecting him."

"Layla, you've got to tell me, are you safe here, from him? Did he ever do anything to suggest he might hurt you?"

She shakes her head, slowly. "No. I... we broke up. He cheated and I left him...."

I step forward again and gently place my hands on the tops of her slender arms. She's staring down at the floor, not meeting my gaze but I need to check she's okay, so I use my finger to gently tip her chin. At the sight of her shimmering turquoise eyes, I'm suddenly pulling her into my arms, gently cradling her small frame.

"I'm sorry. I didn't mean to frighten you," I say feeling like an even bigger asshole than her ex.

She shakes her head, disbelievingly and says, as though to herself, "No one's ever stood up for me like that." Her teeth clamp onto her lower lip and her gaze drops, back to the floor.

"If he gives you any more shit, you tell me, okay. I will personally see to it that he can't get to you. Understand?"

Layla takes one step back. Her eyes are impossibly pure, and she nods. "Thank you."

Her vulnerability makes me want to pull her back into my arms but I hold myself still, allowing her space to compose herself. The silence is eventually broken by the sound of Layla's cell phone vibrating across her desk and it makes her flinch.

Once she's checked the caller ID she says, "It's just Jessie.

I'm supposed to be meeting her and Skyla for lunch. They're saving me a space."

"I'll walk you," I insist, expecting her ex has been expelled from the premises but also unwilling to take the chance of her running into him again.

Once I have delivered Layla to her feisty friend and my sister-in-law, I head straight to the security desk and make sure the entire detail know her ex's face and the consequences of him gaining access to her.

CHAPTER 29

LAYLA

*T*he rest of the week improves after Jonathon's visit, but I'm still floored after Logan stormed into my office and threw him out. I've never seen Logan so angry, so formidable. It was like he was possessed, but he was also protective, kind, and concerned about my welfare. Ever since it happened, Logan has been sweeter, smiling more and rather awkwardly asking me if I'm okay, if I have heard from Jonathon or if he is bothering me.

Of course I haven't heard from Jonathon. He's probably too afraid to come anywhere near me since Logan warned him off. My mother, on the other hand, heard all about it and I received three voicemails back-to-back warning me that I had made the "mistake of my life" turning Jonathon away when he was *willing to give me* a second chance.

I delete the voicemails and throw myself into work where there's a catching buzz in the air about the upcoming party and my mood gradually lifts.

By Thursday morning, I'm feeling so much better that when I get to the coffee shop, instead of ordering Logan's usual, I grab him the coffee shop's special concoction, since it sounds delicious with soy, spices, and a big helping of cocoa on the top and then I head into the office, sure that today will be a good day.

Logan's sitting in his office when I stroll in and put his breakfast and coffee on his desk. I'm about to leave but remember there was something I wanted to thank him for. "There was extra money in my pay."

I noticed yesterday there was an extra deposit in my account, and when I looked it was from Blingwood Enterprises, marked: Coffee, etc.

"You're welcome. I appreciate you bringing me breakfast. Without it, I hear I can get quite grumpy." He full on smiles instead of smirking and it sends a thrill right through me.

"You're welcome but you gave me too much. It's almost twice what I have spent."

He waves his hand, unconcerned. "Call it recompense for your additional time."

Logan's lifting the cup to his delectable lips as I tell him, "I got you the special today. It's the soy choco and sounded amazing. If I wasn't being careful not to gain weight before I need to wear not one but two new dresses, then I would have treated myself to one." I'm grinning. I do that way more than usual lately but I just can't believe my luck in finding this job and it working out perfectly—with the exception of quietly lusting after my boss.

Logan's hand flies to his throat and the cup drops on the marble floor, spilling out like brown sewage. His face goes suddenly red and he chokes out the word: "Soy?"

"Oh crap. Is that bad?"

He buckles to his knees and I'm at his side in a heartbeat. "What do I do?"

He's choking and having some kind of seizure at the same time. I snatch the phone from his desk and dial 911. "Ambulance," I scream into the receiver and then follow the instructions of the dispatcher.

"Don't you dare die on me, Logan Blingwood," I order, but I don't think he can hear me as he shudders and rocks beside me.

CHAPTER 30

LOGAN

"*M*om, I'm fine, please stop fussing."

My entire body throbs like a son of a bitch and my throat feels like it had the crap punched out of it—from the inside—but I'm alive, which is more than can be said for Layla, who is an uncomfortable shade of gray.

"I swear I didn't know." She wrings her hands, then wraps her arms across her body in a self-soothing manner. "Honestly, I wasn't trying to kill you. I stopped wishing for your death weeks ago!"

"Layla, it's fine," I choke out as smoothly as I can. My voice is gravelly and doesn't sound like my own. "I don't believe the poisoning was a premeditated attack."

"Why didn't you tell me you're allergic to soy?"

I shrug. "You always bring me straight black; I wasn't expecting anything different."

"Poor Logi," Mom says, killing any chance I had at

making my allergic reaction and subsequent brush with death seem manly and cool.

"They gave me the shot. I'm all good. Let's get out of here." I climb off the hospital bed. There's no way I'm staying here another moment; this place still takes me right back to when we lost Dad.

The second Mom starts shaking her head, I know I'm going to have a battle on my hands securing my discharge. "You need to stay overnight so the nurses can keep an eye on you. Honey, your body just had a massive shock." Above her folded arms, I can just make out the slogan on her T-shirt: *Crazy Dog Lady.*

Sounds about right.

"I'm fine," I repeat but it seems everyone around me has suddenly gone deaf to the sound of my voice.

"Logi, you need to stay in the hospital."

"Not doing it, Mom. I'm fine."

Except my damn face has puffed up like a blowfish.

"Layla, honey, can you stay with him? I'm booked on a redeye flight to go see Tate. He had a wardrobe malfunction at some awards ceremony and the ogres are ridiculing him, poor boy."

"Trolls, Mom. The trolls are ridiculing him." I massage my temple to try to soothe my aching head. "You go deal with Tate. I am absolutely fine and do not need a babysitter."

Mom ignores me, telling Layla, "I'm at a loss with what to do with my boys these days. I turn my back for a second and there are break-ups, a marriage, trolls and ogres... near death experiences."

"Of course I'll look after your son, Mrs. Blingwood. It's the least I can do. I feel so responsible—"

I interject. The last thing I need is Mom railroading Layla into feeling like she has to look after me. "Layla, you don't need to do that—"

"Oh, honey—thank you. Thank you so much. That'd be such a weight from my mind." Mom turns to me. "Logi, you've had a terrible shock. Layla has too. You need to look after each other." She turns back to Layla. "I know these things are scary. Why, I nearly died of fright the first time Logan had a reaction, but you did the exact right thing and called for the ambulance. You saved his life!" Mom hugs Layla and I'm left feeling like a spare part. Then she leans back, gripping Layla's shoulders and tells her, "Thank you for agreeing to watch him while I'm gone. But are you sure you'll cope? He'll be cranky—"

"Mom, I'm not a baby—"

Mom continues talking to Layla, cupping her hands in hers, talking to her like she's family—which is not something I ever noticed her do with Dana. The gesture and seeing them join forces, causes a strange, warm feeling to spread across my chest, which I chalk up entirely to the drugs the doctor pumped into me.

"My Logi can be so stubborn, always has been. Even after his first reaction, he was adamant Tate and Drew must never know about his allergies."

"Because they'd poison me for fun!" I huff.

"I know he'll be in good hands with you, my dear," Mom says, reaching her arms around Layla's shoulders as she pulls her into a hug.

Layla grins back at Mom and reassures her she won't leave my side.

Meanwhile, neither of them listen to my protests that I. AM. FINE!

* * *

"Here, sit forward. You look uncomfortable. Let me put this cushion behind you."

"Layla, stop fussing."

As soon as I got back to the penthouse, I went to change into my sweats and a T-shirt. Even I was spooked when I saw my reflection in the mirror. My eyes are mere slits in my balloon-shaped face and my pallor is an insipid shade of burgundy.

The nurse said the meds should kick in over the next twelve hours, but meanwhile I look like John Merrick after he went ten rounds with a truck.

"I can't help it. You look like…"

"Shit? Melted shit? Like a truck rolled over some shit and then drove over my face?"

"You look like you need some rest," Layla says, her tone still set to worried and concerned. "How do you feel physically?"

"I feel fine." *Aside from the thumping headache and horrible embarrassment at the state of my face.* "Can you pass me my laptop, please? It's on the coffee table."

"I already told Skyla to spread the word that you are in the penthouse, sick. Any urgent calls will be directed through my cellphone. Your *only* job today, Mr. Blingwood, is to rest."

"There's really no need—" Layla pulls my legs up onto the sofa and begins rubbing my feet. I freeze. My instinct is to tell her to stop, that she doesn't need to feel guilty or care for me. But watching her hands work my flesh, it's sensual and oh so relaxing. I relent briefly, telling myself if it eases her guilt, I'll allow her to do it for a minute. Two tops. Three at an absolute maximum. Then, I close my eyes and focus on the heel of her palms working the ball of my foot.

"You're going to rest and recuperate. You need to be healed for the party. Your body had an enormous shock."

Despite my slumber, concern dawns on me that if Layla continues rubbing me, shock won't be my only enormous thing. I pull the comforter that's thrown across the back of the sofa over my lap.

"It's a great place you have. The steel and bare brick walls —it's so fancy," she says, but her voice doesn't contain her normal level of enthusiasm when something pleases her.

I open one eye and reply, "You don't approve?"

"I don't not approve of anything. It's just, well, it's a hotel room. A very fancy hotel room, but still, a hotel room no less."

"And your point is?"

"Well, it's not a home, is it? You could live anywhere. There's this great little house that I saw on one of our walks. It faces the ocean to the front and the mountains to the back. Wouldn't you prefer to live someplace like that?"

When I thought I was going to be a father, before I found out it was all a lie, I was looking for houses with enough land for a pool and a swing set. Since then, I have resigned myself to living at the hotel.

"It's convenient," I reply simply, allowing my eyes to drift closed again.

"Don't you find it annoying, though? Living where you work. It must feel like you're always on duty."

"I am always on duty."

Layla's fingers splay my toes and a groan leaves my throat.

"But you have staff. Good staff. Don't you trust them?"

"I trust the staff just fine. I have everything here at my fingertips. Besides, since it's just me, what would be the point in my buying someplace just to rattle around inside it on my own?"

Layla quiets for a moment, seemingly satisfied with my reply, while I shift my other foot until she takes the hint and begins working that one. I wonder if her interrogation is over, but then she asks another question.

"I suppose when you marry you'll move—" She stops talking, realizing her faux pas. Her hands have stopped massaging and when I open my eye to check, her expression is stricken.

"You heard what happened with Dana."

She nods and parts her lips, pulling a sorrowful expression that hits me straight in the gut.

"I'm sorry. I didn't mean to bring it up. I know you don't like to talk about what happened."

The bereft look on her face is more than I can take, so I open up, if only to make her feel better. "It's okay. Dana leaving me on my wedding day is hardly a secret around here."

"Are you okay now, though? I mean, obviously you weren't at the time, but are you over it? It must have been a shock."

"Dana told me she was pregnant. So, we planned the wedding."

"You were standing by her."

She begins rubbing my feet again.

"Of course." *Does she think I'd up and leave if a woman was carrying my child?* "Hey, I might be a grumpy asshole sometimes—"

"Most of the time," she supplies with a cute smirk.

I nod and attempt a smile, though with my face this swollen it probably resembles a grimace. "I stand corrected. Most of the time I am a grumpy asshole, but if a woman is carrying my child, I'll be there in whatever capacity she wants me."

"You're very decent," she says, humbling me with what I am sure is a lump in her throat.

"I didn't feel very decent when I found out it was all a lie," I admit. "You may not have heard this part from the rumor mill, but Dana told me and her whole social media following she was pregnant but she wasn't. She was, however, trying to get pregnant. I found out in the final hour, moments before the wedding that there never was a baby, and she fled, making it appear that she had left me at the altar, and humiliating me in front of everyone I know. Now she alludes to her followers our relationship broke down because I was a workaholic son of a bitch. Decency, it seems, doesn't always extend both ways."

"You know, I looked her up online and I think people see through her. She comes across as a superficial fool and that guy she's dating is a total tool!"

I grin at her. "Graham Grieves and I went to school together—never did like the guy."

"Oh?"

"He acted like a chump because I was captain of the football team and he got benched." I smirk, remembering how he'd try and sleep with the girls I dated or spread rumors about me.

"Sounds like they deserve each other."

"Bowers, you speak sense sometimes—"

She grins and it's dazzling, right up until the moment she corrects me. "I speak sense all the time. And I'm so glad you're finally seeing my wonder."

"So, how about you? It's unfair that my private life, or rather the false parts of it are so public. What have you been up to?"

Layla shifts uncomfortably in her seat and asks, "What do you want to know?"

Everything.

I shrug noncommittally.

"Something. Anything. I mean, I already know you can't hold your liquor and that you snore like a freight train, but I'm missing the finer details." I wink and it hurts like a bitch. "What else should I know about Layla Bowers?"

She stops massaging my toes and I wonder if I said something wrong. The last time I found out an intimate detail about my assistant's private life was when I threw her ex-boyfriend out of her office. I suppose she wouldn't want to talk about him.

"Not much to tell really. Pretty average." She slides my legs off her lap and stands before propping my feet under a cushion. "You need to eat." She looks toward the kitchen. "Am I likely to find any food in your fridge?"

I sheepishly clamp my teeth down onto my lower lip. "I normally eat in the cafeteria or order room service if I miss the staff sitting."

Layla slides her cell out of her back pocket and dials. "Fernando, are you busy?... Good. Can you send me the following ingredients…"

She reels off a list and then hangs up. "I am going to make you Layla's finest chicken soup."

"Just like momma used to make, huh?"

She looks away, turning her petite frame toward the kitchen. "It's a recipe I learned in cooking class. It's good, you'll like it. Now, stop yapping and rest."

"Hey, I don't yap," I complain, but then she turns the lights down in the living room and suddenly the heavy weight of exhaustion takes over.

* * *

I MUST PASS out for a while because when I wake, I'm facedown on the cushion. When I look up, Layla is standing barefoot in my kitchen stirring some kind of goodness and a growl forces its way past my lips.

"Good, you're awake," she says. "I hope you're hungry because dinner won't be long. I hope you don't mind? I opened a bottle of this." She points to the 1930s Chenin that arrived awhile back as a wedding gift.

"No, I don't mind at all."

"I'd pour you a glass, but I don't think you should. Not after—"

"After you poisoned me?" I quip, raising a playful brow.

Layla points the spoon she is holding at me. "If you tease me, I might just poison you for real." She smiles sweetly, her voice is higher pitched than normal as she moves about my kitchen—her skin glowing from the heat. She's removed her sweater and is wearing a cami that temptingly hugs her chest.

She takes a sip of the wine and I sit up and watch her take control of my kitchen while I wait for my post-nap hard-on to relax.

When the oven beeps, she sings to herself, "That'll be the bread." I watch as she inserts her tiny hands into a pair of oven gloves and deposits the loaf onto the counter. As she bends to deeply inhale the scent of freshly baked bread, I'm afforded a great look at her breasts.

The sight makes me salivate.

"Where did you learn to bake bread?"

"I took a course while I was working in this auto shop in Connecticut a couple of years ago. If you think this is good, you should taste my snickerdoodles."

I'd love to taste her snickerdoodles.

"My mouth is watering," I say, keeping my tone dry.

"You may mock, but my snickerdoodles are the best in town."

Yes. Yes, they are.

"Come sit," she orders. "I've poured you a water."

I pull myself up from the sofa. My body feels heavy but I should be feeling back to almost full strength by tomorrow.

Layla pours soup into bowls and slices the bread into

thick chunks. It's difficult to take my eyes off her, but when I do, I'm impressed with the meal she has cooked.

I try not to think of Dana but can't help compare the difference between the two women. Dana barely ate, and as such, had a willowy figure that resembled something that might snap to reveal sharp, pointy edges. On the rare occasions Dana and I dined together, the food was always delivered or we ate out. Conversely, Layla has a figure with soft, round edges that dip in and out in ways that send my mind spinning out of control. She eats lunch every day and looks strong and healthy and always seems to have an abundance of energy.

I shouldn't allow my mind to wander to such places like how energetic she would be in the bedroom, yet somehow, I can't seem to help myself.

"This looks really good," I admit, returning my focus to the food, instead of admiring the way her tight pants are molded to her ass as she leans across the table to pass out cutlery.

"Just something I rustled up." Layla shrugs, but I can tell from her smile that she's pleased with herself.

She sits opposite me, holds up her wine glass and I mirror her action by lifting my water glass.

"To that amazing view." She points her thumb to the wall-sized window beside me, and I don't need to look to know she is referring to the ocean that's romantically lit by the setting sun. Cast in the glow, with her face flush from the heat of the kitchen, I wonder if she has ever looked more beautiful. "And to being alive. May we never forget how lucky we are."

I follow her wondered gaze to the ocean I have passed a million times without admiring and then turn back to face Layla.

"To spectacular views."

CHAPTER 31

LAYLA

I'm unable to stop staring at him. He looks better than a male model or movie star—even with his face all swollen and puffy from his reaction to the soy.

"I know, I look like the Hulk. My face should go down by tomorrow," Logan says self-consciously.

"Was I staring? Oops, I'm sorry. I still feel bad about the whole thing," I reply and my cheeks flush, or maybe it's the wine making them warm—it's going down nicely after all the stress of the hospital and also from noticing Logan's enormous boner beneath his sweats.

"Staring?" He chuckles. "Layla, you haven't stopped staring. You don't need to feel bad; it was an accident. I still feel quite embarrassed."

"You feel embarrassed?" I repeat. "Why?"

He waves his hand that still clutches his spoon. "Seizing in front of you, losing control like that, my mom and her inability to call me by my given name, my failing to see Dana for what she was… the list is getting longer by the day." He rips off a chunk of bread and soaks it in his soup. "This is delicious, by the way."

"It's okay to be vulnerable. You let your guard down and embraced Dana telling you you were going to be a father, that's noble," I tell him. "And you couldn't help your medical reaction to the soy—you were sick, and the way your mother dotes on you, it's…" My eyes moisten. I'm trying hard not to gush but I'm seeing so many different sides to the man I thought was just a mean boss, that it's difficult to keep my emotions in check. "Your mother is a lovely woman. You're lucky to have her."

His mouth turns up at the corners. "You're right, she's a good mom. She's been struggling since Dad died, we all have."

"What happened?"

"Sudden heart attack. The shock was unbearable. Dad was in good shape, could outrun anyone of us on the track. It was—crushing. Worse for Drew. They'd had an argument before he died, so he took it the hardest, but he's healing now." Logan twists the spoon around in his bowl, his eyes mist, then he blinks and shakes his head. "I don't know why I'm telling you all this."

I hadn't even realized I moved my hand, but suddenly, there it is, atop of his, my thumb stroking back and forth. "I'm sorry, it's hard to lose a parent."

His gaze moves to my hand and pauses there for a while. I wonder if I should snatch my arm away. After all, he's my boss and holding his hand, even to comfort him, is an intimate gesture, but no worse than rubbing his feet and watching his hard dick beneath his sweats. Before I have time to decide, Logan's other hand reaches out and cups mine between his. Then his gaze returns to me. "You lost your dad too. I'm sorry I was such a dick during your interview. I'd had a bad day. A bad year, actually. But it's no excuse." The sadness in his gaze holds me to the spot. "Were you and he close?"

I slide my hand back to my cutlery and look away while I load my spoon with soup. "We were when we saw each other," I admit but the sentiment feels lacking. "He was a photographer and worked all over the world, so I mostly grew up with my mother and my various stepdads. It wasn't practical for my father to raise me." I shift uncomfortably in my seat and confess, "Even if I might have preferred that."

I spoon more soup into my mouth to distract myself from Logan's burning gaze, then deftly change the subject by gesturing my hand at his amazing suite to the balcony, beyond which lies a first-rate resort in an idyllic location. "Your dad must have been very proud of you. All of this. It's really something."

Logan smooths his softer than usual, floppy hair back away from his face. His styling products are now long since dissolved. "Dad, or rather, his dad, founded all of this. I had it handed to me since Drew, the oldest of our clan, never cared for it. I reno'd it, built a second resort, and elevated its status from four- to five-star, but the meat and bones of everything was handed to me."

I feel the space between my brows crinkle.

"Logan, you run an empire and built that from something far less significant. In the past two years alone you increased your net worth five-fold and you were listed in Forbes three years running. That is impressive and something to be proud of."

He shrugs and then I watch his eyes sparkle as they narrow on me. His lips tilt up in a barely there smile and he asks, "Sassy pants, have you googled me?"

Caught out, I almost choke on the wine I am sipping.

"It's prudent to know who I am working for." Mostly I

looked at the images of him and somewhat disregarded most of the text. Logan stepping off a yacht, Logan in a tux at an awards ceremony, and my personal favorite, Logan in ripped jeans and a mucky T-shirt helping to rebuild a homeless shelter after the 2022 wildfires.

"So, you weren't checking me out?"

"No!" I choke, horrified at how he might react.

"Fair enough," he replies with an air of disappointment. "The resort my grandfather and father built were remarkable for the times, but the old man was happiest at home surrounded by all of us. Not that he didn't appreciate a hard day's work." There's a fondness in Logan's eyes as he summons the memory of his father that touches my heart.

"You were lucky to have him."

"Yes, he was a good man." He sips his water then asks me, "What about yours?"

"Mine?"

"Your father. What happened?"

I push a piece of bread into my mouth and hold up my hand in a gesture that suggests I need more time.

"He came home from Zambia with a stomach ache and got checked out. A few scans later and we found out the cancer was in his pancreas. He'd lost touch with most of his family and, as his only child, I quit my job and flew home to take care of him. He hung on as long as he could and I got to spend time with him."

"But…"

Logan is looking at me expectantly like he knows there's more to my story. His gaze also burns with understanding, like I can tell him anything and he won't judge me, so I explain my divided feelings.

"I've been carrying some resentment that I feel incredibly guilty for now that he's gone."

Logan pushes his empty bowl aside and leans forward. "How so?"

I push my bowl aside too and try to ignore the sting in my heart.

"It'll probably sound cruel, to speak ill of the dead," I dismiss, putting my bowl inside Logan's and preparing to clear the table but Logan's hand lands on mine to make it still and he says, "No one's perfect, alive or dead. What happened?"

I pause, the weight of his hand grounds me in the moment and then I explain, "My mother wasn't all bad but she could be a little selfish. Mom worried more about how I made her look in public, rather than my feelings. We lived wherever her new husband lived, no matter if I had to change schools and start over. And I could have tolerated it if she actually spent time with me, but she was always at the country club. I never even had a birthday party; I share the same birthday as my mom and so she was always busy that day." I laugh pathetically and swallow the lump that has formed in my throat, and then I look back at Logan and am met with brown eyes so warm I feel comforted. "At least Mom was there for me, I owe her credit for providing for me and keeping a roof over my head. My dad had the opportunity to give me a different life and chose not to."

"Yet when he needed you, you dropped everything and came to help him."

I nod. "I don't regret being with him at the end. No one should ever have to go through cancer alone, but there was this nagging feeling that I pushed aside, making me wonder if he would have done the same for me. It's probably why I settled with Jonathon. The feeling that I owed him something... I mean, he drove me to the hospital multiple times."

Logan chuckles but it doesn't meet his eyes. "A few car rides does not make him deserving of someone like you." He shakes his head. "You're an amazing, independent woman and you care deeply for those around you." His tone is completely devoid of sarcasm.

I shrug, not feeling remotely amazing but appreciating Logan's compliment nonetheless.

"Jonathon helped me get through a really tough time, and I wasn't an abused child or anything like that. Mom didn't hurt me and she was there for me. Maybe not in the way I needed her but she was there. We had nice houses, even went to Europe one summer. Her husbands were, for the most part, nice to me. But she didn't know how to be with me, you know? Dad knew what she was like. It's why he left her. I just wish he'd put me first."

"One day, you'll meet someone who will put you first in everything they do, I guarantee it."

I chuckle lightly and reply, "Well, that would really be something."

Logan's stare is so heated, I start to hope he'll kiss me— even though he is across the table. Nerves envelop me and my eyes dart around the room looking for a distraction until I settle on Logan's dish.

"You ate it all up. Well done, Logi Bear." I stand and fluff his silky hair while reminding myself that no good will come of kissing my boss.

I need my job and this place to live, and kissing Logan will no doubt ruin everything. As I tidy, I replace the fleeting moment with jovial chatter. "Your momma's going to be so happy when she calls me later for an update." I plaster a grin on my face that feels forced and by his curious stare, he can tell.

I take our bowls to the counter and he asks, "My mother has your number?" He's suddenly behind me, carrying the rest of the tableware.

"She's calling me as soon as her flight lands. We're buddies."

"You know she'll be recruiting you to walk the rescue dogs all the time now?"

I begin filling the sink with hot, soapy water. "I don't mind. I like helping her dogs get started on a new path."

"Yeah, I feel sorry for them too."

I stop what I'm doing and tilt my head up to Logan's full height. "I think you should get a shot every day. It's like it's transformed you into this new, sweet man."

He steps forward until he is in front of me and my mouth goes dry.

"There's much you don't know about me, sassy pants."

"Is that so?"

"Let me put these in the dishwasher and then you can ask me anything you like," he offers, brushing past me to grab the dishes I am about to wash and causing my skin to vibrate with excitement.

"Okay. But how about I wash, you dry? If you even know how to?" I tease, but I need something to do with my hands that isn't touching my boss. "I bet you never washed dishes in your whole life." I stick out my tongue and his eyes light up.

"Take that look off your face." He's so close I can smell the spice of his cologne mixed with his sweet shampoo.

"What look?" I say innocently goading him.

His mouth widens to a full-lipped, heart stopping smile. "I've washed plenty of dishes. In our house Mom withheld dessert from the kids who refused to clean up."

"In that case you know they have to get good and wet." I swish the water a little too zealously and it splatters up his white T-shirt.

"Hey!" He grabs both my wrists with one of his. "That's it!"

I let out a roaring cackle as he pulls my hands downward

until they're in the water-filled sink and swooshes a wave toward us.

I try and free my hands but his are large and more easily able to grip mine, but then a move I learned at self-defense takes over my body and I use a flick and scooping motion to take his leg out from beneath him. He falls back, but his grip on my wrists doesn't loosen, so he pulls me down with him. Momentarily we're suspended midair and his arms wrap around me so that when we hit the floor, I am protected from the blow by his embrace.

I somehow land on top of him, his arms still around my waist, holding me firmly.

"Disarmed by a woman," he says shaking his head with mock disappointment.

"Not just any woman," I reply, raising my brow smugly, but pressed against him like this, I don't just feel smug, I feel wanton and needy.

I wonder if he feels it too and am sure he does as his gaze darkens, our faces just a few inches apart.

"No, not just any woman."

He leans forward an inch and I do too. The tension is thick, my need for him growing beyond what I can deny. His lips part, while mine pucker.

I want him.

I want to feel the pressure of his lips on mine and taste his mouth.

Logan's chin dips, and his lips barely brush mine teasingly. But I want more and I'm no longer prepared to wait. I push my mouth against his and a burst of adrenaline rocks through me.

I'm kissing Logan Blingwood and it feels divine.

Our tongues tangle, my hands reach into his hair, making his escape impossible. Okay, so maybe not impossible, but if he tries to move away, I'll fight him.

As I lay on top of him, my hair falls over us like a curtain and it's like we are the only people on earth. No concerns about work, accommodation and non-fraternization policies, it's just me and him, taking what we need, and my god, do I need this. Logan must too, because he grips the flesh of my ass and squeezes while my hands tangle in the hair I have obsessed about touching for so long. It's silkier than I imagined, his mouth is tastier than I was prepared for, and his body, beneath mine, sexier than anything I have ever come across.

He's making me so damned hot for him that I grind against him, making it obvious what I want. Logan responds like a champ, flipping me over until I am pinned beneath him and he's posed over me, his weight spread between his knees and one arm. The hand of his other arm is busy sliding up my thigh, beneath my skirt. I widen my legs to give him access and he's suddenly brushing against my panties, making me gasp and threaten to come on impact.

"Fucking you is all I have been able to think about ever since I first laid eyes on you." His voice is guttural, his eyes trained on my breasts that are almost but not quite revealed by my shirt that got pushed up in the carnage. "You're all I've been able to think about."

"I've been distracted too. I've been trying to ignore it, but —" he slips his finger beneath my panties, making me gasp as he slides it along my wet slit. He teases my opening for a few seconds before moving back up and twirling his finger slowly around my clit. I moan and grab his wrist to make him move faster, but then he begins to move back down and gently inserts a finger. It feels so good all coherent thoughts have left the building.

His mouth trails kisses and nips down my neck, and I arch my back as he inserts another finger, pushing my body towards where I need his touch the most.

Knowing he wants me like I want him, after thinking about him like this for so long, it's the most powerful turn-on I ever encountered and as though to prove it he says, "So fucking wet for me, Layla. I thought I could resist you but I don't have the strength anymore."

"We need to get it out of our systems," I pant, feeling the threatening climax heighten as I grind my core against his fingers. "We'll just do it once. Fast and hard and then we can stop imagining it. It'll be done. It'll be over."

Logan inserts a third finger, hitting *that* spot that no other man has hit before, and I spasm out of control, wrapping my arms around his neck without strangling him like I have imagined.

"Fuck!" I yelp as I come hard on his fingers. The pulsating heat and friction has my vision blurring and senseless sounds forcing their way past my throat.

As Logan continues to ride out the waves of my orgasm by playing with my clit, and when the last delicious ripples of pleasure have rolled through me, I catch my breath and notice Logan watching me with wide eyes that are borderline crazy.

"I need to fuck you, Layla." He hoists me to my feet and lifts me onto the kitchen counter as if I weigh nothing. My skirt is already hitched around my waist and he's unbuttoning my shirt. "Sweet baby Jesus," he says almost to himself. His vision is laser focused on my breasts, and he's licking his lips. "I knew they were epic, but fuck, Layla, I'd have taken you first chance I got if I knew they were this perfect." His pushes aside the cup of my bra and his mouth is suddenly covering my right nipple, while his hand works the other one.

I fumble, pulling his shirt over his head and then his mouth goes straight back to nuzzle my chest. His torso is tanned and rock-hard, ripped with only a few manly hairs in the center. I've seen it in photographs on social media, but none of those pictures could prepare me for its feel beneath my hands, and I can't stop myself from biting his shoulder to feel his flesh in my mouth and savor his taste.

"You turn me on so fucking much," he says, pausing. "Your smart mouth and your tight body, Layla, you're going to be my undoing."

Our mouths come together in hot, frenzied kisses. My hands roam his body, squeezing his shoulders, running my palms over his pecs then squeezing his biceps. Logan's hands explore me too, skimming my jaw then neck with his fingers before running them over my shoulders, down my back and squeezing my ass. Then he slides his finger across the skin of my waist and goes south to caress my thighs. Finally his hands seem to decide where to settle. One cups my breast while his mouth captures my nipple again; the fingers of his other hand settle at my entrance, slowly running up and down between my folds.

It's measured but hurried, like we're trying to sample everything the other has to offer before the clock turns twelve and the magic runs out, when suddenly we will turn into boss and employee again and the enormity of our predicament will need to be faced.

But that's a concern for another time, because Logan inserts two fingers, and I become incapable of concerning myself with anything that does not involve feeling Logan inside me.

Instead, I focus on the comment he just made and I do indeed become his undoing as I untie his sweat pants and slide them down over his hips, arching back and to the side to stare in wonder at his cock that's long and thick and deeply colored like it's threatening to explode.

I grip him and a growl forces its way past his throat.

"Good?" I check.

"Fuck, Layla, I need to be inside of you." Logan leans back, but his fingers continue their torment, bringing me closer to the release that I crave. "Shit. I need to go get a condom."

My hand grips his bicep and I nuzzle against his chest, tempted to bite his pec. "I'm clean and on the pill. Have you been checked out?"

"I'm clean," he replies and I believe him instantly.

Logan fleetingly wrestles with the decision, his forehead rests against mine while my hand encourages him to decide by gripping his thick erection, sliding my hand up and down his length easily thanks to the precum that's leaking out. The entire time, I'm imagining how good it's going to feel deep inside me.

"Fuck it." He takes ahold of himself while I go back to gripping his shoulders. Like a delicious prelude, he rubs the crown of his dick back and forth against my sweet spot and along the length of my folds.

My entire core spasms as he eases the smooth tip into me by an inch, slowly stretching me. "God, you're beautiful," he says, his voice low and sexy, his warm brown eyes pinned on mine while he pushes in deeper. "So tight."

"You feel so good," I admit, as he moves inside me with long, gentle strokes. I whimper and pant his name. "I think I might—" I cling to him, kissing his neck and feeling his pace quicken. "Logan, I—give me all of you. Please don't stop!"

He drives into me and my hands reach down behind him, my fingers curling into his muscular ass. Smooth and firm, my nails sink into his butt as he lifts me by my ass and takes control, pushing me down onto him, forcing a delicious friction to rub at my clit.

I must hit the fruit bowl on the counter because it wobbles forward and smashes on the floor, but neither of us even glance its way.

My chest is pinned against his heated skin and my entire body aches for release.

I'm gazing in his eyes when he says, "I couldn't have imagined you'd feel so perfect." He lifts me and spins us around, taking two short steps while still buried deep inside me. "I want you on your back. I want to watch your beautiful face and your perfect tits bouncing as you come for me."

"Yes. Yes, *Mr. Blingwood*," I whimper, though in all honestly, I can't imagine objecting to anything at this point.

He uses his foot, one at a time, to discard his sweatpants and then takes a few more strides until he is lowering me down onto the designer sofa. He uses the arm that isn't gripping my ass to swipe away the throw cushions—and in the process, the lamp from the side table gets thrown across the room.

"Watch the furniture," the good girl in me says, and he grins.

"I don't give a fuck about the furniture. I only want to see you come again, and on my cock this time." He circles his hips and the promise of his threat intensifies the sensation.

I swallow hard and every nerve ending reacts. "Oh, well… I definitely think I can rise to that target, Mr. Blingwood." I raise myself up to meet every thrust of his hips. Our bodies move together so perfectly, I wonder why we waited this long, and then I remember. "What about the non-fraternization policy?" I blurt, and hope he didn't hear me.

He's so deep inside me my entire body belongs to him.

"Fuck the non-frat. I'll never fire you, if that's what you're worried about. But I am going to fire into you and you're going to scream my name when I do."

My mouth goes dry which makes sense since all the liquid in my body is now between my thighs. "Thank you for clarifying," I say between pants. "If you stopped now, I'd be writing a strongly worded letter of complaint to management."

He chuckles into my neck. "There's no hope of me stopping. You better hold on, sassy pants. I'm so fucking close."

Logan's tongue dips inside my mouth, probably to shut me up, so I widen my legs and wrap them around his hips until his cock hits the sweet, magical spot that makes me cry out in ecstasy.

"Logan. I—" but I can't finish my sentence because he steals my breath by quickening his thrusts, looking sinfully pleased with himself as he drives into me, detonating the orgasm inside my body. All of my muscles vibrate and spasm out of control and my toes curl. I grip onto his slick body and, as though he's been waiting for me to come, he stiffens and I watch as his climax blasts through him and his expression turns ethereal. It's sexy as hell. His eyes flutter closed and then open, pinning his stare on me as his pumps slow and his cock twitches before finally he collapses over me, hugging me into his body.

"Sweet Layla. Holy fucking Layla. That was… you were… it was… perfection."

We're tangled, sweaty messes.

There's a tingling throughout my body and my muscles ache, feeling like I just had an amazing workout—even my inside muscles.

Logan's nuzzled in the crook of my shoulder and neck and we cling to one other, lightly panting until our heart rates return to normal. Then he lifts his head and smiles before kissing me gently on my lips. "You're gorgeous. Incredibly gorgeous." He kisses me again and a wave of emotion crashes over me.

"It was incredible." I can't help the smile that creeps on my lips. "I definitely won't be writing that letter of complaint. Maybe I'll write a positive review on *Tripadvisor* instead," I gush, and blame my discombobulated post orgasm thoughts on my talking utter nonsense.

Logan grins and strokes my hair back and I lean into his touch.

"Is it going to be awkward, now? Working together."

He shakes his head despite the fleeting look of concern that flashes across his face. "No. We'll make it work. I would never treat you any differently."

I cock a brow at him, wondering if he means, "I'm going to treat you like crap, just like I used to," or, if he means, "I'll make you feel like my most precious staff member," but since it feels weird asking him to clarify, I nod and shift my body an inch away from him and his cock twitches inside me.

Logan's finger and thumb suddenly grip my chin. "I'll take care of you…" his eyes momentarily close and then he continues, "as an employee. Layla, I don't want this to change things. I'm getting used to having you around, and well, I like you."

Like.

"Oh. Well, that's good." I nod. "Who doesn't want to be liked by the boss, huh." I can feel my cheeks warming and suddenly I need some space. "I need to clean up," I say, accidentally clenching around him and his eyes flutter like he enjoys the sensation.

Logan's lips graze mine and it feels nice, like he's ending our tryst on a sweet note and then he slides out of me and points to his bathroom.

I pull my bra into place and button my shirt on the way to clean up, then straighten my clothes, and splash cold water on my face, trying hard not to focus on what this means. I'm not looking for a relationship and neither is he. Casual sex is okay, it doesn't have to change anything.

When I walk back into the living area, Logan is still shirtless but he has pulled on his sweatpants and his hand is thoughtfully scratching the back of his head while he takes in the aftermath of our encounter. The fruit bowl is shattered across the wood flooring, apples and bananas haphazardly launched in all directions; the table lamp, pulled from the socket lays in two parts; his T-shirt and my shoes that I never even felt come off are littering the floor, and cushions lie strewn in front of the sofa.

Logan glances at me and smiles. "We made quite a mess."

"You have a broom or do you need me to call the cleaning crew?"

"It's fine. I'll clean that up—"

The sound of the elevator opening draws our attention and I turn my whole body in Sally's direction. "Knock, knock. Mr. Blingwood, are you here?"

I gawk at Sally. Had she walked in five minutes earlier she would have seen everything. Not to mention, Sally is the biggest gossip at the resort and if she figures out what happened tonight between me and Logan, the entire resort will know by morning.

"I hope you don't mind me coming up like this, but the doctor's script was delivered for you and since I was about finished on my shift anyway, I thought I'd bring it up."

I stare at Logan, stricken as Sally's feet shuffle against the hardwood floors near the carnage that is broken fruit bowls and discarded shoes. Logan darts toward her with the expression of a forbidden lover caught in a clench—which is not what this is. We're not forbidden lovers; he is my boss and now that's out of our systems we'll never need to have sex again.

I'm almost certain we won't.

"Am I interrupting something? I can come back," Sally says, her tone inquisitive, looking around Logan and staring at the lamp before looking at me and then Logan again. "Mr. Blingwood, would you take a look at your face! You look like something the cat dragged in. And this room? Did you have another seizure."

Logan chuckles, then covers it with a cough while I bite my lip, feeling like a naughty school girl.

Overtaken by desire, I'd forgotten all about his puffy face.

"Thank you for bringing the meds. I don't think I'll need them, but you can leave them on the counter and go enjoy your evening."

"Layla, is everything okay?" Sally asks, narrowing her eyes on the smashed fruit bowl.

"Everything's fine, Sally," I reply, clearing my throat to buy time to think of an excuse as to why the penthouse is in such a state. It's common knowledge that Logan and me have a love/hate relationship and she probably thinks an argument got physical, which I guess is partly correct. *Things certainly got physical.* "Mr. Blingwood was unsteady on his feet from his reaction when we got back inside the penthouse. All of this was just an accident."

"I'm going to clear all that up," Logan insists. "I'm perfectly fine now."

"Oh, you poor thing," she says to Logan. "I heard all about it. You were in such a state. Good thing you didn't lose control of your bowels, I hear that sometimes can happen during a seizure."

I'm looking at Sally incredulously, wondering how on earth the woman no filter when she talks about our boss shitting himself, but Logan laughs.

"Bowels are thankfully still functioning normally, thank you Sally. Now, if that is all, Miss Bowers and I have quite a lot of work to get through."

"Oh, of course. I'll leave you and Miss Bowers to get on with all your important work."

The reminder that I am indeed *Miss Bowers*, Logan Blingwood's assistant, is jarring after the night was starting to feel like more.

I shift on my feet, wondering how awkward we'll both feel once Sally leaves. Logan is probably already regretting giving into temptation, even if it did feel incredible at the time. Not to mention, I rely on Logan for accommodation and employment. Even though he says it won't, banging my boss will undoubtedly complicate things, and most likely not in a good way.

"Actually, I should probably go too. You seem to be doing much better, Mr. Blingwood, and it's been a long day. I'll send for housekeeping to help you with this mess and ask Simon to come check on you later." I slide my feet into my shoes and grab my purse.

I'm getting in the elevator next to Sally in seconds. When I look back, Logan's rubescent face makes it difficult to tell if he is disappointed I am leaving, or if he regrets fucking me entirely.

I suspect it's the latter.

CHAPTER 32

LOGAN

*L*ayla left right after we fucked. I don't blame her, she's probably upset because I completely overstepped the mark. She'd had some wine, okay, so just a couple of glasses—but still, I know she can't handle her alcohol intake—and I... What even was that? One moment we're toying with each other, and the next, I'm pressed up against her and devouring every dip and curve.

"Loag, are you even listening to me?" my oldest brother, Drew, asks from the counter in his kitchen. I came to see him as a distraction, but he's already noticing that my thoughts are far away.

"Sorry, brother, I was miles away. But I get the gist of what you're saying. You love married life. You guys want to add a baby to the family. And you're tired of hearing Mom complain that I hardly call her back.... Blah, blah, blah."

At least, I think that's what he said. Drew's only been back from his honeymoon two weeks and already he's up my ass about me working too much and hardly having time for people. Drew looks at me with a glint in his eye that tells me he knows exactly who I'm thinking about.

"Should I call Miss Bowers? See if your hot assistant can pay attention while I explain the finer details of living a life outside of work. I might as well since I spend more time talking to her than you. Why is it that she never puts me straight through to you on the phone, anyway?"

"Shit! I forgot to unpress it," I hiss, then clarify. "There's been a problem with the, um thing…" I make a mental note to fix the intercom between our offices and then return to what Drew said. "Don't call Layla hot. She's my assistant. Don't be a jerk."

Drews brows shoot up. "Jerk? I know you noticed she's hot and judging by what Skyla told me…" He leaves his sentence hanging in the air so long I get impatient and my eyes bore out of my head at him. Then he shrugs and holds up his palms. "I probably shouldn't share. It's not my place."

"You better fucking share. What did Layla say to your wife?"

"Nothing. Nothing at all." The bastard grins, enjoying my discomfort.

"Don't fuck with me, Drew. What did she say about me?"

"Skyla might have mentioned that you and Miss Bowers are getting along better, after a shaky start, I might add."

"What do you mean, *getting along better*?"

Drew shakes his head, curiously. "Just that she was at the penthouse with you last night. Mom called and said I should check in with you because of what happened. I mentioned it to Skyla and she said it was fine because Layla was spending the night with you. Anything you care to add?"

I shake my head and pour more coffee from the pot into my cup.

"Where's Callie?" I ask, checking on the whereabouts of his daughter.

"At school." Drew blows on his coffee then takes a sip. "You feeling okay? You don't seem yourself."

"I'm fine. Can't a guy visit his older brother?"

"You're always welcome here, you know that. It's why you're here that concerns me. You never visit anyone socially during work hours."

"I needed a few hours away from the office, that's all." I shrug, then admit, "Okay, so I'm avoiding Layla—just while I figure out how to handle this. I emailed her and told her I'm working from home until my face goes back to normal and in her reply she sounded… disappointed? Unsure? I don't know. I think I screwed up."

Drew puts down his coffee. "How so?"

I thrust my hands into my hair, remembering her gorgeous body, wishing I hadn't wanted her as much as I did, and then I blurt it out, hoping Drew has better advice than the Nike tagline I submitted to last night.

"I screwed Layla."

And now I can't stop thinking about her tight little body wrapped in mine and the taste of her mouth when I dipped my tongue inside.

"So? What's the issue? You like her, I assume she likes you?"

I scrunch up my nose. "You're not getting the fucking point. She's my assistant. The power imbalance alone makes it untenable."

"Loag, seriously? Half the resort is knocking boots. An office affair is hardly the worst news to come out of the Blingwood Resort!"

At him mentioning news, my thoughts automatically veer to Dana and the shitshow of covering up a wedding that nobody was supposed to know about so the press wouldn't report on her departure and pan me in the tabloids and online.

"I'm still trying to get my reputation back on track. A boss who fucks his pretty assistant is hardly going to get me another nomination for business man of the year."

"Fuck that. Logan, do you like her?"

"I've been asking myself that same question all night. I can't stop thinking about her. I'm an idiot in her presence. She makes me laugh and does sweet, nice things for me. She's fucking unbelievable at her job—well, with the exception of nearly killing me—and she's the most beautiful girl I've ever seen. But she works for me."

"Oh, is she your assistant? I didn't realize."

"Are you even listening to me at all?" I huff and the bastard laughs.

"Logan, I get that she works for you but that only seems to matter to you—no one else gives a damn. Is Layla even into you?"

I nod then shake my head. "I doubt it. I look like the fucking elephant man thanks to the meds still doing their thing. She's way too good for me, man. Besides, I have a ton of work to get through, not to mention..."

"What?"

"I asked her to attend the Gee Awards with me. I wasn't going to go, and then in a moment of madness I decided I shouldn't stay away because I have done nothing fucking wrong, and if I don't go, it'll look to the industry like I don't have the guts or I don't believe I can win. I told her to book us a suite at Gee Towers. We leave Sunday."

"Well, I guess a couple of days together will give you a chance to decide whether it could work. Though, won't Dana be there? I mean, Gee Towers is her father's place and he is hosting the awards."

"I'm hoping she won't be, but it's possible."

Drew hides his smirk beneath his coffee cup while he drinks and then says, "That won't be awkward at all. But if you want to show the world you moved on, then showing up with a hot woman on your arm is a great way to do it."

"You sound like Tate. I'm not using Layla; I want her to come. But now I'm having second thoughts. The sex, it complicates things. I barely even know Layla. I don't want to get into anything, and after Dana, well I'm not sure I'll ever want anything serious again."

"You think she's like Dana? After you for your money or fame?"

"No." I shrug. "But I never thought Dana was like that either."

"You need to talk to Layla. Clear the air. But don't be afraid to listen to your gut. That's what I did in the end with Skyla, and it's been worth it."

I shake my head and push my fingers into my hair. "I doubt Layla will want to talk to me, anyway. No, I need to give her space. Besides, I can't go through something like I went through with Dana again. I could have lost everything. I overstepped the mark with Layla. She's probably already regretting it. I'm her boss."

"If you think that's for the best, but in my experience the feeling doesn't go away when you like someone. It gets bigger."

I stand to leave, my decision made, when Drew reminds me, "Mom said to remind you you're walking Yogi while she's away visiting Tate."

* * *

ON THE MORNING of the party, I use one of the hotel vehicles to travel to the park. My hair is styled, and I'm wearing a casual pair of shorts and a polo, and thankfully my face has returned to its usual size and shape.

I spot my niece, Callie, who is helping my mother out by handing out the rescue dogs to the volunteers for their daily walks, but there is no sign of Layla.

"Hi, Uncle Logan. You here for Yogi?"

"Unless you'd rather hand me a proper dog?"

She giggles and plays with her hair. "Nanna told me you'd try to sneak that one past me. I'll be back in a sec." She skips away and I look around for Layla again. When Callie returns with Yogi—who is tugging at the lead and barking at a seagull in the sky—I ask her, "Did Layla Bowers call in sick?"

She probably doesn't want to see me.

"Oh no, Layla came by early. She's already done walking Cindy."

So, she's avoiding me?

Great.

Disappointment settles around my solar plexus.

I already planned my apology. I don't want to have to do it at the party tonight, but I suppose now she's giving me no choice. I have to put this situation to bed, eat humble pie, and get our working relationship back to exactly that—a working relationship. I had no business fucking her and she probably hates me again now—even more so since I haven't exactly been the easiest of bosses.

"You look disappointed, Uncle Logan," Callie replies too perceptively.

"What? No, not disappointed, not at all. No, I just like to know that all these…" I stare down at Yogi, who is trying really hard to lick his own butt… "delightful animals get their steps in."

Callie's stare reminds me of her father's when he's about to call bullshit. "Layla is like, really pretty. It's no wonder you want to run into her."

I'd like to do more than run into her... but I'm not telling my niece that.

I shrug dismissively. "I hadn't noticed."

"You hadn't noticed? Are you for real? Unless you went blind, you noticed she's hot."

"Callie, she's my assistant, that's all. There can never be anything between us." I'm starting to feel like a parrot repeating the same line of defense over and over but the truth is, I barely know Layla. Okay, so I'm getting to know her pretty damn well, but still, I have no idea if I can trust her.

"Okay, well if you're gonna talk crap, you'd better take some potty bags so you can pick up after yourself." Callie holds out the dog potty bags and I take them somewhat begrudgingly.

"The apple doesn't fall far from the tree," I say, referring to how much she is like my brother Drew.

"You remind me of Dad too. He wasted all that time resisting Skyla, but you can't resist love, not when it's written in the stars. Sometimes you just have to wait until it goes dark to see it."

I close my eyes to humor her. "All I see is darkness but I can smell..." I flare my nostrils and nudge my head toward her. "Are you wearing perfume?"

I open my eyes in time to see her blush. "Ben Bartlett is meeting me here. We're going to have a picnic once were done walking."

"Does your father know?"

She punches my arm and I retaliate by mussing her hair. "Dad knows. You can call him and check if you want to."

"I believe you." Even though I know Drew is still coming to terms with his daughter having a boyfriend. "Should I hang around and wait for Ben to show up? I can chaperone you both."

Callie glares at me in horror. "Uncle Logan, don't you dare!"

"Don't give me that look. I'm cool. I wouldn't dream of embarrassing you by… showing him your baby photos." I'm trying to keep my features neutral but Callie's disgusted expression is making it difficult.

"Yogi is getting impatient." She pushes me with her hands while telling me, "You'd be way cooler if you were dating Layla. She could be my new aunt." Callie seesaws her brows up and down while I shake my head.

"Callie, I—"

"I know, I know, assistant." She rolls her eyes and then looks around, noticing the adolescent boy of her dreams walking across the grass. "Go," she hisses, and finger combs her hair. "I'll see you later."

I'm tempted to stay and mess with her some more but honestly, she seems flustered enough. Besides, Drew and I looked into him and couldn't find any dirt so we're not booting his ass unless he says or does anything wrong.

I start walking and, when I look back, I see Callie and Ben standing three-feet apart.

Wise kid.

"Just you and me then," I say to the dog and begin the walk around the trail.

Yogi seems equally as pissed off as me that Layla isn't here, and he shows me by attacking the laces of my sneakers as I walk, causing me to stumble.

"And you wonder why nobody's adopted you yet," I scold.

Yogi retaliates by moving into a squatting position—and I swear he looks me right in the eyes and smirks as he poops.

CHAPTER 33

LAYLA

I didn't see Logan at all on Friday.

Our email exchanges were short, to the point, and professional, but each time I looked at his empty leather chair, I felt a sense of loss.

I miss him.

I hoped to see him while I was walking Cindy, but I had to do it earlier than planned after a call late last night from the baker about the cake for the party. There had been a terrible accident—she dropped the cake and it is completely unsalvageable. Then the cool cover band I booked had to cancel because of a stomach bug, and the fire breather canceled due to a sore throat. And that's when panic firmly set in.

I multitasked while walking Cindy as I called and begged every entertainment provider in Santa Barbara. I rebooked as much as I could—and though some of the replacements weren't quite what I had in mind—and we now have a 90's themed disco, complete with glow sticks and neon face paints, and an entertainer named Rory the Dinosaur, who specializes in juggling dung. I'm still hoping the party will be a success.

And God I hope it is, because if we wind up playing musical chairs, pin the tail on the donkey, or dung from the juggler winds up flying into Logan's flawlessly styled hair, my boss might actually kill me this time.

After the walk I collect the cake that Fernando agreed to bake and take it to the venue, leaving me exactly one hour to get ready before I need to go and set up. I shower, making sure to shave my legs until they're looking sleek, style my dark hair with a few curls, and apply my makeup as expertly as I can.

After banging my boss on Thursday, this will be the first time I've seen him since and I don't know what to expect. Will he want a repeat performance? Maybe he'll tell me it was a huge mistake. Perhaps he'll pretend like it never happened. I'm second guessing everything and so nervous that a swirl of butterflies is making a break for freedom from deep inside my stomach.

I try not to read too much into Logan's absence from work yesterday. After all, he did just have a near-death experience. So what if Jessie saw him on his way to Drew and Skyla's place on Friday? It doesn't mean he was well enough to come into work. It's natural for him to want to spend time with his brother when he's sick.

He's not avoiding me.

Logan Blingwood doesn't avoid people. He shakes salt and pepper on them and eats them whole. And holy glow sticks, during our encounter, I wanted him to eat me. I was moments from begging.

Stop thinking about him, Layla!

Logan obviously regrets it. I need to push it to the back of my mind, too, and pretend like it never happened—just like he has.

And with the party events balancing on a knife's edge, I need to divert my attention to the matter at hand. Hopefully Logan will appreciate that I pulled out all the stops to ensure the three-year anniversary of him taking over the Blingwood Resort goes as well as it can.

Maybe he'll be so happy he'll kiss me when the fireworks go off at midnight....

I shake my head in an effort to empty the red-hot fantasies building up in my imagination.

He regrets it. I almost definitely wish we hadn't complicated our existing complicated relationship by screwing.

It is not to be repeated.

Even if it was the hottest sex of my life.

* * *

I DOUBLE-CHECK that my suitcase is ready for the business trip with Logan tomorrow and then I lock my apartment door, swing around, and am ready to kick off my shoes and run to the venue when I spot Skyla and Jessie atop one of the resort golf carts, ready and waiting.

"We thought you'd be stressing and in need of a lift," Jessie says.

They're both dressed up to the nines with Skyla in a sunflower-yellow dress with straps that tie at the back, while Jessie has opted for a pastel-blue ensemble that complements her eyes.

"I'm running late. Thank you!"

I jump onto the back of the golf cart and Jessie stomps her foot down on the pedal. We careen left and right, past the coffee shop and Logan's penthouse, all the way to the building that is used to host weddings and conferences.

Too quickly, Jessie pulls the golf cart to a stop and we disembark.

"By the way, Layla, you look beautiful. With your gorgeous dark hair, the red of your dress is definitely your color. And the fabric, you look incredible," she gushes, having no idea how much I needed the boost.

I'm nauseous with nerves and excitement.

"Thank you! Ladies, I need your help. This is the first party I have ever planned. Hell, it's pretty much the first party I have ever been to. Please help me make it a success."

Jessie and Skyla agree and I'm overwhelmed with gratitude.

While they go and check on the catering, I show the DJ where to set up then greet some of the members from house-keeping who helped me decorate the room with streamers, banners, and balloons last night. And finally as the lights dim and the music, upbeat and loud, starts to play, I grab two flutes of champagne from a tray and go and welcome the first guests—Mike and his colleague Tim.

"You scrub up good, Layla." Mike's eyes rove about me appreciatively as I hand him and Tim champagne. "You want to dance?" he asks.

"I won't have time for dancing tonight," I lie. "I have to make sure the champagne fountain is full and..." Over his shoulder I see Logan and my legs weaken. He's wearing a dark navy suit sans tie and a white button-down shirt with the top button undone, perfectly showcasing his tan skin. His gaze fixes on me as he walks in the direction of the bar, and every hair on my body stands on end as though reaching to be closer to him.

In my peripheral vision, Mike waves his champagne flute in front of my face to get my attention and then his other hand grips mine, bringing it up to his lips in an awkward and overly friendly gesture. "Are you listening,

Layla? I said you look beautiful and asked if you wanted a drink."

"Huh?" I turn to face him, pulling my hand away. He's lifting his glass to his lips and is obstructing my view of Logan.

"I said, would you like a drink?" he repeats loudly over the sound of the music.

"Oh, no thank you. I'll grab myself one once I have welcomed everyone. See you later." I walk away and immediately look back to where Logan was standing but he's no longer there.

An hour passes while I welcome everyone inside and am accosted with various issues I need to go deal with until, finally, the party seems to have taken on a life of its own and I am able to relax.

I scout the room for Logan, but it's packed, so I can't see him. After grabbing a cocktail as I pass a waiter, I go find Skyla and Jessie—my wing women.

"Are you having fun?" I ask, joining them in the line to take a turn hitting the piñata.

"It's amazing! I'm happy my mom agreed to have Macy overnight. The music, the vibe. I love the party games. I just saw Silvia and the others from marketing do the conga around the pool!" Jessie lets out a deep laugh that she cuts off halfway. Then she covers her mouth with her hand and says from beneath it, "Hey, did you piss off Mr. Blingwood again?"

My insides turn watery. "I don't think I did, why?"

"If looks could kill, we'd be saying your eulogy."

I glance around. "I don't know where Logan went."

"He's over there talking to Betty." Jessie nods in his direction and says, "Seven o'clock. He's staring at you."

My face heats until it surely matches my red dress, as he looks directly at me. Neither smiling nor angry, his expression is sheer brooding. Then, as though dismissing me entirely, he shakes his head and turns his back to me.

"Weird. Well, whatever you did it can wait until Monday, right? It's a party and we're here to have fun, and I for one am going on the bouncy castle!" Skyla says, taking my hand and leading me outside where there is a 20-foot, pink inflatable castle.

"Shoes off!" the attendant orders, and we each kick our shoes off and go bounce our troubles away.

* * *

A WHILE later we visit the petting zoo and a photographer takes pictures while we handle snakes, colorful birds, and cute little fluffy bunnies. Whenever I pass a colleague, I get a thumbs up and compliments at what fun everyone is having —except Logan. Whenever I catch a glimpse of him, he looks like he'd rather jump off a cliff than be here.

"What gave you the idea to theme the party on three-year-old's?" Debbie from accounting asks while I am at the chocolate fountain.

Hearing her complaints, it occurs to me the party I planned probably seems primitive and childish to Logan. I got the theme of *fun* completely wrong. He meant sophisticated and demure, an event fit for a luxury resort. Instead, he's surrounded by balloons, jugglers and blaring 90's pop music.

Logan probably wanted an orchestra—not a disco complete with an enormous ball dangling from the ceiling throwing out blinding specks of light. I organized the party I wanted instead of something that fit Logan's brand.

My voice sounds choked. "I suppose I was focused on it being fun… rather than classy."

More like me than him.

241

No wonder he is looking at me like he wants to kill me. I've embarrassed him.

"I messed up, didn't I?"

She bites her lip politely, but then adds a measure of sarcasm. "I'm sure Logan is having a great time."

Across the dance floor, I see Logan and beside him is the mime act that seems to be annoyingly copying everything he does. Logan doesn't seem to be enjoying it one bit.

His eyes fix on mine and he turns his body in my direction like he's about to come over, but the mime mirrors him and blocks his path, earning him a furious glare. Then I see Betty go over to him and I relax since she'll probably keep him talking awhile. After he's finished talking, I decide I'll duck away through the linking door to the reception to get some air and hide. Hopefully, I can avoid him all night.

CHAPTER 34

LOGAN

*W*hen I asked Layla to arrange the party, I expected something quite unlike the formal, boring affairs of previous years.

But I didn't expect this.

The place is decorated up like a color explosion of glitter and neon. There are jugglers, blaring music, mimes, and a fucking bouncy castle!

I've never seen the staff letting their hair down in such a way and each and every one of them seems to be having a blast—with the exception of Debbie from accounting, who just might have found the only wasp at the petting zoo.

Still, with all this going on around me, I find myself seeking out Layla at every opportunity—which is infuriating because I have decided to put two nights ago right out of my head.

I am a stubborn bastard and it normally serves me well.

When I decide I won't do something, I don't do it. Layla is in the "don't do" column. I have weighed the pros and cons and ruled out anything further between us as an unnecessary risk. Yet still, I've spent the entire evening watching her and waiting for an opportunity to apologize and clear the air.

My toying with approaching her is moot anyway. Every damn time she moves anywhere, she is accosted by a staff member. I even loitered by the bouncy castle waiting for her to finish jumping. I thought I had seen everything, but that was a sight I will never forget, one that I will be revisiting nightly for years. Frolicking, laughing, and her enormous breasts bouncing up and down.

Layla Bowers in that fucking delectable red satin dress—the one I imagine myself ripping from her body just to see if she looks as good in the underwear she had delivered to the office as I imagined.

My balls are still twitching.

"Mr. Blingwood," Betty greets me. She's retired now but worked at the resort for decades under my father's reign.

I instantly smile. For a long time, Betty was the glue that held this place together.

"How are you, Betty? You look wonderful; retirement suits you."

Betty smooths the fabric of her floral gown and twirls. "Thank you very much, Mr. Blingwood. I wish I could say the same for you but the circles beneath your eyes are even darker than before I left this place. When are you going to learn that all work and no play will see you heading to an early death?"

I put my palms up to jovially defend myself from her onslaught. "It's been a difficult few months," I reply.

"Yes. Made more difficult by your dilly-dallying around your new assistant, I hear." At her mentioning her, my gaze flicks in Layla's direction. "I've seen you watching her. You look at her like you can't drag your eyes away."

I force my stare back to Betty and divert the subject. "How's Bob?"

"He'll be better once his rash goes away. Now, don't change the subject. When are you going to bend your assistant over your desk like we all know you want to?"

Her stare is prying and I check no one heard her.

"Betty, it's not like that. Our relationship is strictly business."

She laughs and bats my arm with her hand. "If you say so, Mr. Blingwood. But we all know you want her. And who wouldn't, she's a knockout!"

I smile politely. At seventy years old, Betty is batshit crazy, but I adore her and her inappropriateness. "She'll be a great catch for the right man someday," I reply placatingly.

"Catch. Catch?!" Betty elbows me in the ribs. "She's not a fish, Mr. Blingwood. You can't stick a hook in her mouth and reel her in. You've got to wine and dine a lady like Layla, show her she's special."

"Yes, except Layla's my assistant. A relationship wouldn't be appropriate."

"Appropriate," she rolls her eyes dismissively. "Appropriate won't get your heart racing. Appropriate never did anyone any good. What you need is—"

"Pussy?" I raise a brow at her, remembering how she suggested that was exactly what my brother needed just a few months ago.

Betty smirks and winks at me over the top of her glasses. "I like your thinking, but I'm a married woman." She flashes me her ring finger to prove she is indeed married.

"Betty, I wasn't suggesting..." I'm truly lost for words and need to escape before the rumor mill grinds its gears and gossip spreads that I propositioned Betty.

"What you need, young Mr. Blingwood, is to woo Layla. Now, you'll have your work cut out since she is out of your league—"

"Out of my league? I'm a man in my prime—"

She shakes her head. "You work too much and you get too stressed. You don't relax enough and sometimes you're snippy—"

"I am not snippy!" I reply, rather snippily.

"Show her the fun and carefree young man I remember from before he got bogged down with investment portfolios and profit margins." She smiles at me fondly and I can't help smiling back. "You're smitten for young Layla, that much is obvious."

I'm already shaking my head as I reply, "I'm not smitten but I'll keep your suggestions in mind. Now, if you'll excuse me." I back away, still keen to straighten things out with Layla when I am immediately accosted by someone else.

"I was just talking to Layla. I can't believe she arranged such a stupid, childish affair," Debbie from accounting says, as I try to navigate around the mime act to go find Layla. "What was she thinking?" She laughs and rolls her eyes like the fun police she believes herself to be.

I turn and face Debbie, wondering how someone so ordinary became so pathetic. "Really, you think my party is stupid?"

She stutters her reply. "Well, I… um… I didn't think you would like it."

I plaster a smile over my look of disdain. "I think it's fun."

While I wait for her to reply, my gaze flicks to Layla. She's talking with Jessie and Skyla but has spent the entire evening working the room, making people laugh and getting to know everyone. I'd bet my Bugatti that Layla knows the name of every person here and that they have learned her name; I'm certain they all already adore her.

Conversely, I turn back to Debbie and wait for her to change tact as she no doubt will now that she knows I approve of the party.

"Oh yes, well, it is a great party, but aren't you worried about the hangovers and the debauchery." Debbie raises her fluffy, mousy brows in an upward path and I grin knowing my prediction was right.

Debbie gets her work done, but I've noticed her bitching in the office, putting a downer on everything in her path—yet always reserving a little brown nose upbeat fake attitude for me.

"No. I'm not worried about that at all. It's good to see people goofing around and having fun. You should try it."

Noticing the mime moving toward some other poor soul, I leave Debbie determined to finally seek out Layla. On top of needing to apologize, now I need to make sure Debbie hasn't made Layla worried. My plan is to speak to her privately where I'll congratulate her on a lively party. Then I'll apologize for seducing her, and we'll agree that in future we will keep our relationship strictly platonic.

I won't even notice the way her dress is cut perfectly to emphasize the length of her neck, the softness of her skin, or the fullness of her breasts. And when she opens her mouth to tell me she agrees that it was all just a momentary lapse of judgment that got out of hand, I won't be thinking of how beautiful she looked as she came on my cock.

* * *

AFTER GETTING ACCOSTED by almost every employee in the resort, who seem to want to personally thank me for ordering such a fun shindig, I duck around some dancers in time to see Layla slip outside.

I follow her, batting away the people who try to talk to

me, until I throw open the doors and a cool breeze fans my face. Away from the booming music, I hear Layla's name mentioned, and I stop behind one of the ornamental pillars.

"She's definitely getting some action tonight!" I hear Tim tell one of the groundsmen, and white-hot fire flares through my body.

"Nah. She's way out of his league. Mike doesn't stand a chance."

"Seriously, dude. Mike's banged half the women here—he told me as much. I don't know how he does it, but he's got game. I'll bet she's in his bed before the night is out."

I rocket around the pillar and am in both guys' faces in half a second.

"Layla Bowers is off limits!" I growl and the two men take a step back. I take a deep breath before attempting—epic fail—to contain my anger. "What I meant to say is, what sort of chauvinistic fools am I employing here who talk about women like this? Layla is my assistant, and like every other person here, she is to be treated with respect!"

Tim's mouth pops open and the rage I am barely holding back urges me to fill it with my fist.

"Sorry, boss. Beer talking." He holds up his beer as though it is a tangible excuse and my lips curl up, revealing what I am sure is a snarl. "Mike wants to bang Layla, and according to him she's up for it but it's probably just bravado. Locker room talk. We'll rein it in."

The image—even imaginary—of Mike's hands on any part of Layla has every muscle in my body stiffening until I think I might explode from the pressure.

"Where is he?" I demand.

Tim points. "Mike went to take a call in the lobby where it's quieter."

As I turn my head in the direction of the lobby, my anger

burns irrationally when I see the suggestion box is still over-flowing, even though I keep asking people to deal with it. I see Layla walk inside, and the overfilled box is the last thing on my mind as my fury propels me forward.

CHAPTER 35

LAYLA

"*H*ere you are," Mike says as I walk through the hotel lobby to go and relieve Sally so she can join the party. He seems wobbly on his feet as he throws his arm over my shoulders, pulling me into him. "Best party ever! The free bar was the best part! Usually we just get a sit-down meal and an orchestra capable of sending you to sleep, but this is way better."

My body starts to overheat and not because of Mike's drunken closeness.

I feel like a complete fool. I should have asked people what type of entertainment is typical for a staff party.

"I've had seven Porn Star Martini's but next I want Sex on the Beach."

I unhook Mike's arm from around my neck and step away from his boozy breath. "Better get to the bar before it closes, then," I reply.

"Layla, you look gorgeous. Can I have a little kiss, just a little one."

"Mike—" My sentence is cut off as he lunges at me, grabbing my shoulders and forcing his lips against mine. He tastes of salt and the unpleasant stench of too much alcohol. I'm gripped in a vice-like hold, and while I have my lips pried shut, I can feel his tongue pushing against the barrier and it's turning my stomach. All my self-defense knowledge momentarily leaves me and all I hear is white noise.

Sally's still on shift. I think I hear her voice but I can't be sure. She's behind the counter at the far end of the room. The security guards are outside working. I know this because I was present when people drew straws to decide who would need to work tonight.

I am safe, I remind myself as Mike forces himself against me. *This is temporary.* I try to push him away. But my body is trembling, and my heels are sliding against the marble of the floor. I lift my arms to push him but I stumble back, one, two, three steps, trying to untangle myself from his grasp when—

"Get your fucking hands off her!" In a blink Logan has a hold of Mike's jacket, yanking him back from me and swinging his fist straight into Mike's face, sending him crashing to the floor. He throws himself down on top of Mike and is about to land another heavy blow when I screech, "Logan, NO!"

The blow lands and Mike's face hits the marble of the floor. I scramble down to stop Logan from beating Mike to a pulp, but it's like he doesn't see me, landing blow after blow.

My actions are frenzied, my hands reaching out to grab Logan's, and when I finally have the palm of mine against his fist, Logan pauses and turns his face to mine—blinking three times like awaking from a nightmare.

I'm frozen with sheer shock and confusion at what just happened.

Logan blinks away his fury and pulls Mike to standing. Security are finally standing around us, waiting for their orders, when Logan tells them to get rid of Mike immediately. He's fired. Behind them stands Sally, wringing her hands. "I called security right away."

At their boss's instruction, security escort Mike away and after looking on awkwardly for a time, Sally returns to her desk.

"He just…"

"I know. Are you okay?"

"I'm fine, but you look…" Logan's fists are still balled, and the one he hit Mike with has a smear of blood across the knuckle.

"I could kill him. I wanted to."

"I'm safe. I'm okay. He was just drunk—"

"He wasn't *just* anything. He's been hovering over you since you arrived. I should have known he was capable of something like this!" His hands go into his hair and he paces about the place like a man possessed. "This is what happens when I take my eye off the ball. Shit like this—" He paces again and I tentatively approach him—rage seems to come off him in waves.

"Mike misjudged the situation. I could have handled him. I'm fine. I'm not sure Mike is, but he was drunk so he probably won't even remember this in the morning. I've handled worse men than Mike from accounting." And it's true, it's why I took self-defense classes.

Logan sits on one of the plush sofas and I sit beside him, leaning forward onto my knees so I can see his face. Right now, I don't know if he is angrier with himself or Mike. "I was jealous."

My mouth pops open.

"I was jealous and this has to stop." He shakes his head

and stands. "You're just my assistant, Layla. This is not what I want."

His words take time to penetrate my brain.

You're just my assistant.

This is not what I want.

Fury fills me and I stand to face him. "I'm so sorry this isn't what *you* want!" My voice is a high-pitched hiss, sarcastic and shaky, but righteous anger carries me forward. "This isn't what I want either. I don't need you to protect me, and it isn't my fault you're a jealous asshole!" I'm angry that he just admitted he doesn't want me and is pissed off with me—when I haven't done anything wrong. My eyes begin to water and my nose tingles but I refuse to cry in front of Logan so I turn my back and wipe my eyes.

As I'm plugging the waterfall, Jessie and Skyla burst into the lobby. "Layla, what happened? Are you okay?" Skyla asks.

Jessie pins Logan with a cold stare. In her hand is a bottle of champagne and three glasses.

"Layla, I'm sorry," Logan says, his voice full of remorse, but I don't turn to face him. Instead, I ball my fists and try to breathe through my fury. When I don't answer, he asks Skyla, "Will you look after her, please? I'm going to make sure Mike is gone."

And as though it suddenly goes dark, I can feel when he turns away from me because I immediately feel cold. The electronic doors whoosh open, and as he walks out of them, Logan orders, "And for God's sake, can someone deal with the suggestion box!"

Poor Sally, who is standing behind reception, moves to get the overflowing box but I stop her. "Leave it. I've got it. You go and join the party."

"Layla, are you sure? You just…"

Sally looks me up and down, unsure, but I plaster a reassuring smile across my face and tell her, "I'm fine, honestly.

Mr. Blingwood and I argue all the time. We'll be fine tomorrow."

She nods her head and looks longingly in the direction of the party. "We're not expecting any check-ins this late into the night, so it should be dead and I already switched the room service line through to the kitchen. All you need to do is stand here looking pretty, deal with the suggestion box, and take any calls."

"Easy-peasy. Go on, Sally. Go and find Doug and get a drink," Skyla says, grabbing my hand. "Layla, Jessie, and I will deal with the suggestion box."

I stare at it; sheets of white paper are poking out from the box with the Blingwood emblem. Then I drag it over to the reception desk and relieve Sally from her duties.

"Mr. Blingwood likes anything of note placed on his desk," Sally says.

I nod. "I think I can handle that. Go on, Sally." I shoo her away, faking an enormous smile. "Go have fun with Doug. I don't feel much like partying anyway."

"Thanks, Layla. You're the best!" Sally replies, before adding an extra coat of lipstick and heading out the door.

Once she is gone, Jessie pours three glasses of champagne and places one in front of me. After prompting, I explain to Jessie and Skyla what happened with Mike and how Logan reacted.

"I feel so responsible. I should have warned you about Mike," Skyla says.

At her regretful expression, I ask her how she could possibly have known. She tells me her and Mike used to date before she fell in love with Drew and that he was a less than stellar boyfriend. "I knew he was a jerk, but he never did anything like that to me. He just told everyone I was frigid, even though it was he who couldn't perform—if you know what I mean."

I make a sickened face and assure her she couldn't have known Mike would try and force me to kiss him. "If I know Logan, he's already plotting to make sure he won't get hired anywhere else."

"The guy is a douchebag!" Jessie announces.

"Who, Mike or Logan?" I joke even though I can't quite bring myself to laugh.

"Mike, of course. Logan was being protective. He's probably pissed off with himself for talking out of turn, but for what it's worth, I think he cares about you, even if he's too scared to show it," Skyla says before cryptically adding, "I know he's been talking to Drew about you."

"Really? What's he been saying?"

Skyla's mouth tightens like she's already said too much. "Bro code. I don't know the details. But he likes you, that much is obvious."

"I knew Mike was a jerk but I didn't for a moment think he'd try and force himself on you," Jessie says.

"It's okay. I was safe. The asshole will probably tell himself I lead him on. Besides, Logan stopped it. He fired him."

"He looked furious when I walked in."

I nod, then I tell her how Logan hit Mike. "Logan told me he did it because he was jealous. That I was just his assistant and that he doesn't want to be interested in me."

"I could literally punch Logan Blingwood in the face right now," Jessie says, clenching and unclenching her fist.

I chuckle half-heartedly. "I'm fine. He's right, I am just his assistant. We should never have—" I stop speaking immediately. Jessie and Skyla don't know that we had sex, but from the look on their faces they do now.

"You…," Skyla says tentatively.

"Oh my God. You banged the boss, didn't you?" Jessie says incredulously.

I don't confirm it, but I don't need to. My face is on fire.

"It didn't mean anything." I shake my head.

"I'm betting it felt like it meant something?" Skyla asks.

I nod. I feel like a love-sick idiot.

"You like him?" Skyla checks.

"Not anymore," I lie.

Jessie's fist lands on the counter causing the vase beside it to rattle. "Well, fuck them! You put everything into the party, and they ruined it."

I throw her a watery smile. "Meh. Parties are overrated."

Jessie looks sad. She had to beg her mom to watch Macy tonight and I hate knowing she's not making the most of one of her few nights without parenting responsibilities so I tell her, "You go and rejoin the party. I'm fine here."

"Fuck that! I'm not leaving you. I'll help you."

"I'm only dealing with the suggestion box and then I'm going to come find you two and we're going to dance until our feet get blisters, deal?"

"No deal, we're staying," Skyla insists.

"But if we're doing this, we're making it fun, and we're drinking this champagne, courtesy of Mr. Grouchy Pants." She chinks her glass against Skyla's and then mine.

"Deal." I grin and take a big gulp of the champagne.

CHAPTER 36

LOGAN

I've been awake all night dissecting every moment of my conversation with Layla and I still cannot excuse how I behaved. The only thing that makes it worse is I have to spend the next three days with her on a trip I wish I could avoid attending for a plethora of reasons.

Despite replaying it from every angle, I still don't know what came over me last night. I saw Mike forcibly kissing her and I saw red. I was capable of killing him and he buckled right beneath my fist.

I had every intention of finding Layla, politely and respectfully telling her that while I think she's very nice, I took things too far. The plan was to apologize if I misled her and overstepped my professional boundaries, and that was supposed to be the end of the matter.

Instead, I arrived at the party and saw her wearing that silky, red dress that clung to every delectable curve like God himself had created her to perfectly fit my every fantasy. I saw her speaking to that asshole Mike—not that she seemed even slightly interested—but it reminded me, she can be interested in anyone she likes. It is none of my damned business. I am not in the market for another woman in my life and particularly not someone who has the staying power of an anchorless boat.

But the way she moved around the party, looking exquisite, she had me in a chokehold. Everyone she spoke to was entranced by her. She makes me feel like that too, like winning her attention—good or bad—is a special gift. Not to mention, I knew what she was wearing beneath her dress and the image was driving me crazy.

I bite my knuckles, getting the pain to help knock thoughts of Layla in lingerie out of my head. Mike deserved the beating and getting fired. However, Layla did not deserve my tactless comments and I will have to apologize and explain myself—it's the least I can do. Her face when I said she was just my assistant still haunts me.

I hurt her and I fucking hate myself for doing that.

THE LIMOUSINE WILL MEET me here in a few minutes, but I need to grab my travel documents from the safe in my office. Once the car arrives, we'll drive around to the employee housing and pick up Layla—who is probably furious with me —then head to the airport.

Seventy-two-hours with her.

It's going to be hell.

I'm strangely excited.

I twist the dial and access the safe, snatching up my documents and my eyes catch the box with my late grandmother's diamond necklace inside. It's a priceless piece. I have no idea why she left it to me. My sister got most of her jewelry in the will and my brothers got my late grandfather's watches. I got a diamond necklace that's been in her family for generations, and Tate and Drew have ribbed me endlessly ever since. But as I slide open the box and take in the exquisite charm of the piece, I find myself imagining it on Layla's slender neck. The heart shaped centerpiece would sit so tantalizingly in the dip between the voluptuous curve of her breasts and suddenly I can't bring myself to close the box, not when it deserves to belong somewhere better.

I slide it in my pocket—perhaps letting her borrow it for the awards would serve as a gentle peace offering that may make the trip more palatable.

Then I notice the empty suggestion box on my desk. Atop the pile of notes is one with my name, doodled in sharpie by either a fourth-grader or an intoxicated employee. And I have a very good idea who the culprit is:

WE HOPE you enjoyed your stay at the Blingwood Resort. Please tell us how we can improve our service:

YOUR SERVICE WOULD BE GREATLY IMPROVED IF I DIDN'T HAVE TO PUT UP WITH LOGAN-THINKS-HE-KNOWS-BEST BLINGWOOD. **URGH!** HE'S SO:

L – LIPPY

O - OFFENSIVE

G – ~~GORG~~ GRUMPY

A – ARROGANT AND ANNOYING!

N – NEANDERTHAL

B – BOSSY

L – LOATHSOME

I – *IRRATIONAL*

N – *NEFARIOUS*

G – ~~*GORGEOUS*~~ *GROWLY*

W – *WOW*

O – *OUT OF LINE*

O – *OAFISH*

D – ~~*DESIRABLE*~~ *DISAGREEABLE*

THANK YOU FOR YOUR COMMENTS.

THE FACT she wrote and attempted to write *gorgeous* not once but twice has me grinning from ear to ear and more than makes up for the slants she has written against me. I snatch up the sheet of paper and fold it, sliding it inside my jacket pocket.

Our work trip is about to get a lot more interesting.

CHAPTER 37

LAYLA

I throw back two Tylenol and down half a glass of water. Some people might think I drink too much —but it's not true! I barely ever drink in normal circumstances; however, since spending time with Logan Blingwood, I get tense, like my whole body is one great big knot and nothing helps me relax.

Which is why not even the champagne and several cocktails worked.

I am so angry with him, treating me like this is all my fault. I like him, *and* I get jealous—but I don't go around punching people.

You're just my assistant.

This isn't what I want.

Well, I don't want you either, asshole!

How can he treat me like it isn't killing me to have to work with him every day?

It's not fair, and I won't stand for it.

A wise woman (his mother!) once told me not to take any shit from him, and I'm not. If it all goes south, then I'll rent someplace cheap while I look for a new job.

I only have two weeks left in my contract, anyway. I refuse to quit, if only to prove to Mr. Snippypants that Layla Bowers is neither flaky nor flighty and will not be run out of town. Besides, I made a commitment to Cassandra to walk her rescue dogs while I am here and I'd hate to let her down.

My phone pings a text and like I expected, it's him:

See you in five.

LAYLA:

YES, BOSS.

ON THIS TRIP I am going to be the absolute personification of the professional assistant. He wants a business-like relationship, then that's what he's getting. No small talk, no smiling, no batting my lashes at him, and no damn flirting! I'm not going to even make eye contact with him unless absolutely necessary.

* * *

THE CAR HORN beeps outside and the driver comes to my door to get my suitcase. I can see Logan in the rear passenger seat of the limo answering his emails on his damn phone.

"It's okay, I can manage. Thank you," I tell the driver in a show of independence.

I nearly pull my back out throwing my borrowed luggage in the back next to his Louis Vuitton and then I seat myself beside him.

"Miss Bowers," he says without looking up.

"Mr. Blingwood," I reply, keeping my gaze trained firmly on the back of the driver's headrest.

We head toward the airport, and I swear time slows.

Logan's invested in his emails. I don't look, but my God can I smell him, and it's that deep woody cologne I have become used to. I open my window to clear my lungs and then pull out my phone.

"I trust there are no eggplants today, Miss Bowers?"

I spin my head at his audacity at mentioning the dick pic I'd received and could kick myself for breaking my vow to only make eye contact with him when absolutely necessary.

I smile at him sweetly. "Not yet. I've issued an official request that all *eggplants* be saved for after dark."

He lets out a growl and his eyes return to the screen of his phone. I notice he has a coffee in the holder between our seats. "I trust there's no soy in your coffee, Mr. Blingwood? It'd be a shame for you to choke to death." I smile cheerfully.

"No soy. They didn't even graffiti the cup with *asshole* boss. You may need to retrain them if this continues." His face is stoic yet amused, handsome but incredibly annoying.

"Did I mention? I invested my last paycheck into soybeans. I hear it's a growing market."

"Really, Bowers? How quaint. Perhaps I'll buy up the other shares and the company just so I can close it down."

"Sounds like something only a bossy asshole would do." I grin.

"Hmph. Maybe you should write a list of the issues you have with your asshole boss and address them with him directly. You could try making it more solution-focused than this…." He pulls something out of his pocket, unfolds it, and drops it on the armrest between us.

My mouth pops open, suddenly remembering the list. I was double pissed; pissed with him and half a bottle deep in Moet. It seemed a perfectly reasonable—hilarious—way to let off steam with Jessie and Skyla. But I could have sworn Jessie threw it in the trash.

Logan wasn't even supposed to go into his office today.

Sitting this close to him, I have nowhere to run or hide, and my face engulfs in flames but his expression is one of perfect, business-like temperament. My only saving grace is that he doesn't know I wrote it.

Okay, so he probably has a good idea that it was me, but he'll never prove it, unless he has some kind of handwriting analyst on payroll—which I would not put past him.

A nervous twitch develops above my eye.

"Mr. Blingwood, who would write such terrible things?" I snatch and crumple the paper into a ball, throwing it into my purse, hoping beyond hope out of sight really is out of mind! "I'll launch an investigation to find the culprit. Don't you worry, no stone will go unturned. I will not rest until—"

"Layla, it's fine. I was an asshole last night, and I deserved it. I'm sorry."

I search his expression for any sign that he is tricking me, that he might be about to press some kind of ejector seat button reserved only for baddies in the movies, but he looks entirely sincere in his apology.

"I mean it. I said some hurtful, unkind things you didn't deserve and I suppose that," he points his thumb toward my purse, "was the consequence."

"Oh," I reply, nodding as though he just told me there might be a chance of rain. "I appreciate your apology."

He nods.

A pregnant silence hangs between us and I am filling it

before I have truly thought through my retort. "I apologize for saying you were loathsome; you're not loathsome... all the time and almost never a Neanderthal. Arrogant and annoying, well yes, but I shouldn't have written them down, that was unfair of me—"

"Layla—" he interrupts but I continue.

"You're not offensive and your manners are improving, so I'm glad you're working on that."

His lips turn up in a delicious smirk. "Apology accepted, sassy pants. Now, let's try and have a nice business trip."

"Let's." I smile, noting his emphasis on *business* trip.

The rest of the journey is thick with silent tension. The kind that makes any sane person want to stick their head out the window and scream. But I remain professional as I kick off my shoes and use my toes to rub the ball of my feet.

HALF AN HOUR later and I'm still being 100 percent professional as I reapply my lipstick while we wait to board the plane. I didn't realize we'd be traveling by private jet to New York, which negates the need to check in in the normal way.

As fabulous as it is to walk the tarmac like some celebrity with a flight attendant waiting at the stairs to the plane, it's intimidating as hell.

Onboard the plane is a mix of white leather seats and high-gloss wood. My eyes go around like saucers, taking in the multiple TV screens, a well-stocked mini bar, and an enormous table with swivel chairs around it. There are maybe ten seats and some look like they lie all the way down —and for someone who has only ever traveled coach, it's impressive. More than that, however, is my brain conjuring images of joining the mile high club.

Scratch that thought.

Business trip, Layla!

Maybe I'll sleep the entire way and ignore his grouchy, gorgeous ways.

A flight attendant is waiting at the entry of the plane ready to greet us. She has her blonde hair in the most perfect French chignon I've ever seen. "Good afternoon, Logan," she says in the breathiest of tones while holding a tray with two champagne flutes.

"Sarah," he replies, helping himself to a glass. "Beautiful day to hit the sky."

I'm surprised he's on a first name basis with the flight attendant. It makes me wonder what other sorts of familiarities he has with her.

Probably the mile high variety!

"George says we'll be taking off in ten minutes."

"Thank you, Sarah." Logan gestures with his hand for me to move along the plane.

"Champagne?" she asks me as I pass. Her skin is utterly flawless, and her lipstick so perfectly pink that she could be Barbie's sister.

"Thank you." I take the glass and choose the seat in the middle that faces the cockpit, since I do not want to go up backward. The nerves in my belly are already bubbling more than the champagne I am holding. The white leather seat is incredibly decadent and to my left are a variety of magazines conveniently placed in a holder, which will help take my mind off the journey as I read the celebrity nonsense.

I delight in pushing the button and pulling up the footrest until the back support is optimal, and I grab the most salacious magazine I can find.

Logan sits opposite me and tries his best not to look annoyed—his attention on the magazine's front cover. I hold it higher so I can block out his face since it commands my attention, and the bonus of irritating him a little bit sends a secret thrill through me.

I promise myself I'll stop taking sneak peeks at him over the magazine, but it's a tiny space and I can't avoid noticing him press a button that pulls a table down between us. Then he leans over, flooding my nostrils with his scent, and pulls his laptop out of his carry-on.

While the pilot does his pre-flight checks, I try really hard not to think about how small the plane is or whether flights are safer on bigger or smaller jets.

"We'll be taking off soon, sir," Sarah says awhile later, and she helps Logan push up the table by leaning over him and sticking her cleavage right beneath his nose, and I wonder if she could be any more obvious about it.

"Ma'am, can you please…" She points to an illuminated sign, but I find myself studying her perfectly made-up face that for some reason is incredibly annoying to me. She raises her pink lips at me expectantly.

Please what? Refrain from choking on your overbearing perfume? Please jump off the plane at the earliest convenience so you can bang my boss? Please do something with my unruly hair because it's making the place look untidy?

I stare and wait for her to clarify.

"She wants you to put the footrest away and fasten your seatbelt," Logan interrupts my internal diatribe.

"Oh. Of course, I didn't know you did that on private planes. No problem, doing it now. Don't want to plummet from the sky because someone left a footrest out of place." I laugh sarcastically but obviously my two companions have had humor transplants. I press the button that returns my footrest to its tucked away position, put on my seatbelt, and lift my magazine to read a fascinating article on whether anticipation makes humans happier while sipping champagne.

I don't miss Sarah putting the palm of her hand on Logan's shoulder, her polished nails perfectly matching her lipstick. "I'm sorry, Logan. We're on a rotation order—I didn't notice," she says to him but I pretend to be engrossed in the magazine, not listening.

Logan waves his hand and I glimpse over the top of the magazine to see him watching me.

"It's fine, really," he replies to Sarah, who nods her head like one might at a funeral, and she takes away our empty champagne flutes.

I wonder what I am missing in the exchange between the two of them.

"Salmon for lunch. Thirty minutes," Sarah says when she returns.

Then the pilot's voice filtrates through the cabin and he announces that we can expect to touch down in NYC around 6 p.m. The weather is unfortunately cloudy with a chance of showers.

"Great," I mutter beneath my breath. We're leaving high temperatures and glorious sunshine. Of course I didn't pack a raincoat or an umbrella.

"Something annoying you, Miss Bowers?" Logan asks mockingly as the plane begins taxiing for take-off.

I tip the magazine down just enough so that he can see me raise a pointed brow. "Whatever could be annoying me?"

He chuckles, but it doesn't reach his eyes, and I feel even worse for my earlier list. He's not annoying me really, it's just my nerves for the flight we're about to embark upon are getting the better of me.

"If you must know, it's the weather," I say. I feel too foolish admitting my fear since Logan Blingwood, bajillion-aire, probably travels to the liquor store in his private jet. "I didn't pack for rain, and I was hoping to get out and do some sightseeing after we've checked in."

"Layla, Layla, Layla, how very *lax* of you. Some might even say *amateur* to travel without adequate preparation." He pauses as he thinks and then adds, "Perhaps it is a consequence of your *youth*." He's smirking again, and the use of *L*, *A*, and *Y* word starters doesn't escape me. He's probably making his own list for me and it's vexing, that is until the jets fire and the plane lurches forward. I squeeze my eyes shut and grip the magazine tightly, even though it'll make a useless parachute should I need it.

The ascent seems to take forever. My palms are sweating and I swear I can hear every noise inside and outside the plane—seriously, someone needs to tell the pigeon I saw earlier to stay away from the propellers.

By the time my seated body is in the upright vertical position and I have unclenched my eyelids, Sarah is back, and Logan is looking at me with concern.

"You okay, Bowers?"

I swallow hard and nod. "Fine." My voice is a squeak.

"Can I get anyone more champagne?"

"Water please," I say since I don't drink and fly as it makes my anxiety worse.

"Whiskey, please, Sarah," he says to her and she toddles off with a cute wiggle, then he turns to me. "Not a fan of flying?"

"It's not the flying that I mind, it's the up and down part— I don't like that."

"Not a fan of up and down. Noted." He taps his nose and a helpless smile breaks through my impeccable professionalism.

I waste time playing with the footrest and back support, flicking through the magazine, and sipping my water while Logan once again works on his laptop, looking up to check on me every few minutes. Then I scroll through the program options but find myself restless with too many choices.

"Bowers, can you please stop fidgeting," Logan says and I barely even huff despite him being so annoying.

When Sarah returns wheeling a cart that contains our meal and I notice real, metal cutlery, I try not to look too shocked.

I suppose if I had to, I could use them as weapons against Logan and claim self-defense.

I throw my copy of *Celebrity Gossip* down on the seat beside me and Sarah helps me find the button to pull my table out. She serves us our meal, and it looks and smells better than three quarters of the meals on *Food Network*. She pours me more water and Logan wine and then disappears with her trolley.

"Sassy pants, did you just huff at Sarah?"

Did I?

"No, of course not."

Perhaps I did. She's all over Logan; they should get a room. Okay, so she's not all over him, but she's smiling too much. It's unprofessional.

He nods like he doesn't believe me.

"Bon Appetite."

I turn to reach for my napkin and as I do, I see the front of the magazine I have been clutching. When I turn back to him, practically stricken with guilt, Logan shakes his head. "It's fine."

"It's not fine. She's there, on the magazine. I was holding it up right in front of your face, waving it around and... I'm so sorry."

"Don't be. I'm fine. The magazine is a subscription I arranged for when we took flights together—she was partial to *Celebrity Gossip*." He shrugs like it's no big deal and forks a piece of salmon into his mouth, but I feel like shit. Beside me the headline reads, "Heiress Dana Gee on love, life, and her new engagement."

"Dana's getting married?" This news has got to hurt. Being left at the altar is one thing, but for her to move on and get engaged so callously after just a couple of months is outright cruelty. "Did you know about her engagement?"

"Not until thirty minutes ago." His mouth twitches as though he finds either the situation or my reaction amusing.

"I'm so sorry."

"I'm not. They deserve each other. How's your salmon?"

I fork a piece into my mouth while I think. "But the way she treated you, aren't you angry?"

He thinks awhile and says, "No."

"No?"

He shakes his head. "Nope."

I continue eating, feeling a sense of strange pride and satisfaction he isn't affronted by this revelation—or my part in it.

"Don't you want to go on social media and tell everyone what a horrible cow she is? Or find him and punch him right on the chin?"

His lips tip up. "I don't normally go around punching people." Then, he clenches and unclenches the fist he used to hit Mike, and after scanning my reaction he adds, "Excluding last night."

"Do you regret punching Mike?"

"No. I've wanted to punch him for quite a while."

"So, it wasn't about me?" I bite my lip and study him curiously. "You said you were jealous."

"It was about a lot of things. I was jealous but I was also angry. I knew he was no good and I didn't act soon enough. I'm sorry for the things I said to you last night. I was out of line. What happened between us… well, I've never been romantically involved in the workplace before. I'm not that type of boss. I want you to know that."

I nod, feeling a wave of disappointment fall over me. It's

just as I thought, he regrets Thursday night even though I know he enjoyed it.

"But for the record," he continues, "you can do much better than a guy like Mike. I've seen him being overly friendly with you, waiting for his moment. You seemed to keep him at arm's length, but I knew he was biding his time and waiting for an opportunity."

"And that bothered you?"

He pins me with a stare that has me forgetting to breathe. "We have a strict nonfraternization policy, Layla."

A nonfraternization policy that we set on fire when we screwed each other's brains out in his penthouse three nights ago.

Suddenly I forget that we're talking about Mike and only see Logan, delicately informing me he will never want me like I have come to want him. I force myself to breathe and try not to be too disappointed he's such a stickler for the rules. He might be the hottest boss I—or anyone else on this planet for that matter—ever had, but that doesn't make it wise to bang the boss. Nonfraternization policies were probably designed to stop women like me from making fools of themselves over men like him.

"M'kay. Well, I'd quite like to punch Dana," I say to take my mind off banging my hot boss.

He outright laughs and I do too.

"Now there's something I'd pay to see."

The rest of the flight is mostly comfortable silence, whereby I restlessly try to get comfortable while doodling horns on Dana's face and coloring in her teeth. Logan intermittently praises my artistic prose and then suddenly Sarah —the footrest police—is back to arrest my reclined position. But this time, as we descend, Logan asks, "Would you like me to hold your hand?"

"Oh, no, I'm fine."

The plane lurches and I think I may lose my lunch.

"Give me your feet," he says in a commanding tone. "Not that I have a strange foot fetish or anything like that..." His voice sounds less steely than usual, like he actually cares if I think him odd. "My father would rub my mother's feet to alleviate stress; it seemed to work and it's preferable to watching you break out in hives. Besides, I owe you a foot massage."

When I don't move, he bends and scoops up my legs with his arms, peeling off one shoe at a time and tossing them on the floor and then he orders me, "Close your eyes."

That's an order I will happily obey, so I close my eyes and concentrate on Logan applying just the right amount of pressure, starting at my heel, and then moving to the arch, and then finally, when he hits the magic spot and splays my toes, I groan in ecstasy.

"Um. Miss Bowers, we've landed," Sarah says, breaking me from my reverie. Opposite me, I see Logan biting his lip to keep from smiling. I quickly but carefully unlatch my feet from Logan's lap and slide them into my pumps while the heat of a thousand flames boils my skin.

Logan pulls his jacket and laptop bag off the hook and tosses them over his arm.

As we disembark, I thank the pilot, George—who is standing at the exit—for not plunging us to our deaths and also Sarah for her "hospitality." It's then I notice their matching wedding bands and the way they stand with their bodies touching and George's arm on the small of Sarah's back.

"What a nice couple," I say to Logan as we descend the steps.

"Quite." He grins as though having the punchline to a great joke and follows me down the steps.

CHAPTER 38

LOGAN

"*W*hat do you mean there is only one room?" I ask incredulously. "My assistant obviously did not book just one room for us to share."

The receptionist taps the mouse of her computer again and then looks up at me blankly.

"When you book a double, it is two rooms, isn't it?" Layla asks, and I turn to her in a slow, measured manner.

"No, Layla, a double is two beds. You work for the best hotel resort in the world, please tell me you are indeed aware that a double room is—"

The reddening on her cheeks tells me everything I need to know.

"All right, then." I turn back to the receptionist. "Can you please add an additional room to the reservation." I don't ask as a question; it's a demand. There is no possible way I can stay in the same room as Layla.

The receptionist's smile deteriorates and I know I'm doomed.

"Anything," Layla says with a desperate plea. "I'll sleep in a cot in the lobby if need be?"

"I'm sorry, ma'am. It's the awards ceremony tomorrow. We're booked. I could get you something on Tuesday? Or you could try a different hotel—but we've already called multiple hotels and unless you travel over to Hoboken, you're not going to find anywhere with multiple availabilities."

I nod my head, knowing the receptionist is telling the truth. While we may be able to find something in the city with availability, it will be a one star in areas I would never allow Layla to stay in. I massage the throbbing vein in my temple, and all I can think about is the boner I got giving Layla a foot massage. I *need* a room to myself or I'm going to have a headache coupled with a massive case of blueballs.

"Who doesn't know that a double is two beds in one room?" It comes out like an accusation.

"She asked if I wanted a double. I thought it was like the penthouse, with two rooms that connect. Whenever I've booked a hotel room, I've booked a single, so I assumed…"

She tilts her head and pins me with her innocent blue eyes.

This was a genuine mistake. I can feel it, and I can tell Layla is embarrassed as hell about it. But Good Lord. First the sandwich, then the photocopy guy, then the attempted murder, and now she is really digging my grave by forcing me to sleep, not sleep, with her. I grind my teeth together, take five breaths and will my dick to relax.

"It's fine, it's fine. You saved the company around seven hundred dollars, and it is only for two nights. We'll just have to… tolerate each other."

Two nights, sharing a confined space with Layla Bowers.

Breathing her in and out, watching her prance about the space all delicious curves and smooth limbs. Cramped in a room with not one but two beds. *The universe hates me.*

We're supposed to be keeping things professional, but I can't think straight when she is around me. My gaze continuously returns to her lips, urging me to remember her face as she came apart on my cock—and I want to make her come again to check if I imagined how good it was.

"I'll carry your bags," she says, straining her voice as she attempts to pick up my suitcase. "You won't even know I'm there."

Then, as I'm leaning down to take it from her, she drops the suitcase right on my toe.

* * *

"It's only for two nights," she reminds me.

"Two nights of your constant talking and intermittent snoring. I've finally reached paradise."

I unpack, noticing the dust on the hanger rod while I hang my tux and Layla's dress. It's still perfectly packaged and I get a glimpse of it as I slide it onto the rod—I can't wait to see her in it.

"Stop saying I snore; I do not snore!"

"You absolutely do snore. Had I known we'd be sharing, I'd have bought ear plugs. I'd ask reception to send some up, but if the state of this room is anything to go by, they'd be a previously worn pair."

Layla pops her full mouth open and makes a two fingered puking gesture. "The room isn't so bad, you're just spoiled."

"Spoiled?"

I walk around the room which takes all of five long strides, check out the bathroom, and then move to the window. "Yes, you're right. I'm being facetious. The toilet doesn't flush properly, the faucet has an unsteady flow of intermittent yellow water, and dust mites are already eating my underwear, but it's a small price to pay for this unbelievable view." I gesture to the brick wall of the building that's right beside ours.

Layla joins me, her sweet scent filling my lungs.

"You know there are people out there with no place to stay who would give their left testicle for this place!"

I sigh. "You're right. I'm sorry. I'm just feeling..."

"Grouchy?" she supplies, rising a delicately arched brow.

"Out of sorts," I correct, massaging my temple. "I should probably warn you that Dana will be staying in this hotel and she might be at the event tomorrow. Her father owns the place. I'm hoping she'll leave us alone, but she can be something of a—"

"Bitch?"

I chuckle and turn to her; her head barely comes past my chest, so I have no choice but to look down at her. "That's an accurate description."

Layla's hands fly to her hips. "Good. Because there are some things I'd like to say to that disrespectful cow. You know she said in the article that her ex-boyfriend—not ex fiancé, ex-boyfriend—was clingy! You thought she was pregnant! She was expecting you to be distant and aloof?! She made you sound like a schmuck, and after what she did, that is not cool."

I'm unable to contain my smile. "You're defending my honor?"

Her arms are now crossed over her chest and she's beginning to tap her foot in place. "I'm defending she is a piece of shit and you deserved to be treated better."

"Interesting, particularly since you have your own special list of my flaws."

"If she'd said you were grouchy and annoying, well, that'd

be different." She stops tapping her foot and pauses for a moment. "But she told outright lies—to kick a man while he was down." If I didn't know better, I'd think she is more irritated with Dana than I am.

"Anyway, I've got to get moving if I'm going to cross off all the places on my list," she says abruptly changing the subject.

"List?"

"Yes. I've never been to New York and I want to see some things! Empire State, Rockefeller Center. I want to see Lady Liberty, and I have got to sample New York cheesecake, and there has got to be pizza on this trip. Oh! And bagels," she licks her lips in anticipation. "And I only have tonight and tomorrow before the event. There is no time to waste, Blingwood."

"Layla, it's 7 .pm., there's very little you'll fit in tonight and tomorrow you're booked in with a stylist to prepare you for the awards."

Her animated expression drops and my previous good feeling vanishes.

"I mean, you don't have to see a stylist. You'll look perfect without one, but I booked it on the basis it might make you feel more… comfortable. Women seem to like these things leading up to fancy events." I wave my hand uncomfortably. Layla doesn't need styling; she always looks amazing and I'm trying hard not to offend her. "I booked it because Dana had always insisted it was necessary. I'll cancel it. You can take tomorrow off."

"A stylist?" She looks oddly excited and I'm so relieved. "I think I could tolerate being pruned and polished." She pulls a list out of her purse and pulls on her lower lip. "What time do we leave on Tuesday?"

"First thing," I reply.

278

"Oh." She folds the paper. "That's okay. Maybe I'll come back one day and do all this then."

I think of Betty and how she reminded me I used to be more fun and snatch the list, open it up and scan Layla's delicate scrawls. "Some of this is doable. We'll start with the Statue of Liberty."

Her eyes are sparkly and warm. "We?"

"If you can tolerate your annoying asshole boss? I have some connections that might allow us to squeeze some of this in."

She bites her lip to hide her smile. "Oh, well if you have connections…."

I fire off a text and tell her, "Come on, Bowers, let's go be tourists."

CHAPTER 39

LAYLA

*M*y face is aching from all the smiling and laughter.

"You're so much more fun when you're not at work!" I tell Logan whose silky, caramel hair is an unruly mess, just like it was when he gave me not one, but two orgasms.

"Touché, sassy pants. Oddly, you're much less annoying, too, when you're not sitting on sandwiches and arranging meetings with the printer guy," he replies, gesturing for me to go first through the revolving door of the hotel.

We get in the elevator and the doors close behind us. The stuffy music playing through the speaker clashes with the buoyant excitement pulsating beneath my skin following a sensational day.

"I can't believe the helicopter took us right around Lady Liberty! She's so beautiful. Powerful. Amazing! And the skyline, I swear I could look at that view every minute of every day and never get bored. I feel giddy!" I gush, still on an exuberant high.

Logan's face is lit up with a wonky smile as he studies me spewing my excitement. And I figure he either really enjoyed the trip or thinks me a little insane—perhaps both.

"Liberty Island… Skyla and Jessie won't believe I saw it. My feet are aching, but it's been worth it to see all those places I've only ever seen on TV and the internet. It's a shame we didn't get to do Rockefeller Center, but I am definitely coming back! I got the New York City bug."

Beside me, Logan's thoughts seem elsewhere as he watches me from the side. The doors open and we both move at the same time, squishing into each other as we attempt to pass through them. "After you."

Logan retrieves the keycard and we enter the room, and suddenly my nerves are fizzing deep in my belly. I'm about to sleep with Logan Blingwood. Kind of. I mean, there's no plan to have sex, but I will be sleeping in the same room as him. *I hope I don't snore.*

My palms are sweaty as he flicks on the light.

The room is almost exactly as we left it. Logan's side is impeccably tidy with his shoes neatly placed side by side under his bed. My side is a little less tidy with my makeup bag on the bed and my sweater from earlier tossed on the floor—except, now there is a huge magnum of champagne in a silver bucket on the dresser.

"Did you…?" I check, allowing my voice to trail off while I wonder how he could possibly have found the opportunity to arrange champagne for our return. He's been off his phone and didn't leave my side all day.

I've spent the evening awkwardly reminding myself that it was not a date, even if it felt like it. Even if a part of me wanted this most romantic of nights to be a date with the hot, gorgeous—sometimes grumpy—man beside me. To end the day in his bed would be like something out of a movie.

Logan strides to the champagne and picks up the note attached to it. His expression turns stony and then he crumples the paper into a ball and throws it in the trash can.

"Do you want to use the bathroom first?" Logan's jaw is strained, his face a perfect imitation marble. He doesn't make eye contact when he addresses me, instead his eyes are glued to the champagne.

Something deep in my gut stirs. Instead of being pleased to see the huge bottle of fancy bubbles, he's staring at it like someone came in and took a shit on the dresser.

"You can use the bathroom first. Is everything okay?" I ask, remembering this is Dana's father's hotel. "Is the note from Dana?"

Logan nods, grabs some items from his half of the dresser and then disappears into the bathroom, locking the door. Suddenly, all the excitement and fun of the day is gone and left in its wake is a man who was reminded that he had his heart broken, which just reinforces why I can never tell him what I did.

CHAPTER 40

LOGAN

I despise her.

I despise her new fiancé.

I despise her father.

I despise all of them, this godforsaken hotel and its cold fucking water!

But most of all, I despise myself for allowing them to get to me and for spoiling what was otherwise a perfect day.

What gives Dana the fucking nerve to do this. To say those things about Layla. Dana knew I was coming here today. Blingwood Resort has been nominated for the prestigious resort of the year award—but so has Dana's father's Scottsdale resort.

It's a two-dog race and I'm the underdog.

If I don't win then it'll be a double humiliation. Showing up here and facing a bunch of industry members who believe my ex-fiancée left me at the altar is bad enough, but losing to a lesser resort is one step worse than I can handle.

I wasn't going to come. I shouldn't have come and I certainly shouldn't have dragged poor, sweet Layla into it. I hit the wall in frustration and the tile cracks. Now it matches the other cracked tiles in the bathroom. I'm tempted to blow the whole damn thing off, but people have already seen me, and I'd look like a fool who can't handle the heat.

I switch off the shower and notice there is just one fucking bath towel so I dry myself with the hand towel and save the bigger one for Layla to use. We were having a great day. The best day I've had since, well, this angry, I can't remember a better day.

Layla hasn't stopped smiling. Like a kid at Christmas, she skipped right through the city, taking photos of anything and everything. A grate with steam coming out of it, gotta get a picture of that! A squirrel coming close in the park, yep—that too! With anyone else, it might have seemed annoying, but it was captivating. She was captivating. I spent the entire evening wishing I could pull her into my arms and kiss her.

And I almost did.

Had she stayed still long enough, then I would have broken my resolve and taken her in my arms and kissed the crap out of her full red lips. I held back because a small part of me—the wiser part, perhaps—couldn't bear to spoil her day.

I suppose it's moot now, since her day was spoiled the moment we got back into our room and I found the champagne. Dana's dig at Layla has me even more furious:

Logan!

So great to see you booked a room in Daddy's hotel—but why did you book the cheapest room? Is it because the little loser PA you're dating isn't worth a suite?

HA!

Still, I suppose you'll both be losers together this time tomorrow.

Dana

XoXo

DANA CAN SAY what she likes about me but to involve Layla in her spiteful game is too much. I leave the bathroom wearing only a fresh pair of boxer shorts since I didn't know I'd be sharing a room with Layla, and I normally sleep naked.

Layla's turned down the lights and the champagne is gone from the dresser. She's bending over her open suitcase and has changed into a mega-short sleepshirt that is riding up over the cheeks of her peachy ass. When she hears me, she spins around and her pretty mouth pops open with her surprise. Her shirt, though baggy around her small frame and faded from washing, looks adorable and I imagine peeling her out of it, but instead I focus on the slogan that covers the swell of her breast: *Saturyay!* Beneath it is a picture of a bear jumping in ecstasy.

Cute.

"Wow!" Layla says simply, her mouth hanging open as she glances up and down at me. "I mean, all done in there?" She rearranges her expression to a nervously tight grin that displays all of her pearly-whites.

"Is something the matter?" I check.

"No. I mean, you... you look so different all dressed for bed—not that I thought you wore a suit to bed but hmm, huh-hmm. I wasn't expecting..." She gestures her hand at me. "I'll go wash up now that you're all clean, and naked, and um... yeah..." She blinks slowly as though mustering the strength to reopen her eyes. Then she shakes her head and darts into the bathroom and I find myself grinning like a fool, alone in the room.

Layla Bowers, so flawlessly put together yet so awkward and bashful at times. Aloof. Endearing. Enchanting. Completely out of bounds and utterly unprepared for tomorrow's debacle, which is why I decide to send her home tomorrow—she doesn't need to be party to the unpleasantries, and I should never have made the decision to expose her to them in the first place.

CHAPTER 41

LAYLA

When I walk into the bedroom, Logan has climbed into bed and turned the lights down low. I hop into the bed that is mine and stare up at a crack in the ceiling. The only sound is the soft in and out of Logan's breathing and it's strangely comforting. However, every time I close my eyes, I see the insult that Layla scrawled on the note she wrote:

Logan!

So great to see you booked a room in Daddy's hotel—but why did you book the cheapest room? Is it because the little loser PA you're dating isn't worth a suite?

HA!

Still, I suppose you'll both be losers together this time tomorrow.

Dana

XoXo

I SHOULDN'T HAVE TAKEN it out of the trashcan while Logan was in the bathroom and read it. It was private, meant only to rock his confidence, but I couldn't help myself. The mood changed so fast that I had to investigate to know how best to support him.

I roll on one side, annoyed by Dana and the lumpiness of the mattress.

How dare she write those things!

I can take it. I've been called worse, but to try to rock Logan's resolve after everything she put him through is unforgiveable.

I punch the pillow a few times to try and force some air into it and then I make a decision. No matter what Dana says or does tomorrow, I'll be with Logan through the awards every step of the way. She won't make him feel uncomfortable or lesser than, and even if he loses, I'll be there, holding his hand and making sure he knows he is supported. I'll do it for all his employees who adore him and will be cheering him on at home.

Yanking the blankets up, my toes stick out the end and a draft makes me shiver.

"These blankets smell funny," I complain aloud.

"They probably haven't been washed since JFK was shot. Go to sleep, Bowers. We've got a long day tomorrow."

The sheets rustle and Logan's mattress groans so I do the same and reposition myself while he is getting comfortable. I end up on my side, facing him and the low moonlight is just bright enough that I can make out the angles of his jaw, lips, and cheekbones.

"I thought you were asleep," I say.

"Between the stench of unwashed linens, you assaulting your pillow, your muttering, and the constant threat you may start to snore, I'm finding it difficult to relax."

"Sorry," I whisper-hiss. "But I don't snore."

"You snore like a chainsaw, but I'm trying to stay positive. Maybe it'll drown out the sound of the dripping tap and toilet flushes of the room beside ours."

I'm grinning despite his teasing, glad his mood seems to have improved since he read Dana's note.

"Logan."

"Yes."

"Good night."

He sighs and whispers, "Sweet dreams, sassy pants," and my smile widens.

* * *

"Layla, are you decent?" Logan asks, from behind the door to our room. He left around ten this morning to go make arrangements with reception and told me he'd be gone long enough for me to change out of my pajamas and get ready. What he actually said was, "It's Monyay! You'll need to change before I return," in his gruff voice.

He's obviously still feeling out of sorts, but I am here and will distract and bolster him until we get back on the private jet home. It's the least I can do after he took last night off to show me the sights—and as much as I hate admitting it, I care about him. I can't help it. Underneath his gruff exterior is a man who is decent and kind.

"Yep, come in." I throw myself on the bed and pull out my cell like I've been there the whole time, not thinking about shitty little notes left by shitty little people.

"Good." He strides in holding a large, flat box that he throws on the bed beside me.

"You brought pizza, for breakfast?" I try to contain my excitement but the smell is amazing and exactly what we both need to overcome our funky moods. "In all the places I have lived, I have never had freshly baked pizza for breakfast," I tell him with a grin.

Logan's lips curl up at the corners just enough to demonstrate that my reaction pleases him. "The room service menu is basic at best and the offerings in the breakfast room are even worse. I thought pizza would be preferable."

"It is!" I squeal and unfold the box to be met by gooey cheesy goodness and salty salami. "New York pizza!" I snap a photograph, take a selfie of me loading it in my mouth and I send it to Skyla and Jessie. When I look up, Logan has a curled brow of intrigue so I explain, "I've been sending Skyla and Jessie my snaps. They won't believe I'm getting fresh pizza for breakfast!"

"So easily pleased," he says dryly though his eyes are warm.

Logan yanks the pants of his suit up to sit on the bed beside mine, leaning down onto his knees with his elbows and watching me expectantly.

"You want some? No way I can eat all this."

He gestures no with his hand.

"Suit yourself but don't throw away what I leave. I'll eat it cold later. Not wasting a bite of this baby."

"The car will be here for you soon."

"I'm eating as fast as I can. You think the salon will mind if I bring it with me?" I ask around a mouthful of pizza.

Logan's smile has completely vanished but his eyes remain warm. "Layla," he starts and I sit up cross-legged on the bed and put my slice of pizza down. "I chartered George to take you home. The car will be here soon. It's not taking you to the salon, it's taking you back to the airport."

"What? But we've got the award ceremony tonight. You'll miss it if we go now."

He opens his mouth and then closes it.

"When you say *you*, you mean *me* and not *us*." I shake my head at the ridiculousness of my comment. Of course, he means me. He's sending me back. He's not taking me to the awards. He's going alone. I let the information sit and drop his gaze. Hurt makes my chest constrict.

"It's the note, isn't it? I embarrass you."

Of course, he's embarrassed. I don't have money. *Celebrity Gossip* magazine wouldn't want me on their cover in a million years. Next to Dana, I'll look like I'm wearing Target despite the Dior label.

"What? No. I'm saving you from dealing with those vile cretins," he says, but his words don't fully penetrate. I'm staring at the pizza, but all of my excitement for it has vanished so I close the box and climb off the bed.

"It's good I didn't unpack, then. I can be ready in no time." I flip the lid and zip up the suitcase. "See?" I pull the handle up and stare at my bare feet. I painted my nails a shimmering ivory color to prepare for the event. I tell myself my eyes are getting wet because it's a shame I won't get to show them off in my strappy heels.

Logan moves from the bed and stands before me. "You do not embarrass me. It's better this way so you don't have to deal with Dana's unkind remarks that will be designed to make you feel small but will essentially be aimed at hurting me. It's what she does. She picks on those weaker than her. I tolerated it when I believed she was having my child, but you shouldn't have to."

I meet his eyes. "Weaker than her? *Weaker*?"

He runs his hand through his hair and takes a step closer. "You know what I mean. There are people who treat others like shit, and I don't want you to be treated like that."

"You think I need your protection? Because I can tell you this for certain, she can do her absolute worst and it won't be in anyway comparable to the shit I have overcome. She can fucking say and do whatever she likes and I will laugh in her stupid face. But ultimately, it's you who can't take it. It is you who think I'm a loser or you wouldn't be trying to hide me from her."

His voice is incredulous. "I don't think you're a loser! Layla, you blew into my life like a fucking hurricane and have put up with all kinds of shit from me. I'm just grateful you only tried to poison me once!" It's a sweet gesture to lighten the moment, but the sad smile on his face makes my heart hurt. "There will be people from the industry who have heard Dana's version of the events. There will be photographers, most of whom Dana courts in her circle. The award ceremony is covered by the press. Knowing Dana, she will be plastering everything about the night all over her socials, and we have no control over how you will be portrayed. I'm sorry I brought you into this."

"You're sorry you brought me, you mean."

"No." He shakes his head, adamantly emphasizing the word. Then his voice softens, "I just didn't think this through."

"You're trying to protect me and go it alone, even though I want to be there for you."

"Layla, I'm not trying to hurt you. The exact opposite, in fact. I want to protect you from getting hurt."

Logan's shoulders have dropped and he's staring at his shoes. This is not the man I am used to, but one that is pulling on my heartstrings *hard*. My decision is quick. "Stop being a masochist and let's face it together. A wise woman once gave me this great piece of advice that I think applies perfectly to this situation."

He looks up and cocks a brow. "What was this great piece of advice?"

"Fuck them!" I reply simply, and I'm rewarded by a deep chuckle. His eyes sparkle when he laughs and I wish he did it more often.

He looks me dead in the eye, lifts up his shoulders and takes a deep breath. It's then I know I won. The Logan I know—and am trying hard not to love—is back. "So stubborn, sassy pants. The driver will meet you downstairs in reception. Tell him to take you to the salon on the corner of 51st and 5th."

I nod firmly, grab my purse, slide my feet in my pumps and only release my long-held breath once I have flung open the hotel door.

"Layla," I pause at the sound of my name, then turn back slowly, "thank you."

CHAPTER 42

LOGAN

*O*nce the door closes, I sit on the bed inhaling the sweet scent of Layla that hangs in the air. I lose all sense of time and have no idea if I sit there for minutes or maybe hours, but I can't get the image of her strength and determination to support me out of my mind.

Apart from my mother, no woman has ever been so determined to make themselves uncomfortable in order to help me. Allowing Layla to be vulnerable to the scrutiny she will undoubtedly face feels cruel, and I wonder if I am a sick son of a bitch for allowing her to endure tonight.

In my two years with Dana, she never once attended an event with me unless it directly benefited her—like being covered by the press. I've been afraid of starting anything new in case I got blindsided, but Layla Bowers seems like a woman I can trust completely and that, in itself, is a revelation.

She is the most transparent woman I've ever met. Decent

and kind and so unlike Dana. She is everything I had been looking for, despite looking in all the wrong places and for all the wrong reasons.

I start to wonder if I have been too pigheaded in my determination to keep things platonic.

* * *

WHILE LAYLA IS at the salon, I attend a shareholders meeting in a boardroom at Gee Towers. It made sense to hold our quarterly meeting here since many of the shareholders bought tables at tonight's event in the hope we win and they can brag about it to their friends. Had I known we'd be served lukewarm coffee and stale bagels, I would have asked Layla to schedule a boardroom at one of the rentable offices in the finance district, but I try not to let the drab location of the meeting sour my mood by thinking of Layla who is probably getting naked about now in preparation for her full body massage.

Sweet baby Jesus. What I wouldn't give to take a turn in untying her knots.

I make a mental note to defer thoughts of Layla naked for alone time and focus my attention on greeting the shareholders. Then I seat myself at the end of the long, mahogany table and hope the meeting will be short since it's likely to be so uneventful even the most dedicated insomniacs will wind up snoring.

Snoring.

I grin and the Chair of the meeting casts me a curious glare as she reels off the profit figures for the quarter. She no doubt associates my unusually cheerful demeanor with our impressive profits and, while they are pleasing, nothing is as pleasing as waking up to see Layla, snuffling lightly beside me. Even an uncomfortable night trying to find sleep with a relentless boner was worth it when I woke up to find my sassy assistant in the bed next to mine with her fleshy thigh draped over the comforter and her hair spread across her pillow like she spent the night furiously making love. I adjust my position and try to empty my mind of Layla. The last thing I need is a tent in my pants as we discuss next quarter's projections.

When the meeting finally draws to a close with the obligatory scheduling of our next one, it occurs to me if nothing changes, Layla will be gone by then. I'll have a new assistant. Skyla keeps promising me she is looking for the perfect person, but I'm not sure such a person exists. I only want Layla.

As I leave the room, my head down, I'm already concocting a plan on my notes app aiming to permanently secure Layla with added benefits and increased salary—a deal no person in their right mind would turn down—when I almost walk right into Donald Gee, Dana's father.

"Logan." He pauses before me and his team of entourage abruptly stops behind him.

"Donald," I greet my ex almost father-in-law. "Still working, I see. Will you ever retire?" Despite being in his late seventies and carrying the appearance of a decade more on this earth, everyone knows Donald is too power hungry to retire.

"Retirement is for the weak," he replies.

"All set for the awards this evening?" I keep my tone cordial for the benefit of my board members who have stopped behind me.

"All set to clean up, you mean? Yes, I am looking forward to winning." His tight-lipped smile is cold, calculating, ruthless. It reminds me of Dana's.

"We're competing for the same award, Donald. It seems rather odd that the Gee Resort has been nominated since you are one of the award organizers," I say it loud enough for my shareholders hear, in case they hadn't already considered the competition could be rigged.

"All is in hand. The ethics committee has been involved with counting the votes. When I win, it will be fair and square."

"I do hope so as the media would have a field day with a rigged voting system."

The papery skin of Donald's jaw clenches and his eyes grow even colder. "I don't need to cheat. I have been at the helm of luxury travel for more than five decades, boy."

I smirk because I know it aggravates him, and I lazily drag my gaze over the faded flock wallpaper and offensively patterned carpets. "If your antiquated flagship hotel is anything to go by, you're losing your touch, old man. It's time for you to retire and let those of us with a finger on the pulse of modernity take the reins."

"This is a fine hotel! You'll see what the people want when you lose spectacularly in front of all the industry experts tonight."

"Yes, we will," I reply with arrogant confidence.

I take a step forward and Donald grips my bicep, lowering his voice so only I can here, "It could have been different. If you'd taken care of my daughter, we could have combined both our enterprises. We'd have been unstoppable."

"If your daughter hadn't lied and tricked her way into my life, you mean," I hiss.

Donald doesn't even have the decency to look shameful that his daughter lied about a pregnancy to trap me into marriage. Instead he smirks like I was a meaningless casualty of war. "To succeed in business you have to be willing to do what it takes."

"You knew what she was doing?" I check. It seems crazy

even for a devious bastard like him, but I also know from my previous interactions with him that he is nervous his legacy will die with him if Dana inherits it all, and he has no other family to leave it to nor anyone worthy to manage it.

"I make it my business to know what everyone beneath me is up to, including you. How is that pretty little assistant you're poking? Layla, isn't it?"

I nudge forward and loom over his short but stocky form. "Keep my assistant's name out of your mouth and I'll keep your daughter's name out of a lawsuit."

This close to him, his head is forced to shift upward to meet my deadly serious glare.

Donald's rattled but covers it quickly with an irate stare. "Silly boy, choosing to slum it with a peasant instead of East Side royalty? You'll see that this new woman only wants you for your money. At least with Dana, you know she has her own wealth and can hold her own around our people. Why, this poor girl you picked up from the gutter will probably embarrass you far more than Dana ever could."

I abruptly shake his hand from my arm. "You're wrong, Gee. And I'll prove it tonight when I beat you by winning your own award in front of all your investors and peers with the smartest, most beautiful woman in New York city on my arm."

I don't give him the chance to reply. I stride down the corridor with renewed vigor, hoping I win tonight, but strangely comforted by the fact that even if I don't win, Layla will be there and somehow that makes me feel okay with losing.

So long as she's smiling, nothing can bring me down.

CHAPTER 43

LAYLA

*T*he car pulls up to what I can only describe as a sleek, pamper palace, and I'm met by two smiling and welcoming women wearing aprons marked with the gold emblem of their company logo.

"Miss Bowers, come in. Let me get your..." Woman number one looks at me, coatless despite the damp temperature. "Well, let's get you a glass of something nice." She takes my hand and pulls me inside. "You're booked for the full works, yes?"

I force a smile onto my lips and once inside, I take the glass of green juice, which will apparently rejuvenate me, and down it in one hoping there's some kind of alcohol inside that'll steady my nerves. There's not but it surprisingly tastes delicious.

"Your massage is the first order of the day. It's going to help you relax and untie all your knots," lady number two says. "I'm Gabby and I'll be taking care of you during your visit. Come sit here for a minute and let's get you a robe."

She comes back with a robe and slippers, puts her hands on my shoulders and grimaces. "There are a lot of knots that need loosening, but it's okay. Today is the day you come undone." She grins manically and I wonder what on earth I am getting myself into.

* * *

THE DRIVER DELIVERS the box that contains my dress and informs me that Mr. Blingwood will meet me in the hotel lobby before the event.

By the time I'm ready to leave the salon, I have been primped, plucked, waxed, and made over to such an extent, I barely recognize the woman looking back at me in the mirror.

She's the high-end, luxury runway version of Layla Bowers.

My dark hair is swept to the side in long, cascading curls, and my eyelids have dark, luscious extension lashes that enhance the blue of my eyes.

When I arrive at the hotel, my nerves are on fire and I'm fretting over everything from the gown and the shoes to the way I should stand, and if I remember how to use cutlery properly.

If chopsticks are involved, forget it.

"You ready?" the driver asks, and as though he can tell I am most definitely not ready for tonight, he informs me, "Don't get out until I open your door and give you my arm to hold. You're certainly going to make an entrance."

My pulse quickens.

Make an entrance? I feel ridiculous, like a child playing dress-up.

Does he mean a good entrance or the type where people stop and laugh?

I don't get the chance to worry since in no time at all he is opening my door and there is the flash of a camera right in my face. I try to stand tall, hold a pose and then enter, but all of the lights are making me dizzy and I feel like I might trip and fall.

But then I see him.

Logan Blingwood stands at the top of the steps to the lobby waiting for me and looking dashingly handsome in his dark tuxedo and a crisp white shirt. His eyes dazzle as he stands frozen, watching me ascend the steps.

When I reach him, he merely says, "You look perfect," in a throaty, deep voice that has my heart beating out of my chest. "Turn around, I have something for you," he says, and I do, holding onto the ornate iron banister. "It'll look exquisite against your ivory skin."

Logan drapes a sparkling necklace around my neck. It's heavy and the metal is cold against my skin. The center stone is the size of my thumb and it sparkles in every direction as the light passes through it.

"It's beautiful. I can't believe you had time to shop for a matching necklace. It looks so real!"

"I'm a man of many talents." He grins boyishly and my heart flutters from inside my chest.

"Yes, you are." I throw him a wide, affectionate smile to show my gratitude.

The flash from the photographers is dazzling, and when I catch sight of myself in the dark window, I am mesmerized by the huge stone that is made to look exactly like a diamond.

"Mr. Blingwood, pose for a photograph with your lovely guest, please?" someone calls, and Logan leans down into my ear until his scent fills my lungs and asks, "Do you mind?"

I shake my head and he takes my hand, lifting it to place a chaste kiss on the back. We pose for the photographer and a shiver runs down my spine as Logan slides his arm around my waist, pulling me toward him. The whole thing feels surreal, like I am at a movie premiere with my love and not a hotel awards ceremony with my boss.

"Come on, let's go inside," he says without letting go of my hand, pulling me through the crowd where people jostle for his attention.

We're handed champagne from the waiters as we enter an enormous hall filled with floral displays and tables beautifully dressed with white table cloths and fine china. There's a huge stage with cameras already set up and an orchestra is playing off to the side of the stage.

I'm out of my depth, but Logan's hand is an anchor to which I am tethered, and it makes me feel capable and safe.

"How was your day?" he asks, his eyes flicking up and then down and then up again until he settles on my face. "I almost didn't recognize you. You look incredible."

"Thank you," I stutter. "I feel like a princess."

He comes closer to my ear. "You look like one, but that's not to suggest you don't always look beautiful. You do." His eyes pin mine with a stare so heated that it has my knees turning to jelly and my heart filling with the power of a lioness. "Layla, if you want to leave at any point this evening, just say the word and we're gone. I don't care about the award enough for it to make you feel in the slightest way uncomfortable, do you understand?"

I nod and let go of Logan's hand, looping my arm through his, catching sight of Dana in the distance—watching us.

Logan takes a step forward. He hasn't seen her yet but I can feel her stare, so I hold firm on his arm. "Dressed like this, not even God himself can intimidate me."

Logan's delectable lips part and his eyes, unwavering in

their supportive stance, widen. In case he needs one, I give Logan a confidence boost, too. "You look handsome. Actually, you look hotter than the devil himself."

I lift my palm and rest it against the side of his face and say, "We've got this." Then I reach up onto my toes, meaning to kiss his cheek, but Logan moves and I catch the side of his mouth with my lips. I pull away quickly, but it's too late. We both know I just kissed his mouth in full view of everyone.

I'm about to apologize, but I see there's no need. Logan's grin rises up rapidly into a bashful smile. His tongue darts out to gently taste where my mouth touched his lips, and I'm a goner.

A smugness washes over me, and I grin as I glance around the room, knowing that Logan is smiling too, and when I see Dana staring us down, I pin the bitch with a wink and a smile.

Mine.

CHAPTER 44

LOGAN

*L*ayla leads me toward a crowd of people and I am dumbstruck.

She kissed me.

It was the lightest brush of her lips against mine, but still, it was heart-stopping.

She had to feel it too.

Okay, so she didn't mean to kiss me, but she did and holy hell it vibrated all the way through my cold, dead heart.

"Good evening. I'm Layla, how do you do?" she introduces herself to Stan Connault, one of the sponsors and he's so utterly bewitched by Layla's beauty, it takes him a full minute to find his words.

I can't even bring myself to be annoyed at the way he stares at her, I'm bewitched too.

Stan takes her hand in his. "You can call me Stan, my dear." After a moment he notices me and we engage in some light pre-dinner chat.

Layla's sweet, chatty, polite and at times vivaciously funny. Her ability to keep a conversation going with strangers isn't just impressive, it's entrancing. After hearing the announcement that dinner is about to be served, Stan says, "You must both come to the Hamptons when the season is over. Jean is holding her famous fall ball."

"I'd love to," Layla replies graciously, and it dawns on me that unless I manage to persuade her to stay, Layla will be gone by fall. Her contract was for six weeks, four have already passed.

"According to the seating plan, we're at the first table," Layla says, glancing over to the dining area.

Before us, Dana is already taking her seat.

"There must be a mistake," I reply. "They know better than to put me and her at the same table."

She grabs my hand. "We can handle it."

Her confidence astounds me and I let her lead me, enjoying the way her slender hand feels inside mine.

The table is marked with place cards, and I suspect Dana was responsible for the seating arrangement. I'm not sure what game she and her father are playing, but if she does anything to make Layla uncomfortable, we are leaving—award or not.

As we approach the edge of the table, I find my card is two seats away from Dana's, placing Layla directly between me and my ex. I glance around the room for Donald but figure he is probably backstage or he'll be working the room right up to the moment the winner is announced.

The only tell that Layla is in anyway nervous is the way she fidgets with the napkin before placing it on her lap. It takes all of my restraint not to grab her hand and pull her away from the prowling hyena.

Our table seats ten and as other guests sit, they chat to their partners and make introductions. The music and raucous chatter inside the hall is loud enough that one would have to raise their voice quite loudly to be heard on the other side of the table.

"And you are?" Dana says, curling her lip distastefully and glancing at Layla. She's wearing a skimpy gold dress that barely covers the essentials. It's held together by metal loops and gives the appearance that it could slip from her body at any moment. Beside her, Layla turns to me with a full-lipped smile that makes my heart thump inside my chest and I'm captivated by her grace and elegance in the dress she chose. The way the fabric clings to her curves and the muted turquoise color accentuates her soft ivory skin—it's making it difficult not to reach out and touch her. Even her hair looks flawless, cascading down her back in glorious ebony waves.

To my left, a guy named Caleb introduces himself, and I do a hasty introduction and then go back to monitoring the conversation to my right.

Layla introduces herself to Dana but she is rudely dismissed when Dana leans around Layla—practically pushing her back in her seat—so she can look at me. "Logan, you came. I didn't think you would after... that unfortunate business." Dana at least has the decency to look somewhat apologetic but still, I don't dignify her comment. I just gesture with my hand for her to leave it since it's not the time for me to tell her what I really think.

Layla fixes Dana with an icy stare, while I slide my hand beneath the tablecloth to find Layla's hand and reassuringly press my thumb in tight circles.

"I hear you're engaged, Dana. Congratulations." Layla's voice sounds pleasant enough, but I know there is sarcasm behind every word. "Where is the lucky man?"

"Thank you for asking. Graham has multiple meetings in

Europe this week. He was sad to miss seeing Daddy win best resort, but you know how it is."

"Maybe Graham didn't want to watch him lose to Logan. Your father's resort, after all, isn't the only resort nominated, unless you already know the results of tonight's award?" Layla's grin is innocent, like she didn't just insinuate the voting could be rigged.

I can barely keep the smirk from my face. Not only is Layla correct, the results could be fixed—unless Donald's toxic confidence led to him failing to rig the vote—but she figured that out with no interference from me. It pleases me to know that other people will likely come to that conclusion should Donald win.

Dana laughs loudly like Layla told a joke.

I forgot just how irritating Dana's laugh can be.

"Oh, honey. You must be love struck to have such faith. Daddy always wins." Dana takes a sip of her champagne, watching Layla over the rim of her glass. "You're wearing this season's Dior. However can you afford that on an assistant's wage? I was going to get that dress too, but it looked gaudy. You wear it well though."

"It was a gift from Logan," Layla replies, unruffled.

I lean into Layla and murmur into her ear, "You look sensational."

Dana turns to me. "Logan, did you buy her the dress? You're so sweet, always out there doing charity work."

A growl rises up in my throat, calmed only by the feel of Layla's hand as it moves to caress my thigh.

"Logan has impeccable taste, *these days*," Layla replies, squaring Dana with a don't-fuck-with-me smile. "Don't you, darling?" She cups my chin with her hand and rubs my cheek with her thumb, looking at me adoringly. "Why, he even found time to shop for a necklace for me."

It doesn't escape me Layla is behaving like we are more

than just PA and boss—probably to annoy Dana—but I don't care because each time Layla touches me or smiles at me, I'm drawn closer to her.

Layla smiles victoriously as Dana's expression becomes thunderous and the tension is somewhat defused by the arrival of the first course wine. Layla takes her glass and confidently holds it up, then puts her other hand in mine and addresses the table, "A toast to a lovely evening."

The evening passes and the meal is mostly boring talk about peak season stats, airline price hikes, and sales figures. Even so, I pay close attention to every word coming from Layla's lips. She is fascinating and her smile, the genuine one she gifts to our tablemates, is mesmerizing. But it doesn't stop Dana from unleashing sideway glares at her.

When the main course is over, Layla excuses herself to go to the restroom and I'm so anxious about her leaving my side, I offer to accompany her.

"Logan, I'm fine." She grins, putting her napkin on the table and cupping my cheek.

I lean into her touch. "If you're sure?"

Layla lets out a cute, tinkling giggle that is probably for Dana's benefit.

I'm tempted to follow her anyway and pin her to the wall to kiss her. Not because I care about people believing we're dating, but because I've been in a trance watching her for the past hour, and now all of my thoughts start and finish with how much I need to have her again.

"So, are you screwing her or did you just bring her here to make me jealous?" Dana says, scooting into Layla's empty chair. This close, I'm accosted by her perfume. "It's working, if you did."

"That's none of your business, Dana."

"You did, didn't you? She's here so you can save face. I didn't think you'd date the help, not after dating me."

Deep chuckles erupt from my chest. Dana's pompous confidence is comical, especially when I know beneath this bravado is an insecure child-woman whose daddy didn't show her enough love. It makes me almost feel sorry for her, almost, but not quite—she still tried to ruin me.

"In case you hadn't noticed, I gave Layla my grandmother's necklace—the one you wanted for yourself. What does that tell you?" I delight in watching Dana's face scrunch up. I had intended for Layla to wear it just for the event, but after watching her face light up when she assumed it was some cheap bauble as well as all the support she gives me, I've decided I want her to have it. I think my grandmother, who appreciated loyalty above all else, would have approved.

"Are you insane? You can't waste a priceless piece like that on some cheap assistant you're screwing. It's criminal!"

"What's criminal, Dana, is you seem to think you have the right to comment on my decisions, on my life. You're engaged to be married. Isn't it time you moved on?"

"I'm only engaged to Graham because Daddy arranged it. He wants male lineage to pass his empire to and after things didn't work out between you and me—"

"Didn't work out?" I laugh again but this time it's laced with a bitter edge. I lower my voice to a growl only she can hear. "You tried to trap me with a pregnancy. You lied about a baby and then, when you were found out, you told the world I was a cold, calculating workaholic, implying I was the cause of the miscarriage."

She drops her gaze and stares at her wringing hands on her lap. "I'm sorry," she whispers. "Daddy won't give me the business. He'd have me marry anyone, so long as they can run a resort. But I loved you, Logan. I loved every part of you. But you wouldn't commit. You backed me into a corner."

My eyes widen at her nerve. "That's not how love works,

Dana. You can't manipulate it with power-hungry lies and fictional babies. What if I hadn't found out? Do you really think either of us would have been happy in a marriage built on a crumbling foundation of deceit."

Dana's stare becomes watery and I back off. I have no interest in making her cry.

"We could have been happy. It's taken me losing you to realize what we had," she replies softly, her hand reaching for mine but I pull it away.

I inhale a deep breath and close my eyes in a long blink as I tell her, "We didn't have anything, Dana. My advice to you is to stop being led by your father and figure out what will make you happy because it isn't me. It will never be me."

"It is you. Logan I can change—"

"I think you're in my seat," Layla says, smiling politely and I've never been more pleased to see my sassy pants back.

"Darling," I greet her with my most exuberant smile. "Dana was just leaving."

Dana stands suddenly and glares at Layla. "It won't last. You're too different." Then she leaves and I rejoice in taking Layla's hand back inside mine.

"You okay?" she checks.

"I am now that you are back. I missed you," I say, the accuracy of my statement catching me off guard.

With Dana gone the rest of dinner has the conversation besieged by Stan and Fred until the music stops and the announcement is made the awards are starting. As is usual, they inform us the overall resort winner will be announced at the end of the evening, and meanwhile the waitstaff do a great job keeping our glasses topped off until the main event.

My discomfort grows as the peak of the evening arrives and Donald joins our table, sitting in his daughter's seat and chugging back brandy.

Layla takes ahold of my hand and tells me, "If you don't

win, you and I are going to drink every drop of champagne in this place, agreed?" She lifts our hands up to shake on it, and I lower my voice and say, "And if I do win?"

A blush creeps up her neck.

"I'm going to sit on your lap and kiss the hell out of you," she replies right as the entire hall goes silent while waiting for the announcement of the winner.

My mouth falls open and not because Layla announced to the entire table that she is going to kiss me, but because I've been thinking about kissing her all night.

I can feel the burn of the stares on us, but I don't care.

"Until two minutes ago, I honestly didn't care if I won. Now, I'd trade my life for it."

CHAPTER 45

LAYLA

"...*A*ND THE PEOPLE HAVE CHOSEN! THE AWARD FOR THE BEST HOTEL GOES TO..." I squeeze Logan's hand knowing what this means to him and all the staff at the resort. "THE BLINGWOOD SANTA BARBARA RESORT!"

The crowd erupts in applause and I drop Logan's hand and begin manically clapping. I turn to Logan and he seems to be in shock.

"You did it!" I'm overwhelmed with pride for him. "You did it!"

His lips turn up and he smiles wider than I've ever seen. "Miss Bowers, I believe we made a deal." His grin turns sinful.

"What? You mean...?" I glance around casually, every pair of eyes in the entire room are on us. "Seriously?"

Logan nods slowly, his eyes are heated and fixed on mine. "Deadly."

I'm so attracted to him that it seems criminal not to kiss him while he's giving me permission. I'm up and out of my chair in a nano, flinging my arms around him and pressing my lips to his. His lips are soft and every bit as good as I remember. The inside of his mouth is warm with the faint yet intoxicating taste of wine.

Electricity pumps through my veins and the zing of pleasure has me wanting more. My hand cups the back of his neck while his arms pull me closer until I'm sitting on his lap. Time passes, maybe just seconds, maybe whole minutes, but I lose the ability to count or link thoughts together. It's divine and I don't want to stop, but I hear his name being called out from the speakers and I reluctantly pull back.

Logan rests his forehead against mine, his arms still pinning me in place.

"Well, you didn't need to be asked twice," he jokes and then his tongue dips out and he licks his lower lip.

I wipe away traces of my lipstick from his lips and then move to stand but he holds me in place. "Layla, you might need to stay where you are a moment." He chuckles but suddenly I can feel him, hard beneath me, and we're surrounded by people. "Would you join me on stage and stay very close. Hopefully the skirt of your dress will hide my arousal."

My cheeks are warm from the workout of kissing him and now from knowing I gave him a boner. I chuckle.

He stands and loops his arm through mine, keeping me to his left so that as we embark upon the stage, his groin is sheltered from the crowd. I don't know how long these things usually take to return to normal, but Logan keeps his speech to a minimum. "Thank you to the Gee Foundation for nominating us, for all of the wonderful guests we've had that voted for us, and most of all thank you to all my incredible staff who deserve this award far more than I do."

When we get down from the stage and look back at our table, he says, "Do you want to get out of here?" I know exactly what he means.

"Yes," I say breathlessly and his face lights up.

"You're sure?"

I gaze into his eyes as I say it so there can be no mistake. "Logan, I'm certain I want to sleep with you tonight."

He bites down on his lower lip while grinning the most dazzling of smiles. "I was going to suggest pizza, but if you insist."

A cackle leaves my lips as I playfully slap his arm. Then with his award in one hand, he grabs my hand with the other and we flee.

Destination: Fraternization. Level 100.

CHAPTER 46

LOGAN

*D*uring the pause while we wait for the elevator in the empty foyer, I study Layla's expression for any sign she wants to back out, but instead of doubt I see mischievous side glances and sultry pouts of her lips.

I still can't believe Layla spent the entire evening defending me, showering me with affection I don't deserve, and even going so far to act as though we are a couple—it's more than I deserve and shows a level of loyalty I haven't seen in a partner before.

I'm the most aroused I have ever been.

The second we're inside the elevator, I pull her body into mine and thread my fingers into her hair to move it aside, giving me access to her neck. Layla's head falls back and she moans as my lips meet the delicate spot beneath her ear. It makes me wonder what other sounds I can draw from her on my journey exploring her most sensitive parts.

The doors open too quickly and we pause.

My erection is strained against the zipper of my pants while Layla's nipples have hardened through her dress. She smells so good, so unbelievably sweet that my mouth is watering and my cock is painfully hard.

"Last chance to back out, sassy pants," I offer, running my tongue along my bottom lip.

Layla licks hers in response and then grabs a fist of my shirt.

"No way I'm backing out now, Blingwood. You won your award, now I want my bonus."

Fuck.

I throw her over my shoulder and she shrieks as I carry her to our room.

We pass an elderly couple shuffling across the carpet of the hall. I call out to them to move aside because I have a very naughty girl on my shoulder and they chuckle.

Still waiting on the floor outside our door is the champagne, but the sight of it doesn't bother me at all since what I have in my hands right now is far more important than a bitchy gift and a spiteful note. The keycard works immediately and I dash into the room and slide Layla down onto her feet. Her skin is dewy and flushed right down to the swell of her breasts.

For all the rush I was in to get here, now that she is before me, I want to take my time and worship her properly.

"Your bed or mine?" she asks, her gaze skimming down my body.

I make a show of looking at both. "How about yours? You can admire the view through the window if you get bored."

She smirks filthily. "Yes, you're right. You paid a lot of money for that view; it should be appreciated."

I stroke her neck, then slide the zipper of her dress all the way down. "The best view of all is right here. You look beautiful tonight."

Her dress slips from her shoulders and down her arms, slowly unraveling until it pools at her feet. She looks down and I can tell she's self-conscious, emotions she has no business feeling. I cup the back of her head and angle her face with my other hand until I can see into her eyes.

"I mean it, Layla. You were the single most beautiful woman in the room. In any room. I can't take my eyes off you."

Her cheeks flush and knowing I'm responsible for her pride fills me with longing to continue making her feel good. I kiss her, slow and deep, tasting her and teasing her body with my hands. She's wearing turquoise lace underwear that matches her dress and makes her eyes sparkle. I pull her close by the straps of her bra, then slide them down her shoulders. Goosebumps prickle her skin as I whisper her name.

The anticipation is killing me but in the best possible way. A gift to unwrap. She's radiant. When her breath labors beneath my lips on her skin, she clings to my shoulders and I can no longer control myself. I want her. I've wanted her ever since I first laid eyes on her and even more since I gave in back in the penthouse. I don't even know how I thought I could keep resisting her.

I reach down, and in one quick motion, I sweep her up and she falls back on the bed—which happens to be mine. "I changed my mind. You aren't looking through the window tonight, but I promise you'll see stars."

CHAPTER 47

LAYLA

*G*loriously naked, Logan leans over me on the bed, using his elbows to support his weight. His lips brush my ear before he trails his mouth along my neck in a downward path.

"Fuck. You smell so good."

"It's a perfume I bought at the thrift store," I brag breathlessly as his erection grazes my navel. Delicious anticipation has my nerve endings on fire. Even the movement of the necklace against my breast has my arousal heightening. "It was almost a full bottle. Five bucks!"

Logan growls. "You smell like a million bucks, sassy pants." He kisses a trail down my neck and then leans on one elbow to cup my left breast. "You look more than a billion." He cups my nipple with his mouth and electricity zings down my spine, making me arch my back. "I bet you taste even better."

He lowers his body and nestles himself between my

thighs, parting me wide and perusing my core like a wolf stalking its prey.

"I'm feverish just looking at you. Every part of you is beautiful." He shakes his head before dipping his tongue in to taste me.

A frenetic sensation builds and I raise my hips to meet his mouth stroke for stroke. His tongue enters me, and then his finger. One, two, he's stretching me and working me into a tangle.

"Priceless. You taste priceless."

"Thank you," I pant and feel him grin. My fingers dance into his hair, needing something to hold onto, something tangible to keep me anchored in case I buckle and float away. The sensation building at my core is growing and my body is becoming possessed by his touch.

"Logan, that feels—" I move my grip to his shoulders, my fingernails digging deep as he embarks on an act so heavenly, I think I am among angels. "If you keep—" My core clenches around his fingers, my hips buck, and his tongue circles until I'm consumed by a scalding heat that's threatening to explode. "Logan Blingwood, so help me God, I'm going to—"

All coherent reasoning vanishes, replaced by reckless need and a surging ache so acute that when it peaks, I throw my head back and call his name as my entire body undulates in a perfect release.

The aftermath is tingles and sunshine and a gentle tickling of his fingers at my entrance. I may have come back down to earth, but I'm still entranced by the angel.

When I look down at him, there's a flush to his face. A dark foreboding look in his eyes. "I'm going to need to see you do that again," he says and his jaw twitches.

"I'm not sure my heart can take another one," I admit.

He pulls me up by my hands, so we are both sitting on the bed. My body is Jell-O but he easily guides me onto his lap until I am facing him with my knees on either side of him. His mouth is suddenly on my breasts. I gaze down and watch as he sucks and nips, arching my back so he has full access. When the sensation becomes too much, I pull away and my gaze settles on his cock. Long and thick, with rope-like cords running its length, it strains past his navel. My core starts to throb. I need him inside of me NOW. Pushing him back just a little, I lift up and then line him up to my entrance before I push myself down on him until he is filling and stretching me, a glorious burn of friction. Eye to eye, he says, "Fuck, Layla. You're so fucking tight!" I rock up and down on him, adjusting to his size, enjoying the way it hurts. "You feel so fucking good!"

I feel it too. It's perfection. Looking in Logan's eyes, feeling how hot he is for me, knowing how good we are making each other feel, there's a total loss of abandon and I can't bear to spoil it by considering what will happen afterwards. Instead, I ride him like my life depends on it. Hell, maybe it does because soon after I start to feel like I might actually go into cardiac arrest if I don't come again.

Our bodies are coated in a slick sheen. His warm mouth takes mine, my clit slides against his body with every thrust back and forth while my nipples graze against his solid chest. I feel connected to him in body and spirit, like we are one, working toward the same goal.

"You going to come for me again, sassy pants?" he says, watching me lose my mind.

"Affirmative," I pant.

His mouth tightens like I amused him, but from the strain on his face, I know he is close too.

My fingernails dig into his shoulders and I throw my head back, arching my back to try to fend off the spasms of pleasure rocking my core. Logan's hands grip my hips and when I lose momentum, he drives me up and down until a guttural growl is forced from his throat. We cling to one another, riding the waves, lost in the moment. The moment seems to go on forever and I have no idea how long it is until we float back to reality, but his cock twitching within me somehow keeps me grounded.

"That was…" Logan breathlessly kisses my shoulder, my breast, my neck, my mouth. His tongue enters my mouth.

"It was." I grin and nod my head. The endorphins are making me crazy and lightheaded. I don't know whether I should kiss him again or break into song. The happiness and relief flooding my veins is like nothing I have ever felt before.

Logan uses his thumb to tip my chin up until I meet his gaze. "I love seeing you like that. I've never seen anyone more beautiful."

I'm in a dream and filled with post-sex-euphoria but still, hearing him use the *L* word has my heart filling and my throat tightening.

"I take it you… you liked it too?"

My face breaks into a huge, shit-eating grin.

That was the best sex I ever had!

His grin is a half a shade shy of bashful. "Am I to take your grin as affirmative?"

I let out a shriek of laughter and feel Logan's cock twitch within me. "Affirmative. I have no idea why I said that! You fucked the sense out of me."

His gaze darkens and his dick tenses again. "Perhaps I should fuck it right back into you."

My swallow is loud, my temperature rises. "Yes. Definitely. I'm going to need all the sense I can get."

* * *

"Housekeeping!" The maid knocks loudly on the door.

"Late check out!" Logan commands from the bathroom.

The maid mutters something and leaves while I stretch my sweater over my head and fasten my pants. My body is sore in all the best places from an entire evening, morning, and midmorning shower of being ravished. Each time I thought we were both sated, that we couldn't possibly find the energy or have need for any more of each other, the lightest lingering touch or mischievous flick of the eye would initiate sex all over again. Our bodies responded animalistically, like meeting a need so primal that it's essential for survival. Do or die, that's what it felt like.

Now I'm hovering by the bed that's creased sheets still scream of sex despite my flattening them out and tucking them in a dozen times.

"You know the maid's going to just rip them off and put on fresh ones?" Logan grins, then glances at the drapes that are grubby from the passing of unlaundered time and his perfect smile falters. "At least that is the hope. Probably best we don't think about it too deeply." He winks and I forget to breathe.

"I want to leave the room looking tidy," I reply, staring back at the bed with a stirring deep in my belly as I recall the sheer and utter release of coming apart beneath his expert touch. "You think they'll notice we broke the lamp?" I don't dare meet his eyes but my cheeks must color like a beacon, drawing his eyes to me.

At the apex of my desire, my arm shot out and the lamp somehow ended up getting blasted across the room. It's back on the bedside table and I've turned it around, but the back of it's almost entirely missing, having shattered on impact —*much like myself.*

Logan creeps closer and his finger runs down my neck, along my collarbone, sending a delicious shiver through my body. "I doubt they'll notice a broken lamp. You did an excellent job of hiding the damage." He lays his lips down onto the nook of my jaw and I turn into his arms and face him. "I've had a wonderful trip, truly surpassing anything I expected— and I'm not referring to the award." He tucks a piece of my still wet hair behind my ear and tells me, "Layla, we fit together perfectly." Logan covers my mouth with his kiss, blocking my reply and rendering me speechless. Then he breaks away and says, "But we didn't use a condom again. You sure you're covered?" His hand travels to my waist where he lifts my shirt and tenderly touches the soft skin of my abdomen.

We were so hot for each other that neither of us seemed to consider the repercussions and, given his past with Dana, I can understand why it could be triggering for him.

"I'm on the pill and I never forget to take it, so don't worry."

His smile lights up his face. "I wasn't worried." His fingers still lazily graze my stomach as he adds, "You'd look stunning swollen with my child."

His sweet comment takes me off guard and I reply, "You'll make a wonderful father someday."

He drops my shirt and meets my eyes with a bashful shrug. "Maybe one day." Then he shifts and pulls on the handle of my suitcase.

"So, we're good, then?" I ask.

"We're good."

We smile at each other and then our eyes flick to the bed. "Have we got time for one more?"

The noise from the maids outside cuts off my suggestion. "Maybe later." He looks at me again, his eyes lazily flicking up and down my body. "Definitely later. You ready?"

I double-check my suitcase is zipped and wonder, having been so intimate, how we will navigate this next stage. I'm walking a tightrope and don't know which way I'll fall.

"Shall we go?" he asks. He smells divine, making him

impossible to resist, but he's got his phone in hand, suitcase by his feet and looks ready to leave, but suddenly my feet won't move. "What's the matter?" He strides toward me, lowering his head and looking me straight in my eyes.

"I just... well, we blew up the nonfraternization policy. Again."

Logan nods slowly. "Yes, we did. You regret it?"

I shake my head.

"Perhaps I haven't been clear. I don't regret it either. So I guess that leaves you with a decision to make," he says through seductive lips. "You can forget last night happened, return to Blingwood and to our professional stance of brooding stares and playful tit-for-tats, or—"

"Or..."

His hands cup the sides of my face and I lean toward him, wanting more of him even though I already had my fill.

"See where this goes. There're two weeks remaining on your current contract, but I emailed you a new contract. I want you to stay—you've more than proven your ability. If you'd prefer, you can transfer to a separate section of the company: marketing, reception, HR—whatever you want. We always need good, reliable admin staff, though I'd miss looking at your face each day."

It's a great offer, yet I am terrified.

Sensing my discomfort, he brings his arm around my shoulder and kisses my temple. "How about we concentrate on today by finishing what we started."

My eyes flick to the bed and he smiles.

"There'll be time for that later. First we need to check out of this hell-hole, and I'm taking the only view worthy of looking at with me." He bends and picks up my suitcase. "You." He grabs his own suitcase in the same hand—giving the appearance that they weigh nothing—and then, Logan Blingwood leads me out of the room.

"I don't get it, how are we finishing what we started if we're not..."

"We're finishing your sightseeing list. I had George reschedule our flight to a redeye back tonight."

"Oh."

He stops and turns to me. "You okay with that?"

"See where it goes, the option of a permanent job, sight-seeing?" I check.

"Yes."

I inhale deeply and then my lips tip up. "I'm okay with everything."

* * *

WHILE LOGAN CHECKS us out at the reception desk, I loiter by the gift shop, checking out the trinkets. Row upon row of diamonds stare back at me, but none of them hold a candle to the costume jewelry still around my neck.

I use my hand to pick up the faux diamond and run it between my fingers, marveling at its weight and also remembering how it swung between my breasts as I mounted Logan. Blowing out a breath that fans my face, I look over at Logan standing at the front desk and he glances back at me, grinning while his face does a slow perusal up and down my body that leaves me tingling.

When he returns to me, he says, "Apparently Stan wants to congratulate me. We left in a rush last night." He grins. "Do you mind waiting here while I speak with Stan? We have to wait for the car and then for the bellhops to load our luggage."

"I can keep myself entertained for bit. Go on, talk to Stan and I'll meet you in the car when you're done," I reply and Logan brushes his lips against mine in a kiss that makes my stomach somersault.

"I'll be five minutes, tops."

I nod and watch as he walks toward the bar and shakes hands with the man I remember from last night.

Last night.

My body still tingles.

"You're still here." The voice is a mix of boredom dripping with malevolence.

I stare after Logan, silently willing him to turn around but his back is to me. My best option now is to ignore Dana, so I focus on reapplying my lipstick and grab the small, handheld mirror I keep in my purse.

"You know Logan's never brought his assistant to any other award ceremony before. You're only here because he wants to make me jealous," she says.

I try not to allow her words to penetrate. I willingly played the part of Logan's plaything last night. I was trying to show his peers Logan has moved on, and to show him that the sting of Dana's public humiliation is long behind him. I hadn't expected the evening to end the way it did, but I'm glad Logan and I came together. There's something between us, I can feel it. No matter what Dana says.

"You know, you sound utterly desperate," I reply finally, unwilling to allow Dana to believe she's in any way close to the mark.

Dana studies me and I let her.

"He'll never love you, you know. He couldn't even love me and I gave him my all. Logan Blingwood is incapable of romantic love. He'll do the right thing if he's in a bind, but he'll never love you deeply, especially since you have nothing of value to offer him."

"I might not be rich, but I'd never sell him down the river like you did."

"Oh, come on. You're with him for his money and if that isn't selling out, then I don't know what is. You're no better than me, at least I can hold my own in his world. Why, even the necklace you're wearing is worth more than you'd make in a lifetime. I have a dozen such pieces. You'll never be more than his assistant."

I stare at the necklace in the gift shop window, suddenly feeling like a fool for not noticing its worth. "It's costume jewelry," I say, mostly to myself.

Dana rolls her eyes. "So stupid and poor you can't even identify a diamond when it's staring you in the face. I guess you'll realize how worthless you are when he asks for it back. He's foolish, but not so foolish to waste a priceless family heirloom on a nobody like you."

I turn and face her. This bitch needs some truths!

"You faked a pregnancy." I shake my head in disgust. "And you have the audacity to speak ill of *him?*"

"Well, he isn't Mr. Perfect. You think I'm the bad guy, but he kept me dangling, refusing to commit. He also refused to go public with our relationship right up until the bitter end, and I knew he'd break things off if there was no baby. People think I'm just this pretty little thing with no brain, but I forged a career from nothing. And while I'm on the cover of *Celebrity Gossip*—"

"*Celebrity Gossip* only wants you because of who you used to date. They don't want you because you are interesting or even more than averagely beautiful. You're a fake. And Logan is very, very happy without you."

"That's not true! Logan refused to do most of the interviews with me. He wouldn't even have our wedding covered by the media. We were only pictured in one magazine together, the rest of my fame I slaved over alone."

"Yeah and they're already getting bored of you. Come to think of it, so am I—" I step around her but she grabs my arm.

"Maybe when they do get bored, I'll snap my fingers and take Logan from you."

I pause, teetering between walking away from this vile woman and punching her square in the face. I search for any sign of remorse but there isn't any. "You humiliated a good man."

"Oh, he'll get over it. Or maybe he won't. Maybe one day I'll feel sorry for him and take him back. *Celebrity Gossip* could do a piece with our 'we've reconciled' baby." She grins sadistically and I wonder if she is so shallow that she would do such a thing, but I immediately know the answer as she looks at herself adoringly in the mirror.

"He'd never take you back."

"I guess we'll have to wait and see." She smiles saccharinely and walks away.

A few minutes later, I'm still reeling when Logan approaches me. "Eyeing up the baubles, I see?" He nods his head at the gift shop window.

"Oh, not really. They're a little out of my price range."

"That reminds me. We should probably pack the necklace away for safekeeping."

I look down at the giant disco ball between my breasts and turn my back, swiping my hair to one side so Logan can reach the fastening. When I look up, Dana is standing at the reception desk watching us and giving me a know-it-all smirk.

"It's SOMBER, yet beautiful at the same time," I say, finding it hard to put my feelings into words as we leave the World Trade Center Memorial at the Freedom Tower. The day has turned to dusk, and it's as though the loss of light is a mark of respect to all the lives lost. "All those people, it's harrowing."

Logan's holding the car door open and the light dusting of rain in the air now clings to him like a second skin. But he doesn't rush me, instead he opens his coat and wraps me against him.

"No matter how many times you watch it on TV or visit the memorial, it's never less emotive, less utterly devastating. Are you okay?" Logan brushes away a tear from the corner of my eye.

"I'm fine." I lean up onto my toes and press my lips against his, needing his closeness. And it works. Each time, his mouth comforts my heart.

"You ready for Rockefeller Center?"

I nod.

We clamber inside the car, making out along the way, and before long Logan's connection has come through and we have gotten into a private elevator, making our way up to the Top of the Rock. The views are unparalleled and give us a sight across all of Manhattan and New Jersey.

Logan's arms are around me, his body against my back and his chin resting on my shoulder.

"The most beautiful skyline in the entire world," I murmur.

"For once, I'd have to agree." His arms tighten around me, snuggling me and before us is the magical view of the city that never sleeps. "I wish we could stay here."

"Me too," I reply. So much has happened since we left Santa Barbara. The uncertainty has me in a chokehold, but here in Logan's arms, I feel safe, and dare I say it, it feels like home, but I'm also terrified our sweetness will turn bitter, just like it did with Jonathon.

Now that Logan and I have formed this tentative relationship, it feels dishonest for me not to disclose my breakup and leaving Jonathon at the altar, but I'm too afraid of ruining this moment. I decide to do it when we get back to the resort.

I swivel in his arms and kiss him one last time on the Top of the Rock.

"Do you think it'll be weird when we get back?"

He shakes his head. "No. I think it'll be perfect."

"Come on then, let's pull up our big girl pants and go face everyone."

"I'd rather you took off your big girl pants," he says with a sexy wink.

* * *

WE BOARD the plane way past midnight and are both exhausted. In fact even Sarah looks less than put together, and I wonder if she and George had a NYC trip that was as spectacular as mine and Logan's.

"We'll be serving beef, if that's okay Mr. Blingwood?"

We ate some over-the-top New York-style Philly cheese steaks on the way over here, and so Logan replies, "Actually, Sarah, we already ate. You can travel in the cockpit with George. Take the night off. We can get our own drinks, can't we, Layla?"

"Yes. We'll be fine. You took such great care of us on the way over here, but we're so tired we'll probably sleep the entire way home." I smile reassuringly and Sarah looks delighted at this turn of events. She reminds Logan to press the assistance button if we need anything, and before long we are taxiing down the runway, only this time our chairs are set to the full recline position and Logan is holding me tight, spooning me, and stroking my hair as we take off.

"Not much longer," he tells me as the plane hits a forty-five-degree angle and my dinner lurches deep down into the bottom of my belly. His grip is so powerful I feel tethered to him, as though the jet could actually crash and I'd still be safe in his arms.

When the plane steadies out into something that resembles a horizontal trajectory, Logan's fingers stroke down my neck, along the fabric of my shoulder, following a path between my breasts.

"Ever since I first saw you in the break room, I've wanted you."

I think back to that day, him walking in and catching Mike asking for my number. "I thought you hated me on sight?"

"I hated what you represented. Temptation. I wasn't ready to feel anything. I certainly wasn't prepared for what you'd do to me." His hand moves lower, undoing the button on my skirt while his teeth nip my neck.

"I was unprepared for you too."

Logan's finger pushes my underwear aside and he circles my arousal. It takes me moments to fall apart in his arms and then I swivel to face him, kissing him deeply and reveling in his touch.

"I hope you're prepared for turbulence, Blingwood," I say.

His gaze darkens. "I can handle turbulence. You, on the other hand, sassy pants, will definitely cause me to crash and burn."

Then I straddle him, wondering how many times we can join the Mile High Club.

CHAPTER 48

LOGAN

*T*he photograph the sponsors decide to put on their website is one of me and Layla standing on stage while I accept the award.

Thankfully, the raging hard-on I had at the time is covered by a strategically placed fifteen-inch glass award that I happen to be holding over my groin. Beside me, Layla looks a picture of stunning elegance, and if you didn't know—as none of my employees do—that she had been kissing me senseless just moments before the photograph was taken, then you would never guess.

And so, life returns to a familiar routine. Layla, sitting opposite me while she completes her duties. Me staring at her, marveling in each and every smile she affords me, and casually stroking her inner thigh when she brings me my morning coffee. Not to mention working late and my eating her for supper on my desk.

Life feels perfect, except she has yet to show we are

together in front of the team. Each time I gravitate toward her or attempt to touch her with affection in public, she balks. And she has yet to spend a single night with me—she's always gone by morning and I am left wanting. I'm unsure what bothers me most, the secretive nature of our relationship or her reluctance to stay at the penthouse with me.

I close the document I am working on and realize my mistake, I haven't clarified the terms of our agreement, and we have immediately fallen into step. Shrouding our relationship—perhaps it's what she thinks I want? Not to mention she probably still thinks there is some nonfraternization policy.

She also hasn't replied to my email containing her new employment contract—whereby I doubled her salary.

"Let me take you to dinner tonight?" I say, loitering at the corner of her desk, keeping my voice casual.

Layla looks up at me through dark lashes. Crystal blue eyes so clear you could dive right into them. "No can do, I'm afraid. You've taken up every evening since we got back from New York last week and I have laundry to do." She sniffs her shirt and pulls a face like she doesn't smell divine.

"Bring your laundry to my place. I'll have someone take care of it for you."

She chuckles. "I'm not allowing someone else to do my laundry."

"Why?"

"Are you serious? Someone else washing my panties? No, I'd rather do it myself."

At the mention of her panties, I'm already imagining sliding them off. "Delay it by one day. There's somewhere I really want to take you. A friend of mine opened a restaurant, let me introduce you to both. I'll pay," I add in case it is cost that is keeping her away.

"Hey, I can buy my own dinner. But I really must do laundry. I already wore this shirt once this week and today I'm without panties."

My jaw drops. "Right now?" I point to beneath the desk, my cock already hardening at the thought.

She nods slowly and any logical thoughts I have fly right out of my head. All I can think about is how quickly I can get her to some place where I can check for myself.

"Logan, the team's ready for you in the lunch room," Skyla says, hovering in the doorway, but I can't take my eyes off Layla who looks positively smug.

"Be there in a moment," I reply over my shoulder, but Skyla doesn't get the hint. Instead, she starts talking to Layla about something or other while I pretend to gather the envelopes.

When it's evident that Skyla's waiting for Layla, I walk on ahead hearing the women chatter behind me as they follow. They're discussing meeting up for drinks this weekend, and I try not to feel affronted at the ease in which Layla agrees when she declined my dinner invite.

Inside the lunch room, those of the team that were due their breaks have assembled; I'll catch the rest on the next few break times. The idea of calling today's meeting came about after I'd suggested to Layla that I was going to award surprise bonuses to the workforce for their hard work which certainly contributed to winning the award.

Layla thought it would be prudent for me to say thank you—in person—when normally, I post a blanket thank-you email to all the staff and add an additional lump sum deposit to their bi-weekly paychecks.

I liked Layla's idea of a more personal approach and wondered why I have never done it before—apart from the fact I was always consumed with being busy. Lately, I seem to be able to find time to pursue more fulfilling activities, like filling Layla at every opportunity. But I digress: she was right, and a personal thank you is warranted.

I kick things off by pointing to the award that's on the counter. Eventually it'll go in the hotel lobby. Then I start the speech I prepared last night while Layla dozed on my lap on the sofa—before she woke up startled and went back to her apartment, that is.

"You've all worked your socks off and this is an award that you all earned," I say, walking around the room and handing out envelopes with notes of gratitude and also their checks. When I get to Layla, she crosses and uncrosses her legs and my mind goes totally and utterly blank. I can feel the burn of the stares of my employees, waiting expectantly for me to continue, but I know she has no panties on and it's doing insane things to my resolve.

I mean, she said she didn't, but with her crossing and uncrossing her legs, like a certain Sharon Stone movie, I see she actually doesn't.

"Logan, is everything okay?" Layla asks. To anyone else, her smile may appear polite, placatory, but then her tongue dips out to moisten her pretty pink lips, making my balls ache for her.

Without looking at anyone else, I say. "You have each earned a 10 percent bonus. Your checks are inside the envelope. Have fun spending it. Miss Bowers, my office. Now!"

I stride from the room. The team are all too busy opening their envelopes to care that my speech was cut short, but I catch Sally asking her, "What on earth have you done now?"

"Beats me," Layla replies and I can hear the smile in her voice followed by her heels clicking as she follows me out.

CHAPTER 49

LAYLA

*W*hen I get to Logan's office, I notice the blinds to the windowed wall are pulled down and he catches my wrist the second I get inside, spinning me around and pinning me against the wall.

"You flagrantly disregarded the company uniform policy."

I bite my lip and innocently reply, "But Mr. Blingwood, how can you be so sure if you don't check?" My gaze is doe-eyed. Logan's is red hot and brooding.

"Good point, Bowers." He roughly hitches up my skirt in a powerful move that has me instantly wet for him, then he drops to his knees and glides his hand across my thigh until he pauses at my entrance making me needy. "Fuck! Layla, you're bare."

I grin widely.

I thought he might appreciate that.

He blows out a breath that grazes my moist flesh. "As I

thought. Such insubordination can't go unpunished." His hand reaches around until he is roughly squeezing my ass.

I insert my index finger into my mouth seductively. "Whatever will you do with me, Mr. Blingwood."

He hitches my right thigh over his shoulder and suddenly his mouth is at my core, his tongue forming a long stroke of my seam before circling my desire. A groan leaves my throat and Logan growls his appreciation.

Outside of the office there's the sound of talking as staff walk the corridor and I press my lips together and try to be quiet, but that becomes impossible when he inserts two fingers inside me, curling them up and hitting my sweet spot while his tongue rhythmically suckles my nub.

"God, Logan," I pant, pressing my back into the wall and using the leverage of my leg that's over his shoulder to prevent me from falling. "I'm going to... don't stop!" My hands latch into his hair, the feeling of his tongue is too much on my tender flesh. It starts as a ripple, subtle yet strong, making my legs tremble until the sensation builds and delicious energy pulsates right through my body. His expertise between my thighs, diligently feasting on me like I am his favorite treat has me tumbling over the edge. I cry out and gasp, having no concept of volume and when I gaze down at Logan, he's grinning right back up at me looking decidedly pleased with himself.

"My desk. Now!" he orders.

I'm not in a position to argue with him as he unbuttons his pants, so I totter on my heels right over to his desk and bend over, looking over my shoulder in time to see him release his cock. Hot anticipation has me widening my legs while Logan stalks over to me with a firm grip on the base of his erection.

"You've been such a good girl, Layla. Taking your punishment like a champ."

I'm drenched and aching to feel him inside me. If that's my punishment, I'm already thinking up ways I can disobey him.

Logan steadies himself behind me, toying at my entrance, sliding in by just the tip, making my eyes flutter closed in a long blink. "God, yes." I pant through heavy breaths and his arm reaches around, inside my shirt and bra to cup my breast. "Double yes," I respond, pushing myself into his hand while also pressing my ass down onto him. His other hand finds my clit and my voice becomes guttural. "Yes. Yes. Yes."

"You're fucking unbelievable, Layla." His hips pick up pace and I buck against him, joining his thrusts. Long, punishment driving all the way back and forth so I feel every part of him exactly where I need him.

"Unbelievable?" I pant. "In a good way?"

"In the best way possible. You're amazing." His hips undulate, increasing the pressure.

"Best PA you ever had?" I'm whimpering now, the tension in my body is like an elastic band stretched to the max and it feels like I'm about to snap.

"The best everything I ever had," he replies and my core tightens around him. I hold onto the edge of his desk like it stands any chance of keeping me grounded and he drives into me faster, harder and my climax threatens to tear through me.

"You're going to come for me, Layla," Logan rasps, plunging into me faster. The tension in my body climbs to searing heights, crushing me beneath the power of his expert touch until I can't hold back anymore and my body instantly surrenders. I'm powerless not to cry out as ecstasy vibrates through me, making my body tremble and my nerve endings combust. I'm momentarily trapped between paradise and heaven and all I can do is hold on and let the pleasure roll through me. I'm still struggling to catch my breath when

Logan lets out a guttural groan as his solid arms pull me in tight against his body and he jerks and shudders until he is spent.

He kisses my temple then rubs his cheek against mine. Then he softly tells me, "I don't want you to leave, Layla."

"Well, I suppose I could try to work in this position but—"

"You know what I mean. You haven't responded to my contract offer."

With him still deep inside me, it's affecting my ability to think straight.

"I'll reply soon," I say and ease myself forward so he can slide out. Then I turn to him and kiss him chastely. He's looking at me so adoringly, his gaze starts to hurt and I look down at the floor.

I can't accept his offer, not while I still haven't told him about what really happened with Jonathon.

KNOCK. KNOCK. KNOCK.

At the sound of someone banging on the door, I turn and gape at Logan, pulling my skirt, bra and shirt back into place as quickly as I can while Logan tucks himself away. His cum is sliding down my inner thigh when the door flies open.

"This had better be important," he sternly tells Sally as she walks inside.

I smile kindly at Sally and lean down, picking up some random papers from Logan's desk and pretending to be busy. "If that'll be all Mr. Blingwood," I say to him, "I'll get back to work."

Logan nods and I've barely taken two steps when he says, "Miss Bowers?"

I turn back and smile at him expectantly, noticing that his hair is ruffled and his cheeks are flushed.

"Excellent work."

I fight to keep my expression neutral and reply, "Thank you, Mr. Blingwood."

* * *

LATER THAT DAY, even doing laundry in the staff facility, I'm still smiling.

"There you are! I've barely seen you since you came back from New York. Where have you been?" Jessie says, walking in with an overflowing laundry basket in her arms and an exhausted-looking Macy attached to her hip.

"Oh. Just keeping my boss happy."

Jessie lowers Macy down onto one of the plastic chairs at the side of the room and hands her an iPad complete with headphones.

"Don't judge me for the virtual babysitter, it's the only way I can get this done without a meltdown." She nods her head to the laundry basket and begins filling one of the vacant machines. "So, tell me all about New York!"

I excitedly gush to Jessie about the awards ceremony, leaving out that Logan and I ended the trip with a big bang, but somehow, she can tell.

"You are lit up like Christmas. You got the glow." She slams the washer door, presses the button and slinks down onto the chair beside me.

"What?" I shrug nonchalantly and focus on watching the drum of the machine go around.

"You are totally banging him, aren't you?"

I smile instead of denying it.

"I had my suspicions it was headed that way when he carried you home from the beach bar and from watching the way you two look at each other, and Mike... oh my god, Logan was a jealous man, but I wasn't certain it would actually amount to anything, not after..."

"Dana," I supply. "And the fact we are worlds apart." I shrug suddenly feeling a weight in the pit of my stomach.

I hadn't really thought about the differences in our lives when he was just a man who was exceptionally hot, off limits, and who also happens to be my grouchy boss, but since we got down and dirty in NYC and now we're getting closer at home, there's a gnawing in my stomach telling me that it won't end well.

"Worlds apart? You guys live a few hundred yards apart. You're staying now, right? The temp job has got to be going permanent or else... are you friends with benefits?" Jessie holds her hands up. "No judgment. I'm just glad one of us is getting some."

I chuckle lightly. "I'm not sure what we are. I mean, he has offered me a permanent job here, but then what? We're so different. He has a private jet and I have... I don't even own a suitcase, I had to borrow yours!"

"Sorry, it's got a wonky wheel."

I laugh. "It suited me perfectly. Besides, it would have been terrible to arrive in New York with my clothes in a trash bag."

Jessie's hand reaches for mine. "You have an infectious personality, a beautiful smile, and tits to die for! I know Logan notices everything about you. Damn! That man is into you, I know it. What's stopping you from staying?"

I throw my hands up. "I'm being dishonest. I haven't told him yet that I left Jonathon at the altar. He was badly hurt after Dana walked out on his wedding day and now I can't bring myself to make him doubt me. What if it's a deal breaker? I don't want to ruin what we have."

"Honey, you left that asshat at the altar for a reason. Dana did it because she's a selfish bitch with no care for anyone else. You're not like her, and Logan knows it."

"You think he'll be cool with it?"

Her smile waivers. "I think he'd be a dumbass not to hear you out."

I laugh. "That isn't a yes."

"It ain't a no either. Only one way you'll know."

"I lined up another job with the agency, just in case."

"Why did you do that?" Jessie looks pissed, and I feel guilty.

"I have to have a back-up plan. Logan's my boss but he could let me go in a heartbeat. I mean, I already broke the nonfraternization rule. Okay, so it was with him, but still, it doesn't make it okay." Jessie shakes her head as though she doesn't understand so I clarify, "The nonfraternization policy. You know, that employees aren't allowed to bang each other."

Jessie shakes her head and lets out a guffaw of a laugh. "Girl, if that's the case, there's a whole lot of banging going on around here and not a lot of firing."

It must be my turn to look confused because Jessie elaborates, "Skyla and Drew, the boss's brother. Tim and Susie in accounting. Sally and Doug. Jeff from security and Michelle from housekeeping. This one will surprise you, Daisy the yoga teacher and Roger from payroll… they're all at it. Work together, play together. Everyone's banging, except me, it seems. And now you and Logan are too."

I find myself grinning even though I've been duped.

"Who told you there's a nonfraternization policy?" Her mouth pops open with realization. "Logan? He did, didn't he? To keep you from banging anyone else. Oh, he's got it baaaad!"

I nod then shake my head with disbelief.

Jessie cackles a belly laugh. "Oh, he got you good."

The bell above the door rings, drawing both of our stares. It's Logan, carrying a basket of laundry.

My tongue pokes the side of my mouth.

Logan doesn't do laundry. What is he up to?

"Mr. Blingwood. Fancy seeing you here with laundry."

His brow furrows. "Hi, Jessie. Why so surprised? This is the laundromat, isn't it?

He looks unsure, and I can't keep from grinning.

"Why don't you take Macy home and tuck her into bed. I can toss your laundry in the dryer and bring it back later."

Jessie regards me. "You sure?" she asks.

I nod.

Jessie looks Logan up and down before whispering to me, "He ain't here to do no *laundry.*"

"I know," I reply laughing.

Jessie picks Macy up and carries her out, using a singing voice to say, "See you later, Mr. Blingwood. Have fun!"

The bell rings as Jessie and Macy exit and I look away, unable to contain my smirk. While I compose myself, I focus on the task at hand, ignoring Logan. The washer finishes and I transfer the load to the dryer.

Logan stands near me, staring at the machine. "I decided to come do laundry too."

I shut the door to the dryer and it starts the cycle, then I sit back on the plastic chair and watch as Logan attempts to figure out how to open the door to the machine—knowing he likely has no idea he has to put four quarters in the slot before the door will open, and I'm pretty sure he doesn't have any quarters on him at all. Hundreds, probably. Change? Hell no.

"Have you used the laundromat even once since you moved here?"

"Of course, I have." Logan turns to face me and I meet him with a challenging stare. "Okay, I admit, no I haven't used the laundromat before, but I decided it was time I should learn." He wrestles with the door again. He's in real danger of breaking it and rendering one of the machines out

343

of order, so I move to help him, pulling some coins out of the pocket of my jeans. "You'll need to insert four of these." I hold up a coin.

"Oh." He looks at me curiously. "Do all the machines take coins?"

I splutter out a chuckle. "Pretty normal for a laundromat."

"Right." He palms his pockets. "I don't have any change."

I flip him a coin at a time and he catches them. "All yours."

"Thank you." Once he's opened the door, he begins filling the machine with colors and whites. I'm tempted to let him screw up his clothes with some pretty tie-dye, but I know his shirts cost hundreds of dollars and my conscience won't allow it. I grab his hand as he's about to toss in another shirt and notice something off. I pull the shirt out and bring it to my nose, noticing the starched fabric. It smells like fresh soap and clean bed sheets.

"You do laundry funny," he says watching me inspect his shirt with a guilty smile.

"And you clean laundry when it's not dirty." I pull what he has stuffed in the machine out, and hold it up as proof before dropping it back in his basket.

His smile falters and he raises both his palms. "Guilty."

I can't help chuckle. "What are you doing here?"

Logan bites on his lip, looking adorably sheepish. "I wanted to see you. You didn't want come to dinner with me, so I… ordered pizza. I know it's not New York's greatest, but it's hot and will be here soon."

I take a step forward and cup his face, leaning up to kiss him. Then I take a step back. "I told you, I have to do my laundry—I really do—it's not that I didn't want to eat—" I wink. "—with you."

He laughs at my innuendo and pulls me in close. "That's what I was hoping for tonight. And since I had no choice but to follow you here, can we do laundry together?"

Jessie's machine finishes the spin cycle and I transfer her stuff to the dryer. "You don't need to do laundry, whereas I have no clean clothes left."

"Maybe I want you to teach me to do laundry," he says but then I feel his hand brush my ass. By the time I've spun around, he's over by his machine, filling it.

"You just touched my butt," I accuse.

"I'm way over here," he says with faux innocence. "Maybe you want me to touch your ass so bad, you're imagining it. Where do I find the soap?" He makes a show of looking around.

I nod to the bottle on the other side of me.

When Logan walks past me, I feel his hand on my butt again, only this time he slows to a stop and I push back as though I am checking the machine is indeed working. A thrill rushes through me. He came all the way here to see me. It's sweet, and if I'm honest, I was missing him.

Logan's minty breath is on my shoulder and his hand, no longer playful, rolls over my cheek. "I missed you tonight."

"It's only been three hours since we got off work."

"I know. I'm never going to get those three hours back."

He continues squeezing my butt cheeks, only with both hands now, and my core heats at the lack of attention.

"You could have come to my place after I finished."

I widen my stance, giving him better access to where I need his hands.

"Oh, baby, I plan to come, right after you have finished."

Logan's fingers reach around and circle me through my jeans until my core is throbbing. His other hand slips beneath my T-shirt and he cups my breast, forcing a mewl through my lips. The sound is all the green light he needs to pop open the button of my jeans and insert his finger right onto my nub.

I scan the room but we're still alone. Opposite me is the

door to the room, but his hands are well hidden by the industrial-sized machines lined up in the middle of the room. Even if someone walked in they wouldn't see, so I let him have at it and thank him by reaching back and palming him through his shorts.

It isn't long before my legs start to shake as my orgasm nears. Logan must feel it too. His fingers reach hyperspeed and my body tenses as waves of pleasure flood through me. I reach inside and grip him, briefly enjoying how slick he is, then gasp as the crest of my orgasm rolls through me.

"Look how good you are at multitasking, sassy pants," he whispers. "Good girl."

My legs are so weak, I'm barely able to stand as the last shudder rolls through me. I'd never considered a laundromat as a fantasy location before. But now I'm here, I appreciate the perfection of the cover provided by the machines coupled with the risk of getting caught. It's joined my list of favorite places, along with Logan's office, the copy room, his penthouse, and the mile high club.

I'm so turned on, I spin and kneel in one fluid motion, pulling down his workout shorts. Face to face with his length, I know exactly how much he enjoyed making me come and now it's his turn. Taking him in my mouth, I roll my tongue over him and his cock twitches.

"Fuck, Layla, that feels so good," he murmurs and it's all the encouragement I need to take all of him. I salivate, making myself good and wet for him and slide him into my mouth. His hands are in my hair, then one is cupping my chin, guiding himself into me.

I look up and relish the sight of Logan's eyes fluttering open and shut as though he can't decide whether he wants to watch or succumb to the pleasure. I feel strong and desirable having this power over him and then the little bell over the door rings and I hear the shuffling of feet.

"Where do you want your pizza, boss?"

Logan pushes my head back but I remain latched onto him. Hidden from view, I'm suddenly curious to push the envelope of the "nonfraternization policy."

"Just put it down where you are and go." Logan's voice is strained but not as strained as the length I am teasing with my tongue.

Shoes tap on the tile and the door moves an inch and then the voice says, "By the way, all of us working in the kitchen are really glad of the bonus."

"Is that all?" Logan bites back.

"No. We're really stoked about winning the award too."

I go deeper and Logan grips the counter. "I didn't mean… go, now!"

"How come you doing laundry, anyway? Don't you got people to do that stuff for you?"

I hum against him as I stifle a laugh and feel him stiffen as I almost send him over the edge.

"Eric, get out of here. Now!"

"All right, I only wanted to say thank you," Eric huffs and finally I hear the door close.

"You are a very bad girl."

I look up at him innocently through my lashes and then I go down all the way until Logan grips my shoulders and releases his pent-up arousal.

* * *

LATER, with piles of folded laundry in baskets beside us, we sit on the floor of the laundry and share the pizza. "You know Eric probably thinks I come to the laundry to jerk off," Logan says between bites and I crease up with laughter.

"Logan Blingwood: hotelier, international playboy, secret sex pest."

"You could have stopped what you were doing, stood, and let poor Eric know you were in here too. He might have left sooner if you did."

"Ah, but then Eric wouldn't have had the chance to tell you how grateful he is for the bonus."

"Layla, I will never again be able to look poor Eric in the eyes."

A belly laugh pushes its way through my body and I gaze at him. When we're like this, together and having fun, it's difficult to notice the vast differences between us. Logan's hand grips mine as I lift another slice of the pizza.

"Your particular brand of gratitude was spectacular."

"My aim is to please."

"Where did you learn—" He stops himself. "I mean, have you had many partners?" He tries to keep his voice casual, but I can tell he's invested in my answer from his penetrative stare.

"Does it matter?" I reply.

"No, the number of partners you have had doesn't matter, not at all. I've gotten to know your body intimately, but the rest of you eludes me. I find myself curious. You already know so much about me; I'd like to even the score."

The air suddenly becomes too warm; the moment intense. Every fiber of my body stiffens and my instinct is to resist answering his questions.

"There's not much to tell," I say flippantly though honestly. "I've had a few sexual partners, of course. No one as good as you, obviously."

"Obviously." He smirks then leans forward over the pizza box and his finger casually trails a path on the underside of my knee. "And Jonathon…"

Unease creeps up my spine. It feels like our get-to-know-you conversation is quickly leading to a destination lined with traffic cones and hazard signs. I need to tell him about

Jonathon, explain. Yet I'm nauseous at the idea of him looking at me differently. We're already different enough.

He's a successful businessman. I'm a temp with a history of taking one fleeting role after another. He's my boss and I am merely his employee—and not even a permanent one. He has this amazing family who seem to support each other. I have just a few friends and very little experience of what it means to have family. He has a home and a life. I'm basically a nomad.

But most of all, Logan Blingwood is a person who comes through for people. He stayed with Dana because he thought she was having his baby, even though she was horrible.

When I fled from Jonathon and the wedding, I felt relieved I didn't have to go through with it, and now I'm torn between running to someplace new or staying right here where I feel safe. A place that feels in my very bones like it has the promise of home.

"You can talk to me," he says, sensing my distance.

"I'm fine," I assure him, standing up.

The look he gives me tells me he knows I am lying.

"I'm exhausted. You mind if I turn in early?"

He closes the pizza box and stands. "Of course. I'll walk you home."

"No. You have your laundry to go put away and I need to take Jessie hers. I'll see you tomorrow."

I grab the two baskets piled on top of each other and get two paces before he says, "Layla, wait…"

I carry on walking, needing the air promised by the door before me. "I'm fine. I've got a headache. I'll see you tomorrow, promise."

And then I rush from the room angry with myself that I chickened out of telling him.

CHAPTER 50

LOGAN

I'm at the office at 7 a.m. on a Saturday because I couldn't sleep.

I was too busy thinking about Layla. She was different. After we did laundry and I asked her to tell me about her ex, her body shrank in, she stalled, she was... I can't put my finger on it but there was a switch.

I already know he cheated on her when I overheard them talking in her office. Maybe she hasn't moved on. Perhaps she's still hung up on him and his behavior still hurts. That option doesn't sit right either because when I'm with her, there is no indication that she's thinking about him. She's into me, and that's not just my ego talking; I can feel it. It's like looking in the mirror the way she looks and responds to my every touch.

So why did she shut down?

I check my cell. She still hasn't responded to the text I

sent last night wishing her goodnight and asking that she join me for dinner at the penthouse this evening. I stare over at Layla's empty desk through the glass wall that divides our offices and my chest constricts.

There's only one week until Layla's temporary employment contract ends. Skyla hasn't mentioned lining up a new assistant for me, and I know it's because everyone hopes Layla will decide to stay. But she hasn't formally accepted the permanent job offer and the more time that passes, the more I become restless that she isn't going to.

I flick through Layla's resume. It's been sitting in the drawer of my desk since her interview. For some reason, I never stacked it on the filing pile. Job upon job, all fleeting until the one she worked at with her ex when she moved back to take care of her father. Her longest job by a mile. I know he passed away six months ago in his hometown; she told me as much. And then her boyfriend cheated and she went back to her transient ways. And now I fear she is about to repeat the same pattern.

The phone on my desk rings. It's not Layla. The caller display notes it's a local number and I relent and pick up before it's diverted back to reception. "Mr. Blingwood. This is Tony Blackwood from Safe Bank. I'm glad I caught you on a Saturday."

"Tony, hi. Is everything in order?"

"The safety deposit box is ready. Miss Bowers just needs to come in to the bank to go through the paperwork and so we can check her ID."

"Good. I'm seeing her this evening so I'll ask when she's available."

"Mr. Blingwood, where is the item now?"

My eyes flick to the safe that's hidden beneath the painting on my wall.

"It's safe."

Tony chuckles nervously through the phone. "Well, yes, I imagine it is. One doesn't leave a fifteen-million dollar necklace lying around in trinket boxes. Would you like me to arrange our security team to escort you both with the piece?"

"No. It's fine. Thank you."

An image of Layla wearing the necklace as she mounted me pops into my head—the enormous diamond bouncing atop her full and perfect breasts. The necklace might be expensive, but that image is priceless.

"Okay, well I will wait to hear from you then, sir."

I hang up the call and turn off my computer. I can't concentrate anyway, not when I have this sense of foreboding looming over me.

That's when my cell starts blowing up. Text messages from Mom, Drew, my sister Tabs, all with links to an online app.

Shit!

On my screen is a video of Tate naked, running from a bunch of paparazzi.

I call Tate right away.

"What the fuck is going on?"

"Thank God you called, man! I'm in a whole heap of trouble."

"Yeah, I saw! All the news channels are covering you with your butt out, running down the street. People are pausing it, swearing they can see your nut sack!"

"Fuck, man. I don't know how this happened. My agent told me to go get changed before the photoshoot, I get in there, get undressed, then I can't find my suit, so I go and look for Chad but he's disappeared. When I come back, all my fucking clothes are gone and then someone whips the towel away. I'm in deep shit, Logan."

"Where are you?"

"I'm behind a dumpster at a Starbucks. Sending you my location now. But Loag, don't you come. Mom said there's a bunch of ogres outside her house and the pound. Drew's got a bunch of them outside of his place too. Skyla couldn't even get out the driveway to get to her Pilates class. Can you send one of your security guys? If I'm seen, I'll never shake them."

I pinch the bridge of my nose.

Fuck being famous!

"Sure. No worries. I'm sending Simon your location now. He'll be driving a black, unmarked sedan."

"Cool. Thanks, bro. Can I take a room at the resort? If I go to my place or Mom's, they'll find me—just until the fuss dies down."

"No problem. You can have the penthouse Drew and Calli stayed in. I'll tell the staff to keep your identity locked down, and you can lie low and eat up the room service. Anything else you need?"

"Some clothes would be awesome."

A strangled chuckle forces its way up my throat. "You got it."

* * *

A FEW HOURS LATER, I'm still in the office and Layla finally replies:

> I'll see you at the penthouse at seven. Can we talk tonight? There's something I need to tell you.

I reply immediately:

> Sassy pants, there is not a single thing you can tell me that won't make me want you more.

Her reply comes through a full four minutes later like she wrestled with her response:

> I hope that's true.

I PUT Layla's text to the back of my mind and reassure myself she isn't like Dana with her silly games. It might be a concern or an insecurity, but the topic she wishes to discuss will be surmountable, of that I am certain.

"Mr. Blingwood," Sally says from the doorway to my office. She has a fresh coffee and a donut in her hand, and so I put down the document and give her my full attention. "You have a... um... visitor in the reception."

"Who is it?"

"It's... please don't shoot the messenger."

I chuckle at her uncertainty. "Who has come to the office on a Saturday to see me?"

"It's Miss Dana, sir."

"Tell her I am busy." I flick my hand away. I have no desire to see Dana. "She's wasted a trip."

"Sir, she's quite adamant. She wants to see you."

I twist in my office chair. Sally seems more nervous and unsure than ever, so I offer her a smile. "What does she want?" I ask.

Sally shrugs and places the coffee and donut on my desk. "She says it's important. Well, she demanded it was important and that I wasn't doing my job if she didn't see you."

Important.

One can only imagine the mundaneness Dana finds

important, though why she is here when she and I already spoke at the awards dinner does have me somewhat curious.

Sally looks beaten down and nervous. "Send her in."

"Yes, boss."

As she heads for the door, I stop her by calling her name and she turns to face me, her look unsure. "Thank you for all your hard work. I know you've been pulling extra shifts during the peak season. It doesn't go unnoticed."

Sally grins widely. "Thank you, sir. It's the least I can do after you gave me and Doug your wedding."

The reminder of my *gift* of the ill-fated wedding to Dana unsettles my stomach. The gift was a ploy to hide the fact I ever intended to marry the succubus that is Dana. Still, our closest friends and allies knew it was a ruse. I just hope it isn't in anyway a bad omen for Sally and Doug, they're a cute couple.

"You're welcome. Send Dana in."

I sip my coffee while I wait and imagine Layla sitting at her desk. Would she approve of me seeing my ex? I'm not sure I'd be content with her having clandestine meetings with hers; perhaps it's a sign, and I should talk to her about a level of exclusivity in our relationship.

"Logan," Dana purrs, shuffling into my office in her too tight pencil skirt. She sits before me, making the assumption that she will be here long enough to make herself comfortable.

"What do you want, Dana? Do I need a restraining order as well as a non-disclosure agreement?"

"Baby, don't be like that. I know things didn't go down well between us at the end, but it was never my intention to hurt you."

"I'm not your baby, Dana, and setting me up to wait for a bride that fled was in no way caring. What you published after the fact was downright libelous."

"I know I can be a handful sometimes, but it didn't go down how you thought."

I stare at her incredulously.

"You already admitted you tricked me. If Jessie hadn't found the negative pregnancy tests and alerted me to your plot to become pregnant and use me, I would now be married to the liar before me—without a prenup."

"Jessie's a bitch!"

"Jessie is worth a thousand of you."

So is Layla!

"I thought I was pregnant. You were so excited when I told you. You wanted the baby, how could I have told you I was wrong?"

I scrunch my nose and shake my head.

Is she for fucking real?!

"Well, there's this nuanced concept—you may need to look it up in the dictionary—but it's called honesty, Dana. Crazy, I know, but there are people walking around using it all the time. You should try it!"

"If you weren't so inflexible, I would have been honest but we both know you would have ended things with me if I told you the truth."

"All the more reason not to lie!"

"Logan, I did think I was pregnant. It was right before Damien's party and I was doing that diet to lose twenty pounds in two weeks. Remember? I had Fernando cook all those cabbage recipes and you said it was stinking up the penthouse worse than socks soaked in puke."

What I actually said was socks soaked in shit. The smell was so nauseatingly foul I thought I'd developed parosmia.

"Yet when you found out the truth that there was no baby, you didn't just keep it from me, you tried to make it real. And when I discovered the truth, you ran and tried to publicize you leaving me at the altar. What was it you said in the Instagram post that I made you take down? 'Logan Blingwood is cold, distant, and a workaholic and caused me to have a miscarriage.'"

Dana has the decency to lower her eyes and look abashed.

"Only one of those things I said was a lie. I was hurting too. I wanted a baby with you. I wanted you to want me."

"It doesn't work like that and besides, we discussed enough of our disastrous past at the awards dinner. I don't need to hear anymore of your lies. You need to leave."

"Look, I know I screwed up. I'm sorry. I see that now. I've been reflecting on my behavior; I've changed."

I can't help scoffing.

"I mean it. At the awards, you seemed so happy. I want that for you. I want that for me, too, but Logan, I can't bear for you to make the same mistake again."

I roll my eyes.

"There are things you don't know about the woman you're screwing, and I couldn't live with myself if I didn't at least try and protect you." Dana's face is downcast, her thickly made up eyes pleading.

I stand. "Get out, Dana. If you slander me, my business, or Layla, I will sue you. I will make sure that your reputation matches your personality and no one will ever offer you so much as a sandwich board at a pizza house by way of work."

Dana makes no attempt to move, instead she reaches into her purse and pulls out some papers.

"Do I need to call security?"

"It's true. Look, Logan." She points to a photograph of Layla and an older woman who looks just like her. Layla's smile on the photograph reminds me of the one she used to give me when I was just her asshole boss.

In the photo Layla is wearing a wedding dress.

"Dana, well done. You excel in spinning lies and figured out how to use photoshop. Now leave." I walk around the table, ready to throw her out, but she begins to scatter the papers over my desk, pulling up another one for me to look at.

"Look. It's her! I had Daddy's private investigator look into her and I spoke to her ex, he said she left him at their wedding after she found out he was penniless. His father is an ex-football player. She thought he had money." She sifts through the papers again until she finds a printed screenshot. The picture denotes a text from Layla asking: **Where's all the money?**

I grab Dana's hand and tug.

"Logan, wait! This one, see." She points to a printed article in some local rag that states: "Jonathon Snell, son of local hero, Rupert Snell, to marry local girl, Layla Bowers."

Then she pulls out another. "Son of Rupert Snell stranded at the altar."

"Seems she's just like her mother," Dana says and holds up another sheet for me to look at. "Bridezilla, Judith Ball, marries fifth husband, owner of car sales business."

"According to Jonathon, Layla's mother has married richer each and every time. He says she's been training her daughter. Layla left Jonathan because she found out he didn't have as much money as he led her to believe. That's on him. He admits he was trying to show off, making out he was as rich as his daddy, but she left him when she found out he didn't have any money. Jonathon was utterly heartbroken." Her eyes are pleading. "Doesn't all this tell you something? Logan, I flew across the country to save you from making another mistake. You knew what you were getting yourself into with me, but do you really know this woman?"

"Layla told me he cheated."

I recall meeting Jonathon. Layla was pissed to see him but the guy behaved like a jerk.

"She walked out and left him because she found out his

bank account was empty. She ghosted him and when he found out she was here, he came for some answers. He was devastated to be left at the altar—I imagine you can identify with how that feels."

Dana's hand cups my arm that still holds the evidence she has gathered, but I shrug it off.

"Layla is nothing like you," I insist.

Her voice softens. "No, she's not. I come from money. Anything I took from you, my daddy would have left me in the will anyway. He was never going to disinherit me, not when push came to shove. What I actually wanted from you was your love and support. What Layla Bowers is after is something quite different. Why, she probably looked you up online and saw you in Forbes and her eyes lit up like Christmas. She's a gold digger looking for a meal ticket and you're her next victim."

I shake my head.

Dana's lying. She must be.

"Just please, tell me you didn't sleep with her?" My face must say it all because next she says, "But you used protection? Tell me you fucked her wearing a condom?"

My gut spins and my mouth falls open.

Don't worry, I'm on the pill.

"Oh, Logan." Dana's voice is pitiful.

"No. She's not pregnant."

There's something I need to tell you.

"You sure about that?"

"Get out, Dana! Get the fuck out!" I growl.

Dana takes one look at me and has the sense to back away.

"I'm going to give you some time to process this, but Logan, I still care about you. Seeing you at the awards made me realize, we're the same you and I. I'm ending things with Graham—because I never stopped loving you. I don't even care if you need to pay Layla off. You don't need to see the baby; we can make our own. I just need another chance."

I don't answer because I can barely speak.

I pour a tumbler full of Macallan and seat myself in front of the evidence.

Have I been duped again?

CHAPTER 51

LAYLA

*M*y cell is ringing, I'm running late, and I can't find a damn thing to wear to dinner with Logan!

I thought I'd see him while on my dog walk, but his mom said he hadn't showed up, but not to worry as he was probably sorting out his brother after some kind of celebrity misdemeanor.

"Hello," I breathe into the receiver having answered it without checking the caller ID.

"Layla?"

"Mom." I stop what I'm doing and sit on the bed. "How are you?"

"I'm okay," she replies, but she doesn't sound okay. "Actually, I'm thinking of divorcing Roy."

"Oh, Mom. I'm sorry to hear that. What happened?" I may not like my mother sometimes, but it still hurts to hear she's upset.

"He got the credit card bill and went bananas. I don't think I can live with a man who would have me shop at Walmart. It's like he doesn't know me at all. Layla, he thinks I shop too much."

I gasp and try not to chuckle. "Mom, you do spend a lot of time shopping. Do you think you can compromise?"

"Compromise. Layla, I haven't worked all my life to make sacrifices now."

"But Mom, you haven't had a job since you were seventeen."

"I have a husband, Layla. I keep the house nice and I keep the garden all by myself, if you don't count Phil who does the lawn. I'm an honorary member of the country club and president of the bridge society. When would I possibly find the time to work?"

"Maybe you could work at the country club. It could help fund your Cordyline obsession?"

"Layla, dear. I know you enjoy working, lord knows you won't take a husband, but honestly, is that what you want for your mother? To be run ragged by the rat race?"

I imagine my mother, with her tailored pant suit and impeccable manicure, packing bags at the minimart. "Roy's right, Mom. You can't spend beyond your means. You're getting older and you need to plan for your retirement. Mom, people's medical debts alone can make them homeless."

"I'm as fit as a fiddle," Mom replies. "Fitter than Candace Hyler from the bridge club who just started blood pressure medication!"

"You are now, but what about in a few years. Roy's a good man, but he shouldn't have to work his fingers to the bone to keep you in plants. Why not try cutting back a little? There are some resources I can send you. TikTok, Insta, they're all full of life hacks to help you save for a rainy day."

"Okay, send them along. I'm rather enjoying Booktok and Bookstagram, perhaps these money-saving life hacks will interest me too. And, I'd rather not have to look for another husband. It's incredibly time consuming and the adjustment period can be quite annoying. Besides, Roy does have his charms. He checks the oil and water on the car and brings me fresh coffee before he goes to work. He even built me a custom gazebo overlooking the pond that blew Deidre Bartmoor's out of the water."

"I like him, too. Stick at it, Mom. Good men are hard to come by."

"Talking of men, I saw Jonathon last week."

"Oh?" I wait for her to mention him telling her all about his spat with me and Logan.

"He told the whole town that you were marrying him because you thought he was rich!"

"What? Mom, I knew he was penniless! He spent the last of the money from our joint account. It was all I had left from Dad's will. He never gave me a penny!"

"Don't you worry. I told him he is not a good man. Not good enough for my daughter. The audacity, rolling around in a 2009 Ford and making out like my little girl wanted his money! I set him straight, and everyone at the country club backed me since they've always been so fond of you, darling. You know his father had the repo guys come take his new car? Not a penny to spare between them. You had a lucky escape."

"I'm not sure about that, Mom. I've got about a thousand dollars to my name and that's only because I got this job."

"Don't you worry about that! I'm having lunch with Deidre—her daughter's a lawyer. I'll have her sue that dingbat for your money back—"

"Mom, I'll deal with it."

"No, you'll let me. I have had quite enough practice

dealing with men and lawyers to know you are just too kind and sweet to go for the jugular. It'll be my pleasure, sweetie."

"Are you disappointed I'm not married? You seemed to be when I fled the wedding."

"I was just shocked, darling. I sometimes make the mistake of thinking that you are like me, that you need a man on your arm. But you're not like me. You're better than me. So independent and able, I wish I was more like you. I miss you."

"I miss you too, Mom," I reply and realize that I mean it.

"The guest room is always available to you. Parsnip can sleep in with me, and Roy can take the sofa if you need it."

"You'd kick the cat out of the guest room for me?"

"Layla, you are my daughter. I'd kick Roy out of the house if I needed to. I'm sorry about all that business at the wedding. You're so independent, it worries me. At your age I had you and a house and a husband to take care of. You seem content flitting around from one place to the next. I worry you'll end up alone."

"I'm actually seeing someone," I admit.

"Oh." Mom's voice raises nine octaves. "Pray tell."

My mom is many things, but no one can ever say that she is not a romantic at heart… even if her romances can be fleeting sometimes.

"He's…" *gorgeous, funny, kind, sweet.* "I think I love him."

"Darling, that's wonderful news! Do you think there might be a wedding?"

"Oh, no. It's not like that. We're… it's too early. I've only known him a few weeks."

"Darling, I married Roy after four weeks of knowing him. One of the best decisions of my life."

"But you said you were thinking about divorcing him."

"I may be having a change of heart. I'll consider cutting back on my spending first, if only to placate him."

"Well, that's a great start, Mom." I laugh to myself. "I have a new job lined up, and if I leave, I think that'll mark the end of us, so we need to have a serious conversation."

"Then why don't you stay?"

"I want to but—"

"Darling, the delivery man is here with my new car. I'll call you later."

"Mom, are you sure you need a new ca—" The phone cuts out.

When I look at the time, I am in danger of being late, so I throw on my dress and dash all the way to Logan's place.

* * *

I WAVE at Sally as I pass through the lobby on my way to the penthouse. She's with a hotel guest but tries to get my attention. I keep walking since Sally has a tendency to talk for hours and I am already running late.

The doorman lets me through the private entrance and I hit the button on the elevator that opens right into the penthouse living space. I haven't heard from Logan much today. He's probably been getting a ton of work done so we can make plans for tomorrow. I just hope my well-rehearsed talk with him goes to plan and he's not too hurt that I'm a runaway bride.

As soon as the door opens, I see him, sitting on the sofa, a bottle of Macallan whisky in his hand.

He doesn't look up.

"Logan," I start. "Day drinking? That's not like you."

He stares up, not bothering to move or greet me. His eyes are dark and glassy, his expression cold.

"Is everything okay?"

"You tell me, Layla. Is everything okay?"

"I thought it was," I reply. "Am I wrong?"

He laughs deeply. "Are you wrong? Not as wrong as I was, it seems."

I approach him with caution, sitting at the far end of the couch that faces the massive sliding glass doors with the view of the ocean beyond.

"You're in a mood. Why?"

"You said in your text you have something to tell me. Let's start there."

Swallowing becomes difficult. My nerves make my voice sound strained.

"Come on, Layla. I'm waiting for your huge, life-changing revelation. You can relax, I think I've heard it before."

"You're drunk. I'll speak to you about it when you're sober," I say, standing to leave.

"But I'm waiting for the punchline. The joke is right in front of you." He gestures to himself.

"What are you talking about?" I ask and he stands.

"I know you dumped your boyfriend at the altar, Layla. I know you've been looking for someone new to get your claws into, someone richer. I've been shown all the evidence." He gestures to a bunch of papers spread across the dining table.

Curious, I go look.

There's a picture of me and Mom taken by the photographer on the morning of my wedding to Jonathon. There's a printout of my text to Jonathon, asking him what he did with the money I put in our checking account. And then there's a gossip piece from the local rag that was written by Roy's former wife, claiming that my mother is a serial bride and is now marrying her fifth husband.

Then I see an article that states I left Jonathon stranded at the altar. "I don't understand. Who gave you these?"

"You're not denying it then?" He *tsks* and takes an unsteady step toward me.

"Denying what? That I left Jonathon at the altar? Yes, I did after I found out he was cheating on me. He spent the money my father left me. He left me penniless. Logan, I've been tying myself up in knots about telling you."

"Ah, yes. Your sob story about your father. Was it to lower my defenses and get me to feel sorry for you?"

"What? Why would I do that?"

"So you could get your hooks into me. You admitted you googled me. What did you read that I was worth? Your information is probably out of date by now, it's a lot more than the last time Forbes did their calculations."

"What? No. I don't care how much money you have. I never asked you for a penny."

"No. You're good, I'll give you that. I didn't even realize I was giving it to you. A twenty grand dress and a fifteen-million-dollar necklace, and you got me to give you those things without me even noticing."

Anger flares deep within me. "You took the necklace back and I asked for a cheaper dress. You took me to a fancy-ass store. I never wanted anything from you except a please and thank you!"

He takes a gulp of whisky and sways.

"I'm still waiting for the punchline, Layla."

"What punchline?"

"Are you going to tell me about the baby?"

"What baby?"

He laughs sardonically.

"The one you planned to trap me with."

"Logan, I was coming over here to tell you I left Jonathon at the altar. I didn't tell you before. I kept it from you until now because I was worried it would trigger you after what happened with Dana and because honestly, since I met you, I have barely thought about Jonathon. But I knew I had to be honest with you. I knew we couldn't move forward while there were secrets between us."

My throat is in danger of closing up thanks to the tennis ball-sized lump growing inside it, and my vision is blurring with the unshed tears that are threatening to drown my eyes.

I look up at him, still as gorgeous as ever but with a mean glint in his eyes that's making my heart ache.

"You think me capable of using you like that?"

"It's what people do to me, Layla. They use me. Why would you be any different?"

"Because I love you, and I thought we had something special," I admit, walking toward the exit. "I thought you saw me." I press the button for the elevator. "I thought wrong."

Only once the doors have closed behind me do I let myself break down.

Upstairs, there's a huge smashing sound—probably the whisky bottle hitting the wall, but even though it sounds as though it has splintered into a thousand pieces, it can't possibly be as broken as my heart.

CHAPTER 52

LOGAN

On Monday morning, she's not sitting at her desk when I arrive.

I don't know why I thought she'd see out her contract, but I remind myself that it's a good thing she's gone. Still, I'm leveled with disappointment when I see her empty chair.

I refuse to dwell, even though it feels like my heart got ripped out my chest.

"Skyla," I say into the receiver, "I need you to get me a new assistant." I'm still staring at Layla's empty chair when I tack on the word, "please."

"But Logan, Layla doesn't leave for another week. Did she turn down the permanent position?"

"She's gone," I admit. Saying it aloud seems to make it more real.

"Gone? Where did she go?"

"I don't know where she went. But she's not here and I need an assistant. Please."

"Okay. I'll call her. I'm sure we can straighten everything out."

"No need to call her. She's not coming back."

I made sure of that.

"Oh. Are you okay?" Skyla asks, her voice softening with a concern beyond what I deserve.

"I'm fine. It's business as usual. Concentrate your efforts on finding me an assistant who is capable before the week is out. *Please.*" My tone is harsh. Harsher than my sister-in-law deserves and she lets me know this by biting back, "Yes, Mr. Blingwood. I'll put out an ad right away, *Mr. Blingwood.*"

* * *

THE DAY PASSES LABORIOUSLY SLOWLY. Each time someone walks into Layla's office, they seem surprised not to see her there. Sad, even. By the time Drew walks in with a sandwich and a coffee, I am missing her so badly, I swear I convince myself she is out there, sending him in with something to eat for me in case I get hangry.

"What are you doing here?" I ask Drew.

"I popped in to see Tate in the penthouse. He's pretty messed up, but not as messed up as you look. Your head of housekeeping told me to bring you this." He nods at the cup of coffee and sandwich. "I've barely seen you since you turned up at my place, beat down with concern that you banged your assistant."

I remember our coffee. Me torn in knots over whether it was wrong to pursue Layla.

"Turns out, you were right. I should have listened to my gut."

Drew sits before me and pushes the wrapper across the desk with food I can't stomach. His expression is confused. "I thought your gut was telling you that you wanted her."

"It was. It was also telling me I shouldn't go there."

"Why not?"

"Because women use me, Drew."

"How so?"

I throw down the pen I am holding and stretch my legs out beneath the table. My body is so tense, it feels like I might crack and splinter under the pressure.

"Dana came by."

"Dana? What the fuck did she want?"

"She had evidence of Layla leaving some guy at the altar in her last town."

Drew blows out a breath. "What did the guy do to deserve that?"

"Layla says she found out he was cheating. Dana says Layla thought he was rich and dumped him when she found out that wasn't the case."

The skin between Drew's brows pucker and he asks, "And who do you believe?"

"If it was just that, I'd have believed Layla, hands-down, no questions asked. But she kept it from me and there was other stuff too. Drew, Layla was a runaway bride. After what happened to me with Dana, don't you think it's a little like history repeating. Was she manipulating me like Dana did?"

Drew ponders this then shakes his head. "Logan, she's not Dana. It seems reasonable that she'd keep her runaway bride status quiet from the guy who was ditched at the wedding. She was trying to save you from reliving your own experience."

"Layla said she didn't tell me because she was worried she'd trigger me. But there was other stuff too." Stuff that feels flimsy now that Layla's gone, and I miss her so much that my chest aches and it feels like I could die from it.

"So, Dana got inside your head and you broke things off with Layla?"

371

I nod.

Drew looks me up and down, his brow arching in a disapproving way. "How does that feel?"

"What do you mean, how does it feel? Layla lied to me, she knew I'd be pissed if I found out and she kept it from me. Dana says she was doing a number on me. Any day now I'll probably get a DNA request, and a court order for child support."

"You think Layla'd do that?"

"I don't know what to believe," I admit.

"Well, you look like shit."

"Thanks. It's good to know I can always count on you to build me up when my life hits the shitter."

"You're welcome, brother. I'll always keep it real, even when you don't want to hear it. You look worse than when you found out Dana lied."

"I feel worse." I push my hands into my hair. When Dana left, it was easy to throw myself into work to mask the anger I felt. Yet today I haven't accomplished anything. I can't concentrate and there's this gnawing feeling like I'm making a big mistake, but I don't trust it. I don't trust myself. I trusted Layla unquestionably and look where that got me.

"Thanks for the sandwich and coffee, Drew. I'll be fine. I've got a lot of work to get done. Can you tell Tate I haven't forgotten about him, and I'll come by to see him tomorrow. I told Jessie to make sure he has everything he needs."

Drew nods and stands to leave. "One question, though. Did you love Layla?"

The weight in my chest is so heavy it feels like my heart is about to implode.

"No."

"Good. 'Cuz it'd be fucking awful to throw something good away on the word of a jealous bitch with a history of fucking you over. Enjoy your coffee. I'll see you later."

Drew leaves. It's a while before I even reach for the coffee. When I do, I notice the scrawling on the cup in Sharpie:

Dipshit!

CHAPTER 53

LAYLA

"*H*ow's your mother's guestroom?" Jessie asks.
"Worse than previously imagined." I force a chuckle. "Parsnip refuses to share with Mom and Roy, so I'm forced to bunk with a geriatric feline with a penchant for trying to suffocate me in my sleep." Jessie laughs. "Seriously, if I wake up with that cat on my head one more time, I'm calling the pound and warning them of a pending case."

"Aside from the suffocation, how are you? Have you heard from him?"

"No, I haven't heard from Logan. It's over."

"He's a dipshit for treating you this way!" I think I hear her chuckle beneath her breath but maybe it's just Parsnip snoring.

"Have you seen that other guy?"

"Jonathon? Yeah, I went to see him like you said. Demanded my money back. He told me he spent it all on

Brenda in Bora Bora…getting over his broken heart but my mom says she's taking him to court."

"Urgh. Men! I swear we'd all be better off without them. Take Tate Blingwood. He gets pictured running down the street naked, and now he's holed up at the resort, and guess who Logan asks to see to his needs?"

"You?"

"Yep. So far, I've managed to go unseen but if he doesn't get back to his life soon, I'm worried he'll see me."

"Why would you be worried about Tate Blingwood seeing you?"

"Oh, I'm not. I'm totally not worried. It's just he's so infuriating. I have enough to do without having to take care of a spoiled man-child movie star with an ego bigger than Neptune."

"If I was still there, I'd help," I admit. "Maybe Skyla can help you deal with him?"

"I know you'd help. We all miss you. Are you sure you can't just come back?"

"No. It's over. He thinks I'm worse than Dana. There's no recovering from it."

"If it makes you feel better, he's wandering about the place more miserable than ever."

I picture Logan, grumping about the place when I first arrived. Then I remember us laughing together and the way he made me feel when he smiled.

"It doesn't make me feel better. Try to look out for him, please."

"I will. Not that he deserves it after what he said!"

"It's okay. Don't be offended on my behalf. He really didn't know me that well, and well, us becoming close, it happened too soon. He wasn't over what Dana did. I should have been honest with him from the start."

Jessie sneers. "The utter doop should have known you're

nothing like her!" I hear the sound of a buzzer through the receiver and then I hear Jessie sigh. "If Tate Blingwood rings that buzzer one more time, I'm gonna stick it up his—"

I laugh even though it hurts. "Jessie, are you sure you don't like Tate, even a little bit?"

"Nope. He's a selfish bastard and no role model. I'll be relieved when he fucks off back to LaLa Land and me and Macy can relax." I hear the buzzer again and then Jessie cusses. "I got to go. Keep smiling, Layla. Logan's going to realize he's made the biggest mistake of his life and come running. You'll see."

Then she hangs up, and I hear my mother calling up the stairs to ask if I'd like some chamomile tea she ordered specially from China.

CHAPTER 54

LOGAN

"*S*ee, he missed you," Mom says. She turned up twenty minutes ago, swearing she needed to come by because Yogi hasn't been acting himself. Today she's wearing a bright red T-shirt with the slogan: *I woof you.*

"So, if you pet him like this," she demonstrates with her hand, "he really likes it, and it makes him feel safe."

I'm standing by the table Layla and I dined from, wishing I could stop thinking about her.

"Darling, are you okay? You seem a million miles away. If now isn't a good time—"

"I'm fine. Why wouldn't I be fine?"

"I heard Layla left."

"How did you hear that?"

Mom looks sheepish. "So, he's using a special shampoo at the moment. Poor little fella still has a rash but it's almost gone—"

"Mom, how did you hear Layla was gone? Did Drew tell

377

you? Or Skyla, perhaps? Have you seen her? Have you heard from Layla?"

I don't realize I'm holding my breath waiting for her answer, until my lungs start to burn. "Mom. Layla. What did you hear?"

She stops petting Yogi and stands to her full height. Eyes, so pale they're translucent, examine every part of my face. "You love her, don't you?"

My instinct is to deny it. "No. I... How did you guess we were dating—if that's even what it was."

"Oh, son. I could tell the moment I saw you together that even if nothing had happened yet, it was sure going to."

"Layla was here five weeks, Mom. It's impossible. It's moot anyway, she's not who I thought she was...." I throw my hands up. "I can't get her off my mind."

Mom wanders closer. "I was hook, line, and sinker for your father in three weeks. He said it took him two weeks to realize he was in love with me, but he always did like to outdo everyone else."

I puff out a laugh at the image. No one could deny the love my father had for my mother. It was in every look, every touch, every breath he took.

"She might be pregnant."

Mom's mouth opens wide, her eyes alight with sheer joy. "That's wonderful! Darling, I'm so happy. But you're not happy?"

I imagine Layla swollen with my child and a bolt of pride hits my heart. "If she's pregnant, of course, I'll take care of the kid."

Mom frowns. "But not Layla? Even though you love her."

Yogi jumps up at me and I don't even have the energy to push him down. I stroke my hand down his head until I reach his backside and his leg jigs.

"How far along is she?"

I shrug. "She says she's not pregnant."

Mom looks confused. "Why would she tell you she's not pregnant if she was."

"Because maybe she was trying to get pregnant, like Dana did."

"Layla wouldn't do that, would she?"

"I didn't think she would." The dog runs off and makes himself comfy on my Italian leather sofa. I push my hands into my hair. "All I know is that I got duped once. I didn't even want another relationship. I was fine as I was! Then she crashes into my life, getting beneath my skin, and making me fall for her and now... everything fucking hurts."

"Sounds to me like maybe you made a mistake."

"Layla put herself on the line and stood up for me, she told me I was a good man. She catered to my every need, even when I didn't deserve it, and the way she smiled at me, that heart-stopping smile of hers. She's never once asked for anything from me, not like Dana who snapped her fingers and I handed over my Amex. In New York, you should have seen the disappointment on Layla's face when I told her she couldn't go sightseeing, but she sucked it up and was prepared to work over the weekend no less. When I relented and planned for us to go see a bunch of stuff, she was utterly joyous. We ate Philly cheesesteaks in Central Park and Layla was as happy as I've ever seen her. She asked for nothing of any monetary value from me, even though I would've given it to her in a heartbeat." I shake my head and step away. "Not that it matters now."

"Love hurts sometimes. I miss your father every day. Some days the pain is unbearable. But that pain reminds me that it was there and it was real." Mom rubs my arm then says, "I don't remember you in this much pain when Dana hurt you."

"I wasn't." I laugh bitterly. "Sure, I was angry, embarrassed even. I felt like a fool but I was also relieved."

"But you don't feel relived now?"

"Relieved? I feel like I'm bleeding out deep inside my chest, like I could actually fucking die."

"Logi, what if you got it all wrong? What if Layla is in her mother's guest room up in Oregon feeling just as terrible as you?"

"How do you know she's in Oregon?"

Mom shrugs innocently. "It's just a hunch I have."

I can't stand the thought of Layla feeling just as miserable as me.

"I screwed up. No way she'll even talk to me now. I said awful, unforgivable things."

"Yes, you did. You acted rashly and there is no defending that. It'll take a lot of work for her to forgive the things you said. But if you don't try, you won't ever find out if you could earn her forgiveness."

"I don't even know if I am wrong about her or right about her. I'm going crazy."

"Are you sure you don't know? Sounds to me like you know her pretty well."

"Maybe I got it wrong. I let Dana get inside my head and I…" The more I think about it, the more I know I was wrong.

"What does your heart tell you?"

"That I'm a fucking idiot."

"Hmph. Yes, I think that's an accurate description. You are an idiot who is in love."

"I don't know how to fix this."

"You know exactly how to fix it, Logi. Now, would you like a cup of tea, or would you like her mother's address?" Mom says, reaching inside her purse.

CHAPTER 55

LAYLA

*T*ime drips by, filling the room until I am certain I might drown.

I feel Logan's absence, painfully so. I wish we could go back to the playful jibes and tender kisses of last week.

Keep busy, Layla. You're normally so good at staying distracted.

An email alert arrives on my cell and I open it immediately.

Miss Bowers,

Further to your inquiry, I can confirm I have viewed your resume and am happy to assign you the temporary post in Peach Lake. The vacancy is with a construction company— accommodation included. You can reach out to them on 914-040....

I CLOSE THE EMAIL.

Peach Lake sounds nice. It's got the sort of name that would ordinarily incite pangs of excitement and have me completing a dozen internet searches. But my gut feels cold and bleak, not a pang of anything to be found unless you count the nauseating churning of uncertainty.

"Layla, darling. There's someone here to see you," Mom calls upstairs and I uncurl myself from the comforter and trudge toward the staircase.

I feel Logan's presence before I even lay eyes on him. Even his scent is the complete package: deep, delicious cologne complimented by undertones of starched cotton and polished leather.

Perfectly designed, every inch of him is alluring, tempting.

He stands still at the base of the stairs when our eyes meet. The intensity has my breath stuck in my throat.

"Layla—"

"Logan… I mean Mr. Bling—"

"You're back to calling me Blingwood. Is that what we've regressed to?"

A flame flares beneath his eyes and my heart swells. He's right. I'm being ridiculous, but I don't know how to navigate this situation.

"Logan," I correct. Just saying his name hurts. "What are you doing here?"

"We need to talk." He holds his hand out for mine and unshed tears brew in my eyes.

I shake my head involuntarily but he makes no attempt to leave.

"I'm not leaving, not until you hear me out."

"I'll go prune my petunias," Mom says, making herself scarce.

"Logan, I'm not pregnant. You had no reason to come all this way—"

"I had every reason to come. I made a mistake. A huge, fucking epic mistake that I'm afraid will haunt me for the rest of my life."

I take two steps down the mahogany staircase. "It's fine. You don't know me and you got burned before—"

"I do know you."

"No, you don't, or you would never have thought... we're different. Too different. That's why it would never work—"

"I know you and I know you are nothing like Dana. I got spooked. I questioned shit I had no business questioning and I came out with the wrong answer. I was wrong."

"It's okay. I'm not pregnant. I'm not after your money. You're safe. I appreciate you coming all the way out here to apologize. Thank you. You can go now," I say and unbeknownst to me I've taken another three steps down.

"Go? Layla, I am just getting started. You still owe me a week."

I stop in my tracks, no more than two steps away, and look at him like he's lost his mind. "Logan, you can't possibly expect me to come back to work. It'd be... awkward."

"Awkward for who? The staff? Layla, you already know, there isn't a nonfraternization policy. I made it up because I couldn't stand the thought of Mike or anyone else making a play for you. The staff don't give a shit if I date you—in fact, they'd be grateful since I'm a grouchy asshole without you around. Half the staff are screwing anyway. It's like an episode of *Love Island* out there. Or, does it concern you that it'll be awkward for me? It's been awkward since the first day you arrived, staring at you, pretending I don't want you when every move I've made has been an indirect move to have you— even if I didn't realize it at the time." Logan lets out an exasperated sigh and lowers his voice. "Or, is it too awkward for you because then you'd actually have to stick around and let something play out?" He blinks away a pained scowl and tells me, "I've fallen for you. I said some fucking awful, heinous things I regret all the way down to my soul. Dana presented me with a bunch of shit she dredged up, and I fell for it because believing her lies was easier than admitting the truth to myself. I love you and I am terrified I have fucked up and lost you forever."

My lips quiver. My reply is automatic, "It's over, Logan. I'm not coming back. It's the only way. You can deduct a week's pay or sue me, or do whatever the situation warrants but it's done."

Logan holds out his hands but doesn't come closer. And I don't know why I can't back down and accept his apology when all I want is to throw myself into his arms.

"It's not the only way, Layla, it's the absolute worst way. I miss you. I tried to do laundry but it's beyond me. Now I have a pink shirt and shorts two sizes too small. Jessie ended up helping me—man, she's strict, apparently the temperature and setting matter. I helped her fold sheets and she told me she misses you too. We all do. I much prefer how we do laundry…." He smirks at me and I can't help but press my lips together with the memory of that night. "I can't bring myself to eat pizza with you gone. I have memories of you everywhere I look. Whether it is in the penthouse or sitting at my desk, I see you. I suppose it's not the same for you, in a new place with no reminders of me. I look at the picture of us at the awards—I have a copy in a frame on my desk now. Every time I look at it and see you wearing the turquoise dress that somehow made your eyes glow, I remember peeling you out of it and feeling like I had discovered treasure—because you are treasure to me. I'm not sure how I didn't realize it sooner, but now that I know, I'll do whatever it takes to get you back."

I take two more steps down toward him and then pause. My voice sounds angry reflecting the pain I felt—a million times worse than what Jonathon inflicted. "You compared me to *that* woman and you decided I was the same. Or worse? Which is it Logan, do you think I am as bad or truly worse than the person who tried to destroy you?"

He blinks twice and his throat bobs with his swallow.

I've hurt him like he hurt me but it doesn't make me feel better, I feel worse. But I can't stop because this might be my only chance to say the things I have been dwelling over and also because maybe it will stop him from making this mistake again in his future. "What have I ever done or said to you to make you believe that I would, that I could ever hurt you like that? Am I shallow and spoiled and spiteful like her? Do I make you feel like my needs are greater than yours?"

He shakes his head. Beneath his eyes are dark shadows. I've never seen him look so… defeated. "No. You made me feel alive for the first time in as long as I can remember. Even when we were at each other's throats, fighting, I knew you were loyal and kind and pure. If you just give me another chance, I can show you—"

"Give you another chance? To what end, Logan? For me to wait around until you compare me to her again? You fucking broke me!" My voice hitches on the final word and Logan steps back like I hit him with a physical blow.

"I promise you, I will never doubt you again."

"Really? What if Dana turns up next week with some news from my high school years. Or some random person recognizes me from a place I used to work and tells you something you don't like about me. Logan, I am not perfect and I can't go through my life worried that parts of me are deal-breakers."

"You're perfect to me. There are no deal-breakers. Not anymore."

"I'm not perfect enough or you would never have believed Dana in the first place."

"Layla, please. I'm begging you. There is nothing anyone could say that would make me question your intentions ever again. I already made that mistake and I swear, I nearly died from the fallout."

It's taking every ounce of my restraint not to make the few last steps and fall into his arms.

"I have a new job lined up; I leave at the end of the week."

"Layla, please, don't take the job. Come home with me. Live with me at the penthouse. You want a house, a place of our own, we'll get one. That little house you liked, I'll buy it. I'll buy you whatever you need. Please, trust me."

He looks so genuine, so hopeful that it breaks my heart to turn him down.

"This isn't about money! You can't buy your way out of hurting me," I say simply but it's the truth. "I didn't think you'd ever truly hurt me, not like that."

"I know and I'm so fucking sorry. If I could take back those things I said, I would. I don't blame you for not giving me another chance, I don't deserve it. All this time, I have been trapped, thinking about what Dana did to me—haunted by it, worrying about how I almost lost everything, when really I was worried about losing the wrong things. I listened to the wrong runaway bride." He reaches into his pocket and holds something out. On closer inspection, I see it's the necklace he gave me in New York. "On the best night of my life, I gave you a gift. I took it back because I wanted to keep you safe. I didn't think it'd be wise for you to be walking around New York with a giant disco ball tied around your neck, but I want you to have it. There's a bank in Santa Barbara with a deposit box set up in your name to keep it in, if you want to. They just need you to show up with some ID to finalize the account. Layla, I set that account up the day after we got back from New York. It's yours. The diamond alone is worth over fifteen million dollars."

My mouth falls open. "Have you gone insane?!"

He shifts uncomfortably then laughs. "Yes. Since the second I set eyes on you."

Logan takes one last look at me, his eyes pleading and I've never felt so wretched as I do watching the color drain from his face as he loses hope. I never thought I'd hear from him again. I didn't even dare hope for it, but now he's here, sticking with my decision to protect myself by pushing him away feels like I am amputating my own heart.

He lowers the diamond necklace, placing it on the bottom step where it glistens like my eyes and then reaches into his pocket and puts a folded sheet of paper beside the necklace.

Logan's mouth tips up on one side and he says, "I wrote my own list from the letters of your name. It's cheesy and not as good as yours but I owed you a list." He lets out a sad chuckle and takes a step back, thrusting his hands into his pant pockets. "If you ever change your mind, you know where to find me. I love you. I'm sorry it took me screwing everything up for me to realize your true value. You're priceless and you're right not to let some schmuck like me tell you differently."

Then Logan turns around and walks out the door.

CHAPTER 55 APPENDIX A

- L- LOVELY. Kind, charming, stunning inside and out.
- A- ALLURING. So powerfully mysterious, you fascinate me.
- Y- YUMMY. Since you sat on my sandwich, I've been hungry for you.
- L- LUMINOUS. You shine brighter than any woman, anywhere.
- A- AWE INSPIRING. I've been awestruck since I set eyes on you.
- B- BEAUTIFUL. This goes without saying but I needed to mention it.
- O- OPULENT. You're utterly priceless.
- W- WOW—each time I look at you, my heart says, "Wow!"
- E- EXTRAORDINARY. Better than a rare diamond, there is only one you.
- R- RAPTUROUS. You have my rapt interest, always.
- S- SEXY, sumptuous, scintillating, sweet.

Beneath his list, Logan has added:

There aren't enough letters in your name, or indeed the alphabet, or even words in the dictionary to describe what you mean to me.

CHAPTER 56

LOGAN

*M*y legs are dead weights but still I put one foot in front of the other. As I near the car, I shake my head to demonstrate to the driver that Layla hasn't forgiven me—that she's not coming with me. He opens the door to the passenger seat door and asks, "Should I instruct George to ready the jet."

I nod, unable to find the energy for words.

I spoke from my heart and said everything I could to try and make Layla see how much she means to me, but in the end, it wasn't enough.

"Wait!"

I turn around to face Layla's mother's home and don't even dare hope.

Layla is running toward me with bare feet, the bauble in her hand darting left and right as she approaches.

"I can't accept this," she says, slowing as she reaches me.

"It's yours. I don't want it. If it's because it's expensive or because you don't want to be reminded of me then... donate it."

Layla stares up at me through thick lashes made darker from the moisture of her tears. Knowing I'm responsible for the tears is like a punch to my gut.

"How could I not want to be reminded of you." She smiles but it's so watery, I can't enjoy it like I normally do.

There's a wind whipping up her glossy, ebony hair, as well as her short pajamas that instantly make me smile as I read the slogan: *Amazing In Bed*.

"I'm going to miss you and your utterly absurd pajamas." I take a lock of her hair and thread it through my fingers, just because I can't not.

"I'm going to miss you and your stuffy suits." Layla winks and my heart swells.

"You could come with me? I know of a decent, permanent job opening. Great perks, idyllic location. You could name your terms and your salary."

"Yeah, but I heard the owner is a real bossy asshole." Her full lips slowly tip up into a smile that lights up my soul.

"He is but he's trying to change."

"Maybe he doesn't need to change too much."

I shake my head and try not to get comfortable with the shoots of hope inside my chest. "He has a lot of room for improvement."

"Maybe we both do. I should have told you I ran out on Jonathon."

"You did nothing wrong. That happened before you even met me." I resist the temptation to pull her into my arms.

"I knew it wielded the power to hurt you. It's why I kept it a secret."

"Maybe one day, you'll trust me enough to tell me all about it."

Layla nods, her eyes all sparkly and warm.

"Where's this new job?" I ask.

"Peach Lake," she replies.

"Sounds fucking awful, if you ask me."

Layla laughs and, after the last few days without her, the sound is sweeter, richer than I remember.

"You know, if you poison your new boss, I'll be deeply, deeply offended."

"It's funny, there's only ever been one person I've considered poisoning."

My hand goes to my chest. "I'm touched."

"You should be."

"What's this new, awful company called, anyway?"

"Creel Construction," she says flippantly and I pull out my cell and immediately search for it.

"What are you doing?"

"Seeing if it's for sale."

"It's not," she replies, batting her hand jovially at the phone in my hand. It drops down onto the pavement but I don't care; the feel of her touch sends me reeling. And judging from the look on Layla's face, she felt it too.

I take ahold of both her hands including the one that still has her necklace wrapped inside. My grip is light enough that she can break away if she chooses to but firm enough that she steps back with me until her back is against the car.

Her gaze is right on mine as I tell her, "I know you feel this thing between us. I love you. Tell me you don't love me and I'll go. You won't have to see me again, but please... don't send me away if you want me too."

She blinks a long, slow blink and then levels me a look of sheer adoration.

"I've never felt like this before with anyone. Yes, I love you."

My mouth dries, I lose the ability to think straight, and I'm pretty sure my hearing fails, but it doesn't matter because if the last words I ever hear are Layla Bowers telling me she loves me then I will die a happy man.

"Don't send me away. Come with me, please?"

She glances over my shoulder at her mother's house and then back to me. "Things will have to be different."

"They will."

"I want to feel equal to you."

"Sassy pants, I'll treat you better than equal. From now on, you are my sun and my moon."

She grins. "But I don't want you to treat me differently at work."

"I'll be the asshole boss of your dreams, I promise."

A chuckle escapes her full and inviting lips. "You know what I mean."

"I do and I've got it, loud and clear. I'm not risking losing you again."

My mouth crashes against Layla's and I hoist her up until her long limbs knot around my waist. Feeling her against me, tasting her mouth and breathing in her sweet scent is everything, and I know I'll never be the same again. Irrevocably changed from a grumpy asshole to a content, happy, ecstatic man.

"I fucking love you," I tell her, pulling away for just a second before tasting her again.

"I love you, too," she replies, breaking apart our kiss, "but I think we should take this inside, your poor driver has my ass squashed against his window."

"No finer view in the world," I spin her around and stride toward the house, "but your ass is mine now and I'm not sharing it."

EPILOGUE

LAYLA

When I wake up in a huge bed with sheets white and crisp, I wonder if I died last night and went to heaven. Then suddenly, I realize I am in heaven when my eyes rest on the deliciously handsome man who mere hours ago made me come three times.

Logan snuffles lightly and I stroke my finger down the length of his back, over the divots, smoothing my hand over his perfect rump.

The bedroom is massive with a huge veranda that over-looks the lake.

Three nights ago when we arrived at the airstrip, Logan told George to take us to his lake house. When I asked about it, he told me he wanted me to himself for a while, and since I still owed him a week, it didn't seem prudent to argue. Besides, I missed him and I wanted us to have the time to reacquaint.

And reacquaint we have!

Letting Logan sleep, I slip on his shirt and go explore the house, remembering I saw some beans and a deluxe coffee machine somewhere in the kitchen. I pass the en suite with the copper tub placed right in front of the window so you can soak while admiring the view.

The primary bedroom opens out onto the sweeping staircase that leads down to the stone fireplace and leather couches. It's so perfectly presented, so cozy I feel right at home wandering about the place in just Logan's shirt.

"You're up early," Logan says and I look up and see him descending the stairs like a fresh-out-of-bed runway model.

"I know, right? After last night, I should definitely be exhausted." *And maybe immobile, thanks to the soreness between my thighs.*

Logan takes my hand, and with his other, he lifts my chin so I am facing him.

"Do we get to stay here the whole week? I mean, shouldn't we get back to work?"

Logan shrugs. "I'll take you wherever you want to go, but since you agreed to live with me, I wondered if you'd consider looking for a house with me? I don't think we should live in the penthouse—I want somewhere we can both be off duty—a place that anchors us both—"

"You anchor me."

His lips stretch into a wide grin that makes me want to kiss them.

"Maybe so, but we need a home. Yogi needs some place where he can go do his business outside—"

The grin lights up my face. "We're keeping Yogi?"

"And Cindy. Those flea-ridden shit machines hold sentimental value, don't you think?"

I nod. "They do! I like to think of that first walk with them as our first date."

"I like the sound of that too. So you'll choose a house for us? A place we can grow, as a family."

"You want that? After Dana, I thought you were done with pregnancies and kids...."

"Layla, I'm not going to lie to you, and maybe this is a deal-breaker for you, and if it is, I accept that, but Dana was trying to get pregnant and it never happened. In the back of my mind, I have wondered... what if I'm shooting blanks?"

I ponder it for a moment and stroke my hand across the scuff on Logan's jaw.

"No way you're shooting blanks, I could taste your fertility just fine last night."

"But if I am?"

I stare deeply into his warm, chocolatey eyes so there can be no mistake and tell him, "Nobody knows what's around the corner. We take every day as a gift, and if I am only ever blessed with your love, then I will be the richest woman in America."

He laughs with his eyes and lifts my hand to kiss it. "Of course, I could be wrong. We'll need to test my theory to make sure. We should probably start right away."

Chills skate down my arms. "I'm still on birth control, and maybe I want to enjoy you for a while longer before we go forth and multiply."

"I want you to know I trust you, Layla. I trust you with my heart and if it ever comes to it, I'll trust you with my baby. And I'm happy to get started just as soon as you want to." He winks at me devilishly.

"I knew you just wanted in my pants."

"Sassy pants, I want in everywhere, but you already let me in your most sacred place, your heart. Now I suppose I just need you to let me make it official. I wasn't going to do this here, but the timing feels right."

Logan lets go of my hand and reaches right into his

pocket, pulling out a small, black box. "If you don't like it or you want something different, we can get you whatever you want. But please, say you'll do me the honor of becoming my wife?"

"Logan, this is crazy. You're crazy. We've only known each other—"

"Long enough. Layla, I know everything I need to. I already spent too long chasing the wrong bride. You. Are. The. One. For. Me. That's all there is to it. But am I the one for you?"

I don't even need to think about it. "I love you."

"I love you too."

"But..."

"But what?"

His perfectly white teeth clamp down on his lip and he looks adorably nervous from me to the ring and back again.

"Yes. Yes, I'll marry you!"

His hands reach around my neck and he pulls me close, kissing me deeply.

"Sassy pants, I promise you won't regret it. I'm going to take such good care of you."

"I believe you," I tell him. "I love you and I believe you."

"What do you say we go upstairs and celebrate?"

Heat flashes in his eyes and my smile lights up. "Okay, but then I've got to call Jessie and Skyla and tell them we're getting married," I say, realizing that suddenly, I have everything I ever wanted.

IF YOU ENJOYED THIS STORY, please consider leaving a review HERE.

. . .

FIND out how Tate and Jessie react when they finally come face to face HERE.

THE END!

ACKNOWLEDGMENTS

To the one and only Randie Creamer, my editor-in-chief extraordinaire! Thank you for your relentless pursuit of perfection and all your encouragement, love and support!

Kari March, the mastermind behind my cute, fun cover. I love it. Thank you!

Ellen Montoya, your proofreading prowess is as sharp as your wit! I adore our chats and banter. You help make my heart full and I can't wait to see you!

Christina Gamboa, the queen bee of all things bookish! You're a legend, and I cannot thank you enough for the work you put into this book. I adore you <3

Sandi from BookDragonHeart (seriously, check out her epic socials!), your enthusiasm and support keeps me smiling. Thank you!

Ana Rita Clamente, the Portuguese tigress with a heart of gold. I flipping adore you!

To Ann Bang for enjoying my words and cheering me along.

And to my beloved readers, who are the true heroes of this story. I wasn't sure I was worthy of this journey. By picking up my books/reviewing them/recommending them, you've shown me such incredible kindness. I'm truly touched. Being an author has healed my soul. I'm humbled, grateful and crossing my fingers that my book enabled you to escape this wild world for a time, and that it left you smiling.

Sending you ALL the love!
XX

ALSO BY EMILY JAMES

The Blingwood Billionaires series
Book 1—Sorry. Not Sorry
Book 2 – Chasing the Wrong Bride
Book 3 – Catch a Falling Star

The Love in Short series
Book 1—Operation My Fake Girlfriend
Book 2—Sexy With Attitude Too
Book 3—You Only Love Once
Book 4—Leaving Out Love

The Power of Ten series
Book 1—Ten Dates
Book 2—Ten Dares
Book 3—Ten Lies

ABOUT THE AUTHOR

Emily James is a British author who lives on the south coast of England. She loves to travel and enjoys nothing more than a great romance story with a heart-of-gold hero. On the rare occasions that she hasn't got her nose in a book, Emily likes to keep her heart full by spending time with her bonkers yet beautiful family and friends.

Facebook
  Goodreads
  Amazon
  Newsletter

Made in the USA
Columbia, SC
11 October 2023

24261788R00248